THE
YESHIVA

Also by Chaim Grade

THE AGUNAH
THE SEVEN LITTLE LANES
THE WELL

THE
YESHIVA

by *Chaim Grade*

Translated from the Yiddish,
with an Introduction, by

Curt Leviant

The Bobbs-Merrill Company, Inc.

INDIANAPOLIS   NEW YORK

First published in Yiddish in 1967, copyright © Chaim Grade
English translation copyright © 1976 by Chaim Grade
All rights reserved, including the right of reproduction in whole or in
part in any form
Published by the Bobbs-Merrill Company, Inc.
Indianapolis   New York

Designed by Ingrid Beckman
Manufactured in the United States of America

First printing

Library of Congress Cataloging in Publication Data

Grade, Chaim, 1910–
   The Yeshiva.

   Translation of Tsemakh Atlas.
   I. Title.
PZ4.G73Ye   [PJ5129.G68]   839'.09'33   76-11608
ISBN 0-672-52264-0

CONTENTS

TRANSLATOR'S NOTE

I WOULD LIKE to thank my father, Jacques Leviant, for his advice and assistance with what I considered difficult Yiddish words and idioms during the lengthy task of preparing the translation of this novel. Also, my gratitude to the author, his wife Inna, and Mary Heathcote for their painstaking care and suggestions.

INTRODUCTION

THE FIRST PAGE of *The Yeshiva* states that Tsemakh Atlas, a yeshiva scholar and rabbi, doubts the existence of God and the divinity of the Torah, thus announcing a theme never before attempted in Yiddish literature. At the very outset of the novel, which is set in the Jewish towns of Lithuania after the First World War, the reader realizes that he is in the presence of a work that will touch him deeply through both action and thought. Indeed, that combination of an exciting story and the drama of the mind and soul is the special signature of Chaim Grade's fiction. And the opening of the book, with Tsemakh in spiritual turmoil, is the overture to a work whose challenge and fascination are sustained and heightened as the novel progresses.

Tsemakh Atlas, the protagonist of *The Yeshiva*, is unlike any other Jewish hero in any fiction. He is a pious man whose life is powerfully affected by a triangle of antinomic forces: religion, doubt, and eros, all of which give him rich, scintillating dimensions. Tsemakh is not only a yeshiva scholar; he is also a follower of the Musar movement, whose goal was ethical perfection and whose mode was rigorous self-discipline. A Musarnik constantly tweaked at his thoughts and behavior to seek out flaws in his character; he plumbed his good deeds to hunt out the tiniest ulterior motive lurking therein; he tried to subjugate undesirable tendencies (finding, for instance, that he had an overlarge appetite, he would purposely limit the size of his meals). A Musarnik had to be more critical of himself than of others; he participated in group sessions in which students criticized and evaluated one another's behavior.

The Musarniks censored, reined in, muzzled every wayward trait to make it conform to a predetermined—perhaps impossible—ideal. The psychological damage from such merciless curbing of all one's natural impulses (especially when begun at the age of eleven or so), and the callousness toward human feelings that can result when a system supersedes the individual, are documented and dramatized in Grade's novel.

Tsemakh Atlas is more than a scholar and a Musarnik. He is a Musarnik from the most fanatical of the Musar schools, Navaredok, where Chaim Grade himself was a student. The Navaredkers, as they were called, concentrated on breaking one's will, one's vanity, pride, love of material possessions; they even held clothing in contempt, purposely going about sloppily dressed to show their defiance of, and spiritual removal from, the world. While the Hasidim found joy in the service of God, the Navaredkers immersed themselves in a pious, angry gloom, symbolized by their mournful chant as they studied the Musar books in dimly lit meditation rooms.

Seething with this Navaredok fire, the Musarnik Tsemakh Atlas steps into the secular world. (Interestingly enough, Chaim Grade tells us that one can never be an ex-Musarnik: once touched, he is infected forever, no matter how far from religiosity he strays.) Even when Tsemakh is in the home of nonobservant Jews, his scrupulous Musar honesty overrides bounds of social decency. In his passion to tell the truth, he publicly humiliates people by pointing out their hypocritical behavior. But in so doing Tsemakh Atlas violates the Torah precept which forbids a person to shame his fellow man lest he lose his share in the world to come. At that point, Grade deploys his basic esthetics of fiction—balance and perspective—and Tsemakh uses his Musar fury in a relentless battle to get justice for a pregnant serving girl, against the rich family who would abandon her to save their reputation.

This is the first novel in Yiddish or any other literature whose central theme is the yeshiva—that institution of Jewish learning which inspired, shaped, and sometimes stained the lives of countless Jewish youths. Unlike other Yiddish writers who rebelled against yeshiva life and depicted it in passing with enmity and venom, thereby distorting its reality, Grade records this life in all its aspects, both positive and negative.

In *The Yeshiva* there are saints and charlatans on both sides of the religious fence. There is the deeply devout fruit peddler, Vella (a loving portrait of Chaim Grade's own mother), and the saintly scholar, Reb Avraham-Shaye Kosover. In contrast are such worldly people as Frankel, the married schoolteacher who has an affair with Tsemakh's future wife, Slava; and Confrada Barbitoler, who leaves her husband and without a divorce marries another man in Argentina and has his children. There are also observing Jews whose behavior makes them sinners: the Rabelaisian wife- and child-beating tobacco merchant, Vova Barbitoler, a drunkard with a mania for ritual fringes; the pious thief and fence Sroleyzer; and Azriel Weinstock, who collects funds for religious institutions while enjoying a gay time away from home. And there are rabbi-politicians who shamelessly angle for—and community leaders who prevent them from getting—rabbinic positions. Innovative and indelible portraits all, comprising a world far less tame and innocent than nostalgic readers about East European Jewish life have imagined.

Even the minor characters in *The Yeshiva* are memorable. They appear only briefly on the ever revolving stage of Jewish Vilna and its environs, but they leave their mark forever. Who can forget Fishele, the adorable little yeshiva boy who eats his meals at Hannah Stupel's house, and on whom Hannah lavishes all her maternal love because she has no children of her own? Or the fastidious yeshiva youth who must read the newspaper fresh, creaseless, or else get no pleasure from it? Or Soyeh-Etl, the old cemetery caretaker who mothers the young yeshiva boys and warms herself with the sound of their Talmud chants?

Doubts, sorrows, tensions tear at many of the characters, from the domineering Tsemakh and his lovely Slava to the pathetic maid, Stasya. Tsemakh can indulge himself in the luxury of existential pain; the suffering of the others is played out in wretched poverty, like that of the unforgettable itinerant peddler who shares his herring and black bread on Sabbaths with a hungry yeshiva boy because he too—like the rich men—wants to help sustain a Torah scholar, and who begs the lad not to leave him lest he be humiliated when others learn of his destitution.

Grade's feat of memory in being able to characterize so many people so fully and clearly is truly remarkable. He re-creates Musar sermons, speeches, rabbinical interpretations. But this awesome memory is merely a servant to the artist, who must shape, hone and polish his material. It is here that Grade's knowledge of and love for Russian literature manifest themselves most unmistakably, for surely the grand design of *The Yeshiva* evinces the beneficent influence of the nineteenth-century Russian masters. Only a work of such massive proportions could do justice to the full blaze of Jewish life in *The Yeshiva*. Reviewing Chaim Grade's previous novel, *The Agunah*, in the *New York Times Book Review*, Elie Wiesel called Grade "one of the great, if not the greatest of, living Yiddish writers."

In *The Yeshiva*, Grade's crowning achievement, we have one of the greatest and most all-embracing novels of Yiddish literature. This translation brings Tsemakh Atlas and his rich cast of characters to a satisfying midpoint in their lives. The second half of *The Yeshiva* is now being translated. Under the title *Tsemakh Atlas*, the novel was published in Yiddish in 1967 in the United States, and it was translated into Hebrew for publication in Israel in 1968.

Chaim Grade is able to depict this panorama of Jewish life because he is the only Yiddish writer of his stature who is intimate with both Torah learning and secular life. Born in Vilna in 1910, and a yeshiva student until 1932—when he burst into the world of Yiddish letters with his first poems—Grade is totally at home in the rabbinic world. He knows the yeshivas, the scholars, the students, and teachers; he knows their lives and habits, their garb and quirks, the predictable rhythms of their lives and the unpredictable flashes of exceptional behavior. But since Grade left the yeshiva at age twenty-two, he is also at home in the secular world, and, unlike the Musarniks who closed their eyes to the world around them, Grade has kept his eyes wide open. He observes all facets of East European Jewish life with an artist's dispassion and an insider's sympathy. Even though he left the yeshiva, Grade has never stopped celebrating, in poetry and prose, the life he abandoned—a way of life which has long been obliterated. As artist and archivist, Grade takes for his mission the resurrection of this world in all its glory and stress, its laughter and pain.

CURT LEVIANT

CAST OF
CHARACTERS

In Navaredok

Reb Yosef-Yoizl Hurwitz—Tsemakh's teacher; also called the
Old Man of Navaredok

In Nareva

Tsemakh Atlas—Yeshiva scholar; since he comes from Lomzhe,
he's also known as Tsemakh Lomzher, or the Lomzher
Reb Simkha Feinerman—the head of the Musar yeshiva where
Tsemakh Atlas studied

In Amdur

Falk Namiot—father of Tsemakh's fiancée
Dvorele Namiot—the fiancée
Reb Yaakov-Yitzhok—innkeeper at Amdur

In Lomzhe

Reb Ziml Atlas—Tsemakh's uncle
Tsertele—Ziml Atlas' wife; Tsemakh's aunt
The three Atlas brothers—Tsemakh's cousins; clerks at the
Stupel flour shop

VOLODYA STUPEL—owner of the flour shop
NAUM STUPEL—Volodya's brother
SLAVA STUPEL—Volodya's young sister; Tsemakh's wife
HANNAH STUPEL—Volodya's wife
FRIEDA STUPEL—Naum's wife
LOLLA STUPEL—son of Naum and Frieda
DUBER LIFSCHITZ—a yeshiva emissary
ZUNDL KONOTOPER—a yeshiva emissary
BERNARD FRANKEL—Slava Stupel's lover prior to her marriage
REB KOPEL KAUFMAN—a community volunteer
REB ENZELE—a community volunteer
FISHELE GRAYEVER—a yeshiva boy, guest at Hannah's house
REB DODYA SHMULEVITCH—a businessman
STASYA—a maid in Naum Stupel's house

In Vilna

CHAIKL—Reb Shlomo-Motte's son; also known as Chaikl Vilner, or
    the Vilner
VELLA—Chaikl's mother, the fruit peddler
REB SHLOMO-MOTTE—Vella's husband, a retired Hebrew teacher
REB SENDERL—a kettlemaker
VOVA BARBITOLER—a tobacco merchant
CONFRADA—Vova's second wife
HERTZKE—son of Vova and Confrada
MINDL—Vova Barbitoler's third wife
REB MENAKHEM-MENDL SEGAL—a shopkeeper: later a teacher
DODYA—an innkeeper
ZELDA—owner of a large fruit shop
ZELDA'S THREE DAUGHTERS—with their mother they are known as
    "the Sennacheribs" after the blasphemous King Sennacherib
KASRIELKE—a tinsmith, Zelda's husband
MELECHKE—Zelda's young son

In Valkenik

GITL—the cook at the yeshiva kitchen
LEITSHE AND ROKHTSHE—Gitl's daughters; they help serve the
    yeshiva students

SHEEYA LIPNISHKER—a student at the yeshiva; a prodigy

YOEL UZDER—known as the Uzder; a Valkenik yeshiva student with a bundle of cash

YOSEF VARSHEVER—the Varshever (the one from Varshe, or Warsaw), a student at the Valkenik yeshiva

REB HIRSHE GORDON—Valkenik's leading citizen; a strictly religious textile merchant. Former son-in-law of Valkenik's rabbi; a leader of the ultra-orthodox faction and a supporter of the Agudah

REB YAAKOV HACOHEN LEV—the venerable rabbi of Valkenik

TSHARNE—Hirshe Gordon's sixteen-year-old daughter

REB LIPPA-YOSSE—the ritual slaughterer of Valkenik; Tsemakh Atlas boards in his house

YUDEL—a slaughterer; Reb Lippa-Yosse's son-in-law

HANNAH-LEAH—Yudel's wife

RONYA—Hannah-Leah's younger sister

AZRIEL WEINSTOCK—Ronya's husband, an itinerant fund raiser for a yeshiva

REB YISROEL—a tailor and yeshiva supporter

ELTZIK BLOCH—the Valkenik rabbi's son-in-law; brother-in-law of Hirshe Gordon; a leader of the town's enlightened religious faction; a supporter of the Mizrachi

THE MIADLE RABBI—a candidate for Valkenik's rabbinic post

SROLEYZER—a bricklayer; a thief and a fence

REB ARYEH-LEYB MIADOVNIK—a candidate for the Valkenik rabbinic post; rabbi from Misagoleh

SOYEH-ETL—the old caretaker of the Valkenik guest house and the Jewish cemetery

FREYDA VOROBEY—Chaikl and his father's landlady

KREYNDL VOROBEY—Freyda's daughter

BENTZYE THE GOLEM—Freyda's husband

NOKHEMKE—Freyda's son

REB MORDEKHAI-AARON SHAPIRO—Valkenik's new rabbi; successor to Reb Yaakov Hacohen Lev

REB AVRAHAM-SHAYE KOSOVER—a renowned scholar, rabbi, and sage; also known as the author of *The Vision of Avraham*, his most famous work

PART I

1

TSEMAKH ATLAS WAS a young Torah student in Lomzhe when he heard that in the Musar yeshiva in Navaredok, the *yetzer ha-ra*—the evil tempter in man—had already been slain. Now there was no need to wait until messianic times when God himself, as the Talmud stated, would destroy the *yetzer ha-ra* in the presence of those who had wrestled with him. So Tsemakh Atlas left his home town for Navaredok, where he struggled to perfect his character. But he soon saw that the *yetzer ha-ra* hadn't been slain in the Musar school either, for it was much easier to observe dozens of laws and customs than to deny oneself one forbidden desire.

During the First World War the yeshiva moved from Lithuania into the depths of Russia. Tsemakh Atlas went through the towns and villages of the Ukraine and White Russia establishing new yeshivas. Not even the post-Revolutionary persecutions by the atheists frightened him away from persuading students at secular high schools to become Torah scholars. Yet at the same time he himself was racked with doubts about the existence of God.

One day he lingered over the Silent Devotion for half an hour, shouting, swaying in all directions, and pounding his fists on the wall. The Talmud students assumed that the man from Lomzhe—the Lomzher, as he was called—was taking spiritual stock of himself. Actually he was grappling with a fundamental principle:

3

he knew that there was a Torah and that without the Torah man couldn't find his way—but he didn't know whether the Torah was divinely given. He had immersed himself in philosophical works that proved the existence of God, and he constantly shouted to himself, "I believe! I have perfect faith"; but he couldn't outshout the demon snickering in his ear: "You have no faith! You're fooling everyone! You're an atheist!" After such a lengthy swaying in prayer, and after poring over a Musar book, Tsemakh Atlas was hoarse and drenched with perspiration. He looked for someone to confide in, and found none other than the mentor of Navaredok, Reb Yosef-Yoizl Hurwitz, or, as his students called him, the Old Man.

Reb Yosef-Yoizl's method was to sow everywhere and to tend the growths. To a youth of weak character, the rabbi would preach at length until the boy burst into tears. To one who loved compliments, the Old Man would offer the highest praise. To a talented but money-hungry boy, Reb Yosef-Yoizl would slip a golden ten-ruble piece, even though he and his family themselves suffered from want. Since Tsemakh knew that the spiritual guide of Navaredok didn't want to lose him, he asked Reb Yosef-Yoizl a question he wouldn't have dared to ask anyone else: "And what if one isn't sure of the First Principle?"

At first the rabbi did not comprehend the question. None of his students had ever asked him if the Creator existed. But he soon grasped what the Lomzher meant and sent his fiery, penetrating glance into him: "You ought to get married as soon as possible."

Tsemakh felt a hot flush on his face as though he'd been slapped. The Old Man evidently considered him the sort of youth who had to be yoked with wife and children to prevent him from thinking about forbidden things. "And if I do marry, will I know the answer? Will my wife tell me?"

The white-bearded old rabbi had been ruddy-cheeked even during his years of hunger. Now, however, he paled and answered sadly, "I know. The burdens of marriage won't save you from the dangers that lie in wait for you. You're too proud to let yourself be broken by workaday cares. But there is only one truth, and that is the truth of the Torah. Man is born a wild ass, as the Bible says, and a wild ass wants to run wild. Then along comes reason to justify every lust. You too, Lomzher, won't be satisfied being just a simple sensualist—that would be too degrading for you. When your blood begins to seethe, it seethes with the hell of heresy. So you have to get married soon to quell that boiling blood of yours. Then your doubts will dissipate like pus from a wound."

Reb Yosef-Yoizl raised a finger and counted his words: "Remember what I'm saying, Lomzher! It's very difficult to die *for* the Torah, but it's far more difficult to live *by* the Torah."

Tsemakh's doubts were gradually overcome as his beard and earlocks grew. The demon in him and the scoffer at his pious ways had apparently been frightened off by the darkness of the Musar yeshiva's meditation rooms, where Tsemakh spent entire nights.

After the passing of Reb Yosef-Yoizl, whose death caused grief among all his followers, Tsemakh became even more devout. Persecutions of Torah scholars intensified in Russia, and the yeshiva teachers and students fled to Poland. Tsemakh began stealing across the border with students smuggled out of Russia. He would offer his last crumb to a student, would give up his bed to one and sleep on the ground. When a lad's weak legs could no longer take him through the swamps along the frontier, Tsemakh would carry him on his shoulders. Then Tsemakh would return to Russia once more to gather children from families unwilling to let them go. He persuaded the youngsters to flee with him at night and consoled them, "One day your parents will thank me and bless you." But in the meantime, mothers cursed him and fathers hunted him like a thief. Among the followers of the Navaredok Musar, however, Tsemakh developed the reputation of one who would sacrifice his life for the Torah. They said in praise of him, "'As an eagle stirreth up her nest and hovereth over her young,' as the Torah says, 'so does the Lomzher watch over his pupils.'"

When they arrived in Poland the Musar followers still burned with the fanatic fire of their struggle with the Communists in Russia. They went about in patched trousers, tattered shoes, and open shirts. Their sallow faces were deathly pale from years of hunger, and their feet were bruised from border crossings. The young pupils whimpered sadly and longed for the parents they'd left behind. Older students grieved over friends who had succumbed to hunger and typhus along the way, and all the yeshiva people mourned the lonely, abandoned grave of Reb Yosef-Yoizl in Kiev.

With this stored-up bitterness—and partly by force—the Musar scholars raged into the little shuls and great synagogues of Nareva and Bialystok, Pinsk, Mezeritch, and Warsaw and established "Beth-Yosef" yeshivas, named after their dead rabbi. From the big cities they went forth to conquer smaller towns. The pale, tattered youths put tefillin bags and Musar booklets into their coat pockets and scattered to the winds. Some went to Lithuania, some to Polesia; others made their way to Volhyn and Hasidic Poland.

As soon as a yeshiva emissary arrived in a town, he would go straight from the train station to the shul, walk up the steps to the Holy Ark, and pound the prayer stand. " 'They that turn the many to righteousness are like eternal stars,' says the Bible. The Jews who help to build a school for Torah study will shine forever like the stars in the sky."And within two or three weeks a small yeshiva would be founded in the town.

Where the Musarniks were not welcomed they sent Tsemakh Atlas, who had settled down in the Nareva yeshiva. His appearance was outlandish, his manner bizarre. He had the aquiline nose of a hawk, and his coal-black eyes radiated sorrow and a touch of anger. When he rose to speak he looked like a prickly fir tree in a thick forest—a chunk of molded darkness. He stood tall and immobile on the steps of the Holy Ark, an otherworldly glow on his pale face. His glazed eyes, seemingly screwed deep into their sockets, gazed at everyone, saw no one. In his sermon he used no melody, no familiar sayings. He demanded endless devotion to the Torah and mocked the man who racked his brain for ways to evade his responsibilities. Suddenly his inwardly turned eyes would flash and sink like a knife into a respected congregant who opposed the yeshiva.

The audience was amazed at Tsemakh's ability to sniff out an opponent and not be intimidated by someone so influential. They even interpreted favorably Tsemakh's praying without a tallis—he had remained unmarried and thus without a prayer shawl, they said, because he had divested himself of physicality.

Having accomplished his mission, Tsemakh Atlas would return to Nareva, sulking and aloof, locked into himself. Even the yeshiva students avoided greeting him. Tsemakh wouldn't say much to the principal, the rosh yeshiva, either, but would merely inform him that a couple of young men should be sent out to launch the new yeshiva. He would then go off to assemble his own pupils.

To them Tsemakh spoke passionately and at length, panting as though his insides were on fire. Suddenly he would stop in mid-sentence and his eyes would glaze, as if the lost thought had plunged from his mind into a windowless cellar. And when he studied Musar, Tsemakh would stalk back and forth alongside the other students in the beth medresh like a powerful beast that paces in a cage with other wild animals but still walks alone. His melancholy chant transported everyone in the house of study, and even at midday it could wrench out of the soul's depths a Yom Kippur night.

Soon few places ripe for new yeshivas remained. Many cities and towns had had schools even before the arrival of the Navaredkers. Moreover, in Poland they didn't have to contend with the Yevseksya—the Jewish Communist group charged with eliminating yeshivas—as they did in Soviet Russia. People laughed at the yeshiva youths for stalking through the streets in groups, their yarmulkes on their heads and their ritual fringes down to their ankles, but at least the students were not persecuted. The Navaredkers in turn calmed down and made peace with the congregants, who at first had refused to let them into their shuls. The head of the Nareva yeshiva induced the community leaders and good-hearted women to provide the students with better food, clean beds, and new clothing. Now that the younger pupils had respite from frequent border crossings, they sank into their studies. One after another the older students married. They outfitted themselves with new gaberdines, shined their shoes, and carefully combed out their thickening beards with all ten fingers.

Tsemakh Atlas, the Lomzher, however, remained a bachelor. He wasn't interested in becoming a Talmud teacher or a small-town rabbi who inspected a chicken's guts to see if it was kosher. He was more interested in knowing if the man was kosher. He was careless of his clothing, let his hair grow wild, and occasionally absented himself in an attic room for private meditation. Tsemakh saw that his pupils' enthusiasm had cooled too and that they no longer spent entire nights listening to his Musar talks.

"You're afraid," he berated them, "that your friends will absorb more Talmud than you and thus make better matches. One can also be a glutton and drunkard with learning. One man wants to gorge meat and swill wine, and another wants to stuff himself with Talmud and commentaries. Basically it's the same kind of overindulgence."

Heads lowered, his pupils listened in polite silence, plucking at the first sprout of hair on their chins. But when their group leader dismissed them, they nevertheless returned to their Talmuds. Tsemakh longingly recalled the years in Russia when the street mobs celebrated with red flags, while in their beth medresh the Musarniks sank their teeth into the prayer stands to avoid being enticed outside by the revolutionary songs. He even regarded the time he spent crossing the borders and risking being shot as a happy one. He had known then that he was living for a higher cause; now he lived in depression, in surroundings without ecstasy. Tsemakh recalled Rabbi Yosef-Yoizl's remark: "It's very difficult to die *for* the Torah, but it's far more difficult to live *by* the Torah."

Only in the fall during Elul could one still feel the old Navaredok exaltation. Small-town rosh yeshivas and their older students, rabbis who spent the year in remote villages or market towns, and young men who had become merchants and storekeepers—all assembled in Nareva during Elul. With the approach of the Days of Awe, everyone was drawn home to the yeshiva. The heat in the beth medresh was so intense it could almost singe one's beard. The Musar melody of hundreds of students reverberated outside. The ecstatic shouting during the Morning Service and the elated banging on the prayer stands were severed by the blowing of the shofar, as though a flashing sword had sliced the air. Night and day its lamps made the yeshiva gleam feverishly as though a live star had landed in Nareva's little lanes.

One of the visitors reported that a small yeshiva could possibly be started in Amdur, near Grodno. However, since opposition existed there, a man of iron determination would have to be sent. It became apparent at once that this was a mission for the Lomzher. Nevertheless, during all of Elul and during the Ten Days of Repentance, Reb Simkha Feinerman, the Nareva rosh yeshiva, looked for someone else. Reb Simkha, a man with a long, narrow red beard and clever blue eyes, didn't like the Lomzher's all-or-nothing fanaticism, especially his conduct with the youngsters he had brought from Russia. Tsemakh kept his students apart and would lead them off for a Musar talk just when Reb Simkha was about to begin a Talmud lesson.

The rabbi had warned Tsemakh a number of times, "You're disrupting the whole beth medresh. You can't run an independent school within the yeshiva."

But instead of defending himself, the Lomzher either was angrily silent or countered with complaints of his own: "The Nareva yeshiva is no longer following the spirit of Navaredok, and what's more, I'm being wronged too."

Hence the rabbi didn't want to ask him to undertake this mission and looked around for another emissary. Nevertheless, no one more suitable than Tsemakh was to be found. On Yom Kippur, after Kol Nidrei, as Reb Simkha made his way to his prayer stand to begin his traditional talk on spiritual awakening, he stopped for a moment next to Tsemakh Atlas. "No choice, Lomzher. After Sukkos, God willing, you'll have to go to Amdur and establish a small yeshiva. For Yom Kippur one must garb oneself in worthy deeds."

Since he knew that the congregation was waiting for his sermon, Reb Simkha strode forthwith to his prayer stand to remove himself from Tsemakh's gloomy silence. Despite his silence, however, Tsemakh at once decided to go, if only to get away from Nareva for a while. He had already foreseen the winter term, when everyone in the house of study would eagerly rush to a new Talmudic tractate while he alone would remain superfluous, like a rotted beam that remains in the water after a flood has washed out a wooden bridge.

2

SINCE THE LAST DAY of Sukkos Amdur had been veiled in a fine, icy autumnal rain. After the week-long downpour, the squat, crooked houses and their soaked roofs looked half-sunken. Tree trunks and naked branches gleamed dark and moist. Clusters of blanched and trodden leaves lay scattered about.

As soon as he left Nareva, Tsemakh had sensed that this time he lacked the strength to succeed. The chill drizzle that greeted him as he entered the town depressed him even more.

He sat in his inn for a long time before he asked the innkeeper, Reb Yaakov-Yitzhok, "Who in Amdur would be willing to support a small yeshiva?"

"I don't know anyone that crazy here! This town has an overabundance of its own paupers, and plenty of wandering beggars besides. Where would we find eating days and beds for the poor students?"

The innkeeper went to the shul for the Afternoon Service; Tsemakh followed later. Since the congregation had already been informed about the visitor and his queer plan, they gave him sidelong mocking glances. An old man with a red, perspiring face and a yellow, snuff-flecked beard approached Tsemakh.

"So you're the fine young man who wants to take the students from us Talmud teachers? And what about the law against encroaching on a person's livelihood—doesn't that mean anything to you?"

In days gone by, Tsemakh would have replied that the old Talmud teacher himself could learn a thing or two in the Navaredok cheder. Now, however, he stood helpless and silent until the old man had finished shouting and departed.

Tsemakh turned to the Amdur rabbi, a heavyset middle-aged man with a curly black beard and a snow-white collar.

But the rabbi didn't look Tsemakh in the eye and replied with an indirect glance, "I'm not going to get involved. In our shul if one congregant says yes, another will say no, and then there'll be a commotion and a fight."

Once more the Lomzher stood tongue-tied. On previous journeys he hadn't asked the town rabbi's opinion. First he had convinced the community, and then the rabbi had perforce agreed.

The congregation remained after the Afternoon Service to hear the visitor's sermon. Reb Yaakov-Yitzhok whispered into Tsemakh's ear as though he were an old acquaintance, "See that young man over there? He's the richest ironmonger in town, influential in the community, and the leader of the local modern Hebrew school. Be careful not to antagonize these progressives, because their leader can order you off the pulpit."

Tsemakh looked at the ironmonger and saw a lively, bony young man who measured Tsemakh with a cold, knowing glance as though to test who was stronger. For a moment the Lomzher straightened up, and his aquiline nose sharpened like that of a hawk when it spies a lordly little rooster on a hillside. Tsemakh knew he could demolish this cocky small-town brat and make his feathers fly. But at once a gnawing feeling of despair swept over him, and he sensed that his hands, ritual fringes, and earlocks were hanging limply, like waterlogged weeds, or as though he himself had been dragged half-drowned from the river.

Tsemakh didn't preach between the Afternoon and Evening Services, but secluded himself in a dark corner behind a prayer stand. The Nareva rosh yeshiva was responsible for his wretchedness, he thought. Reb Simkha Feinerman gave him no money for necessities, didn't invite him to his house, and didn't consult him on yeshiva matters as he did other older scholars. And when Tsemakh justifiably complained and asked why he was being treated like a stranger—after all, he had helped build up the Nareva beth medresh and had brought dozens of pupils over from Russia—Reb Simkha replied that the Lomzher should first examine himself and should not run an independent cheder with his students. Reb Simkha made use of him only during an emergency—for instance, to send him on a mission to a town, as he had now sent him to Amdur. So why should he expend all that energy and contend with the townspeople when he knew he wouldn't prevail anyway? Still, he had to deliver at least one sermon, to keep people in Nareva from saying later on that he hadn't even made an attempt.

The next evening Tsemakh asked the shul's trustees for permission to preach, assuring them that the yeshiva would not be the sole topic of his sermon.

The Lomzher spoke in the Navaredok fashion: "Recognizing what is good and what is evil is not a difficult matter. But it's enormously difficult to locate the evil that has wormed its way into the good. A man's heart must be a red-hot smelting furnace, and in the fire of his own torments he must refine the good from the evil that can be found in his finest deeds, too. A man ought not to think: My evil deeds are separate from my good deeds. A defect in the particular is a defect in the whole. The Vilna Gaon says: 'If a man studies Torah in a house where there is a stolen nail in the wall, he won't succeed in his studies. The stolen nail will creep out of the wall and crawl into the Talmud and tear its pages.' The same applies to our supposedly good deeds in which the rusty nail of an impure intent resides. The impure intent will puncture holes in all our other mitzvas, and rust will devour everything else."

"He's one of ours!" The ironmonger poked his friends from the modernist school.

The enlightened young man assumed that the preacher was reviling the mindless fanatics. The pious congregants, on the other hand, thought that Tsemakh was preaching to those who ran after honor. An old maskil, champion of enlightenment, combed his small white beard with a stiff brush and smacked his lips enthusiastically: "Socrates!"

Sensing that he had won the congregation over, Tsemakh now broached the main theme of his sermon: "Man is evil from birth. But his nature prevents him from finding the evil in his supposedly good deeds. That is why the Torah was given to us—to teach us to lead an ethical life. But one can also interpret the Torah to suit oneself. Hence one has to study Musar from childhood on, and study in a yeshiva . . ."

Tsemakh stopped. He noted that the older congregants were whispering and the younger ones were rattling their prayer stands, ready to shout, "You won't put up a yeshiva here!" A wave of fear swept over him. Before he finished preaching he knew he would not return to Nareva. Since he had lost faith in his own powers and could no longer succeed, the rosh yeshiva would persecute him more, and even his own pupils would no longer respect him.

After the Evening Service a trustee brought Tsemakh a handful of coins and a few paper zlotys. Among themselves the congregants had made a collection to pay him for his sermon. Tsemakh, usually contemptuous of such gestures, was touched by these simple Jews who helped him when he was in need. The next morning the worshipers saw him praying without a tallis and decided that the bachelor ought to be married. Everyone left the shul, and Tsemakh remained alone, studying, immersed in his thoughts. The Talmud teacher with the yellow, snuff-flecked beard approached.

"A young man like you ought to get married. There are no new Talmud students in Amdur, but thank God we've got plenty of unmarried girls."

The teacher and matchmaker had a ready proposal: "There's a man in town named Reb Falk Namiot. He's a widower with a big grocery store and a stone house in the market place. His married sons live in Grodno, and his only daughter, Dvorele, is the sole manager in the store and at home. Reb Falk is offering five thousand zlotys as dowry and two years of free board so his son-in-law can study. The father-in-law will provide the groom with a gold watch, a complete wardrobe made by the finest tailor in Grodno, and a leather-bound set of the Vilna Talmud."

The Talmud teacher seized Tsemakh's arm and pinched it. "Well, what more do you want? Don't hesitate; you'll regret it!"

Tsemakh agreed to meet the prospective father-in-law. Falk Namiot spoke sparingly and had a strange appearance—a low, hairy forehead, a long face, a hairless chin like yellowish sandstone, and a sparse, colorless beard growing from his neck. Beneath his right armpit he held a gnarled cane. He walked stiffly, with measured stride, as though he had just risen from a sickbed.

Tsemakh's first meeting with Namiot left him unnerved. His consolation, however, was that the man seemed the sort who'd stint himself in all pleasures and provide for his daughter instead.

The prospective bride, Dvorele Namiot, was a chubby girl with large gray eyes and auburn hair pulled straight back. Her somewhat puffy cheeks and sallow complexion declared that she was no longer young, but her smile was full of wonder, like a child's, as though she had lain down to sleep as a baby and awakened fully grown, and was still looking for her lost childhood. At her first meeting with Tsemakh she was even more taciturn than her father, but she gazed at him with respect and trust.

Although Tsemakh had previously expressed little interest in matches, he had met some prospective brides, and every one, he recalled, was younger and prettier than Dvorele Namiot. Still, he liked her submissive glance and helpless smile. Moreover, the large, dark rooms of her father's house seemed made to order for him to find repose after his life of homelessness and poverty. Tsemakh felt as if all his years of anguished wandering were gathering like shadows and whispering in his ear, "What are you waiting for? Who else is going to take an interest in you? You're already thirty-three." Tsemakh also figured that if he became an Amdur resident, the very same townspeople who now opposed the yeshiva would help him build one. And the yeshiva would be his—not a branch of Nareva that would enlarge Reb Simkha Feinerman's empire. Reb Simkha wanted another yeshiva under his wing—but not with Tsemakh Atlas as principal.

Hearing that Tsemakh had agreed, Falk Namiot immediately prepared the engagement contract and invited guests to the ceremony. The groom, however, didn't invite his friends from Nareva, or the rosh yeshiva either. Tsemakh felt that even in this matter he'd been wronged by Reb Simkha, who had never proposed a suitable match for him as he had for other Torah scholars. And if no one came from Nareva for his engagement party, Tsemakh wouldn't have to account for his failure to start a yeshiva in Amdur. However, Tsemakh was distressed for the students he had brought over from Russia. After all, he had promised their parents that he would watch them as if they were the apple of his eye. But on the other hand the youngsters were grown up now, and even natural parents let their mature children be independent. He realized too that he had been hindering his students more than he had helped them. They wanted to learn Talmud and the commentaries with an eye toward making good rabbinic matches, while he was vexing them with his sermons on improving their ethical state. The youngest of his pupils was now more expert and keen in Talmud than he, the group leader, who had shouted his heart out over the Musar books.

3

IN HONOR of his daughter's engagement, Falk Namiot's usually dark rooms were brightly lighted. Amdur householders sat around the groom, tasting honey cake and whisky, speaking softly among themselves in a restrained fashion. The bride-to-be sat in the same room, surrounded by girls from the town. A separate women's table was laden with plates of fruit, candies, sugar cakes, and wine in small carafes. The householders' daughters, their hair braided like challa loaves, observed the groom from a distance.

A charming black-haired girl, the prettiest at the table, never took her shrewd, sparkling eyes and smiling glances off Tsemakh. She had heard that the groom was a raggedy yeshiva student, but she saw a young man with a neatly trimmed beard in a pressed suit and white shirt. A dim sadness misted his deep-set eyes, and sharp lines were etched into the corners of his taut lips. The girl was surprised at his tall stature and his broad, manly shoulders. Her amazement at how such a man had come to Dvorele Namiot could be seen on her face.

Tsemakh sensed her curious glances, and the color rose on his pale cheeks. His shoulders straightened and a gruff look came over his sharp profile. The bright-faced girl realized that the young man was warming to her glance and began to turn her head like a bird. She patted her hair and whispered and chattered and laughed with her friends.

In Tsemakh's eyes, Dvorele Namiot looked like a clumsy creature among these well-dressed middle-class girls with their radiant faces and white teeth. Tsemakh noticed that the girls around the table were not really her friends. They spoke more to one another than to her; she sat there as if she were being tolerated, like a stranger in her own house. Dvorele's face looked swollen; her childish smile, full of wonder, had become wrinkled and old, as if she had realized that she and her fiancé were not a good pair. In the well-lighted house her long-faced father with the sparse beard looked even more bizarre. His morose silence during his only daughter's engagement party settled heavily in all corners of the house. The groom noticed that the guests were reserved: they spoke softly among themselves, as though visiting Falk Namiot were torture for them. Moreover, the guests were those who sat in the shul's rear benches. No prominent residents were there—not the rabbi and not even the owner of the inn. Of the bride's four brothers in Grodno, not one had come.

Edging in among the celebrants' elbows and shoulders, the Talmud teacher and matchmaker gasped, "Give us some Torah commentary. A groom should display some of his learning."

Tsemakh offered a prepared interpretation which the simple crowd didn't understand anyway. Even during his discourse he was haunted by the thought that something was fishy here; something had been hidden from him. Yet he was heartened by the girls' looks directed at him from the other table, looks which seemed to say: Don't be depressed; you're still young.

The next day Namiot told him, "Business prevented my sons from coming to the celebration, so I'm going to Grodno to tell them about Dvorele's match."

Tsemakh was pleased that Falk Namiot was leaving. Now he could freely ask about what sort of house he had fallen into. He began by talking to the innkeeper, a man with a tangled beard, thick brows, and tufts of hair in his ears.

"Can you tell me why you and other prominent Amdur folk didn't come to the engagement ceremony?"

Reb Yaakov-Yitzhok shrugged, twisted his neck, stuck his hands into the sleeves of his short fur jacket, and groaned, "Are you an orphan?"

Tsemakh nodded.

"Well, to save an orphan from harm, slander is no sin."

The innkeeper began by saying, "Breaking an engagement is worse than divorce, especially since Dvorele is a gentle soul and her mother too was a quiet dove." Then he turned to the matter at hand. "Falk Namiot is a beast, a werewolf. Once, when his wife said something he didn't like, he didn't speak to her for fifteen years. But this didn't stop him from having four sons and a daughter by her. Finally the wife couldn't take it any longer, and one day she was found in bed frozen to death by his cruel silence. He beat his four sons with the cane he carries under his arm to this day. When they grew up, they ran away—they didn't want to see their father any more. That's why they didn't come to the engagement ceremony. The rabbi and other prominent townspeople didn't come because they hate Falk Namiot like pig meat—he doesn't give a penny to charity. But there's still another reason why they didn't come—they didn't want you to accuse them later of having helped to fool you."

Tsemakh gaped in confusion. "How would they fool me?"

"It's very doubtful," Reb Yaakov-Yitzhok answered, "that your father-in-law will actually give you the dowry and keep his promise of two years' free board. He wouldn't care if his daughter never got married, for she's an unpaid salesgirl in his store. But Namiot himself is planning to get married again and to a young divorcée who doesn't want a grown stepdaughter in the house. People here are saying he's afraid someone else might beat him to the divorcée. That's why he just ran off to Grodno to tell her he'll soon be rid of his daughter. Rumor also has it that this divorcée is a Cossack of a woman. When she was warned what sort of person Namiot is, she said she wasn't afraid. 'If it comes to burying,' she said, 'I'll bury *him*!' The long and the short of it is that the father doesn't even give his daughter money for a doctor."

Seeing Tsemakh's stupefied look, the innkeeper crinked his neck again and pondered whether to say more. But since he had already begun, he continued, "People say the bride is sickly. Maybe Namiot didn't beat his only daughter the way he beat his sons, but she's beaten down anyway—she's a sickly girl, and her dear papa begrudges sending her to doctors. I've heard people say that his stinginess comes from some kind of illness, calluses on the brain. Others think he's just a downright murderer, a cutthroat, a man with the heart of a killer. Well, if you don't believe me, ask someone else."

Reb Yaakov-Yitzhok took his hands out of his sleeves and refused to utter another word of slander.

Tsemakh sat with lowered head, musing that the Navaredok proverb, "He who knows himself knows the world," was impractical and a lie. The Musarniks, he thought, speculate on how to refine the traits of one's character, but they haven't the slightest conception of the like of a Falk Namiot. Tsemakh, then, had gone out into the world blind. A simple little shopkeeper wouldn't have made such a fool of himself. Nevertheless, Tsemakh didn't rely solely on the innkeeper, but went to the shul to talk to the Amdur rabbi about his prospective father-in-law. The rabbi, who didn't want a dispute in town over a yeshiva, was even less eager to start a quarrel with Falk Namiot over a match.

"But it's all over and done with. What do you have to ask now?" the town rabbi said, withdrawing.

Tsemakh returned to the innkeeper and asked, "Why did the Amdur Jews keep quiet when they knew I was being fooled?"

"Did you sit down and consult anyone?" the innkeeper replied. "Everyone in town loves Dvorele, and they want to save her from that father with the calluses on his brain. So everyone thought: It's none of my business. Why shouldn't a religious young man save a Jewish girl who's an orphan to boot? After the wedding he'll take his young wife and go somewhere else, become a rabbi, a rosh yeshiva, a ritual slaughterer, whatever he wants. That's what everyone thought. Even I wouldn't have said a word if you hadn't pressed me and if Reyzele hadn't said that during the engagement ceremony the groom looked at the bride as if he hated her."

Tsemakh felt that his head was splitting. "You mean they decided I should save an orphan girl without consulting me?" he shouted. "They wanted to wash their hands of me just like that? And just who is this Reyzele? Who's the mind reader here who can tell that I looked at the bride as if I hated her?"

The innkeeper shrugged. "Why are you yelling? Reyzele comes from a wealthy home, and she's a fine girl with lots of good qualities. She has only one fault. She doesn't want a yeshiva student and refuses to get married by means of a matchmaker. At the engagement party Reyzele and the other girls noticed that you hardly looked at the bride, and then only reluctantly. Reyzele told her parents that if she'd known before what you looked like, she'd have gotten to know you. The fact that you're a yeshiva student wouldn't have bothered her at all."

At the engagement party Tsemakh had heard the girls calling the bright-eyed young beauty "Reyzele". Some comparison, he thought, Reyzele and Dvorele . . . and he stopped visiting his bride-to-be, spending his time instead at the inn or the shul. He noticed, however, that the congregants who at first had held him in awe paid scant attention to him since his engagement. How foolish had been his dream of opening a yeshiva in Amdur after the wedding and becoming its principal through his father-in-law's prestige. In Amdur he couldn't even be a simple tutor. He would have to leave town before Namiot got back from Grodno. Returning to Nareva was out of the question. He would never be forgiven for failing to start a yeshiva and for not inviting the rosh yeshiva and the older students to the engagement ceremony. Tsemakh decided to go home to his family in Lomzhe.

The betrothed girl was standing in the grocery store, busy with customers, when she saw her fiancé entering. Tsemakh's unexpected appearance flustered Dvorele, and her bewilderment went to her hands. She couldn't weigh the merchandise. She poured out an extra half-scoop of barley, then took back a full scoop, which made the scales fly up and down. The customers smiled: they knew they should leave the engaged couple alone. As soon as the women left, Tsemakh quickly told Dvorele he was leaving. Her cheeks flamed; the color made her look younger.

"Why all of a sudden?" she said. "Father said he would talk with a Grodno tailor about the wedding clothes and would buy the presents there. He's coming back tomorrow or the day after and he's going to wonder what happened."

Fearful that the in-law's presents would bind him even more, Tsemakh bristled: "I have to see my family. Your father said he was going to Grodno to tell his sons about the match, so I too can go and talk with my relatives. It's still too early to order wedding clothes. It's only two weeks after Sukkos, and the wedding is scheduled for two weeks before Passover, six months off." The crimson in Dvorele's cheeks began to disappear, and her big gray eyes slowly welled with tears. The same aged smile he had seen during the engagement ceremony pressed into the corners of her mouth—the smile of a grownup whose last childish hope has vanished.

"All right," she said, and gave her fiancé a long look as her tears dried.

Tsemakh left the store at once, afraid to turn around for fear he would encounter her eyes again. He returned to the inn and told the owner he was leaving. The innkeeper seemed more amazed and frightened than the engaged girl.

"And when are you coming back?"

"I don't know, and it's none of your concern. I don't want to meet Reyzele, or whatever her name is, anyway."

"It didn't even dawn on me to bring the two of you together," Reb Yaakov-Yitzhok said in a wild rage. "A quarrel with Falk Namiot is all I need. You do want to meet Reyzele, but it's beneath your dignity."

Tsemakh considered the innkeeper named after the two Patriarchs a troublemaker, more like the evil counselor Ahitophel, even though everything he had said about Falk Namiot was true. However, everything he had said about the groom was true, too. Aboard the train heading back for Lomzhe, Tsemakh thought more of the bright-eyed, black-haired beauty than of his fiancée.

4

REB ZIML ATLAS, a tall and scrawny man, was perpetually immersed in prayerful ecstasy. Standing next to him, his squat and wide-girthed wife Tsertele looked like the foreshortened shadow that a tall, slender tree casts at noon. In Lomzhe they were called the lulav and the esrog, the palm branch and the citron. Nevertheless, the old couple occasionally squabbled. Reb Ziml considered his wife an immodest wanton, for on weekdays she covered her head with merely a kerchief and not a wig—she wore a wig only for the Sabbath. And furthermore their three sons were like her, both in build and in chasing after the pleasures of this world. Tsertele, on the other hand, considered her husband an idler and made fun of him for always standing with his head thrown back toward the ceiling.

"Any word from the ceiling, Ziml? What's new up there?" she would shout up to him, and Reb Ziml would lift his chin higher.

Tsemakh's father and mother had died one after the other before he was Bar Mitzva, and he had been raised by his father's brother, Reb Ziml. While studying in Navaredok, Tsemakh had rarely come home for a holiday. After his return from Russia he had come back to Lomzhe only once, to visit his parents' graves. Since then the family had neither seen him nor heard from him directly. His uncle and aunt had heard only that their nephew had become a great man and was so busy founding yeshivas he didn't even have time to get married. Hence Tsemakh's sudden return to Lomzhe delighted the old couple. His uncle swayed over him and his aunt tapped him all over with her careworn hands, stroking him and crying, "Oh, what joy you would have given your parents!"

A sweet feeling engulfed the weary Tsemakh as he found himself among close kin, protected and shielded by their devoted love. Behind him stood Uncle Ziml, looking like a long, crooked shofar, like the ram's horns displayed in booksellers' windows in the month of Elul. Before him stood Aunt Tsertele, serving him a fresh egg with trembling hands. Tsemakh tapped his spoon on the shell, immersed in thought. He couldn't understand why for years he'd had to extirpate home and family from within himself. One Simkhas Torah Tsemakh had castigated a student who after a shot of whisky burst into tears because he missed his parents in Russia. "Instead of trying to perfect your character, you're longing for your mama to make you meat dumplings and potato latkes," he had mocked. Tsemakh had treated his students like the Levites in the desert who didn't let kinship stand in their way when they punished those who worshiped the golden calf. But what had he achieved, after all? He was a broken man, without faith in Musar and with no prospects for tomorrow. Tsemakh still tapped the shell, watching his aunt's constantly moving hands.

"Eat, eat," she pleaded, pushing the salt shaker and the bread-basket toward him. "Why aren't you eating? Why are you sitting there so sad and lost in thought? How proud of you your parents would have been now!"

During the day the old people were busy in their grocery store, and Tsemakh remained alone in the apartment. In the bedroom two high, bolstered beds drowsed in patrician repose. On the ancient, cracked chest of drawers stood an old photograph of his grandparents; years of piety shone out of its hazy distance. In the cold parlor where Tsemakh slept, two silver candelabra containing long white candles stood on a table on either side of a large mirror. The gloom of Sabbath twilight, the sadness of a Saturday dusk, always pervaded the room. From the mirror, moist with cold and lackluster with age, Tsemakh saw a lifeless face staring at him. Why, it asked him, wasn't Dvorele Namiot a suitable bride for you? He turned away from the mirror and said to himself, "My uncle and aunt would have liked her, no doubt, but I'd have to live in Amdur with her and her father, who wouldn't pay the dowry or provide the promised two years of free board. I'd be forced to take up the wanderer's staff once more, and this time with a wife and children. No, it's no match for me."

When his uncle and aunt returned from the store that evening, Tsemakh was still sitting in the dark. Distressed that her nephew hadn't touched the prepared food in the pantry, Tsertele urged her husband to heat the oven in Tsemakh's room at once, while she began to cook supper. But before the old couple and their nephew had finished eating, Tsertele's three sons stormed in.

In their youth the three stocky and boisterous Atlas brothers had been members of the Lomzhe Cantors' Choir; they had dreamed that someday they'd be cantors wearing high octagonal yarmulkes and deafening great synagogues with their leonine voices. They never developed leonine voices; in fact, Lomzhers made fun of their size, which would disqualify them for military service. But just because they were considered midgets, Tsertele's children didn't even try to avoid the draft. They let themselves be sent to Polish regiments, where they became the finest marksmen. Returning home on furlough, the brothers wore heavy leather boots with leggings and wide leather straps, and soldiers' caps that looked like little boats. Their uniforms made them look even shorter and bulkier. People in Lomzhe wondered why these three were the finest marksmen in the regiment. Was their eyesight any better? And the double-chinned soldiers laughed. "You don't shoot just with your eyes. You have to use your brains to hit the target."

After their discharge, the brothers had married short, thick-set Lomzhe women, so as not to look up to their wives as their mother looked up to their father. All three became clerks at the huge flour concern owned by the two Stupel brothers. Entering the Stupels' store, a customer might have thought he was in the circus. The clerks dangled in the air over sacks of flour piled ceiling-high, and clambered over the shelves like acrobats over rope ladders.

The brothers ran around in their mother's house, too, tearing open closet doors, turning over jugs and pots, looking for a snack, a piece of cake, laughing and making an uproar. Among them their short, squat mother looked like a frog amid her restless young, and their tall father resembled a narrow-winged stork standing on one leg in a swamp. Soon he'd bend down and with his long dry beak pick up a quivering little frog and lift him to the ceiling. But the sons, not fazed by their father, hovered about their mother. They also spoke to their scholarly cousin unceremoniously.

"We heard that you fought the Bolsheviks in Russia," they said with a little cough and the mocking smile of experienced salesmen. "And the yeshiva boys consider you a hero, a Judah Maccabee. Well, we've seen such swashbucklers before. Be that as it may, the younger Stupel brother, Volodya—the one who used to study in cheder with you—wants to see you."

Tsertele's sons literally jumped with admiration talking about their boss. "He's rich and he treats us very well and later on he's going to help us become independent businessmen. It's an honor for you, Tsemakh, and for the whole Atlas family, to get an invitation from Volodya Stupel."

The three ebullient brothers tumbled out of the house as quickly and merrily as they had entered, and ran off to their short, chunky wives. Hands on the table, Tsemakh's aunt gazed at length into Tsemakh's eyes. "I suggest you go up to see the Stupels. They are very rich, and their only sister, the youngest in the family, isn't married yet."

Tsemakh still hadn't told them about his engagement: he found it extremely difficult to discuss the matter. Now he finally revealed that he had entered into a match, but he had no strength for extended conversation; chills and waves of fever were sweeping over him. "My fiancée is all right," he said briefly, "but people say

my future father-in-law won't give me either the promised dowry
or the two years of free board."

Behind his nephew's back, Uncle Ziml addressed the ceiling. "So
become a recluse after the wedding."

"Very smart! Is that the sort of good advice you get from the
ceiling?" Tsertele shouted up to her husband. "Did you hear that
suggestion from a flesh-and-blood uncle? Marry and become a
recluse right after the wedding!"

Tsertele saw that her nephew was not well and suggested that he
lie down. Tsemakh entered the heated room, shuttered from
within. In the darkness the unlit white candles in their silver
candlesticks gleamed coldly on each side of the mirror. Tsemakh
did not turn on the lamp; with despair in his heart, as though he
had already recited his final confession, he lay down in the bedding
on the sofa. Tsertele groped her way into the darkness with another
pillow, which she quickly placed under her nephew's head, and
covered his shoulders with her woolen shawl. When she left, his
uncle came in and put his fur jacket over Tsemakh's feet. Tsemakh
let himself be tucked in like a child, lamenting the youth which
others had enjoyed amidst their own families, but which he had
been deprived of when he became a Navaredker Musarnik.

5

VOLODYA STUPEL HAD a short, thick neck, a big head with
thick hair, short arms, hairy fingers, and palms as broad as shovels.
While talking in the store with a grain merchant, the thirty-five-
year-old Volodya stood at an angle to keep one eye on the dealer
and the other on the clerks and customers. He loved to dig into his
pocketful of coins and jingle the silver or throw a handful up into
the air and catch it. The clerks knew that if their boss lost a coin
they had to stop what they were doing and quickly look under the

benches, between the flour sacks, and near the customers' feet. Volodya didn't stir from his place; he didn't lift a finger to point out where the coin had fallen. He waited calmly, his hand full of change, until the retrieved copper fivepence or silver tenpence was placed in his hand. Instead of thanking the clerk, Volodya would burst into laughter. His delighted chuckle was the clerks' greatest reward.

Unlike his elder brother, Naum, Volodya didn't involve himself in city affairs. Naum loved to attend receptions for famous people. If a provincial governor or a Jewish delegate from abroad came to Lomzhe, the gray-bearded elder Stupel donned a tail coat, a starched white shirt, a bow tie, and a black top hat. The dandyish tails made him appear even shorter; a tight vest pushed his pointed stomach out even more. When Naum displayed himself in the store in this formal attire, Volodya would pluck at his hair excitedly and giggle. "You look like a chimney sweep!" The incensed Naum would squirm like a bound rooster and run out of the store in a rage.

The Stupels lived in their own stone house in the old market place. The shop was on the ground floor, and their apartments, with adjoining balconies, were on the second. In the summer Naum loved to put on a flowered dressing gown and sit on his balcony in the evening, taking in the fresh air and gazing down upon Lomzhe. At the same time Volodya would go out onto his balcony and begin tossing handfuls of coins in the air and catching them. Naum, on his rocking chair, would tremble lest a coin fall down on the cobblestones below. He actually writhed in pain and shut his eyes tightly—but he still couldn't endure it, and ran into his apartment crying, "I can't take it any longer. He's driving me crazy!"

"It's not a baby, God forbid, or a pussycat," his wife would say. "He's just throwing bits of silver and copper into the air. A coin can't crack its head. What are you making such a fuss for?"

Volodya would be convulsed with laughter. The echo of his thunderous roar resounded over the empty market place and reverberated in the side streets.

Since Tsemakh hadn't accepted Volodya Stupel's invitation, the clerks ran to see their mother in the grocery.

"Mother is at home," their space-gazing father said. "Tsemakh doesn't feel well and she's taking care of him."

The worried Tsertele didn't know what to think. Her nephew couldn't leave his bed but wouldn't let her call a doctor. Was he really sick, or did he just feel depressed and want his aunt to tend to him?

Tsemakh's mind was a fog of memory—childhood scenes, yeshiva days, and rainy days in Amdur—but thoughts of his old school friend, the flour merchant Stupel, didn't cross his mind. Hence his amazement when a young man built like a beam rolled into the house one evening and amiably reached out his hand.

"How are you feeling, Tsemakh? I heard you're not well, so I came to pay you a sick call. Don't you recognize me? I'm Velvel, Velvel Stupel," the visitor said, using his childhood name, and he sat down at the edge of the patient's sofa.

The three clerks, who had accompanied Volodya, were quite staid in their mother's house this time and didn't remove their eyes from their boss. Volodya's visit made them respect their cousin more. Tsertele stood by the door, craning forward as the rich merchant talked with her nephew.

"Tsemakh, do you remember our teacher with the red beard? When he got angry his mouth foamed, so the kids nicknamed him the foaming red pancake." Volodya pulled a handful of coins out of his pocket, jingled them, and threw them up into the air.

His head resting on two pillows, the pale Tsemakh smiled at these incidents recalled from his childhood. Velvel Stupel had adored sticking out his leg and tripping his friends. When someone fell, he would double over with laughter. However, the other children were afraid to get even with him. All Velvel had to do was raise his thick fist threateningly and they'd retreat as though before a bear with an upraised paw. Nevertheless, Volodya was liked. He was good-natured and shared the food in his big lunchbag with his friends. When a pupil didn't know his lessons, the teacher would bang a Talmud over his head. The other children were frightened, but Velvel Stupel, though he knew even less than the next fellow, looked on calmly with a broad smile on his beaming face. He knew the teacher wouldn't lift a finger to him: he was the richest pupil in town; and besides, he was apt to hit back.

Volodya lost one of his coins, and Tsemakh saw his aunt's eldest son throw himself on the floor to look for it. The clerk placed the found tenpence in Stupel's hand; Stupel didn't even thank him. He merely looked pleased and continued jiggling the coins.

"And do you remember the incident with the bugs?" the flour merchant asked.

Once, when the teacher dozed off, Velvel had taken a little box out of his pocket and placed it on the table. Soon little bugs began crawling out, scurrying over the open books until they crept into the teacher's beard. Introducing black beetles into the red beard so delighted Velvel that his wild laughter awakened the teacher, who pounced on the lad with flying fists.

"The rabbi wanted to kill me. So I lifted up a bench, and he retreated, white as a sheet, afraid I'd crush him with it." Volodya once again lost a coin, and the second of his clerks now caught it.

"But the rabbi chased you out of the cheder. He said he'd forego the rich man's tuition, and he threw you out." Tsemakh's eyes flashed angrily. "Why do you have that nasty habit of throwing coins in the air and letting people crawl around to pick them up for you?"

"What do you care?" The three brothers yelled at their cousin as though he had brought misfortune upon them. Tsemakh didn't look at them but continued talking to the flour merchant.

"If you like to have someone crawling on all fours for you, why don't you buy yourself a dog and teach him how to stand on his hind legs? Or train him to jump into the water and fish out a rag you've thrown in? But don't act that way with human beings."

The three brothers were silent. Tsertele too was amazed at her nephew for scolding her sons' employer. But Volodya laughed contentedly and ran his fingers through his thick hair. He slipped the handful of coins into his pocket and stood.

"A dog is a wonderful idea. And how well you remembered that the teacher threw me out of the cheder. When you get out of that bed, Tsemakh, come up and see us. I want to introduce you to my pompous elder brother and my little sister. Good night, Auntie!" he shouted into Tsertele's ear and marched out of the house accompanied by his clerks.

"He's a simple soul but a good man," Tsertele told her nephew. "You should go to see him. His sister is a different sort. Gentle and educated. I can't understand why she's not married."

Tsemakh lay with his eyes closed. While Volodya Stupel lived in vulgar wealth, he himself struggled to live a spiritual life. But basically he couldn't do without a little of the pleasures of this world either. Nevertheless, he had accomplished something in Navaredok. He would never crawl on all fours before a rich merchant.

6

HANNAH, VOLODYA'S WIFE, robust, summer-fresh, calm as a bright village morning in July, knew how to hold on to her husband with her body and with food. Volodya loved to stuff himself and wanted meals to be served by his wife and not by a maid. Seeing his wife carrying a platter of fish from the kitchen, or a tray laden with soup and meat, he whinnied like a stallion in heat and didn't know what intoxicated him more: his wife's plump body, her fleshy arms and massive chest, or her food.

Delighted by her skill, her clean fingers, and her flaming face, he jumped up with outspread arms and grabbed her by the waist, pinched her, and seized a handful of her firm flesh, just as he liked to clutch a handful of coins. Hannah stopped and, holding the laden tray with both hands, patiently waited for her husband to calm down so that she could continue bringing the steaming dishes from the kitchen to the dining room. She wasn't upset and didn't blush as he capered about, sniffing her. She merely smiled and appeased him silently—the winter night was long and the bed in their room was wide enough for two.

Hannah was terrified of only one thing. Under her thick auburn hair was a pair of rosy, transparent little ears that drove her well-fleshed husband wild. When Volodya wanted to whisper a secret into those ears, they perked up like two young fawns raising their heads at a suspicious rustle in the twigs.

"I'm going to drop the tray!" Hannah screamed, and Volodya was very careful not to touch his wife above the neck while she served. But when Hannah sat down at the table, her husband—hairy, sweaty, aflame with desire, and packing away the food from the full plates—turned, pretending to get a piece of bread and, with a swiftness that belied his bulky frame, blew into her ear. Hannah jumped up as though scalded by hot soup. Volodya laughed wildly, and his sister Slava, who was eating supper with them, also laughed until the tears came.

Slava, the youngest of the Stupel family, was a radiant twenty-five-year-old with light blue eyes and a head of blond hair. Her soft, feline gait indicated that she was a pampered only daughter, amiable, warm, in love with herself, and longing to be loved. When she was a young schoolgirl in the Hebrew *Gymnasium* in Bialystok, she had dreamed of being a pioneer in Palestine, but she had soon realized that she wasn't really drawn to the land she recognized on school maps—a thin line for the Jordan River and two blue spots representing the Galilee lakes. In the higher grades she already hated her long, dangling braids and the white-collared black dress that was the school uniform. When she graduated from the *Gymnasium* she no longer wanted to study or to see her former friends, pioneers with healthy faces and thick legs, apparently born for hard work. For a while Slava Stupel went around with the sons of Bialystok and Lomzhe merchants, but finally she couldn't stomach them any more. These young playboys from well-off homes had fat lips and cold eyes and were too crude and ill-mannered for her taste.

In Lomzhe it was said that old Stupel had willed half his fortune to his only daughter, while the two sons received the other half. It was also known that Slava was Volodya's little darling. They constantly joked and laughed together. But when the Stupels entertained, Slava hardly spoke, lest the Lomzhers become too friendly with her. The townspeople had long pondered why the young woman had not married. Then they had discovered that she had a married lover in Bialystok. Her visits to the city were ostensibly to order tailor-made clothes and to attend the theater with her friends, but it was the lover she went to see.

Slava lived in the rear wing of the Stupel house. The corridor led from her apartment to those of her brothers, and she was at

Volodya's almost every evening. Once she found a tall, pale, black-bearded young man sitting at the table drinking tea. Both the visitor and Volodya wore hats. Though the Stupels had a Jewish home—they bought kosher meat and on Friday afternoons closed their store before the onset of the Sabbath—Volodya was by no means religious. He always went around bareheaded, and this didn't embarrass him when a religious Jew came in for a donation. Slava gathered that her brother held the pious visitor in esteem and guessed that he must be Volodya's childhood friend. Volodya had told her that his friend had become a great scholar and ran a yeshiva, and that he couldn't understand why Tsemakh hadn't married.

A young man with a beard? Slava wondered, and immediately the stranger ceased to interest her. In fact she resented his visit. She had gone to spend an evening with her brother to avoid being alone with her confused thoughts, but at Volodya's she encountered a tense silence like that at Rosh Hashana before the shofar is blown.

"This is my cheder friend, Tsemakh Atlas," Volodya said. "He was there when I let little black beetles get into my teacher's red beard. Tsemakh was never a young rascal, as though he knew even as a kid that he was going to grow up to be a Musarnik."

"I've seen Musarniks in Bialystok," Slava said, so that her silence would not be interpreted as a rebuff to Tsemakh. "They go around wearing long ritual fringes that hang out from under their short jackets, and people make fun of their clothes. I've also heard it said that a Musarnik occasionally goes out in the street in the summer wearing a fur coat, a scarf, and galoshes. Is this some kind of religious observance?"

"They do this to train themselves to disregard other people's opinions and to ignore ridicule," said Tsemakh, who himself had on a good suit and a clean shirt and tie.

"And what's a Musarnik?" Hannah asked.

"A Musarnik?" The visitor wrinkled his brow and hugged the empty tea glass with his fingers. "A Musarnik is a man who lives the way he thinks he should live."

"Every man lives that way," Slava retorted, and saw a furtive spark flaming in the scholar's eyes.

His deep glance floated up from an umber distance and his words were measured: "On the contrary! People always complain that they've never really understood how to live. But the truth is, they don't live according to what they understand to be right."

"It's hard—I mean it's hard to live according to the dictates of one's understanding," Slava said, immersed in her own thoughts.

When the guest arrived, Hannah Stupel had quickly donned a kerchief that was too short and too narrow to cover her thick hair, low-cut neckline, and long bare arms. The more Hannah looked at and heard her husband's friend, the more her respect increased, and she kept adjusting her kerchief to cover her naked flesh. Watching him, she thought that he should be fattened up; his cheeks were hollow, poor soul. The conversation now fascinated Slava too, but she was even more interested in the appearance of the visitor, who was evidently much younger than she had assumed. Volodya, however, was already bored by the intellectual turn of the conversation, and his hat felt like a lead helmet on his head. He ran his fingers through his hair and fidgeted in his deep chair, oppressed by his heavy, cumbersome body. But most of all he was tormented by the rosy, transparent ears that peeped out of Hannah's locks like wild strawberries in a forest thicket. Those little ears, those sweet little devils, winked and teased him as if to say: Now you can't squeeze your own wife's waist. And she, that shrewd vixen, she sat there opposite the scholar like a pious-faced rebbetsin.

Volodya saw the gray cat parading through the apartment. He bent down over the chair and put the cat on his lap. He patted her, imitated her meowing, and whispered in her ear, "Have you got a papa and mama?" The cat squirmed free, then shook her head no. Volodya giggled once again, blew into the cat's ear, and repeated the question. Hannah turned her big, handsome head restlessly as if she were being tickled by a straw. Slava caught on to her brother's joke and burst out with a resounding laugh—but immediately cut it short for fear their guest would think it had something to do with him. She looked at Tsemakh again and noted the apathetic sadness of a man who had gone through a great deal. He had neither the face of an innocent yeshiva student nor the self-imposed tragic mask of her friend Bernard Frankel.

"If you have time"—Slava stroked her long throat—"come see us again." She pointed to her apartment down the corridor and displayed her wide, pearly-toothed smile as though triumphant over her brother and sister-in-law, who were surprised at her daring to invite a Torah scholar to her room. Tsemakh gave her a penetrating glance, and Slava moved her thin shoulders back and forth like a playful wave that splashes softly ashore, then immediately retreats.

7

SLAVA STUPEL MADE SURE that her frequent visitor, Tsemakh Atlas, always sat opposite the table with the shaded lamp. She herself sat on the sofa at the other side of the room, her legs folded under her. Cozy among the small embroidered pillows, she talked with him from a distance and studied his profile—sharp, aquiline nose, sensual lips, black beard and mustache—evidently a strong-willed man.

"Why are you always so serious and angry-looking? Are all Musarniks like this?" she asked, her gay voice coming from the other side of the room. "My brother Volodya didn't study in a yeshiva, and he's good-natured and always laughing."

"Wordly people," Tsemakh replied, "can put up a false front until someone steps on their toes. Then one can see the true character of these supposedly sensitive, good-natured people's disguise."

Slava listened and thought of Bernard Frankel—nothing irritated him more than bad manners. His fine manners, however, didn't prevent him from deceiving both her and his wife. Slava had seen enough of Tsemakh's profile; she now wanted to see him full face. So, like a cat, she clambered over to a deep chair, folded her legs beneath her again, and stroked her knees with both hands. From the front, she noted, Tsemakh had an anguished, ascetic appearance and a good smile, like the stone saints in the Warsaw churches which she and Bernard Frankel had seen. Tsemakh Atlas would surely have been appalled had he known she was comparing him with a sculpture of a Catholic saint. But he would have been more appalled had he known that she toured these churches with a married man, her intimate friend.

"But if a Musarnik can't put up a false front, then he can't tell lies," she rambled on.

Tsemakh answered calmly and softly like an adult speaking to a child. "A Musarnik, too, can be led astray and tell a lie. But lying is something the Musarnik learned either at home or in the world at large, not in the beth medresh, the house of study. Besides, a Musarnik can only lie to others; he can't fool himself even if he wants to. But a man who hasn't toiled to know himself can also convince himself that his lies are truth. If a day later it's to his advantage to say exactly the opposite, he says exactly the opposite and again convinces himself that that's the truth."

"When I lie, I know I'm lying, and I enjoy telling a well-turned, polished lie." Tsemakh heard her laugh. "But you're dead serious again! Is a Musarnik forbidden to be happy?"

"In our yeshiva it is said that he who has learned Musar will never again have joy in his life, even after he has stopped studying Musar," Tsemakh said gloomily, as if to armor himself against the magic of her sweet voice. "Perhaps that's why a Musarnik is indeed angrier than a secular person. A recluse can't be good-natured and happy, like the wordly, nonreligious man who submits to all his desires."

After Tsemakh's departure Slava thought: He's angry because he loves me but is ashamed to show it. He's no longer as observant as he once was, but he hasn't yet become worldly, as he puts it. Anyway, a man like Tsemakh didn't discuss his own feelings. He was not as easygoing and frivolous as Frankel. A snowstorm raged in the darkness outside and Slava snuggled into her corner, thinking at length of her lover, a teacher in Bialystok's Polish-Jewish *Gymnasium.*

Bernard Frankel, born in Lemberg, was a ruddy, powerfully built man of thirty-eight. He talked to Slava about books and the beautifully sad Polish autumn. In the midst of his philosophizing he would often become depressed, but after a long silence he would heave a sigh of relief, as though he'd had to console himself over a sorrow he could entrust to no one. Slava liked the contradictions in his character and felt drawn to him. But she was insulted that he didn't bring her into his circle. To this Frankel replied, "Mean tongues can dirty someone's purest feelings, as a beast with an unclean mouth dirties the cleanest water." But he saw that his poetic image didn't please her, and he added with a sigh, "You still don't know everything about me."

Once, Slava made an unexpected trip to Bialystok and waited in Frankel's room until he came back from the *Gymnasium*. On the table she noticed a sealed envelope with a Lemberg postmark and a return address from a woman named Helena Frankel. The landlord had left the letter for his tenant. When Frankel entered the room, instead of being pleased with Slava's surprise visit he grabbed the letter from the table and inspected it from all sides, to see if she had opened it and resealed it. Then, his face red, he quickly tore open the envelope. The further he read, the more his fingers shook. Either because Frankel knew that his behavior had given away the secret, or because he no longer wished to deceive her, he handed Slava the sheet of paper written in Polish. The lines jumped at her eyes; she was scarcely able to read the page. Helena Frankel wrote to her husband Bernard that she would no longer wait for him to summon her. She was taking their child and coming to Bialystok.

"I told you all along that you didn't know everything about me," Frankel sighed.

Slava hadn't yet decided whether she wanted to marry Frankel, but she had always been confident that she could easily do so if she chose to. Now she suddenly discovered that the decision wasn't solely up to either of them: there was a third party involved. She was even more insulted, however, by Bernard's perpetually anguished pose. All the time he had simply been afraid—afraid that she might discover he was married and leave him, or afraid that his wife would come and spoil their affair.

"Don't worry, Bernard. Everything will turn out all right. Bring your wife, and we won't see each other again," she consoled him with a wicked smile.

Frankel was crestfallen. "I've felt it all along. How can you leave me so easily, Slava?" he complained. Then he laughed sarcastically. "You're just a small-town girl, and you want my sorrows to be romantic ones, not the mundane sorrows of a miserable family life." But seeing that this made no impression on her, he began to shout, as though crazed with fear: "There's not going to be any family life between me and my wife anyway. If she comes to Bialystok, I'll go somewhere else. I don't love her. She's always intoxicated with fantasies, as though the whole world were a romantic dark-curtained salon with a grand piano." Then Frankel threw himself at Slava, embraced her, and laughed with joy. "I knew you wouldn't leave me."

Slava was pleased that within a moment she could elicit from him so many different moods, as a struck stone sends out sparks of varied colors. Their constant fear of being seen together gave all their secret trysts a sweet, feverish haste and kept their thirst unquenched. Once, when Slava asked Frankel to show her a picture of his wife without their child, he replied huffily, "You don't want to see my child because you don't love me." She was amazed at his narrowness of spirit. Didn't he understand that she didn't want to see the child's picture because she felt guilty toward his wife? He handed her a photograph of a woman with a narrow face, large, frightened eyes, and thin lips. She wore a flowered kerchief over her head and shoulders as though posing for a painter. Slava looked at the picture and smiled indifferently to hide how hurt she was. She realized that her lover didn't want to be with the mother of his child because she was a bundle of thin bones in a white shirt. There was more to her dress than to her body. Nevertheless, Bernard wouldn't leave her. For his lawful wedded wife he preferred a Lemberg lady with an aristocratic mien over a provincial Lithuanian girl from a merchant family. He liked the Lithuanian woman; it was convenient to have her as a mistress. And since her discovery that he was married, things were much easier for him—he no longer had to be careful about exposing himself as a married man.

For his summer vacation Frankel went home to Lemberg, besieging Slava with letters in which he begged her to join him in Warsaw for the last two weeks of his vacation. On her way to Warsaw she told herself she was going there to explain to Frankel why they must separate—people were talking about them in Lomzhe and in Bialystok. Their behavior was considered scandalous even by those who were open-minded. Her brothers were well-known merchants, and she was spoiling their good reputation.

When she met Frankel in Warsaw and told him they ought to separate, he again climbed the walls with rage and despair. His body trembled with tense desire for their secret meetings. She too became infected with his madness; his inability to get along without her was exciting.

But during their fortnight in Warsaw, Slava saw how false and inconsistent Frankel really was. Realizing that his teacher's salary was insufficient for both his family in Lemberg and the Warsaw trip, Slava offered to pay for the hotel, the theater tickets, and the drinks at the taverns. Insulted at first, he later took even more than she offered him. Slava, by nature gay and full of fun, talked loudly at the restaurants and chatted amiably with the waiters. After all, no one knew her in this big city, so she didn't have to be careful. Frankel blushed and looked around anxiously, as though appearing in public with her were torture and humiliation for him. But Slava enjoyed his nervousness. The gossip about her and the grief she was causing her family didn't matter to him. His only worry was about what was and was not proper among strangers. Slava also noticed that of late he fell more frequently into a sour mood. She realized then that Frankel was afraid she might ask him to divorce his wife and marry her. He feared the familial intimacy that might develop between them and was already waiting for the day when he would return to work.

Before their departure from Warsaw, Slava said, "Show me the Jewish commercial center, where I can see Hasidim in their long gaberdines and little visored caps."

"I have more than enough of these Yids in Lemberg and Bialystok," Frankel snapped. "With my education I could have become a director of an aristocratic Polish *Gymnasium*, but because I'm Jewish I have to be a poor teacher in a Polish-Jewish *Gymnasium* in filthy Bialystok."

When they parted, Frankel was in a good mood again, and he made plans for them to meet in Cracow during the winter vacation: "We'll go to museums and to Vavel, the royal castle, and the adjoining cathedral with its crypts of Polish kings. We'll sit in the little cafés and gaze at the old paintings on the walls."

But on her way back to Lomzhe, Slava decided to break off with him. She no longer loved him; she wasn't sure she had ever loved him. Yet she felt so close to Bernard that it was hard to leave him. It surprised her that she was a lot less frivolous than both she and her family thought her to be. The only person who could help her extricate herself from this maze was her brother Volodya, who loved her very much. Out of deference to him, her sisters-in-law had held their tongues. Slava talked to her brother, and he heard her out, his head at an angle, as when he listened to a merchant and kept one eye on the store.

"Put an end to it," he said curtly, and instead of criticizing the *Gymnasium* teacher, Volodya soon brought the scholar Tsemakh Atlas into the house. Slava compared the two at length until she angrily asserted, "Bernard Frankel is a little nobody."

When Tsemakh Atlas came again, Slava ran toward him joyfully and put her soft hand into his. His limp handshake left her unsatisfied.

"You shake hands like a cripple," she complained. He regarded her outstretched hand with fear and curiosity, as though he had discovered a new and beautiful but forbidden world; then he pressed her small hand with such force that she gave out a little scream of pain. Yet at the same time she felt that with his palm he had covered not only her hand but her whole naked body.

Suddenly Tsemakh dropped into a deep chair and groaned. Slava stood confused. "Are you still so religious that touching a woman is a sin?"

"I'm engaged to a girl in Amdur." He groaned again. A tormented look came over his face; he looked like a hermit who realizes that he can't withstand temptation. Slava laughed softly and sadly. Frankel hadn't told her he was married, and Tsemakh hadn't told her he was engaged.

"That's nice. Then you'll get married," she said.

"It's not nice. Right after signing the engagement contract, I discovered I'd been fooled." Then Tsemakh began to tell her what he had heard about his future father-in-law.

"Don't say a word. I'm not interested," Slava interrupted impatiently. Hearing another story like Frankel's—Bernard was always complaining about his wife—made her grimace with disgust. Tsemakh looked at her, grieved and astonished, but at once he too grew tired of his sighs: they sounded like those of a merchant who had been fooled.

"You're right." Tsemakh rose. "I'm going to go back to Amdur and get married."

Slava saw that he was serious; it wasn't an idle threat. Instead of replying that she wouldn't let him go, she leaped up and huddled against him as though she were sheltering herself against a rainstorm. Without thinking, she raised her finger to his hot, dry lips. Tsemakh did not embrace her, nor did he push her away. He stood with head lowered, wistfully silent. Slava retreated somewhat, looked into his eyes, and smiled. Now she finally understood why he was always so gloomy. He had made a bad match. He had been fooled. He wasn't Frankel! If she hadn't discovered the letter, Frankel would never have admitted that he had a wife and child. But as soon as Tsemakh saw that she trusted him, he hadn't been able to rest until he told her the truth.

8

IN THE EVENINGS VOLODYA stayed at home. Stretched out in his soft easy chair, he would make an inventory of his merchandise in the warehouse and in the mills, and tally his money in cash and in notes. When he finished this mental accounting, he liked to reckon how much time he had to loll about in his chair before crawling into bed and stretching out his limbs. To avoid turning his big heavy head to see the time, Volodya had an apartment full of clocks.

In a corner, encased in a glass-doored cabinet, stood a large grandfather clock with a square white dial and brass weights. On the wall hung a round clock with a lifeless face like a yellow moon, dangling two long chains and a pendulum. Volodya loved to compare this clock to a weak Jew who with a moan wished his enemies a stone-lonely old age. A little clock with a raucous alarm was on one table, while on a second was perched a nickel-cased timepiece. Yet another clock rested on wide, squat legs, panting like an angry bulldog with bared teeth. This council of clocks sounded off the quarter-hour and the half-hour; on the hour, an entire orchestra was heard in the house. In addition to the chime clocks, Volodya had ensconced on the shelves and sideboards clocks that were silent, square-shaped and round, flat and bulging. In the dark their dials and hands glowed with a secret greenish light. Volodya loved to stand next to them in the middle of the night when he came back from the bathroom. He imagined he was looking down into an abyss in the sea, where all sorts of phosphorescent fish were to be found, strange creatures with many eyes. Hannah said her hairy husband was a big baby, but Volodya's elder brother was sure that Volodya had purposely collected an apartment full of clocks for the sole purpose of driving everyone crazy.

The customers treated Volodya deferentially and his employees trembled beneath his gaze, but no one in the store was intimidated by Naum, no matter how much he thrashed about and yelled. Naum suspected that the clerks and customers had no regard for him because of some gesture or wink of Volodya's, a thought which always came to him during suppertime, causing him to tear the white napkin from under his collar and to run to the other wing of the house to quarrel with his brother. At his heels was his wife Frieda—a short, emaciated woman with a worried face, her ears ringing and deafened by her husband's shouts. Behind her ran their son, Lolla, a youth with gluttonous cheeks. Still chewing with a full mouth, he whined like a baby: "I want to eat! Mama, you just started serving!" Naum paid no attention to his wife's pleas to return to the table nor to his son's sniveling.

"The wholesaler from Grayev," he fumed one evening, "was given merchandise even though I issued an order that no more credit be extended to that Grayev bankrupt, while the merchant from Zembrov wasn't given *any* credit, even though I explicitly said that he *should* be given credit."

Volodya let his elder brother rant on until the clocks began to chime. Naum noticed that little bastard with the alarm bell mimicking him. The nickel dog with the squat legs assailed him with yelps. The monstrosity with the brass weights pounded at him as though a hammer were banging against his skull, and that senile thing with the jaundiced face was gasping for air. While

Volodya's huge belly shook with laughter, Naum felt all the clock wheels, gears, and springs turning in his mind, exploding in his temples.

Naum dashed to the door and, once on the other side of the threshold, shouted to his younger brother, "What are you, a ship's captain, that you have so many clocks? And do you know what a compass is, you boor?"

After this incident Naum didn't show his face in his brother's apartment for a week, and Volodya felt sad. Moreover, since Tsemakh Atlas had become a frequent guest, Slava's regular evening visits had ceased too. Volodya, however, was pleased that his sister was seeing his childhood friend and patiently waited to see the results. One evening Slava came in unexpectedly, merry as usual, but Volodya quickly saw that she was upset.

Three days had passed since Tsemakh's last visit. At first Slava convinced herself that she didn't care. Then she laughed indignantly: no doubt the yeshiva scholar wanted her to send a matchmaker. Finally, she felt a gnawing at her heart and was annoyed with herself for missing Tsemakh Atlas. Volodya was right in saying that her brains were not in her head but in her sharp tongue. She had bound herself to a man even before knowing what kind of person he was.

Slava chattered more than usual, then suddenly blurted, "I plan to marry Tsemakh Atlas."

Volodya usually laughed when he was astonished or displeased, but he was quiet now. He slowly turned to his sister and said, "So how will it turn out? Are you going to become a rebbetsin? Or is he going to become like you?"

"I'm prepared to become a rebbetsin. What do I care?" Slava ignored her brother and, with a spiteful smile, spoke directly to her sister-in-law. She suspected that Hannah didn't consider her fit to be a Talmud scholar's wife. "But I won't really have to become religious. Even though Tsemakh studied in a yeshiva, he isn't really a yeshiva bokher."

"I'm sure you'll be a divinely blessed couple," Hannah replied, and her calm, clear eyes bespoke no ill toward her sister-in-law.

Slava saw that her brother wasn't entirely surprised at her statement—it almost seemed that he had expected it. Soon, however, Volodya began to twist and turn in his easy chair as though all the flattened springs were piercing his buttocks. Hannah too moved her head restlessly, as if she were searching for her rosy ears.

"Tsemakh Atlas is already engaged." Slava laughed, as if happy to become involved again with someone else's man.

"He didn't tell me he was engaged. That wasn't nice of him," Volodya flared, red with anger.

"Tsemakh didn't tell anyone, because right after his engagement he discovered he'd been fooled." Slava's features became sharp, as if she were already defending her husband's veracity. "When he saw he'd been fooled, he left his fiancée's town even before he knew there was a Slava Stupel in this world, just as I decided to get married even before I met him."

Volodya and his wife exchanged glances. They realized now that Slava had ended her affair with the married man.

In the darkness outside, a thick snow was falling, covering the Lomzhe houses with an otherworldly whiteness. It seemed to Slava that the snow had been falling for years, and that Tsemakh would never return. Had she insulted him with her behavior? She had chatted and been coquettish, but he was too serious a man for flirtations. Perhaps he was returning to his fiancée. Perhaps he had already gone.

The thick soft snow outside cast a gloom over Volodya. He would have been much happier lying in bed than breaking his back in a chair. He yawned, stretched his arms, and was about to tell the women he was going to sleep, when the door opened and Naum entered. He wore soft slippers and a short red robe of silk with a fringed belt; his voice too was now soft as silk.

"I didn't come to quarrel. I just want all the clerks fired and replaced with people who will listen to my orders."

"From now on you're going to have to treat the clerks as equals." Volodya's eyes flashed with joy, knowing that his brother would soon be climbing the walls with rage. "Slava is going to marry Tsemakh Atlas. He's our clerks' first cousin, and he lives with their parents."

Naum was confident that this was one of his brother's tricks to stir up his wrath. But Hannah too, her face melting with joy, nodded to the truth of Volodya's remark. "Well, wish us *mazel tov*," she said.

Naum untied and quickly retied the belt of his short robe, his hands and feet trembling.

"A relative of our clerks is going to be my brother-in-law? Never!"

"I don't know if he wants me yet. Since he realized I'm ready to marry him, he hasn't come back," Slava said with a quick, nervous laugh.

Hannah looked frightened. Volodya noticed that Slava's face had become thin, as if her impatient heart had made her ill.

Naum modulated his screaming voice, pushed his belly out, and in paternal fashion lectured the youngest of the family: "If you like the young man, you should have brought the news to me, your elder brother. I would have invited him so as to let him see who Naum Stupel is. Then I would have sent a respectable matchmaker to the prospective groom or spoken with him alone. But nobody asks my opinion about a match. Nobody asks me anything about business affairs."

"Where are you going?" Volodya called to his sister, who was making her way quickly to the door. Without replying, Slava went back to her apartment and began dressing to go out. She didn't mind the snow, wind, and darkness outside, and she didn't care what her family and Tsemakh's family would think of her—she had to see Tsemakh and speak to him at once.

9

THE SNOW FELL without letup, reaching the windows of the squat little houses in the lane. From one of the houses emerged a man in a fur hat holding a wide shovel. As he cleared the snow from his porch, the wind spun a whirlpool of snowdust around him, showering him with ice slivers. The man stopped working, stuck the shovel into the piled snow, and returned to the house. Tsemakh looked out the window at the embedded shovel as though envying its stability, and mumbled "Either or!" to himself; it was a phrase he liked to use when telling his yeshiva students that one cannot seize both this world and the next at the same time. He was still engaged to Dvorele Namiot. Hence he couldn't visit the Stupels again until he decided either to go to Amdur and marry or to return the engagement contract. On the one hand, there was no comparison between the rich, vivacious family of the Lomzhe flour merchants and the unfriendly Amdur in-law as there was no comparison between his fiancée and Slava Stupel. On the other hand, he knew quite well that the quiet Dvorele was more suitable for a Torah scholar like him. Moreover, he had become formally engaged to her, and breaking the troth would humiliate her terribly. But was he obliged to destroy his own life just to avoid shaming a girl who had helped her father deceive him?

Every evening Uncle Ziml returned from the grocery an hour earlier than his wife and stood staring up at the ceiling. From time to time he sent a few words down to his nephew: "Take my advice. Marry your Amdur fiancée and become a recluse after the wedding."

"Uncle Ziml," Tsemakh answered, "if you had wandered about away from home until you were thirty-three, you'd understand how hard it is to marry with the intent of becoming a recluse in a synagogue immediately after the wedding."

His hands tucked into his sleeves, the entranced Reb Ziml murmured to the ceiling, "Of course, when you're a recluse you can't be ashamed of living off donations. But when I tell Tsertele that a donation is the most honest wage, she says I'm crazy, and my quicksilver children agree with her. Well, I guess I'm fated not to have any joy of this world. You think being a shopkeeper is worldly pleasure? Sitting in the beth medresh is worldly pleasure. There one prays, studies, delves into one's own ideas, instead of selling herring and salt and a measure of groats and a box of matches."

"Reb Israel Salanter stated that we are recluses out of necessity," Tsemakh said. "According to the Torah, a Jew has to be involved in the world. But since in this world one finds oneself being strongly tempted every day, scholars must be recluses. But you, Uncle, you're looking for worldly pleasures in reclusion."

Tsemakh looked up at Reb Ziml and rubbed his forehead. What

was he waiting for? True Navaredkers would consider even being a rabbi in a small town or a recluse in a little shul too much worldly pleasure. According to them, a Musarnik must marry only to fulfill the mitzva of "Be fruitful and multiply"—and then he must be on his way to spread the Torah of Navaredok.

While Tsemakh was talking to his uncle and silently arguing with his yeshiva friends, his Aunt Tsertele was slowly plodding home from the grocery. But she could not extricate herself from either the snow or her nephew's betrothals. Her sons came daily to the store, whispering that the rich Stupel heiress wanted to marry their cousin. They told her to urge him on so that this opportunity wouldn't slip by him. It would be good fortune for him and an honor for the entire Atlas family.

Tsertele listened to her sons' remarks and replied, "Whatever is destined will come to pass." In her heart she knew she must not interfere. It was as clear as day that her nephew regretted the poor match he had made in Amdur. Although he couldn't be faulted for that, she wouldn't try to persuade him to humiliate a Jewish girl. During the past few days Tsertele hadn't known what to think. Tsemakh no longer visited the Stupels; he sat at home, but couldn't seem to find his place there either.

Then she heard someone asking softly and clearly, "Auntie, can you tell me where Reb Ziml Atlas lives?"

"What do you need Reb Ziml for? I'm his wife," the old woman said.

"Are you Aunt Tsertele?" The voice rang out like silver sleigh bells. "Your sons work at our store. I'm Slava Stupel. How is Tsemakh?"

"How should he be?" the clever Tsertele answered. "He brings us lots of joy."

"Since he hasn't visited us for the last few days, we assumed he was sick." Slava took the old woman by the hand as they entered a little lane. "Careful! There's deep snow here. Let's hold on to each other so we don't fall."

Tsertele let herself be led by the arm. Not bad! she thought. If Slava braves such weather to see him, it's not just for the fun of it.

When the two women entered the house, Tsemakh couldn't believe his eyes. Slava Stupel's nose was snow-covered, her cheeks ruddy, and her eyes smiling. She wore high-heeled patent-leather overshoes that reached to her knees, a short fur coat, a gray lamb's-wool hat, and a muff. Slava immediately removed her overshoes, coat, and hat, and began combing her wet, disheveled hair.

"And I thought you were sick or had left," she said to Tsemakh. The snowflakes on her brows and lashes sparkled like crystals; she looked even younger and more beautiful. Her eyes were radiant with joy, yet anxious lest Tsemakh tell her to leave. Tsemakh stood as though possessed. He wanted to say something but could not. He gazed at her, perfectly immobile, as if he'd seen a robin flying into the house in midwinter and was afraid that one move might frighten the bird away. He knew then that he wouldn't return to Amdur but would remain in Lomzhe and be happy with Slava Stupel.

The roly-poly Tsertele, all bundled up in her furs, couldn't reach the knot of the kerchief at the back of her head. She kept turning in circles like a cat around its tail. She gave her husband a scathing look. Even with such an important guest at home he didn't budge from his stance.

"My husband likes to stare up at the ceiling. He sees the sky there, and birds flying." Tsertele apologized for her idler and for her house. "True, this place is no palace, but if you've lived in a house for forty years, it's hard to leave it, just like one's own child."

But Tsertele still couldn't reach the knot of her kerchief. Angry now, she yelled at her husband, "How come you're standing there facing the ceiling as if in Silent Devotion and haven't yet made a fire in the stove? Tsemakh hasn't had a bit of warm food today."

"I'll help you cook supper, and I'll eat, too. I'm hungry," said Slava, quickly unbinding the knot at Tsertele's back and throwing a glance at Tsemakh, who stood there flustered, amazed, and happy. Slava smiled at him and fussed around Tsertele like a bride who wants to show her future mother-in-law what a good wife and darling daughter-in-law she is going to be.

PART II

1

_____

IN THE BEGINNING of Tammuz, or July, three months after Tsemakh and Slava's wedding, two Musarniks set out from Nareva to bring their friend Tsemakh Atlas back to the yeshiva. The elder of the two, Duber Lifschitz, a tall young man with muscular shoulders, continually ran his long fingers through his broom-stiff little blond beard. Duber Lifschitz was so stubborn and willful that apparently even his beard feared to grow without his consent—and he gave no consent of his to anything physical. Immediately after his wedding he had become a yeshiva principal in the small town of Narevke, which was under the aegis of the big yeshiva in Nareva. The second emissary, Zundl Konotoper, small, thin, and sharp-eyed, was an old bachelor with a long, thick beard and a lion's voice.

On the way to Lomzhe, Zundl had shouted to Duber, the edges of his beard trembling, "Yes, Tsemakh sacrificed himself for his students. But even a blind man could have seen his delight when his students shook in fear of him."

"I suspect he wants to be a rabbi rather than a Torah teacher—like some rabbis of old who bought their post by presenting a town with a gift of money. That's why he married into a rich family, to get the dowry and buy a job," Duber Lifschitz muttered with a shrug. "It's incredible that a Navaredker could have fallen so low."

Upon arriving in Lomzhe the two Musarniks found out where Tsemakh Atlas lived. Seeing the Stupels' stone house, the two balconies, and the large shop on the ground floor, Zundl Konotoper shouted to Duber, "A rabbi, you say? I think a merchant is more like it."

Zundl dashed up the staircase, and Duber Lifschitz had to take long strides to keep up with him. Both wanted to storm into the living room, but a maid held them back.

"Wait till I ask the master if he wants to receive you," she said.

Tsemakh Lomzher welcomed his yeshiva friends calmly, neither overjoyed nor apprehensive, but feeling as if two communal trustees had come asking for a donation. The first thing his friends noticed was that Tsemakh was dressed like a man of the world, not a yeshiva scholar. Instead of the traditional gaberdine, he wore a short jacket, a white shirt with a starched collar, and a polka-dot cravat. He himself looked trim and starched, with his full cheeks and no trace of beard—which he had either clipped or even shaved. Instead of a rabbinic hat or a yarmulke, he wore a felt fedora with a sharp, broad brim, jauntily angled, like a dandy's. Moreover, he wasn't shod in high black soft-leather boots, but in low, laced oxfords; and he sat with his legs crossed, as if to display the thick soles. The bookcase was filled not with the Talmud and sacred texts but with secular works. Next to the window stood a writing desk with turned legs, covered with a green blotter. Pleated heavy drapes hung over the door, and the sofa in the corner was strewn with soft little pillows. Zundl Konotoper's sharp eyes narrowed, and Duber Lifschitz laughed scornfully to himself. If I weren't looking for a wife who would sacrifice herself for the Torah, he thought, I could make an excellent match too.

Tsemakh asked his guests to be seated. He remained sitting in an easy chair, his elbows on the arm rests. Tsemakh coldly asked how his friends were, and out of politeness inquired after his students. Then he fell silent and looked out the window at a tree heavy with leaves.

The chilly reception put a damper on Zundl Konotoper's fury and he asked the Lomzher in a choked voice, "Why did nothing come of the proposed yeshiva in Amdur?"

Duber Lifschitz also forced himself to speak softly and amicably: "I'm still amazed that I wasn't invited to your wedding. As far as I know, we were both utterly devoted to the Torah, right? Perhaps you can tell your old friend why you broke your first engagement and married a different woman?"

Tsemakh answered with sparse and measured words: "As to the match, I had my reasons. As to the yeshiva in Amdur, the people there didn't want one."

Then a woman in a short, tight dress—she wore no marriage wig, not even a kerchief—entered the room. She had an alabaster face, a smooth chiseled nose, and a rather long chin. On her bare throat lay a string of pearls, and a gold bracelet dangled from her wrist. She came in, with twinkling eyes and mincing steps, precisely the way Isaiah described the sinful daughters of Zion. She approached the guests as though totally unaware that a Jewish woman is forbidden to come close to strange men, especially Torah scholars. She was apparently even prepared to shake hands, but the visitors' wrathful faces prevented her.

"I want to invite your friends to lunch," she said, turning to her husband. The emissaries exchanged amazed glances: Was this lewd woman the Lomzher's rebbetsin?

"But how about a glass of tea?" Tsemakh asked his guests, smiling to Slava, who didn't understand that these men wouldn't accept her invitation, for they didn't trust her to keep a kosher house.

"Tea? You don't suppose we came to drink tea!" yelled the astounded Kundl Konotoper.

"You don't suppose we came to drink tea!" Duber Lifschitz repeated, even more astounded.

The woman retreated to the doorway with a fleeting anxiety in her glowing, questioning eyes. Her husband commiserated with a tender glance that apologized for his guests' wild behavior. He looked out the window again, gazing wistfully at the blossoming tree outside, until Zundl Konotoper's grumble wrenched him out of his sweet reverie.

"You're probably aware of the confusion you caused by leaving the yeshiva. To this day your students still seem to be in mourning. The rosh yeshiva sent us here to remind you to return to Nareva and to your group of students for the month of Elul."

Tsemakh smiled. Reb Simkha Feinerman wanted him to come back to Nareva before the High Holy Days and to stand like a beggar at the doorway, so that the youngsters would see how he regretted his past actions and derive a moral from it. Then they would send him away with the excuse that they could no longer depend on him. "I'm not even thinking about returning to Nareva," Tsemakh answered. "But I am puzzled why old friends of mine undertook the mission of bringing me back. The two of you, and indeed all true Navaredkers, should side with me and not with the rosh yeshiva, Reb Simkha Feinerman."

Hearing such impudent words, Tsemakh's friends pushed their chairs back, then at once brought them forward again. "Tell us why we should side with you."

The longer Tsemakh spoke, the deeper the wrinkles cut into his cheeks, as though he had once again become an embittered yeshiva lad. He began by speaking of Reb Yosef-Yoizl Hurwitz.

"The Old Man of Navaredok taught his students that the Torah was given to man to perfect his character. Our sages of blessed memory tell us that when Moses went up to heaven, the angels told the Almighty, 'Give us the Torah,' and the Almighty replied, 'Why? Are any of you envious? Do any of you hate?' Since there is neither envy nor hatred among angels, they don't need a Torah. Man, however, needs a Torah to perfect his character, to recognize his innate badness and uproot it from himself. This is the essence of Reb Yosef-Yoizl's method in Musar, and I was a faithful disciple. I worked hard to do good for its own sake, and not for honor or for a return favor at some future time. Even helping a friend in order to store up credit in heaven—God spare me such a plague!—also smacks of shopkeepers' accounting. A shopkeeper wants God to sign a little receipt after he's helped someone whose store burned down as insurance that his own store won't go up in smoke. I wanted to be one of those upright men who sought a higher sort of life, who didn't fear a fire because they owned no store. Not only did I want to be a perfect man, but I wanted to make my students into upright men too. But since the Navaredkers returned from Russia, they've stopped being Musarniks, and when I spoke to my students in the old Navaredker style, the rosh yeshiva persecuted me mercilessly."

"Because you didn't know when to stop. You're extreme to the point of madness. Your way in life is all or nothing," Duber Lifschitz remarked, twisting and untwisting his stiff little beard.

"You called your students drunkards and gluttons for diligently studying the Talmud and the commentaries. Once, when a boy cried in the beth medresh because his friend was ill and had to stay home, you berated him: 'We have no respect for a weakling who indulges himself in so much self-love that he can't see another person suffering, but lets the tears flow in order to make it easier for himself. Navaredok doesn't want to make things easier; Navaredok wants to make things more difficult.' That's the way you spoke to those youngsters, and everybody in the beth medresh was amazed. Too much is no good."

"I wanted my students' good deeds to stem not from tender-heartedness but from awareness and a profound intellect," Tsemakh answered with a twisted, angry smile.

"And why do you disparage good deeds that come from the heart, from depths of compassion?" Duber Lifschitz looked at Tsemakh as though he were seeing his true face for the first time.

"With one's mind one can *do* good, not *be* good. Indeed, you have done good deeds, but you were never good," Zundl Konotoper told Tsemakh bluntly.

Duber Lifschitz began speaking rapidly in a sharp voice: "You were never scrupulous about the mitzvas. Not at prayers, not with tefillin, not even with the Sabbath laws. What's more, the older people in the yeshiva always had their doubts about you because you always talked to your students about the good deeds between man and man, and completely neglected the mitzvas concerning God and man, concerning worship of the Creator. You even constantly discussed those mitzvas between man and man from a secular and not a Torah point of view, quoting gentile scholars or philosophers as though, God forbid, we didn't have our own Torah."

A cold, mocking gleam lit up Tsemakh's eyes. He was delighted that the Musarniks were excited while he remained calm. Now he no longer had to fear saying what was on his mind.

"It's true," he replied, "that I wasn't too preoccupied with fulfilling the mitzvas. I observed the Code of Law, but had no joy in keeping those laws and customs. I followed the Navaredok method of Reb Yosef-Yoizl to its uttermost limits. The Torah with its six hundred thirteen mitzvas wants man to purify himself from his inherently evil attributes and to live on a higher plane of

discernment. But this is exactly what the Greek and later philosophers teach. The only point that attracted me to the Musar
movement was the concept of being a perfect man. It is for this
reason I spent so many years in the yeshiva, until Navaredok
surrendered to the Talmudic hairsplitters, the pilpulists and the
mindless pietists."

Zundl Konotoper shook his long, thick beard as though to shake
Tsemakh's heretical words from it. He spoke quickly, in a high
voice: "Either you don't know, or you pretend not to know—or
perhaps you've even forgotten since you've strayed from the true
path—that the mind is a public domain where each one leaves his
filth, his offal. The man who lives solely by his own wisdom and
the wisdom of others is a captive of his own self and a slave of
others. Everyone with a twisted mind and half-baked ideas drops
his twisted thoughts on the man who considers himself rational,
just like that sly bird that drops its eggs in another bird's nest.
Torah believers do not agree with the free-thinking philosophers
that good deeds done out of heartfelt compassion are on a lower
scale than good deeds done by a man on the basis of reason. But
whether they're done with one's heart or one's mind, a man cannot
truly perform mitzvas if he forgets the most important principle: to
be good and to *do* good is a commandment in the Torah. Man's heart
and mind don't provide him with enough patience and intelligence
to help his fellow man in the manner prescribed by the Torah.
Without faith that the Torah was divinely given, man wouldn't
sacrifice himself for his fellow man, nor would he know when one is
forbidden to do good. That's what our sages of blessed memory and
Maimonides and the Vilna Gaon teach us, and that's the foundation
of Musar. So now you come along with this brand-new discovery
that one can be good and do good without a Torah, without the six
hundred thirteen mitzvas, but solely on the basis of human reason!"

Duber Lifschitz shrieked and pointed a long hard finger in
Tsemakh's face. "Hearing such words, Reb Yosef-Yoizl would
have rent his coat in mourning. The Old Man lovingly kissed his
tefillin and his ritual fringes, and when he spoke of pure intentions,
he meant pure intentions in fulfilling the laws of the Torah. The
truly God-fearing man has much joy in his life. Every mitzva has
its own particular flavor, but the so-called pious man who is
expedient and has ulterior motives—all his deeds smack of the salty

taste of his arid scheming, like the snake to whom everything tastes of earth. That's the way Reb Yosef-Yoizl spoke. And that's the way his students who follow the Torah and keep the mitzvas speak."

"You latched yourself onto a great tree—our rabbi," Zundl Konotoper shouted. "But now we see that all these years you've fooled our rabbi as well as your friends and students."

Tsemakh jumped up, paced about the room, and hurled the words in all directions: "I haven't fooled anyone. *I'm* the one who has been fooled; Navaredok fooled me. I devoted myself heart and soul to the Torah because I believed that the way of Torah believers is a straight and honest one, but I discovered that Torah believers do the same thing as worldly Jews: through subtle quibbling they come up with dispensations to show that their deeds are in accord with the law. So I left the beth medresh and saw that there are good people even among the nonreligious—even though they never learned Musar. Moreover, if a nonreligious person does something forbidden, he doesn't look for a pious excuse like the Nareva rosh yeshiva Reb Simkha Feinerman, who isn't a finer man at all. He persecutes everyone who doesn't kowtow to him. Now he's afraid lest another yeshiva outstrip his in size; and he's especially afraid of having a yeshiva founded by Navaredok Musarniks become greater than his. This fact is well known by all Torah scholars who themselves have become heads of small-town yeshivas after marrying. Isn't that so, Narevke rosh yeshiva?" Tsemakh stopped briefly in front of Duber Lifschitz, his face contorted. "But your young lads aren't supposed to know this yet," he went on. "Meantime, they run around the beth medresh studying Musar until they too get married and become teachers in small towns. Then they realize that the great Nareva rosh yeshiva is constantly afraid of competition, just as a storekeeper is always afraid another store like his might open up across the street. So I don't want to deceive myself or my students any longer. I suffered until I was thirty-three, and that's enough." Tsemakh stopped at a distance from the men, an indication that his visitors could leave.

"That's the way to talk!" Zundl roared. "Tell us plainly that you've left the path of Torah and that you married into a free-thinking family in order to enjoy an illicit, licentious life. Let's go, Reb Duber. Our mission has ended."

"And you have the nerve to tell us that *we're* looking for a dispensation for everything we want," Duber Lifschitz added. "*You're* the one who's whitewashing a wrong—as the Talmud says, seeking a hundred and fifty reasons why a worm is clean. In order to justify your corrupt ways you rant that at Navaredok no one lets you live by reason, that no one lets you become an Aristotle."

Duber laughed scornfully and the two Navaredkers ran out of the house posthaste, apparently certain that the stone house with its two balconies would soon collapse upon the Lomzher.

2

THE NAVAREDKER EMISSARIES' HARSH WORDS were imprinted in Tsemakh's mind and heart like pins in his body. As much as he tried to persuade himself that his former friends were just idle bench warmers and that their remarks were obviously prompted by envy for his successful match, he still couldn't forget their argument that he had sought an excuse to leave his poor and pious life. In that case, he had to show everyone—and himself above all—that good deeds had been and still were the aim of his life. After three months of marriage it was time to start thinking about a practical goal, and he must discuss this with his wife.

Slava had gone about in a daze ever since her wedding day. Her eyes had become darker; her half-lowered eyelashes screened a secretive smile. She no longer laughed or spoke raucously; her walk had become more sedate. At night a storm swirled about her, and in this storm fluttered a large, hungry bird—Tsemakh—filled with impatience and with the male strength stored up from all the ascetic years of his yeshiva life. Every morning when Slava rose, her body was swollen like a bunch of ripe grapes. She would bustle about Tsemakh and snuggle close to him, already exhausted early in the morning.

But from the day the two strange Jews came to see him,

Tsemakh had become depressed. He paced about sullenly and paid no attention to Slava.

One morning she put on a blue sweater that matched her blue eyes and tucked it under the belt of her skirt. The soft lines of her arms, breasts, and shoulders beneath the thin, taut wool made her look like a nimble, clever, furry-warm house pet with lively eyes. In front of the mirror, Slava gazed at her long white neck and curled blond hair, annoyed that her appearance couldn't banish Tsemakh's bad mood. He didn't love her; her experiences prior to their meeting didn't even interest him. She was ready to cry, to tell him to get out of her sight forever, but a minute later she laughed and entered Tsemakh's room softly, longing for tenderness.

Tsemakh received her with a worried expression and said dryly, "You know I've studied Musar. The upshot of all I've learned is to do good deeds in this world. That's why I see no other course in life than to study medicine and become a doctor in order to help people."

To hide her bewilderment Slava huddled close to him and spoke right into his broad chest. "Why don't you speak to Volodya? He's the practical one in the family," she said, embracing him as though she wanted to make night out of day and put him to sleep.

"Volodya likes money. He's always playing with a handful of coins or with clocks," Tsemakh said, freeing himself of her arms.

"He plays with clocks because he's forlorn without children," Slava answered, feeling forlorn herself. She had often noticed that when Tsemakh spoke about the world and people in general he spoke intelligently; but if he had to say something about a particular matter, he gazed off into the distance and couldn't see what was before his eyes. He didn't know life; he imagined everything according to his books. He was like a blind fortune teller who while able to predict everyone's future had to be led by the hand.

Volodya didn't like to see Hannah leaving the house while he spent evenings at home. Whether he was playing with a handful of coins, winding up his clocks, petting the cat, or even snoozing in his deep easy chair, his wife had to be in the same room. She could do what she pleased—play cards, comb her long hair, knit, sew, anything—as long as she didn't leave him by himself. Hence

Volodya's unexpected request that Hannah visit her sister-in-law surprised her.

"Tsemakh is coming soon for a rather confidential talk and Slava doesn't want anybody to hear his childish ideas. He wants to take up medicine."

A look of surprise flitted over Hannah's face, but she made no comment lest she be accused of interfering with Slava's life.

A depressed feeling came over Volodya as he sat alone in the large apartment. He got up and adjusted all his clocks to chime at exactly the same time. Tsemakh met Volodya as he was turning the hands of a clock and listening intently as the mechanism emitted one sound after another.

"See? When there's people around, all these little chaps make a tumult with their chiming," Volodya told his brother-in-law, as if he too were fond of clocks. "But after midnight they chime furtively and quietly as if they were miles away. If one of these fellows breaks down and doesn't chime, I feel it in my sleep, and I crawl down from my bed to see what's wrong with the patient. Well, what's the good word, Tsemakh?"

Tsemakh spoke so confidently and seriously about his plan that Volodya gaped at him in astonishment, but then he calmly began explaining. "First of all, half a dozen tutors will have to coach you to pass the *Gymnasium* examinations. Then you'll have to be admitted to a university, and when you graduate you'll have to intern at a hospital, and only then will you be able to start practicing medicine. Before you become a doctor your studies will cost a fortune, and you and your wife will use up your share of the inheritance."

Volodya had promised his sister that he would speak softly and gently with her husband, but a joke wouldn't hurt, would it? After all, Tsemakh wasn't a watch spring, and he wouldn't burst. So he began telling Tsemakh about the lot of Lomzhe doctors.

"On the one hand, there's the push from the old-fashioned doctors. On the other, there's the competition between the Russian doctors and those who graduated from modern Polish universities. In town we have three noted physicians. They're chucked about by their women patients like rotten apples. They don't like one doctor because of his long white mustache, which is damp, and yellow with tobacco stains. Another one with a pointy beard the women can't stand because he's as talkative as a fishwife. He keeps asking them about their grandfathers and grandmothers. He claims he has to know this for his prescriptions. They don't like a third doctor because he's bald and because it's rumored that he wears ritual fringes, and a doctor is supposed to be a godless rascal. At the hospital on Sanitarsky Street young doctors wait on the steps, hoping to be admitted to practice just for one month. In every town dozens of diplomaed practitioners rove about looking for spinsters with money so that they can open up an office. These young doctors have command of many languages—Polish, Russian, German, even French. If Slava had wanted a doctor so badly, she could have gotten not one but ten. How come you decided to become a doctor anyway?" Volodya asked, smiling.

"I've decided it's the best possible way to do good for others."

"But you'd have to take money for your work to support yourself. What sort of goodness would that be?"

Tsemakh looked at him, perplexed and surprised. His business-man brother-in-law had posed a question worthy of a Musarnik. If he were paid for healing the sick, it would not be goodness but self-interest. "Then what should I turn to?" Tsemakh sighed.

"Your wife has a share in our business. You could work with us, and then you too could help people who need doctors."

In Navaredok no one was held in greater contempt than a shopkeeper. A shopkeeper couldn't be truly good even if he crawled out of his skin. His god was a kopeck, and he also wheeled and dealed with the Master of the Universe.

"I should become a shopkeeper?" Tsemakh cried in despair.

"But I'm a shopkeeper," Volodya said. He couldn't comprehend his brother-in-law's mood; Tsemakh was as depressed as if he were being forced to go begging from house to house.

Volodya, sick and tired of the talk, looked toward the door, longing to see his snow-white, well-fleshed Hannah appear. He steamed like a piece of drenched earth in the sun after a rain; he perspired with pleasant anticipation and scratched his armpits.

"My little sister is some wife, huh?" He winked slyly. Tsemakh looked at him coldly like a huge fish dragged up on dry land.

The next afternoon Tsemakh went down to the store. Slava waited for his return with large, moist eyes like a cat's. Toward evening it occurred to her that it was high time she became an independent homemaker. Hitherto her sister-in-law Hannah had sent the maid in with their supper. Tonight Slava cooked by herself, working hard and fussing about. When Tsemakh came upstairs he found a prepared table. But he scarcely touched the dishes; he chewed silently, lost in thought. After supper he sat down, shoulders sagging, in a deep chair by the window, as though he had carried a hundred sacks of flour during his few hours at work. Slava sat down lightly on the arm rest, her hand on his shoulder.

"I see that going to the store is torture for you. Other people would have considered themselves lucky."

"My cousins, in fact, consider themselves lucky to be clerks for the Stupel family," Tsemakh replied. "They're little people, and their brains are no bigger than a herring's eye."

Slava laughed. "Why put yourself on the same level as the clerks? You're a partner."

"And what next?" Tsemakh asked gloomily. "What of the future?"

"The future? No different from anyone else's," his wife replied, slipping from the arm rest onto his lap. She pressed her head into his chest and looked up at his clouded face.

His words fell heavily and slowly. "By day I'll tell the customers that the merchandise costs me more than they're offering me. At night I'll reckon up my earnings and aggravate myself because people aren't paying me or because I don't have enough to pay off the notes. Even when I sleep I'll dream of flour and barley. First I'll be a young man taking a Sabbath stroll with my wife as she pushes a baby carriage, and later I'll be an elderly father having trouble with my grown children. And what next?"

His image of her pushing a baby carriage with her husband at her side pleased Slava, but she wasn't ready for that yet. Now she wanted her husband to kiss her and caress her. She looked up at him, tossing her head so that her hair touched his chin, nose, and cheeks. She pressed her thin back into his chest and her buttocks into his belly and his firm legs until she felt his flaring nostrils wafting warm winds over her. Laughing triumphantly, Slava quickly jumped up from his warmed lap. Tsemakh saw the form of her small round buttocks imprinted on her dress as if with a compass, and he embraced her wildly. But she slipped out of his embrace and teased him: "And what next?"

Her lips pouted with desire and her eyes sparkled drunkenly, as if she had sipped old wine and wanted to retain the bitter-sweet taste and aroma as long as possible.

Tense and erect, Tsemakh seized her in his arms and grumbled, "For your sake I'll become a shopkeeper."

3

WHEREVER TSEMAKH TURNED IN the store, there were sacks piled ceiling-high. He felt that not only had his face, hands, and clothes become whitened by the flour, but his very soul had become floury. The clerks, however, didn't let him stay lost in thought for long. Seeing him dreaming in the rear of the store and rubbing some flour between his fingers, the clerks bounded toward him. The eldest one took a handful of flour from a sack and showed Tsemakh the difference between two types of merchandise. Ground corn, even after it had been rolled and milled several times, was still rather hard and crumbly. Wheat flour was always yellowish and fatty, thin as silk and soft as velvet. Tsemakh's middle cousin taught him about bran, the corn's black residue, and about unrefined flour, the wheat's black residue. His youngest cousin, the one with the impudent, lively eyes, counseled him on prices: "Don't give them the lowest price right away. You have to start high and come down slowly. You should also know how to handle situations as they arise. For instance, you can't demand more than seventeen and a half zlotys from a Lomzhe baker for a sack of white flour, because he knows the prices and is likely to go elsewhere. However, from an out-of-town shopkeeper you can ask more. And if a woman comes to buy a couple of kilos of white flour for herself, she has to be charged twenty-five percent more."

"Now do you understand?" all three brothers said at once.

Tsemakh wiped the white dust from his hands and answered, "I still don't understand the various types of flour and the prices that well. But I understand *you* quite well. As time goes by, you'd like to become great merchants. Your mother, however, should pray that you always remain clerks. Because if you grovel on the ground before those stronger than you, you will trample to the ground those weaker than you."

The clerks retreated, thanking God that no one had overheard their cousin's remarks.

Into the store came Reb Kopel Kaufman, a community volunteer. He wore a long gaberdine, shiny with stains from grease, Kiddush wine, and wax from the Havdola candles. Reb Kopel was always busy and bustling about, collecting donations for the Talmud Torah and for the orphanage. Everyone in Lomzhe knew that he didn't take a penny for himself—he was supported by his wife's little store. Tsemakh too had become acquainted with him and didn't like Reb Kopel's lusty groaning while telling about the needy little Talmud Torah children. This time Reb Kopel came in with a mouthful of sighs to collect his monthly donation for the orphanage. He took his notebook out of his pocket, licked his blue pencil, and waited for the Stupels' brother-in-law to tell him how much to write down. Tsemakh gave him a contribution and declined the receipt.

"As far as the money is concerned, I trust you. But I don't trust your goodness. It makes me sad to see people who are so compassionate they literally take delight in their compassion. For a lustful man even compassion is a lust, and you actually sweat with pleasure when you weep over these orphans."

Reb Kopel stood there open-mouthed, his tongue smeared with the blue of his pencil.

"Is . . . is that the way you talk to me?" he stammered and began to sob. "A man who is a faithful servant of the community? I run around day and night collecting charity and eating my heart out before I get a donation."

Tsemakh gave him a searing glance and said furiously, "That's exactly what I mean. When a man helps someone, he should talk as little as possible about it, and not make a big noise or bustle about the needy person as if he were a corpse with no kin. But you, who are supposedly a faithful servant of the community, you make a big noise about your compassion and brag about your kindness. That proves you're motivated by your own pleasure and honor, and not the orphans' welfare."

Reb Kopel Kaufman sidled out of the store as if afraid that wet towels might be thrown after him. Volodya was beaming.

"Wonderful, Tsemakh! You really gave it to him. That's the way to talk to these community busybodies, these public-spirited do-gooders!" the hefty Volodya screeched with joy in a thin, eunuchlike voice. He never refused to make a contribution, but he despised these community workers and also ridiculed his brother Naum: "That showoff has run out again in his frock coat and top hat for some bigwig's reception."

In the afternoon Reb Enzele came into the store. He was a small man with a tiny nose and a tidy white little beard. From his neat and pious demeanor it was apparent that his thoughts were clean and his lips spoke no evil. Even Reb Enzele's occupation was connected with Sabbath holiness. A bronzesmith, he silvered candelabra and gilded the Torah's crowns and little bells. Each time he entered and left a Jewish house he tiptoed to kiss the mezuza on the doorpost. He permitted his tefillin to be examined only by the man with the longest beard in town, and for Sukkos he bought the finest esrog. Now he had entered the Stupels' store to pay for his Passover matzo flour. His kind eyes beamed with joy and trust. Reb Enzele said good morning to everyone and had already taken out his purse.

At the same time a woman entered the store to buy flour for her Sabbath challas. Her face was despondent; she sighed aloud and poured out her heart to Volodya: "I really don't know how I can bring myself to bake and cook. Not even a month has passed since the Nareva River took my sister's one and only child. Oh, Lord, how many doctors and Hasidic rebbes my sister and brother-in-law went to see before they finally had a baby! How the parents tended and fussed over their little boy until he grew up! Then one Sabbath Itzikl never returned. The Nareva had taken him."

Even though Volodya was hearing this story for the twentieth time, he wrinkled his brows and had to strain not to shed a tear. He empathized with the anguish of the parents. Moreover, he was almost choked with gloom that there was no little blond girl in white socks running around in his home.

"What a tragedy! May it befall no other Jews! What a tragedy!" Reb Enzele the bronzesmith sadly shook his head. "But God is just and his ways are just. When a Jewish child goes swimming on the Sabbath . . ."

He had scarcely ended his sentence when Tsemakh turned a pair of blazing eyes on him and let fly a torrent of words. "Job's friends were much holier than you, but still God was furious with them for their remarking that Job had probably sinned and deserved his troubles. When a man feels that the world has crumbled beneath him, it's cruel to console him by saying he will overcome his misfortune. It's even more cruel to justify the heavenly decree—for someone else. And besides being cruel, it's also toadying and hypocritical. One toadies up to God that he is just and his ways are just—for the next fellow—to save oneself from the very same judgment. But God in heaven sees through such phony little plaster saints."

The bronzesmith ran out of the store as though his gaberdine had been set on fire by Tsemakh's blazing eyes. The clerks followed to apologize, but Reb Enzele waved his hands—he didn't want to hear a word. He quickly paid them for the Passover flour and fled through the market. Everyone saw the old man shaking his head from side to side. "No, no, I've never been so insulted in my life, and for no reason."

The aunt of the drowned boy slipped out of the store to avoid being reviled by the Stupels' brother-in-law for baking challas before the thirty-day mourning period for her nephew had ended. But Volodya laughed and told Tsemakh about a superstition that Reb Enzele believed in. "Whenever the bronzesmith passes through a doorway, he bangs three times on the adjoining wall and stamps three times on the threshold. Boys! Give us an imitation of Reb Enzele stamping and banging with his little hands and feet." Volodya barked the order, and the clerks jumped out into the street to mimic Reb Enzele's mannerism. Outside, the clerks saw their boss splitting his sides with laughter. But since they knew him quite well, they realized that he was laughing to hide his anger at Tsemakh for having driven away both an old customer and the woman who wanted to buy flour for her Sabbath challas.

Prickly sun rays brought on hot, dry days that sparkled like glowing hot sand mixed with glass splinters. During these summer days the dark green tree by the Stupel house had become dusty gray, and its heavy, thick-leaved branches weak with heat. Tsemakh looked out the store window at the tree and thought: Another month and the leaves will wither. Trees also grew in the courtyard of the Nareva yeshiva. In the summer he had sat there with students discussing Musar. . . . Outside, in the Lomzhe market, he saw a woman in a flowered dress with a brown-checked kerchief on her shoulders bargaining with a saleswoman. A summer dress and a winter kerchief? Tsemakh wondered and couldn't comprehend why he was so amazed. "A summer dress and a winter kerchief. A summer dress and a winter kerchief," Tsemakh muttered over and over. He imagined he had become a huge fly in the corner of a window. The fly wanted to leave but kept bumping into the pane, buzzing, buzzing. In the market, a peasant sat on an overturned empty milk can next to a full one. Again Tsemakh was amazed: how could a man sit on the sharp round metal edge of a can? A fright came over him. Perhaps he had gone out of his mind. What thoughts ran through the head of a former Navaredker Musarnik!

He turned from the window and saw Volodya talking with a wholesaler about transporting from the train station two wagon-loads of flour they had jointly purchased. Porters were carrying sacks from the store and loading them onto a side platform. Naum was shouting orders at the porters, and the store clerks were waiting on the customers.

A young merchant entered. He came from the village of Piontnitse on the other side of the Nareva River. He had protruding white teeth, a tuft of spiky hair, and a tic around his squinting eyes. He stamped his boots as though there were a frost outside and roared self-confidently, "I've come to buy merchandise!" Volodya, busy with his partner in the flour transaction, signaled Tsemakh to attend to him. One of the clerks rushed over too.

"Let's have a sample of the wheat flour," the village merchant shouted. "And what's the price for a bagful?"

"Thirty-seven zlotys." Tsemakh came out with the lowest price.

"It's thirty-six in other stores," the villager said, guessing.

"If the boss hadn't said thirty-seven," the clerk interrupted, "you wouldn't have gotten the merchandise today for less than thirty-eight. Wheat flour's gone up."

With one eye closed the merchant from Piontnitse sized up the new boss next to the cash register.

"A partner? Oh! I completely forgot. Yes, indeed, I did hear that the Stupels had acquired a brother-in-law who was an ordained rabbi. Is that the way a rabbi looks? With no beard or long gaberdine, and up to his elbows in flour? The Lomzhers love to make up cock-and-bull stories."

The impudent smile on the village merchant's thick, protruding lips combined with his buck teeth to remind Tsemakh of a horse with a bundle of chewed-up straw in the corner of its mouth. From the look in the merchant's eyes and the way he wagged his head, one could see all the stupidity of a sly little peasant who brings a cartful of wood to market and assumes that everyone will be concerned only with him and will be out to fool him. Tsemakh even took pleasure in this young loudmouth's deriding him. Do not both evil and good stem from the Most High, as the Bible says? He had made his bed; now he would lie in it.

After lengthy bargaining, the Piontnitser agreed to purchase the wheat flour at the price specified. Then he asked to be shown the corn meal. He needed five bags.

"If the price isn't too bitter, I'll take ten bags."

Tsemakh again gave him the final price, and one of the clerks added, "No need to bargain over this. Your brother also paid seventeen zlotys per bag."

"That's why he's in the fix he's in. That brother of mine has already gone under," the customer said, laughing. "My brother opened up a store right opposite mine so as to compete with me. But things aren't going well for him—he's gone broke twice. Nevertheless, I help him out. Every week I give him a fiver, and sometimes even a tenner. But I don't put it right in his hand. My bankrupt brother is stuck-up, no less, and would refuse to take it. So I send it to my sister-in-law and say it's for the kids."

"You help your brother out with five or ten zlotys, but you won't help him to the extent that he won't have to depend on you any more," Tsemakh unexpectedly lashed out at him.

The merchant from Piontnitse suddenly lost his nerve and began to defend himself. "So what should I do? Go ahead, you tell me what to do so that my brother won't be my blood enemy. The more I give him, the more he hates me."

"Because the way you help your brother makes him choke on every bite. That's why he's your enemy," Tsemakh said, relishing his undammed anger like a sip of fine wine. "I see the sort of person you are. You don't trust anyone. You constantly rack your brains to discover the other fellow's ulterior motive. You feel good when you're full of suspicions, the way a pig covered with vermin feels good rolling in the mud."

The insulted and bewildered customer slowly came out of his daze. "What's going on here? I come here to buy flour and pay an inflated price, so you abuse me and butt in between me and my brother too? To hell with you, you vulgar louts," he said, finally recovering and shouting the length of the store. "There are plenty of flour merchants in Lomzhe, and for the kind of customer I am, they'll even kiss my hand, damn you all."

The village merchant left, slamming the door. A silent tumult enveloped the store. Volodya's face was dark. The wholesaler standing next to him shrugged, unable to believe his eyes. Naum was waving his hands as though struck dumb. Tsemakh, oblivious to everything, had his elbows on the cash register and his head buried in his hands; he was breathing heavily.

Volodya put his hand on Tsemakh's shoulder and made an effort to speak calmly. "This man from Piontnitse is a good customer, and you've driven him away forever. I don't know how good and wise it is to tell the truth to everyone's face and make an enemy of everyone."

The fire flared once again in Tsemakh's dark eyes and he answered hoarsely, "That's the way it really should be—a man should tell everyone the truth and not be fazed by the fact that he's making enemies. Nevertheless, I'm not such a hero or man of truth. But if a rich brother persecutes his poorer brother and doesn't understand why the latter is his enemy, I have to tell him the truth."

Volodya's big broad face turned hard as stone, but he remained silent. Looking at him, Naum didn't dare say a word either. He just looked daggers at Tsemakh's cousins, the clerks, all of whom were huddled in one corner as though everything were their fault.

4

EVERY THURSDAY a student from the Lomzhe yeshiva ate at Hannah Stupel's house. Fishele, a nine-year-old lad from Grayev, had beautiful black eyes and the high, scholarly forehead of a rabbi. Hannah spent all her days at home alone and yearned for the day when Fishele would come to eat. Hannah sat opposite him, serving him the prepared dishes. She noticed that the boy was always staring at Volodya's clocks and casting glances toward the other rooms. She guessed that he was looking for children his own age but was tactful enough not to ask if there were any. His intelligence and sensitivity made him appeal to her even more.

"You can touch the clocks if you like, but take care not to break them." However, playing the role of an idle youngster who entertains himself with clocks did not befit Fishele Grayever. He finished eating quietly, piously recited the Grace After Meals, and departed, leaving in Hannah's heart a gnawing feeling and a longing: If only she had such a little boy, such a sweet, beautiful, bright little son!

The young student came every Thursday morning for breakfast and came back at two that afternoon for lunch. He didn't want to come for supper, which would take time from Torah studies, but Hannah always gave him a bag of food and twenty pennies to buy what he wished.

"Where do you eat your other meals, Fishele?" Hannah asked.

"I have another good day," he replied. "It's Wednesday at Reb Dodya Shmulevitch's. The yeshiva's policy is that a student gets two good eating days a week, while the others aren't as good. After all, it wouldn't be fair for one student to have six good eating days and excellent Sabbaths and for others to go hungry."

Hannah decided to talk to her husband. She knew that Dodya

Shmulevitch was heavily in debt to the Stupels but was not making any payments.

"Still, Reb Dodya is a fine man," she told Volodya, "for Fishele has excellent meals at his house."

"They're always on a seven-day eating binge over there," Volodya answered. "They stuff themselves like at a rich man's wedding. Always roasting entire oxen. The maids sweat over the pots day and night. The doors never shut there—guests, guests, no end of guests. So it's no big deal for him to give a little yeshiva boy something to eat. But he doesn't pay his debts. We've already extended his notes twice, and if he doesn't pay by the third due date he's in trouble. He owes us a fortune."

Hannah soon noticed that a change had come over the young yeshiva lad. He hardly touched his food and looked anxiously toward the kitchen. Perhaps he's ashamed in front of me, she thought, and left the room. But when she returned she found that he hadn't touched the food.

"If you don't like what I prepared for you, I'll get you something else," she told him.

"I'm full," Fishele answered, but he looked at the laden plate with hungry eyes.

Under other circumstances Hannah would have asked the yeshiva to send her a student with a good appetite—for now Fishele never finished anything she cooked. However, the thought of parting from such a lovely boy, with his black earlocks, round face, and small mouth, grieved her. At his departure, as usual, she gave him a bag full of food and half a zloty. "Please don't forget to come next Thursday," she said.

When Fishele came the next week, Hannah noticed two buttons missing on his jacket and a third hanging by a thread. She removed his little jacket almost by force.

"It's all right," she told Fishele Grayever, "you don't have to be ashamed in front of me. I could have had children older than you."

Hannah sat down with his garment in her lap; the collar and the elbows were torn too, she saw. She pulled the thread through her full, juicy lips and from under her brows looked at Fishele. He wore a white shirt with a high collar; suspenders ran over his thin shoulders, and his ritual fringes were drawn though the noose of the suspenders. He's just a little boy, she thought, practically a tot, and he already knows what's in those huge, thick Talmuds. Volodya didn't know; Naum didn't know very much either; only Tsemakh knew. And what if he did know? He no longer studied and wasn't religious. But Fishele knew and studied and was religious too. She would gladly have put him on her lap and pressed him to her breast—but he no longer looked at women, that little saint. Fishele seemed to sense that a mother was sitting opposite him; he put away his embarrassment and ate everything that had been prepared. Hannah was overjoyed but pretended not to notice. When he had said graçe, she asked him, "What's happened to you lately? You don't eat and you look so frightened. Were you perhaps ill, God forbid?"

Fishele Grayever burst into tears. He rubbed his eyes with his little fists and told her the whole story. "At first my Wednesday people used to stand over me and shout: 'Eat, little boy, eat!' The one who shouted loudest was the master himself, Reb Dodya. 'Eat, little boy, eat!' And he even called in his guests to show them how I was eating, as if I were a beast in the field. But lately they feed me in an empty, half-dark room and nobody comes in to see me, not even the maid. I find a piece of bread on the table and some soup in a bowl, and when I leave there's no one to say good-bye to. So I was afraid that on Thursday, too, I'd be told to sit in the kitchen and nobody would come to me."

Tears welled up in Hannah's eyes. She related the incident to her husband and asked that Fishele eat at their home on Wednesdays, too.

"As long as Shmulevitch hasn't paid his debt," Volodya answered, "it'll be dangerous to start anything with him. He won't like the fact that his student has gone over to the Stupels', and he'll become a deadly enemy of ours."

In the store, Volodya repeated the story about the yeshiva lad whom Shmulevitch was feeding so stingily, even though they still roasted whole oxen in his house. Tsemakh heard but didn't interfere. He had had more than enough of the merchants' world.

When his debt fell due, Shmulevitch came into the store and requested a third extension on the note. Although he stood there with princely confidence, one could tell that he feared being declared bankrupt. Shmulevitch told of his entanglement with

various business enterprises and only in passing let it be known
how great was his wealth. "My mill behind the Zembrove River
can't begin to function until the new motors are installed. The
tenants of my new houses still haven't paid their first installment of
the rent, and the government too still hasn't paid me for the
soldiers' barracks I built for them. So until I can collect all my debts
and begin to build anew, I've got a mountain of bricks lying in my
brickworks and a forest of planks in my sawmill. That's why things
are a bit tight for me. I must admit, too, that I spend too much. I
give too much charity. People are eating me out of house and home.
I'm being cut to pieces. The Guest House Fund says give. The Old
Age Home says give. And when they come around for the Jewish
Hospital, I certainly can't be a swine."

"We give even more. You don't give more than twenty-five zlotys
to all the charity funds you mentioned, maybe even less," Naum
Stupel said sourly. "I'm a member of the community council and
the chairman of many organizations, so I know how much everyone
gives."

"Don't tell me you know how much everyone gives!" the debtor
said. He pushed up his sleeves, and with outstretched hands, like a
kohen whose hands are laved before he blesses the congregation, he
began reckoning on his fingers. "The Old Age Home is one . . .
the Guest House Fund is two . . ."

"You've already mentioned the Old Age Home and the Guest
House Fund," Volodya said, laughing unwillingly.

"My memory is a bit weak lately," Shmulevitch replied in
confusion. "At night when I go to sleep, I remember everything—
but when morning comes, my mind gets soft from the heat."
Finally, however, he began enumerating once more: "Well, and
what about the poor people who beg from door to door; they don't
count, huh? If you tell me the poor only get a penny, I'll tell you
that they come in droves as long as the Jewish exile, day in and day
out, and it all adds up to a mighty big heap. And what about the
charity plate in shul on the Eve of Yom Kippur—that's nothing?
And what about the yeshiva boy who comes to eat? He shows up at
my house every Wednesday and eats the very best of everything.
He's eating me out of house and home."

Tsemakh had listened to the conversation, not caring whether
the sweating man with the big stomach and fat neck paid a penny of

his debt. Tsemakh was fascinated at the way this potbellied mound of flesh was desperately struggling to cite his charitable contributions. But his including the Lomzhe yeshiva boy in the list of his squandered wealth made Tsemakh furious enough to tell him off:

"Every man is a miser, either for himself or for someone else. And if someone is a spendthrift, squandering his money on himself and on others, the miser in him will suddenly spring forth over a penny. Your wife and daughters-in-law and daughters, those fat Kine of Bashan, have new dresses sewn for themselves—that you forgot about. The sums your sons and sons-in-law lose at cards— that you forgot about. The gala banquets you make for your guests, where they glut and swill and sweat and stink—that you forgot about. But that little boy from the yeshiva—him you didn't forget, and you're crying that he's eating you out of house and home."

Dodya Shmulevitch looked around as though searching for an iron bar, a heavy scale, a hunk of wood. At first he couldn't utter a sound. He was certain that the Stupel brothers had incited their brother-in-law against him. Shmulevitch wiped the perspiration from his face and neck, straightened up, and strode toward the door.

"That loafer who insinuated his way into your family like a spider—I'm not even going to answer him. But you, my former partners, I'll say this to you: Even if you were sure that I'd never pay back my debt, you should not have permitted such an attack on me. Send as many treasury officials and collectors after me as you like, but as for you personally, don't you dare show your faces at my door, or I'm going to crack skulls."

Shmulevitch left the store with his shoulders sagging. Volodya restrained himself as if with iron pincers from seizing his brother-in-law by the throat.

"You've made us miserable. I too give to charity, but I'm not a mad Musarnik," he rasped.

Tsemakh looked at him as though awaiting a blow. "You don't give to charity. You hate poor people and call them beggars. You throw them coins like a dissipated nobleman, just to be rid of them."

Naum clenched his fists and ranted, "I'm known in Lomzhe, I'm known in Bialystok, and I'm known in Warsaw too. I'm a member of the community council, and I've been to receptions given by the provincial governor. I've even been a member of a delegation that presented bread and salt to the president of Poland—but never in my life have I heard anyone talk this way to another human being."

Tsemakh addressed Naum softly and with contempt: "I feel sorry for you. You consider yourself so inferior that you're always rushing to be up front so that everyone can at least see you."

"Don't set foot into this store again." Volodya ground his teeth and removed a handful of coins from his pocket. He had ceased doing this since Tsemakh had come into the store and couldn't bear the sight of the clerks throwing themselves on the ground to gather up the fallen coins. This time, however, the clerks stood at a distance, fearing that they too might be sent away along with their cousin.

Tsemakh went up to the apartment and told Slava, "Your brothers have chased me out of the store."

Before she had a chance to ask whether he was serious or joking, Volodya's maid entered and told her that her brother wanted to talk to her. Slava left quickly.

Volodya and Hannah were standing helplessly in their living room, as though they had returned from a celebration and discovered that the house had been stripped clean by thieves.

Overcome by excitement, Hannah pressed her hands to her heaving bosom and told her husband, "Your brother-in-law is apparently not so pious. He doesn't have a beard and doesn't go to the beth medresh. Truly religious people are quiet and gentle."

"That loony Musarnik," Volodya roared, "is going to drive us all to the poorhouse and make enemies of everybody in Lomzhe."

Slava's face was drawn. Volodya had called her husband a loony Musarnik, and her sister-in-law, that village hick, was expostulating on how a virtuous person should behave. Slava shrugged and spoke with feigned astonishment: "I don't understand Tsemakh either. Where does he get the idea of arguing with shopkeepers? What do you merchants know?" Then she headed for the door, her lips pressed together.

Volodya's face turned red and he shouted after her, "Wait! You'll see what trouble you'll have with him!"

When Slava returned to her apartment, Tsemakh met her with ruddy cheeks and joy in his eyes, as if he'd spent the entire day out in the forest by the river.

"That's how you show your love for me?" she sobbed weakly.

He didn't see the charm that glowed through her tears as he replied, "Then I guess I don't know what it means to love. To love apparently means not to stand up for truth and justice."

"You're not so good and you're not so smart," Slava shouted angrily. "What rational person insults strangers who did him no harm and by so doing hurts his own family?"

Tsemakh's radiant face clouded over and his words smoldered like his eyes. "Dodya Shmulevitch is a glutton with a wide-open maw who belches constantly. He's as low-class as a pair of cheap leather boots. A beefy clunk with double rolls of fat on his fingers. One night he couldn't fall asleep. He was missing ten thousand zlotys and couldn't recall where he put them. Finally he remembered that it was the yeshiva boy who ate at his house once a week who had eaten up his fortune—should I spare such a glutton?"

Slava, depressed, said nothing. In their first private conversation, she hadn't taken him seriously when he told her that a Musarnik couldn't enjoy life; now she saw that he was right. The fire in Tsemakh also gradually subsided, and both sat gloomily silent, like a poor couple at a bare table the morning after a holiday.

"You won't be able to make the world over, but you'll ruin our happiness. Ever since time began, people have been both wild beasts and angels," Slava murmured sadly.

"That's just the point," Tsemakh answered. "All my life I've learned that when someone flutters with the wings of an angel, one must look beneath his wings to see if the body of a beast isn't lurking there in a sweaty and hairy hide."

Tsemakh went quickly to the clothes closet and took out the black gaberdine that had been sewn for his wedding. Since leaving sacred studies he had never worn the garb of a Torah scholar. Now, however, he took off his short jacket and swiftly donned his rabbinic cloak, brand-new and pressed as though it had just come from the tailor. In this long, below-the-knee coat, he appeared even taller, thinner, and stronger; he fused with the cloth like a tree trunk with its bark. Tsemakh paced back and forth across the room in the open gaberdine, which fluttered festively after him. His face gleamed in the reflected sheen of the black silk coat.

Slava watched him as though she had just become a bride. "Why did you suddenly get dressed up? Where are you going?"

"I'm going back to the beth medresh. I can no longer deny my previous life."

Since the Stupel brothers had promised their sister her share of the earnings as long as Tsemakh didn't show his face in the store, Slava didn't object to his going back to his religious life. Perhaps there his fire and rage would subside. For days on end Tsemakh paced in the house of study ceaselessly reviling the world: The world's deep-rooted malaise stems not so much from its wickedness as from its phony righteousness. Tsemakh plucked at his chin as though desperately urging the beard to grow more quickly, the beard he had cut off when he married and left the straight and narrow path.

5

LOLLA WAS NAUM STUPEL'S ONLY SON. The strapping twenty-year-old had a pair of beefy cheeks, a short, thick neck, and sticky lips from the sweets he was always eating. His bull neck packed his collar, and his heavy shoulders made his jacket tight. All day long he played soccer or strolled around with a group of loafers. His father called him a good-for-nothing to his face. Naum wanted his grown son to work in the store, but Volodya refused. He called his nephew a wild boar. "Could he weigh a kilo of flour, that wild boar?" he would chuckle.

Lolla sniffed around the Jewish maids in the house but had no luck with them. During supper he would go to the kitchen for a drink of water, and at once the maid's scream was heard in the dining room: "Beat it or I'll throw the soup at you." Occasionally a slap would resound in the kitchen and Lolla would run out, excited and panting. His mother would weep, his father would wave his fists, and the son would defend himself, whining, "What's wrong? What did I do?"

In town, serving girls remarked, "We'd rather carry firewood and be stooped over laundry tubs than work for Naum Stupel. He always flings back his plates and hollers that the dishes are either too cold or too hot, too burned or too raw." His wife Frieda therefore looked for a submissive type, the sort that wouldn't snap back at her husband; and also one that wasn't too pretty or charming, so that Lolla wouldn't cast eyes at her.

By coincidence, Hannah Stupel had seen at a friend's house exactly the kind of maid Frieda wanted. She had an awkward, lumbering figure, unkempt flaxen hair, and a childish face; she didn't look Jewish and was even called Stasya, a Christian form of the Jewish name Stesye.

"Stasya's parents," said Hannah's friend, "were rich villagers who lived in the Zembrove region. They died years ago, when she was still an immature little tyke—whereupon her Jewish relatives and Christian neighbors helped themselves to her inheritance. To prevent her roaming about the village before their eyes, they brought her to Lomzhe and hired her out as a maid. And she was good at it. She knew how to cook and launder, clean and scrub. She did everything she was told. The only thing she couldn't do was serve at table. Seeing even a plain bench in the middle of the room, she would stand petrified, as if she were confronted by a mountain. But worst of all, she never learned how to keep a kosher home, and that's why she doesn't last long with Jewish families. In fact, my husband too is afraid she'll make the kitchen unkosher, and I'm going to have to send Stasya away."

The good-hearted Hannah, herself a village girl, looked pityingly at the silent girl and imagined how Stasya's parents had pampered her during her childhood. She pictured her running around the fields with a blue ribbon in her flaxen hair. Stasya was heavyset and her hands had become rough with toil, but her eyes radiated the tranquility of a forest at sunset. Her face expressed a strange bewilderment, as though she still didn't understand why people had ransacked her home and brought her to a strange town.

At Hannah's suggestion Frieda went to look at the maid. She was satisfied. A girl with such an appearance and such a childlike nature would not attract Lolla, she concluded. To prevent Naum's opposition, Hannah talked with him. When thin, anxious Frieda could not convince Naum, Hannah, with her snow-white neck and

rosy cheeks, always succeeded. Hannah asked her brother-in-law
to take in the dimwitted orphan, and Naum agreed. He hardly
looked at the maid. While the family ate, Stasya would stand in the
kitchen looking dreamily at the open oven. The glowing embers
cast a golden shine on her face, and her flaxen hair took on a copper
hue.

Before his parents Lolla wrinkled his nose in disgust and called
her an ugly beast. But actually he considered her a healthy piece
and subtly began to worm his way into her good graces. Once he
found her sitting in the kitchen with folded hands. He broke off
half a bar of chocolate in his coat pocket and gave it to her. Stasya
hungrily swallowed the chocolate, smearing her mouth like a baby,
and quickly wiped her lips. Another time Lolla threw a handful of
pistachio nuts into her apron pocket. She looked about happily and
at once began to crack the nuts like a lively squirrel. The third time
he gave her some change. She gave him an odd look, and then took
it. She pretends she's a stupid calf, Lolla thought, but she's clever
enough to accept and not say a word.

One morning when no one was at home and Lolla was just
crawling out of bed, he saw the maid bent over in the dining room
washing the floor, her dress tucked up. The warm, rested youth
saw her spread bare feet, her arms naked up to the shoulders, her
full breasts bulging out of her loose bodice—and lunged at her as
though the hair on his body had been singed. The girl laughed
wildly. Even more aroused by her wild laughter, Lolla seized her
broad shoulders and dragged her to the bed. Stasya pushed him
away, looked at him terror-stricken, and crossed herself.

"You're not Jewish?" He gaped at her.

"I'm Jewish," she replied.

With a broad gesture Lolla pointed to the contents of the room.
"You see, all this is going to be mine. I'm an only son. Uncle
Volodya's fortune will also be mine, because he has no children."

Stasya looked submissively and happily at the young man who
was so rich and was so good to her. He lifted up her chin and said
with authority, "Now is no good. My mother might come in. But
tonight I'll slip into your little room, so don't be frightened and
don't start screaming and don't say a word about this to anyone.
You hear?"

Stasya nodded, but her quiet, pensive gaze showed that she

didn't quite understand what would happen when the young master slipped into her room.

Lolla sneaked into her room night after night, until he got tired of her and began to think of other girls standing around outside. He roamed about the house gaily and didn't even see the maid staring at him, wondering why he had ceased coming to her. More frequently, however, Stasya stood in the kitchen, gazing into the oven fire as though seeing there the reflection of a sunset in the windows back home.

Once when Lolla didn't come to supper, she asked her mistress, "Where's your son?"

"He's not here, thank God," Frieda answered and hurriedly left the kitchen, both hands laden with full plates. Frieda knew that when her husband didn't see his wastrel son sitting opposite him at the table he yelled less and liked the food more.

Stasya kept asking about Lolla, but Frieda thought nothing of it until she happened to notice that the maid had become fatter. It was more difficult now for her to bend over to scour the floors. Frieda pushed all her fingers into her mouth to stifle a scream: Oh woe is me, the maid is pregnant! She brought the maid into the kitchen, closed the door, and made long efforts to speak before she was able to utter a word.

"Who is it?"

Stasya understood what her mistress was referring to. Her childish face became mournfully serious as she slowly answered, "Your son."

Her mother's heart had known it all along. Nevertheless, Frieda had hoped that perhaps God would have pity and it wouldn't be her son. Knowing that she would have to break the news to her husband, she began to tremble all over. Yet when Naum came home, Frieda, in dread of him, immediately told him everything, even before he had a chance to change into his robe and slippers.

Naum smiled foolishly: he thought he was dreaming. Then he blinked for a while and finally collapsed on the sofa with his head thrown back. Frieda didn't want to be there when he came to and began ranting. She also knew that Naum wouldn't counsel her on how to get out of this calamity. So she left him on the sofa, staring out into space, and went through the corridor to Volodya, the real head of the family. A while later, when Frieda returned with her brother- and sister-in-law for a consultation, they heard screams from the kitchen. Naum stood there waving his fists at the maid.

"You whore, you seduced my son!"

Stasya paled; she looked Naum straight in the eye but didn't reply.

Hannah came between them and said passionately, "It's not the orphan's fault. She's still a child and trusts everyone."

Volodya stood there like an enraged bear chased out of his den by a pack of dogs. After spending all day in the store, he loved the quiet repose of his apartment; he couldn't stand his brother's house, which was as full of din as a bathhouse is of steam. Volodya looked with disgust at the maid's childish face and her big, lumbering body. He hated bunglers and grownups with childish minds. He silenced the excited family with a roar and ordered everyone except the maid to go into the living room.

Naum paced back and forth in the living room, tearing the hair from his head. "What will Lomzhe say, and what will the world say? They'll say that Naum Stupel's son knocked up a maid."

Just then the door opened and Lolla ambled in. He was about to yell, "Mama, food!" when he saw his mother standing in a corner wringing her hands. His father looked at him and retreated as though before a demon. His Aunt Hannah sat wet-eyed at the table, and Uncle Volodya sat in an easy chair with murder in his eye.

"How can a Jewish boy be so heartless and make an orphan so miserable?" Hannah sobbed.

Before the disconcerted Lolla could put on an innocent face, Volodya marched over and smacked him with his bearish paw.

"You wild boar! You don't make filth where you eat."

Lolla put his hand to his stinging cheek and pleaded, "What's wrong? What did I do?"

Then, to everyone's surprise, Naum—instead of lashing out at his son—pounced at his brother and stamped his foot. "I'm boss in my house, not you! Lolla is my son, not yours! If he deserves to be smacked, I'll smack him, not you! You hear, you big oaf?"

"You overblown balloon, I don't care about you or your wild boar. I care about our family's honor." Volodya turned from his brother and addressed Frieda. "The maid's not going to stay with you any longer. She can't stay in my house either, because she might drum the news all over town. We'll have to ask Slava to take her in and not let her out till we find a place for her somewhere." Then the incensed and disheveled Volodya roared at his wife, "Stop blubbering and come to bed."

Seeing that Volodya and Hannah were leaving, Frieda cowered even more. Now her husband would pour out his entire wrath on her. Lolla still stood in a daze, hand on his swollen cheek, looking around like a man gaping stupidly at the spot where he's just slipped.

Volodya made sure that his loudmouthed brother was not present when he spoke to Slava. Frieda sat depressed in a corner, and Hannah was wrapped in a melancholy silence. She knew not to expect any compassion for the orphan from her husband. Volodya said he planned to find the maid a home with a village peasant, and that's where she'd give birth to her bastard. Slava too was unsympathetic. However, she was prepared to hide the pregnant girl at her place to keep Lomzhe from gossiping about her family.

"And what should I tell Tsemakh?" she asked.

"Don't tell him the truth. Think of something," Volodya answered apprehensively.

"An inexperienced eye, especially a man's, won't notice a thing. You can hardly tell she's pregnant," Frieda sighed, swaying back and forth.

Hannah could no longer restrain herself and began sobbing again. "Why should a deceived, innocent orphan be abandoned like this?"

"Are you still babbling?" her husband yelled at her. "You're the one who brought that calf into the house in the first place. It's all your fault!"

Volodya marched into the maid's room. "From now on," he told her, "you're going to live at my sister's until we find you a home in a village. I'm concerned about you like a father or a brother, but you're not to say a word to anyone. If you tell the master of the house where you'll be living, or anyone in the village, you'll be chased out in the street. Nobody will take in a pregnant maid, and the police will arrest you for immoral conduct."

Stasya listened to him with wide-open eyes and stammered, "I'll do as you say."

Volodya stood for a minute with his back to her, as though to purposely make her remember not only his words but also his broad shoulders, hard neck, and huge, bearish head. Confident of the fright he had cast over the girl, he went down to the store and told his clerks that he was going away on business. That same day he put a hat on his unkempt head and went out to look for a peasant in a village.

Stasya took her little bundle and moved into the apartment of her new mistress. "You're not to go outside or into the room of the master," Slava instructed. Then, fetching something from Tsemakh's room, she told him in passing, "Naum has suddenly discharged another maid. She's a sort of silly girl and has no place to go, so I've taken her in here till she finds another job."

Tsemakh nodded, indicating that he'd heard, but didn't lift his eyes from the sacred text he was studying.

6

THE MAILMAN BROUGHT SLAVA a letter from Bernard Frankel. She looked around to see if Tsemakh had noticed, and with a mixed feeling of fright, curiosity, and guile, like a pet about to snatch some food, she went into her bedroom to read. But as soon as she had torn open the envelope, she felt insulted by Frankel's handwriting. The intertwined lines were apparently hastily and carelessly written. In his style of writing she recognized at once his manner of speaking with sham earnestness and sincerity which cloaked anger as well as scorn.

> Dear Slava,
>
> I wish you lots of luck on your marriage, but I'm surprised you didn't let me know that you had finally found your chosen one. I'm even more surprised that you never let me know about your religious feelings. I heard that you married someone from the Musarnik sect, those poorly dressed and heavily bearded fanatics

whom one finds on the Bialystok streets. But still, I'm sure your husband is an intelligent and gentle man, and I'd be honored to meet the rabbi who has won your love. In my life, too, there's been a change. My wife has come to Bialystok and brought our child, but this has made our relationship even more complex and tense. However, I find it painful to discuss this, especially in a letter.

Admiringly yours,
Bernard

She noticed that he concluded his letter as if he were a tall man bowing before a little girl. Frankel, she gathered, wanted to renew his secret trysts with her, confident that she didn't love her husband. She tore up the letter and entered the kitchen to throw the bits of paper into the oven. Stasya sat on a bench, her big hands in her lap.

"Where is Lolla? He promised he'd marry me," she said with a blank face.

"And you believed that fool, that exploiter, that stupid faker? He would have kept it up as long as he came to no harm and no one knew about it," Slava reviled her nephew, not realizing at first that she was thinking of Bernard Frankel.

She returned to the bedroom, and as she paced back and forth she thought about Tsemakh. Since he had quarreled with her brothers and had begun studying in the beth medresh and at home, he had become calm and gentle. When she called him to eat, he came; when she spoke to him, he replied laconically or merely nodded. He behaved submissively so that he'd be left alone. Occasionally her wild rage at him took her breath away. Then her anger would suddenly evanesce like a bad dream that disappears the instant it becomes a nightmare and begins choking the sleeper. But her brothers loathed him. They wished him all kinds of ill. Volodya and Naum were dragging her into a calamity too. If Lolla's deed and Stasya's whereabouts were known in town, people would say that the scholar Tsemakh Atlas was no better than his brothers-in-law. After all, he had hidden the pregnant maid. They'd say that his wife, too, had had a lover before her wedding. Slava's wrath rose against her family. But she knew now that it was Frankel's mocking tone that had stirred her rage. She was irritated by his sarcastic reference to her husband as one of the fanatic, dirty, and ragged Musarniks.

Suddenly it occurred to her to go to town and buy a pair of shoes. It had been a long time since she had bought herself new shoes. In fact she hadn't bought a thing lately, as though she had indeed become a rusty rebbetsin. She'd buy a hat to match and order a new dress from a seamstress, and she'd have a jacket and a skirt made too. From her tightly packed clothes closet Slava removed a pale blue suit and quickly changed into it. She also donned a pleated blouse with a large white bow. Then she looked into the mirror. I don't even need a jacket or a new dress, she thought, and shrugged. Big black patent-leather purse in hand, she went into her husband's room. Tsemakh didn't notice her as she stood in the doorway looking at him. He sat motionless, studying a holy book. Around his lips hovered the sad smile of a man lost in thought. Then, sensing her presence in the room, he slowly turned to her. His expression showed total indifference to what she would say.

"I'm going to town to buy a dress," Slava said, and Tsemakh nodded apathetically. She left, thinking that Frankel would have noticed the large white bow that flowed over the jacket lapels like sea foam on deep blue waves.

"They make their bellies their gods, their clothes their Torah, and their desires their moral code," Tsemakh murmured from his Musar book on the table. Having sat immobile so long, he felt that his stiff back was broken, turned to stone, tombstone. Nevertheless, he didn't budge and continued dunning himself: Did he not make of his own belly a god, and had he not exchanged the Torah for fine clothes and a well-furnished home? He had acted just like the hedonists depicted in Bachya ibn Pakuda's *The Duties of the Heart.*

Two weeks of Elul had passed. In his mind's eye Tsemakh could see the yeshiva in Nareva. Amid the huge crowd that had gathered for the Days of Awe, in the crush of boys and youths who scurried about the beth medresh studying Musar, he saw his students sitting next to one another. He had always taught them: An individual seeker is a firebrand, an entire group a glowing oven. And because their mentor had abandoned them, the youngsters now huddled together more than ever before. Just as he could see his pupils, they too, Tsemakh felt, could see him. As they turned their heads to him, their faces lined with grief, they moved their lips as though mumbling adjurations that he be rid of his impurity. They were praying for their teacher, who had become an Elisha ben Abuyah, the Talmudic sage who left the path of Judaism. Almost a year had passed since he had humiliated them and broken their hearts by his departure. Nevertheless, they didn't curse him and couldn't forget that he had brought them from Russia and saved them for the Torah. Tsemakh's seekers were prepared to forgive him for shaming them if only he would come back: Return! The Day of Judgment is approaching. As Isaiah said, "Return, O Israel, to him against whom you have deeply revolted."

"Return, O Israel, to him against whom you have deeply revolted," Tsemakh said, bending and swaying. He wrenched from his depths the bitter Musar melody and transported the entire Nareva Musar school to Lomzhe, so as to feel around him and within him the ecstatic fervor of the yeshiva during the Elul days. The Nareva Musar school obeyed him and approached with the force of a flood, with hundreds of upturned faces and voices. And from this vast sea of blending, tumultuous voices the voice of a woman nearby was singled out. Tsemakh pricked up his ears; someone was crying. He tore himself from his chair and went to look through the open kitchen door. The maid was sitting on a bench, sobbing.

"What's the matter? Why are you crying?" Tsemakh called and immediately remembered what Slava had told him. "Are you crying because you've been fired? Don't cry over that! You'll get another job. Meanwhile you can stay with us."

Stasya remembered Volodya's warning not to tell anybody the truth, so she began to stammer, "It was . . . your singing, rabbi; it reminded me of my father. My father too would sing on Friday evening, but not as sadly as you."

"Perhaps my wife can convince her brother to take you back," Tsemakh consoled her. "Why were you fired?"

Stasya lowered her head and began weeping. Her big body, small face, and unkempt hair portrayed complete desolation, as if she'd been living half-naked and barefoot in the river-bank bamboo for years. Tsemakh realized that out of fear or shame she was hiding something. He led her by the hand to his room and sat her down at the table facing him.

"If you want me to help you, I have to know why you were fired. Did you take something without permission?" Tsemakh lowered his eyes so that Stasya wouldn't be ashamed to talk.

As afraid as she was of telling the truth, she still didn't want the fine and kindly rabbi to consider her a thief.

"I didn't take anything from them. Lolla promised he'd marry me . . . and he came to my room every night and I'm . . . going to have a baby."

Tsemakh raised his eyebrows and understood everything. The news came so unexpectedly that for a minute he regretted that his questions had brought out the truth.

The rabbi's silence and his stern look frightened Stasya.

"Lolla's uncle," she whispered, "told me not to tell anyone and he'd find me a house where I can work. But if I said a word to anyone, he wouldn't do a thing for me. I'll be chased away wherever I go because of my big belly, and the police will arrest me because I'm not decent. Lolla's uncle has gone away to find me a place in a village, but I don't want to work in a village. After my parents died, my relatives sold my house in the village and took the money. The peasants also stole many of our things and even laughed at me for not converting. 'You look like one of us, but you have a different faith,' they told me. So why should my baby be called a bastard and all the gentiles laugh at me?" Stasya began crying again, then suddenly kissed Tsemakh's hand, which lay trembling on the open *The Duties of the Heart*.

Tsemakh pulled his hand away. His left eye brimmed with a huge tear, which slowly rolled down his face and remained hanging at the edge of his nose. He rose, pale, a cold sweat on his brow, his heart chilled and his lips compressed, ready to do battle even unto death.

"Will Lolla marry me?" Stasya's eyes shone with trust in Tsemakh; she felt that the nice rabbi would intercede for her.

"Lolla's uncle will not send you into a village among gentiles. You're going to give birth to your baby among Jews," Tsemakh answered, and the girl colored at Tsemakh's penetrating glance, as if at that moment she had outgrown her immaturity.

Tsemakh led her back to the kitchen. "Don't tell my wife or anyone else about our talk. Be patient till Lolla's uncle returns and I speak to him. One word from me and he'll be afraid of sending you to a village, and he'll no longer threaten you with the police, either."

Outside, clouds gathered and thickened, bringing with them the quiet unease that precedes a storm. Slava came in with light, rapid steps, carrying a round hatbox and an oblong shoebox. She was delighted with her bargains and pleased that she'd returned before the rainstorm. At home she found everything the way she had left it: Tsemakh sat in his room, deeply immersed in his text, and the maid sat in the kitchen, hands in her lap, with an earnest expression, as though listening to the baby growing in her womb.

7

EVEN BEFORE THE WEDDING, when Tsemakh lived with his aunt and her sons, who treated him as one of the family, they had passed hints, via words and gestures, about his bride-to-be. "She's a good piece of merchandise," they said, "but slightly damaged. Slava's brothers want to cover up her unsuccessful love affair with your scholar's mantle. So don't be a shlimazel—ask for a large dowry. And don't ever forget that we, your cousins, introduced you to the Stupel family."

Tsemakh had let his aunt's sons cavort around him as though he were a huge fish they'd dragged out of the water. Nevertheless, he saw the truth of their words in the Stupels' haste to arrange the wedding as soon as possible, lest he hear too many bad things and regret the match, just as he had already regretted his previous match in Amdur. Even discounting the gossip around him, Tsemakh perceived that Slava, when she was a young girl, hadn't been a homebody like his first fiancée, Dvorele Namiot. After the wedding Tsemakh noticed that she frequently spoke of her child-

hood and her Hebrew *Gymnasium* days, but quickly skipped over
the years that followed, chattering incessantly all the while to
forestall suspicions that she was hiding something. Distressed that
his wife kept secrets from him, he had nevertheless remained silent,
even though playacting was foreign to his nature. But after
discovering Slava's role in the outrage against the maid, he thought:
The time for revenge will surely come. If a fight ensues, another
matter will be mentioned too. In order not to explode prematurely,
he spoke less frequently to his wife and even avoided looking at her.

Slava too was in a restless mood. She had received another letter
from Frankel, this time a despairing one.

> Dear Slava,
>   I admit that in my last letter I purposely wanted to hurt you. I
> expressed myself crudely, out of fear that you might end our
> friendship. I need your help and can trust only you. You're
> smarter and calmer, and a better person than I. So I'm asking you
> to please come to Bailystok—I promise to spare your feelings. I
> know that you're forbidden to me.

"He's crazy!" Slava told herself in amazement. She was sure that
Frankel now loved her very much, when previously he had merely
desired her. But, she thought, that love-dazed maniac forgets that
his letters can fall into my husband's hands. . . . No, he hasn't
forgotten that at all! Frankel realizes that Tsemakh knows no
Polish. He doesn't even have a *Gymnasium* education, though he
wanted to become a doctor. Instead of studying a little Polish every
day, he rocks and sways over his little books just like an old Jew.
And what's more, lately he's become terribly grouchy. Yes,
Tsemakh exuded a cold air of enmity these days. She ought really
to go to Bialystok and see why Frankel was so upset. Befuddled by
thoughts of her husband and her former lover, she suddenly felt a
desire to dress up.

From the brimming closet Slava removed a brown polka-dot suit.
The tight and rather long skirt rounded her hips, and the folded
collar of the blouse heightened her long neck. She rummaged about
for a while among her more elaborate hats and finally chose a plain
beret, which covered her head and most of one ear. At the mirror
she penciled her eyebrows, lashes, and lids and painted her lips.

Then she slipped into a pair of high-heeled shoes, which made her look supple and slim. She drew on a pair of beige gloves, chose a velvet purse, and went into her husband's room.

"How do you like me in this outfit?" She turned to display the big slanted pockets of her short jacket. In her painted eyes and lipsticked mouth Tsemakh saw so much latent wantonness that he became momentarily confused.

"I'm not a connoisseur of such things," he replied and returned to his book.

Behind his back Slava gave a bitter laugh and with resounding steps left the room. His eyes immersed in *The Duties of the Heart*, Tsemakh sat and thought: How can she dress up when she knows an orphan is sitting in the kitchen bewailing her fate? Because Stasya was too honest and trusted that spoiled brat, both she and her child are being cast away. But if in her youth Slava had become pregnant by such a brat, her family would have spared no effort finding a husband for her.

"And how do you like me in this?" he heard Slava's voice again fifteen minutes later. Once more she pirouetted before him, wearing a long, low-cut, flaring white silk dress embroidered with flowers. A short, wide-sleeved gray Persian lamb coat with an upturned collar was thrown over her bare shoulders. Her bosom was bare to her firm breasts. A string of pearls was around her neck and earrings dangled from her ears. Holding a little purse in one hand, with the other she lifted up the dress, turning happily and passionately.

"When do you wear a dress like that, at a wedding?" Tsemakh asked.

"Yes, at a wedding and a ball." Slava now beamed with joy; her voice bore no trace of the echo of the angry laugh of minutes ago.

"And why don't you have a baby?"

"A baby?" Slava, still looking raptly at her dress, finally realized what Tsemakh had asked her. She grimaced with distaste. "You want a baby? Do you love me enough to want to have a baby with me?" she asked, and without waiting for his reply, she left the room and slammed the door.

The next day Volodya returned from his journey. To prevent the maid from being spirited away secretly, and to be aware of what was happening in the apartment, Tsemakh constantly kept all the doors open. He noticed that Volodya had come in through the dining room, gone to the kitchen, then left immediately. A moment later Stasya's weeping was heard. Tsemakh turned and saw Slava standing in the bedroom, about to close the door to his room.

"Why is the maid crying?" Tsemakh strained to keep calm.

Slava answered quickly, her hand on the doorknob. "Volodya found her a job at the house of one of his customers, but she doesn't want to go there. But I don't need her; I have no patience with her. I only took her in till she found another job."

Tsemakh beckoned Slava with a finger, as though intending to insult her by summoning her with a gesture.

"You can tell your brothers that if they send the maid away to a village, I'm going to go from one Lomzhe shul to another and say that Lolla Stupel seduced an orphan girl and that the Stupel family has sent her packing to a village where the child will end up converting. I'm going to tell everything, as sure as I'm sitting here talking to you."

"Then what should we do?" Slava asked after a long period of silence. "Should Lolla marry the maid?"

Tsemakh was amazed. "Why not? Lolla is a glutton and a drunkard and the girl is a saint. She's been persecuted ever since her childhood. Still, she's remained a Jew, even though her life in the village would have been easier had she converted. So why isn't she good enough to be a Stupel daughter-in-law?"

Slava saw that he was provoking her and deriding her family. "That cow," she yelled, "that promiscuous clod—that whore—should be Naum's daughter-in-law and my niece?"

Tsemakh continued talking calmly, as though wanting his soft-spoken words to hurt her even more. "Why are you reviling her like that? Because she told me the truth while you deceived me? You're a fine one to call her promiscuous! Were you any better?"

At that moment Slava remembered that she must keep calm and not flinch under his gaze. She must remain composed so that her face would express neither anger nor fear. "All right, I'll tell my brothers what you've said," she replied and left the room.

8

EXHAUSTED FROM THE JOURNEY but pleased with his accomplishment, Volodya sat in his deep easy chair and told the women of the family how he had dragged himself from village to village until he had finally found a peasant who for a small fortune agreed to take the girl. "Now we have to send her away as soon as possible and put an end to this business."

Slava waited until her brother had finished, then quoted Tsemakh's warning word for word. Frieda and Hannah exchanged frightened glances. Volodya rose slowly.

"How does he know about this?"

Slava answered with a flat voice and a blank face, like a wooden cuckoo in one of Volodya's clocks. "Tsemakh could have found out only from the maid herself, but he didn't say a word to me till now."

"When I told her I'd found a place for her, she didn't say a word," Volodya panted.

"But as soon as you left, she began crying because she was being sent away, and Tsemakh heard her. You can be sure he'll carry out his threat. He'll go from one shul to another and tell everyone," Slava baited her brother.

Red with anger down to his bulging neck, Volodya went to a black clock cabinet and removed a long brass weight. "I'm going to split his skull open with this."

"Do it," Slava said.

From her talk and appearance Volodya realized that her anguish was now greater than his. He put the heavy brass weight on the table and sank into his chair again, his head lowered. Slava looked at both her sisters-in-law with a distorted smile.

"According to Tsemakh's sense of justice, Lolla should marry the maid. Tsemakh said she's good enough to come into our family and warned me not to say a harsh word about her because I too was promiscuous."

A gentle sorrow appeared on Volodya's full, saucerlike face. He hadn't forgotten how Slava had stood up for her husband when he was driven from the store. But now she herself was talking about him with bitterness and contempt.

"Divorce him!" Volodya roared the thought he had long harbored, and frowned, his brows puffed up.

"Maybe I'll do just that, but not over a maid," Slava answered. "I suggest you find her a Jewish family far from Lomzhe, and then Tsemakh will keep still. And if he wants to talk, let him talk. No sensible person will say that Lolla's obliged to marry the maid just because he made a fool of himself. And since Stasya and her baby will be among Jews, the Stupels won't lose a single friend."

"The shame will drive Naum to do himself harm." Frieda wrung her hands.

"I have a better way out," Slava called triumphantly as though she were outsmarting a foe. She returned to her apartment through the rear door so as not to look at Tsemakh's face.

In the kitchen she told Stasya amicably, "If you wish, we can find a doctor who will perform an abortion. That's a little operation so that you won't have to have the baby."

Stasya immediately burst into tears, and a moment later Tsemakh strode in as though he'd been on guard nearby. Slava felt that he was glaring at her as if she were a demon come to harm a sick babe, but she stared at him with disgust too. Since his repulsive remark, his beard seemed to have become repulsively entangled beneath his chin.

"I don't want a doctor, I don't want an operation, I want to have my baby," Stasya cried, and Slava saw Tsemakh beaming at the maid. He had taken a greater liking to her because she wanted to have her bastard; but to her, his wife, Tsemakh spoke severely and impatiently:

"Well, what did the family decide?"

"If she doesn't want an abortion, we'll look for a home for her among Jews," Slava answered, and looked on as her husband asked the girl paternally, "Are you satisfied?"

Stasya contemplated the expression on his face and realized that she had to agree. "I'll go anywhere the rabbi tells me to go, but everyone'll say my baby is a bastard."

Tsemakh put his hand on her head and consoled her. "Anyone who calls your baby a bastard is himself a low and vulgar person. A tenderhearted Jew and a scholar know that a virgin's baby is a kosher child. Only a married woman's child by another man is a bastard." Tsemakh stroked her disheveled hair. She bent her head beneath his hand, smiling and happy, like a little girl who unbraids her hair under a warm summer sun. Feeling that she could bear it no longer, Slava left the kitchen.

Meanwhile Naum, who had returned to the house, learned that Tsemakh had threatened to make a scandal. Slava watched her elder brother running around the rooms yelling in a choked voice, "A blood enemy has been taken into the family. That Musarnik should be cut up root and branch. What do you mean, he's going to chase all over Lomzhe and tell everyone that Naum Stupel is going to become the grandfather of a bastard? A bastard! A bastard!"

As bad a mood as Volodya was in, he nevertheless beamed with joy at his brother's anger. "Well, what did you accomplish over there?" he asked Slava.

"I advised the maid to have an abortion, but she began bawling like a baby." Slava was laughing with rage, as though little flames were bursting from her mouth. She sat down on a chair, and her laughter dissolved into sobs, tears, screams. "And Tsemakh was even stroking and fondling the girl. He's completely charmed by her. He's crazy for her. I left the two of them there. Let them kiss and cuddle each other. Why are you looking at me as if I'm a maniac? It's not me who's crazy, it's him. He said her baby won't be a bastard. A virgin's baby, he told her, is no bastard."

"Maybe he's right. After all, he's a scholar, so he knows what he's talking about!" Hannah exploded with delight. Then she spoke feelingly to her sister-in-law: "After all, Frieda, the child is our own flesh and blood."

"Shut up!" Volodya thundered at his wife. Frightened, Hannah said nothing more. In the apartment, dense with the anxious silence of the gathered family, Slava's humiliated weeping sounded even more raucous.

After a long while Slava calmed down and returned to her own apartment. Frankel would not have compared her to a maid, Slava thought, fondly recalling the times they had been together, secretly embracing each other and cut off from the world. Frankel had written that he needed her help. What had happened to him? She must go and help him. Yet at the same time she hoped that Tsemakh wouldn't let her out of his sight even for a day.

Slava went to him and said, "Tomorrow morning I'm leaving for Bialystok."

"Go where you please and do what you want," he answered, continuing to pace angrily up and down. Her flaming face and tearful voice did not move him. He didn't even turn around when she left the room with bent head.

Husband and wife didn't exchange a word during the whole evening. He slept on the sofa in his room, and she lay hunched into herself in her bed in the bedroom. In the morning Slava heard him leaving for shul. She got up immediately and chose a black dress with patch pockets and a white design around the low-cut neck. She packed a small valise with the most important items for her journey, put on a flared coat with big buttons, and went to see Volodya, who was preparing to go down to the store.

"I'm leaving for Bialystok. I don't know for how long—I can't stand looking at that girl's face any more. Find her a job with a Jewish family and let her get out of my house and my life as soon as possible."

Volodya remained gloomily silent for a long time; then he growled softly, so that Hannah in the bedroom wouldn't hear, "Your teacher's wife and child are with him now."

Slava looked at him, astonished at his knowledge of the news, and smiled pathetically. "Don't worry, I'm not going for adventure."

Volodya saw that the beloved baby of the family, the high-spirited, giggling prankster, was scarcely able to contain her tears. Her face looked smaller; her skin was pale. There were dark patches beneath her eyes. He pressed her head to his broad cheek and felt her whole body trembling. A murderous rage came over him. He would have liked to take her husband by the throat with his iron fingers and throw him down the stairs. However, he had to wait for Slava to get rid of her plague of her own accord. He dared not request it; she had suffered and been humiliated more than enough.

Volodya looked down at Slava's baggage and wondered: Is that all she's taking with her? She always went with large valises and several hatboxes. Yes, it was clear that she wasn't going for a good time, but just to take a breather. And her husband, that louse, wasn't even accompanying her to the station. Volodya carried his sister's suitcase to the bus station at the old market place and promised her, "I'm leaving soon to try to find a Jewish home for the girl."

On the bus Slava leaned her forehead against the windowpane. Lacking sleep and weary with thinking, she was delighted with the scenery, which for a while freed her from her thoughts. Thin wisps of fog hovered over the houses; then from the low-hanging clouds a shower burst forth. On a little hill stood a windmill. Slava stared at it intently, as if it were a queer great-winged creature that had flown in from another world. Through the smoky grayness along the way, wagons with tarpaulins over their loads plodded along. The bus passed them. Slava was pleased to be moving quickly, while the horse-drawn wagons inched on slowly. Little chains of raindrops formed above the windows. She lifted the window and put her head out into the wetness. A passenger behind her grumbled that the rain was blowing into his face. Slava lowered the window and gazed out once more. She didn't want to look straight ahead lest Lomzhe acquaintances engage her in conversation.

9

BERNARD FRANKEL WAS CALLED to the phone in the middle of a lesson. He heard Slava's voice, and the veins in his temples began to tremble as if an electric current had gone through them.

"I'm here in Bialystok, waiting for you at the Hotel Ritz."

Straight from the *Gymnasium* the teacher stormed into her hotel room and threw himself at her, still in his hat and coat, as though she were anxious to see him, as though she craved him. She sat at the edge of her bed and bent over to remove his hat. The reddish hair above his temples had become grayer and more sparse. Her first thought was that Bernard was already forty, seven years older than Tsemakh. Frankel fixed his hot brown eyes on her; the yellowish whites were streaked with red. His face burned with sweet hope, and Slava felt good at seeing that someone still loved her passionately. She wanted to continue stroking his disheveled hair and hoped that he would not stir or say a word. Suddenly he lifted her skirt over her knees and stockings, and with his nose, mouth, and chin burrowed into her thighs. Then he swiftly threw his hands around her shoulders and pressed her to him.

Slava felt his lips sealing the corners of her mouth, and a thin line of fire ran over her spine. She freed herself from him and sighed, "You wrote me that you'd spare my feelings."

Frankel threw off his unbuttoned coat and sank into a chair. He massaged his flaming face with his hands, like a sobered-up playboy after a week's binge. He rolled his eyes and said passionately, "There you are sitting before me, and I can see you haven't the foggiest notion how much anguish you cause me at night. But when I lie in bed, half-suffocating till you bend over me with those cold eyes, then it seems to me you do realize the anguish I suffer because of you. You want me to suffer even more, so that I won't spend a night without thinking of you. You come naked into my dreams, looking like a tree without its bark, a white, unveiled trunk, and you look into my eyes with a triumphant smile. But I'm afraid to stretch out my hands to grab you. I see that you're waiting for me to make the attempt, and then you'll leave me your body and flee. That's the sort of bizarre feeling I have. You're going to leave me your body but run away as though your limbs aren't a part of you. These are the strange thoughts and crazy fantasies I have— because you never belonged to me completely. You were mine with your arms and hips, with your firm round belly. But you never got sick pining for me. So I'm sick with yearning for what you never gave me, even when your body belonged to me." Frankel lifted himself from the chair and once again spread his arms to embrace her.

Slava pushed him away angrily and with disgust. "Stop it! That's the way you always spoke to me—as if I were a beautiful witch of the forest, or some sort of goddess of lust to whom wild primitives kneel. You always spoke beautifully, but with an empty heart. Nevertheless, your words intoxicated me, and I too became enchanted with what was forbidden . . . until I sensed that I was a woman like all other women. I wanted to be a housewife. To prepare lunch for my husband and lead a family life!" Slava was shouting, anguished that she hadn't become for Tsemakh what she had wanted to become. "Look, you brought your wife to Bialystok, or perhaps she came on her own. In any case, be happy with her."

Frankel grimaced with distaste. "My wife! Since she came from Lemberg to Bialystok she's constantly afraid of losing her romantic mood among the sober Litvaks here. What's more, she's become pious! A nun! Her morality smacks of the tomb!"

"And would you leave your wife now to marry me?" Slava asked.

Frankel began to sway restlessly in his chair. "You know we have a child. Are you ready to leave your husband for me?"

"No," Slava admitted in a soft, depressed voice. "I don't want to leave my husband. I love him. But he can never love a woman so passionately that he loses sight of the world around him."

Frankel surveyed her body. She had become fleshier and rounder but her face looked gaunt and milky white. Her pallor excited him even more. Ripeness wafted out of her, the sweet aroma prior to withering. But she had already repulsed him twice, and she spoke of her husband dreamily and sadly.

"And I thought you came because of me," Frankel said.

Slava remained silent, a smile of chagrin on her face. How little her life interested him!

In a flash his tone changed and he began to reproach her. "What is it that attracted you to your husband? Is it because he's one of those exotic Jews from the Musarnik sect?" He laughed, irritated by her silence.

A cold, wan sheen came over her eyes, like the light that streams into a room when shutters are opened to wintry weather. But the sharp, cold glance faded at once; she didn't have the strength to fight.

Slava handed Frankel his coat and hat. "Go now, Bernard, and come back tomorrow or the day after. I'm in a bad mood today. I'll expect you the day after tomorrow."

What was it that had attracted her to Tsemakh, Slava asked herself after Frankel's departure. Was she so weak and spoiled that she could love only a man who was hardhearted and unbending, one who humiliated her? Frankel had not changed. He saw in her a woman who could satisfy his crazy passion. But was Tsemakh any different? He was never tender to her. He sucked the essence out of her, kneading her body with his hands and devouring her. He raged and stormed about her, while she, unable to flee, was lifted and carried as though on high, tempestuous waves. Yet in the daytime he didn't look at her; she was a piece of meat left on a plate after one has eaten his fill. If she wanted to snuggle up to him during the day, he moved away from her and a cold shadow crossed his frowning face. An abyss was between them. During the day he was ashamed of his nighttime desire even for his own wife, as if it were a sin—a disgusting sin. He denied himself the pleasure of sipping water slowly; he just wanted to quench his thirst. That's the way he was in everything, even in his dealings with people. He either insulted strangers in the store for no reason or was prepared to ruin his own life, his wife's life, and her whole family's life over a maid. And who could tell what he would do next? Volodya was right: she should divorce him. She should hate him for his empty eyes when he grew angry, for the beard and earlocks he had let grow again. Still, deep down in her heart she admired him and was proud of him. She and her brothers were preoccupied only with themselves. Frankel, too—though he was educated and spoke beautifully—was so preoccupied with himself that he couldn't see another person's suffering. Tsemakh didn't think of himself at all; he thought only of others. But if he had compassion for a maid, why didn't he have consideration for his own wife? How long could one live with a person who, because he wanted to correct all the world's wrongs, destroyed his own home in the process?

Exhausted by her helter-skelter thoughts, Slava found no peace in her narrow little room, but to avoid meeting acquaintances, she couldn't leave it. People would ask her about her husband but would assume she had come to Bialystok to meet her former lover. So she sat in her hotel room as though in prison, or went down to the restaurant adjoining the hotel, and returned as soon as possible. She hadn't believed that Frankel could endure waiting until the next day. Nevertheless, he didn't come even the day after that.

He's playing games, Slava thought, glad that he hadn't come. She had no more patience for his outbursts, for his war of nerves and sarcasm. Another day passed and Slava began to think of returning to Lomzhe. Volodya had probably found a Jewish home for the maid and already packed her off. Would Tsemakh calm down now? Then, as if in answer to her thoughts, Bernard Frankel knocked on the door.

"Well, how have you spent the past few days?" he said, patting her arm like an older brother. But he couldn't resist for long; it was as if the mere cloth of her blouse ignited him. He pulled her sleeve up over the elbow and began feverishly kissing the round bend of her arm, where blue veins shone out of her velvety muscle. "I've always marveled at your well-rounded limbs," Frankel said.

"My husband doesn't notice them. Too bad he doesn't see that I'm beautiful," she said, gazing wistfully at her bare arm.

"It sounds like you asked me to come back so that you can go on talking about your husband." Frankel frowned and began to speak about his suffering again. "When you told me you loved your husband, I left with the thought that I'd never return. You see now how long I've been able to hold out. That's my punishment: I can't tear myself away from you. That's my punishment for loving you. It's not for nothing that during our happy days together I was so nervous and agitated. My heart predicted how much it would cost me when you left me."

"I've also paid for it, paid dearly." Slava smiled at him. He had never before seen such a smile on her face: it was the smile of a blind man asking to be escorted across a busy street. "I haven't told my husband that he wasn't the first man for me—you know that's contrary to his moral code. Our life together has become disrupted."

"Did you marry a man with such old-fashioned prejudices?" Frankel stood up in astonishment and immediately sat down again. "Which man asks a woman nowadays if he's the first one? It's not refined. It's incredible!"

"And I find it incredible that I've become the kind of decent housewifely spouse who can't persuade herself to betray her husband even when she wants to betray him." Slava laughed, an unhealthy flush rising in her cheeks. "That's what makes me angry at you. I'm irritated that you can't seduce me away from my husband. The truth is he doesn't ask me to account for my past. I think he's even pleased that my past life is stained as far as he's concerned and that he has an excuse to regret having married me." Slava spoke quickly and gaily, as though she enjoyed describing her humiliation. "Do you need any money? In your letter you clamored for my friendship, so if you need money I'll lend you some."

Frankel jumped up. "Do you think that's why I asked you to come?"

Slava began stroking his face with trembling fingers. "Don't be insulted," she said, smiling. "A teacher's salary isn't enough to support the family that is with you now. Perhaps your wife is pregnant and you need money for an operation. I know I'm just babbling. But tell me, if your wife should become pregnant, would you want another baby, or would you ask her to have an abortion?"

"No, I wouldn't have another child." Frankel didn't take his eyes off her.

"Don't look at me so pityingly, Bernard. I'm not in that fix. I'm not pregnant." Slava touched her throat, forehead, and cheeks to see if they were burning, and continued talking hastily, feverishly. "I just thought of asking you about an abortion because a maid in our house was made pregnant by my nephew, my older brother's son. The maid doesn't want an abortion, and my husband refuses to let her be driven out. My husband and the rest of the family had a fight over it, and that's why I went away. Now do you understand what sort of person my husband is? Why don't you come tomorrow and I'll tell you all the details. Now it's time for you to go. My brother Volodya has come to Bialystok on business and may be here any minute. Before I left, my brother told me, 'Your teacher's wife and child are with him now.' I haven't the faintest idea how he found out. So if you don't want to meet my brother—and I gather you don't—better leave now. Come tomorrow, after work."

Frankel shrugged and left the room looking worried; he had decided Slava was sick.

Slava immediately began to pack, talking to herself. "What a fool I am! Tsemakh will ask me why I went to Bialystok and who I met here. It's too late to go back today. I won't catch the bus. I'll go tomorrow morning and leave Frankel a note saying I had to return unexpectedly. He didn't believe that Tsemakh fought with me and the whole family over a maid. Frankel wouldn't have stood up for a serving girl. After all, he admitted himself that he would have told his wife to have an abortion."

10

STASYA SAT in her little room, her eyes like those of a frightened rabbit. Hearing a knock at the door, she shuddered, but her fear was unnecessary. The kindly rabbi and master of the house brought in a tray with cake, tea, butter, and cheese.

"This is for you. You haven't eaten a thing today," he said, then returned to the kitchen to prepare his own meal.

Later Tsemakh sat in his room, chewing dry bread and hard salty cheese, mulling over the same thing for the hundredth time: There was nothing more for him to do in Lomzhe, yet he couldn't return to Nareva. After the argument with Reb Simkha Feinerman's two yeshiva emissaries, they would no longer trust him there and they wouldn't let him near his group of students. Hence he had to find a small town and establish a little yeshiva on his own. Never before had he had such a desire to teach youngsters and tell them about the world. Oh, and how he knew the world! And Slava? Would she don a marriage wig and go with him? When she realized that he knew of her role in the outrage against the orphaned maid, she had gone away from home to punish him for telling the truth. Could she, then, be the wife of a rosh yeshiva, even if she agreed to depart with him?

"It's my fault." Stasya interrupted his thoughts. She stood before him, a kerchief on her head, as though she already considered herself married and didn't want to appear before the rabbi with her own hair. Yet her hands were pressed together in prayer like those of a Christian girl kneeling in church. "Rabbi, I don't want you ever to fight with your wife and brothers-in-law on account of me, so I'll leave and go wherever my feet take me," she said, not knowing where she would go.

"Don't you dare!" Tsemakh warned. "If you leave the house, there's going to be an even bigger fight. Just wait patiently until Volodya Stupel finds a job for you in a Jewish home."

Stasya returned to her room and Tsemakh to his thoughts: But if he had married Dvorele Namiot of Amdur or any other modest girl from a religious family, he wouldn't have had such a hard decision to make about his wife, who was suited even less to be a rebbetsin than he to be a merchant.

Toward evening Hannah brought in a full tray of cooked food. She watched Tsemakh recite the blessing over the bread, part his mustache with two fingers, and bring the spoonful of soup to his mouth with the gentle meekness of a recluse eating at a strange table. Of late her respect for her scholarly brother-in-law had risen greatly.

"God will repay you for siding with the orphan. My Volodya isn't so bad; he just didn't think about Stasya's baby being converted in a village."

The soup that Tsemakh swallowed burned his insides. He wanted to cry out: There's the nub of his meanness—he doesn't even realize he's committing an injustice. But not wanting to grieve his good-hearted sister-in-law, he slowly stirred the hot soup until his anger cooled. "You'll bring Stasya something to eat, too, won't you?" he asked, smiling at Hannah.

"Of course. I'll bring her something right away. To tell the truth, Reb Tsemakh, I don't understand Frieda. After all, Stasya's baby will be Frieda's own grandchild. How could she have agreed to throw Stasya into a village among non-Jews? But on the other hand, we can't condemn Frieda. She was afraid of Naum—he's so hot-tempered, and he's so embarrassed that he can't look his townsmen in the eye. Slava knew I'd take care of you; otherwise she wouldn't have gone away. Yes, she's proud and a bit capricious, but still she asked us to give in to you and find a Jewish home for the orphan," Hannah said, trying so hard to mitigate and justify everything that she felt a crimson glow in her cheeks, a surge of heat in the little ears beneath the heavy tower of her hair.

Hannah finally escaped from Tsemakh's room, vexed with

herself. Her brother-in-law had a pair of fiery eyes that penetrated down to the very marrow of one's bones. His stern gaze flustered her and made her tongue swivel like a windmill. No wonder Slava was so attracted to him. He was a good-looking man with a character of steel.

Every day, while Tsemakh ate Hannah's prepared meals in his room, he saw her carrying the empty plates back from the kitchen, her face shining with joy at having fed Stasya.

The house was pleasant and quiet until Volodya returned from his journey. Enraged, disheveled, unshaven, he went straight to his brother-in-law and screamed, "I ran around looking for a home for the maid. I was in Grayev, in Ostrolenke, in Ostrove. I even went up to Grodno, but I couldn't find a Jew to take the girl. So why don't *you* go and find a place where we can dump this knocked-up cow? Let them cock their eyes at you as if *you* were the bastard's father," Volodya ranted, leaving the room with a heavy, bearish tread that shook the floor.

Tsemakh listened for Stasya's crying. But she was in her little room, paralyzed with fear. He felt the same responsibility toward her that he had felt for his young pupils when he smuggled them over the Polish-Russian frontier. But where could one find a home for her? He had made no friendships in Lomzhe, neither with Torah scholars nor with young middle-class townsmen. The only house he had frequented was his Uncle Ziml's, and he hadn't been there since he quarreled with the Stupels and left the store. He realized that his cousins must have complained to their parents about him, but he saw no other way out and went to the old couple.

Tsertele heard him out, then asked her nephew, "Doesn't this bother your brother-in-law? People here will soon find out that the Stupels' pregnant maid is in my house. Does your wife's family know that you came to me?"

From his aunt's lack of astonishment, Tsemakh assumed that she'd already heard the story from her sons. Irritated, Tsemakh bit at the hair tufts on the back of his hand and admitted, "The Stupels know nothing of my plan."

Reb Ziml, as usual, stood with his head aimed toward the ceiling, as though dreaming of swimming away to the heavens.

"And what do you say, Uncle?" Tsemakh looked up at Reb Ziml. "Can we let an orphan girl and her baby perish because the ones responsible for her misfortune have murderous hearts and want to wash their hands of her?"

"The smartest thing for you to do would be to pick up the wanderer's staff. I too am yearning to lead the life of a wanderer," Reb Ziml answered, as though he hadn't heard a word of his nephew's question.

Tsemakh recalled that his uncle, whom everyone considered an idler, had been the first to perceive that the Stupel family was unsuitable for a Torah scholar and had advised him to marry his poor fiancée from Amdur.

"Uncle, you once advised me to marry and then become a recluse. Sitting in a beth medresh, you said, was the greatest wordly pleasure. Now you're talking about leading a life of wandering. Is wandering from place to place also a worldly pleasure?"

The tall Reb Ziml shrugged his thin shoulders a few times, then sank gently into a chair, as if his body had no bones. His beard looked as though it were woven of gray spider webs, and he spoke with the ethereal voice of a half-mad Kabbalist living in a dark, dank synagogue vestibule. "Certainly it's worldly pleasure to be a recluse. Because, you see, sitting and studying diligently can surely make a scholar arrogant. He asks sharp questions and offers sharp interpretations. Then he discovers that his question was asked long ago by one noted gaon and his answer has already been given by another gaon and so he becomes conceited. Then the scholar starts writing his own commentaries on the Talmud margins or writes his own books until he becomes haughty. But the scholar doesn't want to be haughty, so he reminds himself that greater scholars preceded him and they too were mortal. But since the scholar takes the trouble to recall that there have been greater men than he, he surely won't forget that less great men existed too. Then he begins to wonder whether he's a great saint or a little saint, whether he's good or bad, a wise man or a fool, a man of feeling or a man of intellect. And the more he thinks about himself, the more entangled his thoughts become, and he can't extricate himself. But there is a cure for this—to pick up the wanderer's staff. When a man leads a life of wandering and sees that no one knows him and that no one thinks about him, he himself ceases to think about himself. That's why so many great men have left their homes to lead a life of wandering.

When a Jew puts his hand out for a donation because he's a poor man, he feels terrible. But when a Jew puts his hand out for a donation because he's poor of his own free will, he feels wonderful." Ziml chanted with a sweetly sad Sabbath-night melody. Then he fell silent, his face ecstatic, as though he hadn't realized that he had stopped talking.

From the shaded hanging lamp a beam of light trembled down on Tsertele's veined, toilworn hands. Both elbows resting on the table, the squat, wide-set Tsertele stood listening to her Ziml. She had laughed at him when he wanted to become a recluse, and had ridiculed him again since he got the idea of leading a life of wandering. She agreed with her idler on one thing, however: that Tsemakh ought not quarrel with his brother-in-law or with her sons.

Tsemakh looked at the old, cracked walls and the furniture, and listened to the sleepy ticking of the wall clock. Everything had remained as it was when he came from Amdur and fell ill in the cold room with the faded mirror.

"Uncle, you've spoken about lofty matters, but what you really meant, no doubt, was that I shouldn't quarrel with my wife's family. But no matter what you meant, in my beth medresh we were taught exactly the opposite: A man must examine his own character and his friends' character throughout his life. He must make demands on himself and others. He must never forget what a man's duty is in this world." Tsemakh turned to Tsertele. "So what's the decision, Auntie? Will you take her in?"

"First convince your brothers-in-law, then I'll decide. People might even say that one of my sons made the girl pregnant," Tsertele answered, laughing good-naturedly to conceal her vexation. Reb Ziml remained silent. Both were upset that their nephew had not given a thought to the sons who worked for the Stupels.

Tsemakh saw that Volodya was right. Jews would not take in a girl who had become pregnant before marriage. Tsemakh, however, needed to widen the rift between himself and his relatives, so that he would be able to wrench himself away. So he left the old couple with a determined stride, as though angry enough to set the town on fire.

11

THE MINUTE TSEMAKH LEFT, Tsertele's three sons stormed into the house. The store clerks had noted that the Stupels had been very distressed of late. Consequently they had insisted that Naum's son tell them what was going on upstairs. "What's the matter with you? You look so worried and down in the dumps—as if all your ships had sunk. We've got a peasant girl for you, peaches and cream!"

"A girl friend is even worse than a wife," Lolla said. "You can divorce a wife but not a girl friend. If you swear you won't breathe a word of it, I'll tell you."

"Word of honor," they declared, and Lolla told them everything.

Instead of being pleased that they had hoodwinked that glutton and fool into spilling the secret, Tsertele's sons were left breathless by the news and ran to their mother with the cry, "It's all your fault. It was from this house that the Stupels took Tsemakh as a brother-in-law. Now we know why our bosses can't stand the sight of us lately."

Later the clerks saw Volodya leaving, ostensibly for a business trip, looking like a man going off to have all his teeth pulled. Then he took a second trip and returned looking like a bound wolf carted into town by a peasant. Volodya immediately went upstairs, and his ranting in Tsemakh's apartment could be heard in the store. All day long Volodya remained in his rooms, not even seeing the important grain dealers. Toward evening his wife came down to lock the store and collect the keys. At the same time Tsemakh left the house, striding quickly away through the empty market place. Assuming that the Musarnik's haste was connected with the secret doings upstairs, the clerks gave chase and followed him to their mother's house. They waited impatiently for Tsemakh to leave, whereupon they immediately burst into the house.

"Mama, why did he come here?" they shouted.

Tsertele hid nothing from her sons. For a moment they stood there dumfounded, their heads pressed together like full sacks of flour.

"Did Volodya send him, or is this his own idea?" they asked.

Tsertele sighed. "It's his own idea."

"Then we'll tell the boss. Let him see how loyal we are to him."

"Don't add to the fire of this family quarrel," she pleaded with them, waving her gnarled old hands. "Don't say a word and I won't take in the orphan."

Their father bent his head and yelled, "Don't you bastards butt in."

But the sons laughed at him and called him "Old Man Moses." They had once seen a picture of Moses with his feet on Mount Sinai and his head in the clouds. In like fashion their father stood with his head among the ceiling's spider webs, wrapped in a cloud of fantasies.

"Woman," they yelled to their mother, "we're going to lose our jobs because of your nephew! Is your little herring store going to support us?"

The next morning when Volodya went down to open the store, he saw his clerks waiting outside. As soon as they entered they told him the news. But instead of being touched by their loyalty, Volodya burned with anger that his clerks knew of his humiliation.

"Get out of here! Go break a leg somewhere. All of you, and your cousin too!"

The brothers stood there blinking, as though someone had struck a match before their eyes in the middle of the night. "What did we do to deserve this bitter brew?" they stammered.

When Volodya's rage subsided, he poured his heart out to the clerks as if they were his equals. "Tsemakh won't let us send the girl away to a village, so I went looking for a Jewish home. But Jews don't want to take in a pregnant girl. So what more can I do?"

The three salesmen were ready to jump into the fire for their boss, if only he wouldn't stand there looking so helpless and forlorn.

"We're going to tell our cousin that we may lose our jobs because of him," they said in a passion. "*Tell* him? We'll *show* him a thing or two the minute he comes back from shul."

"Do it!" Volodya said, his eyes swollen.

The clerks lay in wait by the windows for Tsemakh to return from morning prayers. "There he goes!" one of the brothers called when Tsemakh approached, holding his tallis bag under his arm. Volodya looked at his brother-in-law with lips compressed and hatred in his eyes. The clerks realized that their boss was waiting for them to keep their word. Just then Lolla walked past the store with a jaded expression on his face as if he were sick of living. "Should we take him along too?" asked the youngest and most impudent of the three brothers. Volodya nodded, and the group went out, resolutely hitching up their shoulders.

They surrounded Lolla. "Your Uncle Volodya wants to teach Slava's husband a lesson," they said. "That Musarnik isn't letting him send the maid out of Lomzhe. He's just dying to stir up a stew in town. The shame is going to kill your father, and your mother'll go out of her mind. It'll be even worse for you. Everyone will laugh at you behind your back. Look at the mistress he picked out, they'll say. The maid is carrying his brat, they'll say. Your friends will tell you to put on a baby's bib and slurp oatmeal, not drink whisky. And girls will give you the cold shoulder. What girl wants to have anything to do with a shlimazel who can't even protect himself?"

Naum's son didn't understand why the clerks were talking so much. If his Uncle Volodya hadn't warned him to stay away from the maid and not start anything with Slava's husband, he would have squared accounts with both of them long ago. Head thrust forward like an ox, Lolla bounded up the stairs, the clerks following at his heels. The group tore Tsemakh's door open in a frenzy as if it had been boarded up.

"You're not going to boss our family around!" Lolla roared.

Tsemakh glowered at the newcomers wrathfully, and this incensed his cousins even more. The nerve of him, looking daggers at them as he had when he rebuked them in the store. To show their contempt for Tsemakh, they talked to one another as though he weren't there at all.

"He fell into a fortune, but he doesn't even know how to value it. The lousy bench warmer! Fanatic with piles!"

"He's just like a thief. On the sly he went to our mother and asked her to take in the pregnant maid. If he doesn't stop butting in, we're going to pull that black hat down over his eyes."

"He was engaged in Amdur, but they found out in the nick of time that he was nuts, so they chased him away."

With a faint smile Tsemakh looked at these clowns who thought they were humiliating him with their impudence and scorn. Then, hearing screams from the kitchen, he hurried away. There Lolla was reviling Stasya, but she was looking at him lovingly and blissfully. It was the first time Stasya had seen him since she'd been taken from Naum Stupel's apartment.

"You bitch, you whore!" Lolla stamped his feet. "You had your own room in our apartment and you brought in guys from the street. Who knows who you were tumbling around with? Now you claim it's me you got the belly from."

Tsemakh pounced on the youth and pushed him out of the kitchen. Thinking that Tsemakh wanted to hit her beloved, Stasya began to tremble. "Don't hit him!" she cried. Then the three clerks joined the fray and began shoving their cousin with callous contempt.

"Just watch who you're lifting your hand to. Who knows if you haven't snuggled up to her yourself?"

"He's going to hit me?" Lolla stretched his hand over all their heads and gave Tsemakh a resounding slap.

The soft black hat was knocked off Tsemakh's head. He bent down to pick it up, but when his fingers touched the felt, he slowly withdrew his hand, straightened up even more deliberately, and remained standing bareheaded. His face was ashen, his eyes stony. His muteness and his frozen expression cast a pall of fear on the clerks. A sudden thought blazed in their alert minds. This incident could lead to a tragedy, and they had better leave quickly. But before they even reached the doorway Stasya began wailing frantically. The clerks ran back to quiet her, lest passers-by run up to see what was wrong and discover what the Stupels sought to conceal. Lolla charged at Stasya with his fists; then he had second thoughts and pleaded with her not to scream. But Stasya wailed even louder, her disheveled flaxen locks wisping over her face. Her sobs aroused a feeling of self-pity in Tsemakh, as though he had been buried alive and heard the mourners weeping over him.

Hannah, Frieda, and Naum now stood at the doorway. "What happened?" they yelled, breathless from running.

Stasya pointed to Tsemakh's hat on the floor, as if she were pointing at a drowned person's clothes on the river bank. "Lolla hit the rabbi, he hit the rabbi!"

Hannah burst into tears; Frieda wrung her hands.

Fingers bared like claws, Naum rushed at his son, his voice rattling: "Why didn't you just melt away in your mother's belly?"

"What did I do?" Lolla bleated.

Naum moved his head from side to side as though he were being asphyxiated in a fire: "Oh, woe! Someone help! The whole town's going to come running!"

Hannah hurled herself at Stasya, kissing and stroking her until she began to sob softly, choking on her tears. Hannah chased the men out of the kitchen and gave Tsemakh his hat. Her look was so beseeching that he put it on and went into his room.

He sat there for a long time, lost in thought, stroking his tallis bag, which had remained on the table when the foursome charged in. He heard his heart within him weeping: "Woe is me that I have seen you in such a state." Tears made his eyelashes stick together. How had he come to this, he wondered. How had he reached the point where it took a slap in the face to make him realize that he must no longer stay with such a vulgar family?

12

THAT AFTERNOON SLAVA RETURNED on the bus from Bialystok. As she came into the house, she bumped into Naum. The unexpected encounter flustered him, and he passed by quickly with lowered head. A thought flashed through her: Her brother didn't want to break the bad news that someone in the house had died. She dragged herself up the stairs as if pushing her way through a deep, icy current. She stopped in the foyer, afraid to go farther. She sensed an air of deep gloom in the apartment, then heard whispering in the kitchen. Hannah was sitting there, consoling Stasya.

Hearing someone, Hannah opened the door to look. Stasya, trembling, hid her face in her hands and cried, "It's my fault. On account of me Lolla hit the rabbi. Lolla slapped your husband today."

Slava sighed with relief. She had expected something worse. Still holding the suitcase, she went to Tsemakh's room, opened the door, and met his gentle, embarrassed glance at being seen so forlorn. Slava immediately closed the door and returned to the kitchen.

"Tell me everything," she ordered the maid. Stasya spoke, her face as lifeless and her eyes as dull as if she had already given birth to the baby and buried it as well. Slava realized that the clerks wouldn't have attacked her husband without Volodya's permission.

"My brothers will pay dearly for this," she snarled at Hannah and walked swiftly away.

The next morning Slava sat in her bedroom without preparing any meals for Tsemakh, lest he assume that she wanted him to forget what had happened. She assiduously polished her nails, arranged her hair at the mirror, and fingered a little blemish on her face to see if it was a pimple. She pulled out a chest drawer and turned the linens over, looked for a packet of old letters, which she scanned, and then leafed through a picture album. Her suitcase still stood unopened in the middle of the room. She had a sudden urge to call a handyman up from the street to rearrange the beds, the night table, and the chest of drawers. A moment later she forgot about this and listened to the ticking of her wristwatch. Slava wanted to delay seeing Volodya—she wanted him to know that she had had enough time to think through what she would say to him.

Hannah reported Slava's words to Volodya and added, "For slapping a rabbi the Stupels won't survive either in this world or the next." Volodya saw his wife, a timid village woman who had never opposed him, looking at him with hatred. But he couldn't understand what all the fuss was about. What had they done to that plaster saint? Had Tsemakh's head been lopped off? And who was he, anyway, the Kaiser?

Slava saw her brother sitting as usual in his easy chair, elbows on the arm rests and facing the door as though impatient for her arrival. Hannah sat at the table with a kerchief around her shoulders, gloomily silent.

Slava stood in the middle of the room and didn't even bid them good evening. "Did you tell Lolla and your clerks to beat my husband? They wouldn't have dared to on their own."

"Me? I didn't say a word to Lolla. I didn't even see that wild boar. And is it my fault if your husband's cousins hate him?" Volodya put on an innocent face and tried to take the offensive. "Didn't you tell me you're going to divorce him? So what do you care if he got a little pat on his face?"

"Perhaps Tsemakh will divorce me, but I won't divorce him. Never!" Slava addressed her sister-in-law, and Volodya noticed that the news made his wife's face beam with joy.

"Well, if you like him that much, keep him. I won't live under the same roof with him," Volodya yelled.

"Not only won't my husband and I live under the same roof with you, but I don't want to be a partner in your store, either." Slava's eyes darkened with hate. "Father's will left me half the business, equal to your and Naum's shares. So pay me the money due me. I'm going to sell my apartment here, and I don't want to see your face any more."

Volodya felt he was going to get apoplexy. Nevertheless, he laughed and replied, "You won't have your way on this. First of all, I've been running the business all this time and you never lifted a finger for it. What do you know about business and bookkeeping? You know fashions, not accounting—and you're not a connoisseur of people. Second, I supported you till you got married, then after the wedding I supported you and your husband. And third, you're talking nonsense. Even people who aren't related but who've been partners for years can't divide up a business easily; how much the more so a family! What are you going to do, call me to a rabbinic judgment? Take me to court?"

"To both places," Slava answered as if her response had already been prepared. "You and Naum always took twice as much, three times as much as you gave me. But I didn't care. I knew you had to support a family. Now I want my share, even though I know I'll ruin the business. I want to ruin both of you; then you'll understand what you've done."

The flour merchant turned in his chair, addressing his broad fingers covered with thick tufts of hair. "And even if you succeed in your plan, I'll still find a way out, and I'll be better and quicker at it than you. But you know what burns me up? I've been a brother, a father, and a friend to you—and now you're talking to me as if I were a murderer who deserves to be hanged. And over whom? Over a man you didn't even know a year ago and who brings everyone aggravation. And what do *you* say?" he shouted at his wife. "I suppose you don't want to know me either, huh?"

Hannah remained silent, her face flaming. Volodya was absolutely right. He and his sister had been much too close. All they did was sit together, joking and laughing. It had been high time for Slava to marry and fool around with her own husband. So it wasn't right for her to talk to her brother as if he were an enemy and to say she wanted to ruin him.

But Slava stood still in the middle of the room like a debtor trying to pick a fight, and spoke to her sister-in-law in a dry, rasping voice. "During the week I was away, my anger at Tsemakh dissipated like smoke, and I came to realize how much finer and better he is than others. Now I come home and find out that my brother has incited some people to assault my husband and thus precipitate our divorce. . . . If I were ready to divorce my husband, I'd tell him the truth—that he's too great a man for me and that I don't even come up to his bootstraps. He lives for others, and I need a man who will live only for me. He was and has remained a scholar, and I need a husband who's a merchant. Everyone in my family is a merchant. That's what I'd tell him if I were ready for a divorce. Now I don't have to tell him a thing. Now he himself sees how common and vulgar the Stupel family is. Even by the way my brothers are bursting blood vessels to keep the story from the townspeople, I can see how common and vulgar they are. Truly noble people aren't that anxious to bury and conceal their faults. But vulgar louts who want to put on airs are always nervous for fear people will unmask them."

As Slava spoke, Hannah's face changed color. She saw that Slava wanted to wound them, to cut them to the quick by constantly repeating that the Stupel family was common and vulgar. Volodya, for his part, just managed to keep himself from pouncing on his sister or tearing the clock off the wall and smashing it to the floor.

Slava spoke exactly like her husband, he thought, but that witch had more venom in her than Tsemakh. Volodya waited for her to finish, but he hadn't the faintest idea what he would do then.

Just as Slava concluded, Tsemakh burst into the room. "Where's Stasya? Isn't she here? Hasn't she been here?" Tsemakh looked around. "She's not at Naum's, either. She's run away!"

"Where would she run to? She hasn't run anywhere. She's gone out for a while and will come back soon," Hannah consoled him, hardly able to restrain her tears.

Tsemakh shook his head sadly. "Stasya told me recently that she'll go wherever her feet take her. She didn't want us to fight over her. But yesterday's commotion scared her, and today she was even more frightened because Slava returned. So she took her little bundle and fled."

Silence reigned in the big apartment. Slava felt that all of Volodya's clocks were thumping at her temples. She looked at Tsemakh and thought: Now he'll run away too.

Volodya didn't sleep that night; he was oppressed by the thought that perhaps the girl had cast herself into the Nareva River. He wouldn't be able to walk through any street in Lomzhe. People would stay clear of his store as if it smelled. The next morning the puffy-faced Volodya told his salesmen that the maid had run off, and then began reviling them in no uncertain terms.

"Everyone knows you're informers and sycophants and everything else that's rotten. If I go under, you'll be the first to croak from hunger. So you better start sniffing like bloodhounds and find the girl. And you better take Lolla with you. When that wild boar was tumbling with her, she probably told him who her friends are. So let him rack his brains and help find her."

Lolla and the three clerks looked high and low for Stasya but found no trace of her. Hannah, however, tried to console her husband. "Stasya won't commit suicide. She wants to have her baby. Remember, she refused to have an abortion. Tsemakh too said that the orphan won't harm herself—she takes his word that the baby won't be a bastard. Tsemakh looks like a corpse and is strangely quiet," Hannah added anxiously.

"Because he's preparing to stir up the town against us, as he's been threatening all along. But since he himself has said that the girl hasn't killed herself, I don't care what he'll say or what he'll do." Volodya pushed his hand into his pocket as though he'd hidden a pair of brass knuckles there. "I hate him more than ever now. On account of him Slava has become my bitter enemy. And I'm sick of her, too. I wish he *would* make a scandal; then I'd be rid of both of them. What are you staring at, you pious cow? I'm sick of the lot of you. You disgust me like rotten fruit."

Tsemakh, however, no longer sought any controversy with his brothers-in-law. Two days after Stasya's disappearance he returned from morning prayers and told Slava, "I'm going to look for a small town where I can establish a little yeshiva. Soon the holy days will be upon us. During the Days of Awe Jews are more religious. Now is the best time to persuade townspeople to support Torah scholars. When I went to Amdur the local Jews didn't want a yeshiva. But every obstacle then seemed ten times greater than it really was because I wanted to leave the beth medresh. Now I have to set aright what I have ruined and start a yeshiva and become its principal. But being a rosh yeshiva in a small town means leading a life of deprivation, and I can't ask you to suffer along with me, especially since you didn't know when I married you that I'd return to my old ways. I didn't know it either. So that's why I'm prepared to give you a divorce."

"I don't want a divorce. Your wanting to leave isn't news to me, but I don't want a divorce." Slava's cheeks shone with a lackluster porcelain whiteness.

"Will you join me? Are you ready to put on a marriage wig and wait for the townspeople to send you a bag of potatoes, challa for the Sabbath, and wood for the winter?" Tsemakh accented the discomforts like a rabbi speaking to a Christian who wants to convert.

"We'll see." Slava spoke carefully, eyes downcast.

"And besides," Tsemakh continued, "I have to leave so that you can make peace with your family. Do you see? Even the suffering Stasya no longer wanted to be the cause of a quarrel, so she ran away. I certainly won't let you fight with your brothers and sisters-in-law because of me."

"There will be no peace between Volodya and me." Slava's face looked bony and her eyes seemed to spray blue sparks. "You yourself said that you'd tell everyone if they sent the maid to a village. But now something worse has happened. A brute has hit you, and your orphan may have jumped into the river. Why are you keeping quiet now?"

Tsemakh threw his head back and spread his hands. "Just because a young man slapped me, should I slap him back? Had the orphan been sent away, I would have raised a fuss in town to save her. But since she ran away and can't be found, should I stir up Lomzhe just for the sake of revenge? That's not the Torah's way. And what's more, I don't believe Stasya jumped into the river. She won't do that for her baby's sake. But picturing her straggling along the roads, half-naked and barefoot, with no place to get warm or to eat or sleep, is bad enough. She's roving about, afraid that the gentiles will try to convert her and that the Jews will call her promiscuous. Nevertheless, she's prepared to endure all this as long as she can have her baby and have it be a Jewish child."

Tsemakh's big black eyes became even bigger and darker, like a blind man's. He remained silent for a while, then went on in a pleading voice, "Even though the Stupel family had no compassion for the orphan, I still don't think they're any worse than other middle-class businessmen. In their world it's no sin to chase away a pregnant maid, and if I hadn't spent years in a yeshiva learning Torah and Musar, perhaps I wouldn't have considered it a great sin either. That's why I can't stay with these people any longer, lest with the passing of time I begin to think and feel like them and take on their worldly outlook. On the other hand, if I stay here but can't think and feel like them, I'll have to fight with them. So the only way out for me is to return to the beth medresh. But, Slava, you must reconcile with your family."

In the corners of Slava's mouth was etched the bitter smile of an anguished woman who realizes what bliss she could have had with her husband if only she'd had better luck. Slava would have preferred to see Tsemakh hard and incensed, the way he had been when he drove her into a convulsive rage, rather than see him with this pale, exhausted face and drooping shoulders.

"All right, I'll listen to you and make up with my family. And if this is what you must do, then go in peace. I'm not angry with you for offering me a divorce. I know you did it to have a clear conscience. But what irritates me is that you didn't even ask me why I went to Bialystok." Slava cocked her head fetchingly and her tear-filled eyes flashed a smile. She expected Tsemakh to flare up now, as he had when they'd quarreled and each of his gestures had reflected strength and stubbornness.

But he paid no attention to her coquetry. "Why should I ask you why you went to Bialystok?" Tsemakh rose, groaning like an old wanderer who has taken a short rest and must continue on his way. "You were angry with me and so you went away. Perhaps you had to be there. It makes no difference."

Slava looked at Tsemakh's beard, glistening with drops of perspiration, and almost stamped her foot in anger. She didn't want to see him as an old, broken man. Let him go, then. Let him become a yeshiva principal. She wouldn't become a rebbetsin with a marriage wig. But he would change in time. No matter where he lived and what he did, he'd realize that people there were no better than in Lomzhe and he'd come back home.

PART III

1

CHAIKL, THE SON OF REB SHLOMO-MOTTE the Hebrew
teacher, was a short, heavyset lad who grew wide rather than tall,
like a strong, sturdy shrub. But he had yearning eyes, and a dream
constantly hovered over his full, pale face like a warm mist. Until
he was fifteen he studied listlessly in Vilna's Rameiles Yeshiva.
Among the delicate, refined scholars he stood out as a burly youth,
but on Butchers Street, where he had grown up, the butchers and
porters considered him a bench warmer. He was his mother's only
son and a son of old age to his father—Reb Shlomo-Motte's
children from his first wife lived in America. In his old age Reb
Shlomo-Motte had stopped teaching and from time to time spent
weeks on end at the Jewish Hospital for treatment of his ailing
kidneys. In Reb Shaulke's beth medresh, where the old teacher
prayed, the pious worshipers couldn't forgive him for being a
maskil, one of the enlighteners of the previous generation. Yet for
today's pork gobblers, they said, laughing derisively, he was
already too religious, just like the heretical biblical commentary of
that hunchback Moses Mendelssohn. Reb Shlomo-Motte didn't
respond but merely indulged them with a contemptuous smile
beneath his broad white mustache. In his heart the old master of
Hebrew grammar remained a maskil, and he wanted his son to
become an artisan who could earn money and help his mother. The

old man was distressed that his wife had to support him and Chaikl with her little fruit shop. But Vella the fruit peddler was prepared to toil even harder, so long as her son would put on tefillin and continue his Torah studies.

Chaikl did put on tefillin, but he gradually stopped attending the Rameiles Yeshiva. Still, so as not to be an ignoramus and to please his mother, he studied alone in the evenings in Reb Shaulke's beth medresh. An old artisan, Senderl the kettlemaker, wanted to take him into his workshop and make a coppersmith out of him. But Reb Senderl's foe, the tobacco merchant Vova Barbitoler, who worshiped in the same beth medresh, wouldn't let Chaikl become an artisan.

The tobacco merchant, a man in his sixties, had bent, crooked legs that strained under the burden of his heavy body. He loved the mitzva of the tsitsis, the garment with four ritual fringes—and the bottle as well. He provided ritual fringes for the Talmud Torah orphans as well as for nonorphans. Vova Barbitoler would stop a little prankster in the street and look under the belt of his trousers. Seeing that the rascal wasn't wearing ritual fringes, he would take him by the hand and tell him, "Come with me to your parents." The tobacco merchant would spend a long time in the impoverished house, attempting to prove to the parents that a child who didn't wear ritual fringes would grow up to be a wayward youth. Then he would take one from his pocket and put it on the little boy, kiss his head, and exact a promise that henceforth he'd wear it and recite the blessing over it. Then the boy's parents would bless the fine man who performed mitzvas for poor Jewish children—but they were astounded when they smelled liquor on his breath.

In town it was said that his troubles drove Vova Barbitoler to drink. His first wife had died when he was still in his thirties, leaving him with a son and a daughter. He remained a widower for ten years. When the children had grown up, he finally married a divorcée who was young and pretty but who was also a crude, disreputable woman whose family had connections with the underworld. Good friends warned Vova that she wasn't a suitable match for him, but he was then in the prime of his masculinity and was attracted to the vivacious woman with the coarse, robust appearance.

Even after the wedding, Vova's second wife behaved as if she were a free bird. Confrada spent more time with her shady brothers than at home. She was always attending relatives' weddings and managed to go to these family celebrations without her husband. Even after she had a child she would spend all day and half the night away from home. At first the tobacco merchant tried kindness, then, seeing that this didn't work, he threatened Confrada with his fists. She raised a fuss. Judging by her pleased expression when she screamed, Vova gathered that Confrada had been waiting for him to lift his hand so she could make a scene. To scare him, she sent her brothers to him. They threatened to beat him black and blue, but Vova Barbitoler wasn't fazed by threats or scenes. Confrada began demanding a divorce, and his good friends advised him to consent, but her practiced female antics and their child bound Vova to her as if with tarred rope, and he changed his mind about a divorce.

Confrada stopped talking about separating and asked her husband to let her spend a few months with her oldest brother in Argentina. Just as she hadn't stayed at home before, so she didn't leave the apartment now, and drove Vova crazy with her blubbering. Finally he decided he'd be better off if she had her fling elsewhere and then returned after she'd simmered down. He was certain that a mother would not desert her child. Confrada went off to Argentina, and the tobacco merchant didn't hear from her for a year.

One day he received a letter stating that she wanted a divorce. "When, with God's help, I remarry," she wrote, "then I'll bring my son over too." Vova Barbitoler swore that the sky would fall before he sent her a divorce, and he kept his oath. His wife remarried in Argentina and bore children—without a divorce. But as the years passed, the thought of living with a man against Jewish law frightened her, and her brothers in Vilna considered it beneath their dignity. Confrada's letters from abroad, supported by these brothers, demanded that the Vilna Rabbinic Court intervene. The Rabbinic Court sent out messengers several times to summon the tobacco merchant, but Vova refused even to present his side before the judges. The Vilna rabbis and Vova's fellow worshipers of Reb Shaulke's beth medresh grumbled that because of him a married woman was living in sin with another man. So, to spite them all, Vova took a third wife, this time a poor, timid woman. Since he knew that no local rabbi would consecrate his marriage, he set up the canopy in a remote village and brought his third wife to Vilna to look after the children of his first and second wives.

Berating Vova Barbitoler louder than anyone else in Reb Shaulke's beth medresh was Reb Senderl the kettlemaker: "That troublemaker shouldn't be included in a minyan. As if it isn't enough that on account of him a Jewish woman has dropped a barrelful of bastards, he himself has married without the permission of a hundred rabbis."

When Vova heard the kettlemaker ranting and raving while he himself was sober, he merely pressed his lips together in silence. But when Vova was drunk, he stormed into the beth medresh stamping his feet and shouting, "You worm! Why should you have the same wife for fifty years and have joy in all your children? Why don't you and your whole family drop dead all together?"

The short, spry seventy-year-old kettlemaker charged at him with clenched fists: "I'll take you with me!"

The congregation barely managed to separate them.

Since Reb Senderl had the habit of speaking his mind, he told his fellow worshipers, "I wanted to take that young lout Chaikl into my workshop and make an artisan out of him, but his mother, Vella the fruit peddler, wants him to become a scholar. He'll be a scholar when I'm the Chief Rabbi of Vilna." Reb Senderl laughed, and the others agreed, nodding their gray beards.

The tobacco merchant listened from a distance and didn't say a word. An hour later he stood at the fruit peddler's shop and offered to provide a teacher for her son. "And I'll clothe him too, and even give him pocket money."

Vella didn't want to receive charity; moreover, she was apprehensive about the tobacco merchant and his bad reputation, even though he performed mitzvas.

Vella thanked him graciously and replied, "I'll talk it over with my husband."

Reb Shlomo-Motte was in the hospital again with boils on his legs, caused by his kidney infection. On one of their daily visits Vella reported Vova's offer to her husband.

Reb Shlomo-Motte shook his head of white hair—whiter than the hospital pillow—and said, "If rabbis don't mind having their children supported by the yeshiva, then it shouldn't be beneath the dignity of a millionairess like you."

The fruit peddler could have been the old teacher's daughter and treated him with great respect. Vella was certain that she was responsible for her husband's poor luck, because since their marriage things had begun to go downhill for him. Consequently she looked up to him even more in his broken old age than when he had been the breadwinner.

"If you say so, I'll listen to you, but the people in Reb Shaulke's beth medresh don't think highly of the tobacco merchant."

"They don't think highly of your husband either." Reb Shlomo-Motte turned his head. When his wife gazed at him with her trusting green eyes, without the least complaint at her hard life, he felt even more guilty that she was the provider.

Vova Barbitoler ordered a suit for Chaikl and hired a teacher for him. Reb Menakhem-Mendl Segal was a thin young man with a little blond beard and prayerful lips. In his boyhood Reb Menakhem-Mendl had studied in Navaredok. After his marriage in Vilna he had opened a little shoemakers' accessories shop, but he suffered much anguish at having to be a shopkeeper. Whenever he had a spare moment he ran from the anxieties of his livelihood to the beth medresh, where he hid behind the great volumes of the Talmud. Although he wasn't pleased at having dealings with Vova, he agreed to study with Chaikl. Reb Menakhem-Mendl needed money for milk for his little boy, and as eager as he was to earn money, he also wanted to keep a youngster in Torah studies.

They studied daily after the Evening Service. Standing behind the pulpit, Vova Barbitoler would look on as the teacher and his pupil swayed over the Talmud—and from a distance he would sway with them. He didn't come too close for fear of disturbing them. The congregants whispered, "It's messianic times. Vova's not drinking and Chaikl is studying diligently."

But the tobacco merchant couldn't stay away from the bottle for long. One late summer morning, as Chaikl sat alone in the beth medresh with his Talmud, watching the sunbeams quiver in the folds of the curtain of the Holy Ark, Vova Barbitoler entered. He stood in front of "his" scholar with such a wild look on his drunken face that Chaikl shivered with fright. Outside, dealers shouted and freight wagons clattered over the cobblestones, but Vova Barbito-ler's brows and tangled beard wafted the desolation of an over-grown and forgotten graveyard. With a sudden leap toward Chaikl's bench, he embraced the boy and began to weep.

"You're my only consolation in life—you, and not my first wife's kids and not Confrada's little bastard. Confrada bewitched me. I didn't love my first wife. She bore me two kids and I didn't love her. I don't like my present wife either, though Mindl is a decent woman. Confrada was the only one I loved. She was a healthy piece, a hot one," Vova Barbitoler babbled, spraying spittle on himself, huddling against Chaikl, embracing and kissing him. "Your mother's a saint; your father's a smart, educated man. It's a blessing from God to have a son who's a scholar and not an apprentice to a kettlemaker. Senderl wouldn't even have taught you the trade. You would've been only a messenger boy in his shop. Still, you shouldn't always sit over the Talmud. A young man ought to go out for walks. And when you're ready to get married, marry a girl you love."

His breath smelled of whisky, herring, chopped liver, and onions. He gave a vulgar laugh and began to describe a trick he'd pulled on Confrada. "That slut ran around day and night kicking up her heels and not giving a damn about anyone. Not me, not my first wife's kids, and not even her own bloody bastard, Hertzke. So one night I put a panful of water in her bed and pulled the cover over it. She came home after midnight as usual and paraded before the mirror, teasing me: 'My, did I dance with cavaliers tonight!' Then, still wearing that fancy evening dress of hers, she plopped herself into bed, right into the pan of water. Ha! You should have heard her bawling and sniveling." Vova Barbitoler giggled until drops of perspiration appeared on his forehead. Seeing that Chaikl was silent, he seized him by the shoulders and shook him. "Why aren't you laughing? Been struck dumb?" Then, realizing that it was improper to tell a young ben Torah such stories, Vova fell silent and his hands dropped as if paralyzed. He bit his lips, stood up slowly, and waddled out of the beth medresh.

Chaikl was ashamed to recall what Vova Barbitoler had told him, as though by remembering he would be a guilty partner in Vova's sinful thoughts. Still, he didn't stop thinking about the woman in Argentina for whom Vova had been pining fifteen years.

A couple of days later, just before evening prayers, the tobacco merchant again came to the beth medresh drunk. The congregants were poring over sacred texts, and Chaikl was sitting in his corner waiting for Reb Menakhem-Mendl. Vova's face and his swaying at the entrance showed the state he was in, and the congregants buried their heads deeper in their books, silent and motionless, so as not to give Vova an excuse to make a scene. Even Reb Senderl the kettlemaker hunched into his *Code of Law,* hoping to prevent sacrilege. A few of the worshipers began singing aloud, as if to soothe and calm the drunken man with their Torah melody. Vova Barbitoler sensed his strength: the crowd wanted to avoid a fight with him. He cocked his head in all directions, looking for someone to pick on—and Chaikl's heart sank. The tobacco merchant was advancing toward him.

"Well, isn't the suit I made you too tight?"

"Not tight," Chaikl muttered.

"Get up and walk around and let me see if the jacket isn't too short, and if the sleeves aren't too tight under the armpits."

Blood surged to Chaikl's face. He sensed that everyone in the beth medresh was laughing in his beard at the way Vova was bossing him around like a servant.

"I said get up and walk around," Vova roared, but seeing tears in Chaikl's eyes, he burst into laughter. "Silly fool, what are you crying for? If you don't want to, you don't have to. I wanted to see how well the suit fits you, and you think I want everyone to know I made you a suit. I don't give a damn what Senderl the kettlemaker and his henchmen think about me." Head held high, Vova made his way to the door. As he approached the exit, his head sank lower and his legs pumped higher, as if he were plodding through a swamp and knew that a crevasse came next.

The congregants remained silent for a while, afraid the tobacco merchant might return, as he had on other occasions. Then they decided that if he should come back, the best way to deal with him was not to answer.

Reb Senderl closed his book with a kiss and said, "When that drunkard was insulting me, I was thinking of a saying of our holy sages: Jews are the humiliated but not the humiliators. Whoever remains silent will shine like the sun at sunrise."

That they had observed a precept of the holy sages while getting rid of the drunkard brought the old men into a mood of pious merriment, as if they were at a wedding banquet. But Chaikl was still depressed, vexed with the congregants who had not considered *his* humiliation a humiliation.

Later Reb Menakhem-Mendl came and, having heard of the incident, chastised the boy as well. "And what if you had paced about in the beth medresh to show the tobacco merchant how the suit fits you? If you had studied Musar it wouldn't have bothered you."

Although in Navaredok Reb Menakhem-Mendl hadn't been such a keen Musarnik, he felt that besides studying Talmud with his pupil he should also introduce some moral admonition. Accordingly he began whispering with his pious lips, "Generally, when one puts on a new suit, one has to be very careful about the Torah's stricture against mixing linen and wool. But since Vova provides Jewish children with ritual fringes, he wouldn't order a suit with that forbidden weave. But you must fear even more the forbidden weave of the cloak of pride. In *The Path of the Upright* Luzzatto says that beautiful clothes lead man to pride, envy, and even robbery. People are afraid of vermin that devour their clothes. But one must fear the pride and envy that devour the soul."

Reb Menakhem-Mendl saw that his student had fallen into a gloomy silence, so he too fell silent and began to muse: Having the tobacco merchant as a patron is no good. But if I have to stand in a little store and sell shoe thread, wooden pegs, and glue, then things are no good for me either.

2

HERTZKE, VOVA BARBITOLER'S SON, was a scrawny, bony lad. He had a pale, freckled face, glazed eyes, and childish notions. It was difficult to tell whether he was really foolish or just pretending. "He's clever enough at pulling stunts," his father said of him. While the rage against his runaway wife seethed in Vova, he also saw in Hertzke her wicked eyes and licentious laughter, and then he would pinch his son, beat him until his flesh was raw, and grind his teeth. "You bloody bastard, you have your mother's saucy face and whorish blood!"

Mindl, Vova's third wife, and the children of his first wife couldn't bear to see the cruel beatings he gave the boy. Yet Hertzke withstood his father's murderous fury in a strange way. He would let fly sham screams while looking on gaily, as if the blows didn't hurt at all and his only purpose were to provoke his father even more. In such moments Vova thought he would go mad. His lips frothed as he remembered that Confrada had screamed in precisely the same fashion. Then from such wild rage he would switch to a morbid tenderness, pressing his son to his heart and kissing him with hot, trembling lips. But Hertzke remained unmoved; he would smile slyly, as if pleased at knowing that his father was burning with longing for his mother.

Chaikl's diligence in his studies with Reb Menakhem-Mendl kindled Vova Barbitoler's fury against his own son, who besides being a spiteful brat was also lazy and dull at school. As the Days of Awe approached, Vova became more melancholy. The sound of the Elul shofar every morning after services split his brain and plucked pieces from his heart. In the blasts of the ram's horn he seemed to hear that up in heaven he was being excommunicated for not sending Confrada a divorce. He saw worshipers who had been

angry with each other throughout the year reconciling in honor of
the Days of Awe, but no one sought reconciliation with him. So he
choked on his wrath, as if it were smoke blown back through the
chimney into a heated apartment.

The tobacco merchant entered the tavern on the corner of
Hospital and Butchers streets, downed a few tumblers of whisky at
the bar, and grumbled to the innkeeper: "No matter how much I
beat Confrada's bastard, he still forgets to put on his ritual fringes
every day."

Dodya the innkeeper had a red face, and his stiff gray hair was as
short and bristly as a brush. Though in his seventies, he still rolled
barrels of beer and helped the butchers carry sides of beef into their
ice cellars. All day long he stood with his sleeves rolled up, slapping
corks out of whisky bottles, pouring beer into mugs, and serving
snacks.

Dodya loved to provoke his customers, the young hoodlums who
were always at daggers drawn with one another. But since the
tobacco merchant was an old pal and a well-to-do householder, the
innkeeper said, "Take the advice of a good friend. Send Confrada a
divorce and let her go to blazes. Why should your son obey you and
put on ritual fringes when he knows that rabbis and congregants
don't respect his father because he doesn't give his mother a
divorce?"

"I'm *not* going to send Confrada a divorce and that bastard *will*
put on ritual fringes for me or else he'll be carried out of my house
head first," Vova roared and left the tavern.

He wandered about in the little streets for a long time and finally
stopped in front of Vella's fruit store. Vella rose from her low chair;
she always did so when a bearded Jew came in, and she was glad to
stand up for the man who had hired a tutor for her son.

"Well, your son's studying, isn't he? You see, with Reb
Menakhem-Mendl as his teacher he sits and learns."

"May you live to be a hundred and twenty!" Vella said happily.
"I just don't know how to thank you! First God and then you! But I
ask myself, perhaps it's hard for you to pay Chaikl's tuition?"

"It's not hard for me," Vova muttered and strode away clumsily,
like a huge, forlorn creature that had stopped for a while to sniff out
a strange lair.

The son of Reb Shlomo-Motte the Hebrew teacher was studying

Talmud, Vova mused, but his own fifteen-year-old son was in a class with ten-year-olds and couldn't even keep up with them. Vova plucked at his beard and felt his vexation gnawing at him. His older children were against him too. They still couldn't forgive him for marrying Confrada or for holding up her divorce. His son and daughter had moved out of his house because he drank and raged at Hertzke. Let them live by themselves and hate him and keep away from him. But Hertzke was still under his wing, and he had to thrash Confrada's character out of him. Hertzke *must* wear his ritual fringes. Vova Barbitoler turned into the entrance of the Yavneh Cheder, where his son studied.

Vova had once stormed into the Talmud Torah dead drunk and ordered the orphans to display the ritual fringes he had given them. The youngsters pulled the fringes out from under their trousers, and the tobacco merchant wept with joy, as though suddenly redeemed from the evil spirit that had been tormenting him.

His tears and the whisky-induced sweat made his face and beard damp as Vova delivered a sermon to the Talmud Torah lads: "The ritual fringes are a shield against all sins. There's a story in the Talmud about a free-living Jew who clung to the mitzva of ritual fringes. This man got word of a lewd woman across the sea and sailed to meet her. When he arrived, the woman took him to a golden bed and sat down naked beside him. Just then the four fringes began slapping his face, like four witnesses. . . ."

Reports later had it that the teacher was forced to call for help from his colleagues, who finally managed to entice Vova out, pleading with him not to tell such stories to young Talmud Torah pupils.

Furious and tottering, like a bear looking for the tree where his foe was hidden, Vova Barbitoler looked for Hertzke's classroom in the Yavneh Cheder. Both the students and the teacher—a tidy little man with a flat yarmulke on his round bald pate—were frightened by the way he burst in, and by his expression and the way he was dressed. Only Hertzke, at the edge of the rear bench, bared his teeth as if wanting all the other youngsters to laugh with him at his father. Vova stared at Hertzke, his eyes smoking with the turbid light of a cloudy day. He headed straight for the last bench, grabbed his son by the collar, and began shaking him.

"Are you laughing at me? Show me your ritual fringes."

Hertzke dropped his hands and threw back his head so that his father could choke him. "I forgot to put them on today."

Vova smacked Hertzke's face with his right hand; the lad fell and rolled to the wall. "Blood!" cried a boy, and the teacher clapped his hand to his head as if his eardrum had burst. But Hertzke calmly wiped the blood from his bleeding nose, his eyes flashing with the joy of revenge.

"He purposely didn't put on his ritual fringes to make me blow up," the tobacco merchant roared to the teacher and left the room.

All afternoon Vova wandered about in the narrow streets, stumbling with weariness. His leaden body urged him homeward, but his heart drew him to the beth medresh, where Jews sat and studied, arming themselves with Torah and mitzvas for the approaching Days of Awe. Vova went to Reb Shaulke's beth medresh; he wanted to slip into a corner, sit there unobtrusively, and warm himself with the sound of Torah learning. But he immediately sensed the malice of the entire congregation. All the worshipers averted their eyes. Chaikl, studying with Reb Menakhem-Mendl, turned away too and made a face. The tobacco merchant felt the top of his head surging like a lid on a pot of boiling water. He went directly to the eastern wall and, with both hands flailing, fell upon Chaikl's lectern.

"I'm the only one who paid any attention to you and hired a tutor for you—so you're against me too? Show me your ritual fringes; I want to see if you're wearing them."

Chaikl shivered and tapped his chest under his jacket. Just because he hadn't forgotten to put on his ritual fringes, he decided then and there not to display them. A silence came over the beth medresh. The congregants raised their heads, arched their brows, and stared through their metal-rimmed spectacles.

Although Reb Menakhem-Mendl was quite frightened, he nevertheless plucked up his courage and whispered to Vova, "One must not shame a man publicly, and one certainly shouldn't suspect a ben Torah of not wearing his ritual fringes."

But Vova Barbitoler paid no attention to him. He stared dully at his hands, stained with dried blood, and rasped hoarsely, "You see this, you heathen? This is the way I just beat up my own son Hertzke for not putting on his ritual fringes. So I certainly won't spare you!"

Chaikl leaped up without stopping to think, and raised the heavy oaken prayer stand that held his Talmud, ready to hurl the stand at the tobacco merchant. Astounded and fearing the blow, Vova stumbled back to the first row of benches opposite the eastern wall and sat down.

"You drunkard! You think I'm your Hertzke?" Chaikl muttered and slowly lowered the lectern.

Vova remained sitting with outspread hands and open mouth. Reb Menakhem-Mendl hunched into himself, trembling. The worshipers exchanged glances and shrugged in amazement. They would have been pleased if the drunkard had been thrown out by a pair of strong Jews, but for a young Torah scholar to lift up a prayer stand against an older man was unheard of.

"Well, what do you expect?" Reb Senderl the kettlemaker chortled loudly. "When I wanted to take this young punk into my workshop and make a decent person out of him, people gossiped that I wanted to tear a youngster away from Torah studies because I needed an apprentice. Now everyone can see he's a thug, and everyone should apologize to me on Erev Yom Kippur for falsely suspecting me."

Chaikl, near tears, fled the beth medresh.

Rosh Hashana was a marred holiday for Vella the fruit peddler. Praying in the women's section of Reb Shaulke's beth medresh, she wept more than usual, asking God to forgive her son for having lifted a hand against an old Jew. At home she complained incessantly to Chaikl, "Why are you so touchy? Can't one even ask you to show your ritual fringes?" Fearing that her Shlomo-Motte at the hospital might hear of the incident from others, Vella told him what had happened. On the morning of Erev Yom Kippur the teacher returned home, walking erect. The swellings on his legs had subsided, his blood pressure was down, and the color had returned to his cheeks. He spoke lovingly to his wife, with a gentle light in his eyes. He didn't speak to Chaikl at all, but his eyes blazed at him like burning lamps.

As a child Chaikl had loved to stroke his father's white beard and high forehead and his satin-soft hands and long fingers. Overjoyed at his father's return home, Chaikl now wanted to gaze into his clever brown eyes, guess what he was thinking, and attend to him.

But since his father was angry with him, Chaikl pretended not to see his mother gesturing to him to be submissive and show respect lest, God forbid, there should be an argument between father and son in the awe-filled hours before the Kol Nidrei. Vella remained silent and hurriedly served the last meal before the fast. She was trying hard to keep back the well of gathered tears until she got to the beth medresh.

Reb Shlomo-Motte was already standing with his tallis bag under his arm when, after the meal, Vella approached to exchange good wishes with him. He held her hand a long while, and his lips beneath his mustache grew puffy in the attempt to contain his suppressed sobs. "May you not have to work so hard," he blessed his breadwinner with a broken voice.

"And may you have good health and live to have joy in your son!" Vella's cheeks began trembling and she burst out weeping. "Chaikl, apologize to your father."

Shaken by his mother's tears, Chaikl began screaming, "First Vova Barbitoler told me to parade up and down before the whole congregation to show them how my suit fits. Then the other day he told me to show him my ritual fringes. Next time that drunkard is going to tell me to lie down on a bench so he can beat me. He won't live to see the day!"

Reb Shlomo-Motte banged his cane angrily on the floor. "Then you should have run out of the beth medresh at once, you fool, and not raised a prayer stand against the tobacco merchant. The whole congregation? If you'd think less of the congregation and more of your hard-working mother, you'd have shown more consideration for the man who bought you a suit and hired a teacher for you."

This time Chaikl remained silent, and Vella thanked God in her heart that her son hadn't snapped back impudently at his father. Reb Shlomo-Motte valued this too, and as a sign of reconciliation he handed Chaikl his tallis bag, kittel, and High Holiday prayer book to carry to the beth medresh. The fruit peddler remained at home to clear the table and change into her holiday dress. Since Reb Shlomo-Motte walked slowly, leaning on his cane, and Chaikl walked decorously behind him, Vella caught up with them on the way. But as much as she wanted to walk with her two men, she really couldn't allow herself the pleasure of slowing down for them.

She had many supplications to weep over in her Yiddish prayer book before everyone began chanting the Kol Nidrei.

3

VOVA BARBITOLER STOOD on his feet throughout Yom Kippur, his tallis draped over his head, his face to the wall. He was surrounded by the commotion of Reb Senderl's sons, sons-in-law, and grown grandchildren. So as not to grieve the old man, Reb Senderl's kinsmen wore pious faces, smote their chests during the confession of sins, and didn't talk during the prayers. His grandsons watched him, armed with little bottles of valerian drops in case he should faint during the long, difficult fast. Because of the donations pledged by his sons and sons-in-law, Reb Senderl was given the honor of reciting the Book of Jonah for the Afternoon Service and of opening the Holy Ark for the concluding Neilah Service. But Vova Barbitoler's son from his first wife didn't come to pray. Both he and his sister were angry with their father. Vova was afraid to bring Confrada's son, for Hertzke was always fighting with the other boys in the beth medresh and dashing about among the prayer stands. So Vova stood quietly and sadly in the tightly packed beth medresh like a forlorn tree in a field.

He was also docile during Sukkos; he recited the blessings over his own esrog and didn't say a word to his fellow congregants. And while everyone danced and sang during the Torah circuits on Simkhas Torah, he walked behind the cantor in silence, his face pressed to the mantle of the Torah in his hands. A beth medresh trustee was distributing honey cakes and whisky, but Vova didn't touch any of this refreshment.

"A drunkard can't enjoy a bit of whisky taken for the sake of a mitzva," the worshipers joked.

And Reb Senderl laughed and said, "Reb Shlomo-Motte's little darling took the wind out of that bigamist's sails." Chaikl heard this and felt hatred for the pious kettlemaker, who was a boor and a man without compassion.

Just as his father had made peace with him on the Eve of Yom Kippur, Chaikl's teacher made peace with him on Simkhas Torah. Although Reb Menakhem-Mendl realized that the tobacco merchant would no longer pay for the lessons, he felt sorry for the youth who might go astray, and also pitied the fruit peddler. Vella was an honest woman whose heart yearned for her son to be a Torah scholar. Frankly, Chaikl didn't have the refined ways of a ben Torah, but in Navaredok even wilder creatures had been taken in and civilized in the course of time. In honor of Simkhas Torah, Reb Menakhem-Mendl drank a couple of glasses of whisky, overjoyed that during the holiday week he didn't have to set foot in his little shop. So when he spoke to his pupil he was glad of heart and somewhat tipsy.

"Ay-ay-ay! I warned you about the terrible trait of pride when you first put on Vova Barbitoler's new suit. But you didn't heed my warning and became haughty. And because you became haughty you were indignant when Reb Vova, and perhaps other congregants as well, suspected you of forgetting to put on your ritual fringes. But the law states that if someone is slandered he must not become angry. On the contrary, he must show everyone that he is free of sin. Had someone suspected me of not putting on my ritual fringes, I would have taken them out and shown everyone that I *was* wearing them," Reb Menakhem-Mendl concluded, adding, "We'll resume our lessons the day after tomorrow."

Once again they began studying together, but Chaikl's diligence had greatly diminished. One evening several days after Sukkos, as Reb Menakhem-Mendl swayed over his Talmud, his pupil's eyes wandered over the beth medresh. He saw ten men sitting at a table studying Midrash, a lighted candle on a prayer stand, and a recluse who was chanting dolefully, as though the wind from the chimney in his cold room had penetrated his voice. From a corner came a dry and angry cough. Chaikl imagined a corpse sitting on the cemetery fence and spewing the earth out of his rotted lungs. Chaikl's glance then fell on a tall man standing behind the pulpit. The stranger had a little black beard and a sharp, aquiline nose, and he wore a soft black rabbinic hat.

Chaikl nudged Reb Menakhem-Mendl with his elbow. "See that man over there? He looks like a rabbi, and he keeps staring at you."

"At me?" Reb Menakhem-Mendl stood up for a moment to look at the visitor. "I don't know him. . . . Look here, I just about manage to tear myself away for a couple of hours during the day to learn Torah, but you don't study, and you don't let me study, either. Now let's go over this passage once more; then you'll be able to understand the commentary."

Vova Barbitoler waddled into the beth medresh. His beard was matted and his eyes were empty, like those of a man pursuing the last ray of light in his burned-out memory. He waved his hands as though struggling with high waves or chasing off a pack of dogs. Vova charged toward the steps of the Holy Ark, but slipped and fell to the floor between the Ark and the pulpit.

The tobacco merchant now looked like a harried, tormented soul, a moribund man who wanted to die in a holy place. From all sides the congregants ran to help him and bring him to. They bent over him and heard him wheezing and whining.

Vova began loosening his coat, jacket, and shirt, then rolled from side to side and howled, "Confrada! I wish for you what you've made of me!" The congregants now realized that Vova was drunk and ranting because of his runaway whore.

"He's undressing before the Holy Ark and its Torah scrolls," someone called, grabbing his head.

"Douse him with water!" another yelled.

But Reb Senderl outshouted them all. "Pour the slop pail over him! The slop pail!"

The men brought in pitchers from the washstand and poured water over Vova Barbitoler. He writhed and turned and twisted about, panting for breath, and then vomited green bile. One congregant turned aside and spat with disgust, and another looked for a rag to cover Vova.

Reb Senderl bustled and hopped about. "Take that carcass to the women's section!"

Just then Mindl came into the beth medresh, followed by Hertzke. Younger than her husband by about twenty years, Mindl always wore a marriage wig covered with a kerchief. Neighbors never ceased wondering why such a young and gentle woman had married an undivorced older man and patiently suffered his rages when drunk and his cold-blooded cruelty when sober. Mindl pushed her way through the congregants, knelt beside Vova, and tried to pull him to his feet, not disgusted by the muck he had vomited up.

"Vova! What's the matter with you? You've been drinking steadily for three days. The whisky is going to burn your insides. Come home! Come home!"

Vova opened his bleary eyes, wiped the perspiration from his face with his sleeve, and stood up very slowly. He straightened his disheveled clothes and waddled toward the door, but nearly fell over and sat down on a bench. "My children!" he bawled and once more began tearing at his clothes.

Hertzke was standing in the circle with glazed eyes and bared teeth. "Confrada's bastard, are you laughing at me?" Vova stretched his ten hairy fingers with their big brass-yellow nails toward his son. Hertzke nimbly backed off and stopped a few feet away, waiting for his father to chase him. Vova dashed furiously around the pulpit to get his son from behind, and bumped into the kettlemaker. "Oh! It's you, Senderl! To blazes with you and your whole family! They bought you the honor of chanting the Book of Jonah? They bought you the honor of opening the Holy Ark for the Neilah as a charm for long life, huh? But I'll make it short for you!"

Reb Senderl fled to the other side of the room shouting, "Help! Let's tie him up and hand him over to the police!"

Vova turned to the congregants with outspread hands as though he wanted to seize them all in his arms and crush them.

"Go ahead! I'd like to see you tie me up! Just to spite you, I won't send Confrada a divorce, and I'll come to the beth medresh drunk every day."

The worshipers drew back. The tobacco merchant looked around triumphantly and spotted Reb Menakhem-Mendl and Chaikl standing near the corner of the eastern wall. He glowered at the two as he strode toward them. "Is that heathen who raised a prayer stand at me here too? Now you're not going to slip out of my hands alive."

Reb Menakhem-Mendl retreated, trembling. From all sides came the shouts, "Run away!" At first Chaikl wanted to raise the prayer stand again—and this time smash it over the drunkard's head. But on second thought, the possible results of such a deed flashed through his mind and he was ready to run. But because he was ashamed of having to flee, his feet turned leaden. Vova now stood over him with an upraised paw.

At that instant Mindl ran between them, calling, "Jews, help! He'll murder him!"

"You too? You're protecting him, you lousy cow?" Vova roared and snatched the kerchief and the marriage wig from Mindl's head.

She whined softly and despairingly, as if stabbed with a cold knife. The congregants saw her gleaming skull, totally bald except for a few tufts of hair like withered grass.

"It's not from lice, it's from a sickness. It happened on account of a sickness," she cried bitterly, covering her face with her hands. But Vova still tormented her.

"You've got lice! Which means you're lousy. If you hadn't had lice, you wouldn't have married me. I hate you. You disgust me. It's your fault that I'm yearning for Confrada. She had long, thick hair, beautiful long hair she had, and you've got lice. Get away from me!" He pushed her brutally and turned to Chaikl. "You're happy, huh, you heathen, that I have a wife with lice? Now I'm going to knock your head off."

But before he had a chance to take hold of Chaikl, the tall stranger seized Vova by the lapels and shook him forcefully and angrily. The newcomer was so angry that he could only say, "You wicked Haman!"

Vova Barbitoler lost his breath. Crushed, hands lowered, he looked up at the tall, black-bearded young man in terror, as if over him hovered a huge angel who had leaped out of the Holy Ark to drag him off to hell.

"It's a lie! I don't have lice." Mindl jumped toward the tall man and with head bent showed her gleaming bald pate. "Look and you'll see I don't have lice."

"Maniac, cover your head! You're in a holy place," the congregation shouted.

The tall stranger released Vova Barbitoler and with an anguished face turned away from the humiliated woman. Mindl picked up her trampled wig from the floor, set it on her head, and covered it with her kerchief.

Vova gazed at her at length with the sober eyes of a man who realizes the havoc he has caused by one mad assault. "Take me home," he muttered weakly. Scarcely able to drag his feet, Vova leaned against Mindl's shoulder to avoid falling.

Mindl kept arranging her wig as she cried feebly, "Now all the women will say I'm bald!"

"Don't talk to them," Vova pleaded as he approached the door, anxious to leave the beth medresh as soon as possible. Hertzke trailed them, hands in his pockets, and threw a contemptuous look at Chaikl for not being bold and quick enough to flee.

As soon as the couple and the boy were gone, the congregants approached the newcomer; they greeted him and thanked him for saving them from the drunkard. Reb Senderl told the visitor about Vova Barbitoler's three wives and his children who were his bitter enemies. "He's always in a jealous rage against me because I, thank God, have joy in my children. I'm a kettlemaker, not a scholar, but a scholar once told me that the holy Zohar states that tears of rage, envy, and complaint about a friend do not reach the Throne of Glory—only true tears of repentance reach the Throne of Glory."

The visitor sat on a bench, hands over his eyes, and did not say a word. The congregants left him alone, and the kettlemaker too withdrew in the face of his aloof silence. Then Reb Menakhem-Mendl moved near him.

"Sholom aleichem, Reb Tsemakh. I saw you standing behind the pulpit earlier, but I didn't recognize you."

"I recognized you, but I didn't want to interrupt you in the middle of your lesson." Tsemakh held on to Reb Menakhem-Mendl's hand and sadly shook his head. "When we studied with the Old Man in Navaredok, neither of us imagined that we would meet like this."

Reb Menakhem-Mendl had heard from Navaredker visitors in Vilna that the Lomzher had fallen into bad ways, that he had become totally nonobservant. This news had saddened Reb Menakhem-Mendl greatly; but at the same time he had thanked God that he himself had remained a man of faith and devoted to Talmud study, even though, unlike the Lomzher, he had not been among the leading Musarniks in Navaredok. "Reb Tsemakh and I studied at the same yeshiva," Reb Menakhem-Mendl told Chaikl, hinting thereby that he should thank the visitor for having saved him. But Chaikl stood there like a mummy, biting his lips, thinking that it was all his father's fault. If his father hadn't been angry at him for threatening the tobacco merchant with the prayer stand, he would have given Vova such a shove today that all his bones would have been broken.

"I'd just as soon stop studying altogether and stay out of that drunkard's way," Chaikl burst out, then quickly left the beth medresh.

"He's a knowledgeable boy, but hotheaded and without manners." Reb Menakhem-Mendl sighed and told Tsemakh about Chaikl's parents, the tobacco merchant's generosity, and the reason for the dispute.

Reb Tsemakh smiled as if pleased to hear that the youngster was hotheaded. "Nowadays a ben Torah has to possess a strong measure of rage to stand up to the world. And do you know the drunkard's son?"

"People say, and it seems to be true, that the tobacco merchant's son is a bit touched. Why are you asking, Reb Tsemakh?"

"I've founded a little yeshiva in Valkenik and I'm looking for students. But I've come to Vilna because of you, Reb Menakhem-Mendl. I want you to help me teach in the yeshiva. I asked for you at your store, talked to your rebbetsin, and saw what kind of livelihood you have. Woe is me that I've seen you in such a state. But I should complain more about what I've done to myself. As the Talmud says, 'Woe is me! On account of my sins the world is darkened for me!' My dispute with the head of the Nareva rosh yeshiva and my marrying into a rich family made me forget how much effort Navaredok put into me in the hope that I would accomplish some good in this world. But I've torn myself away, and you, Reb Menakhem-Mendl, must do the same."

"I've been dreaming for a long time of going to a yeshiva, and studying Talmud with the students would certainly make me happy. But I doubt if my wife would agree," Reb Menakhem-Mendl said, tugging at his little beard.

"I've already told her in the store that as a rosh yeshiva you'll earn more than by selling glue and cobbler's thread. Once you get settled in Valkenik you can bring your family," Tsemakh said.

The Lomzher hasn't changed, Reb Menakhem-Mendl thought. He had always spoken self-confidently, and he now spoke with authority too. So perhaps it was destined! If the Lomzher had become a penitent and convinced himself that he should throw over a life of wealth, surely he could persuade Menakhem-Mendl's wife to let him leave his little thread-and-glue business.

The congregants dispersed. Reb Menakhem-Mendl also left for home, and the beth medresh remained empty and half dark. In one candle-lit corner, however, a recluse dozed over a book; and in another dark corner Tsemakh Atlas recited the Evening Service. He lingered over the Silent Devotion, the cries of the drunkard's shamed wife still ringing in his ears. After praying he sat down on a bench, humming and swaying, and his shadow, stretched across the length of the floor, swayed with him. The dozing recluse woke up, for the mournful Musar melody pierced his heart. He removed the melted candle from his prayer stand and entered the women's section, where he slept. Tsemakh remained alone in the dense darkness, lamenting even more intensely: "Woe is me! Because of my sins the world is darkened before me. Adam had eyes that could see to the edge of the world, but his desire for a lovely fruit from the forbidden Tree of Knowledge dimmed the light of his eyes, and the world became dark for him."

Tsemakh sat for a long while immersed in thought, like a flooded cellar full of stagnant water. While living with Slava and her family, he had rarely been disturbed by the old doubts of the existence of God. Although he knew that he had remained a Musarnik in character, and despite his penchant for outbursts, he still gave no one the impression that he was a pious adherent of Musar. But since resuming his ways as a recluse, he was once more tormented by the relentless uncertainties of his young yeshiva years. He felt someone unknown pounding at his mind, as though beating fists on closed gates. "Are you once more masquerading so piously with beard and earlocks, planning again to establish a yeshiva where students will study Torah? Do you even really believe in a Creator who gave the Torah?" Trying desperately to free himself of these doubts, Tsemakh began to burrow into medieval philosophical texts. But the old Jewish philosophers, whose style and ideas were Aristotelian, asserted that it was incomprehensible to conceive of the existence of the world without a Creator, without a First Cause—and that sort of philosophy exhausted Tsemakh; it bored him and made his head ache with despair at finding nothing there to help him. It also left him with a feeling of nausea, as if he were chewing a hard, tasteless piece of meat that did not stay his hunger but lodged in his cavities and between his teeth. Since man was forbidden to conceive of God as simply the First Cause, in the manner of the rationalists' God, as Creator of the world, with attributes like the Beneficent, the Omniscient, the Eternal—what difference did it make, Tsemakh thought, whether such a God existed or not, if in any case he did not grace us with warmth or consolation. But the God of Abraham, Isaac and Jacob, the God of the Prophets, the God of the Talmudic sages and the students of the Kabbala, was above all a God that a human being could perceive and even to some extent comprehend. He spoke the language of his believers and even the mute language of broken hearts because he was a God who lived in our hearts. But the person of wavering faith, or the one who lacked faith and needed a God logically proven—that sort of person regarded the rationally determined Deity as cold and remote, with no links to lonely man, caught up in his misfortunes down on earth. And besides, the existence of such a God could not be proven anyway. Tsemakh kept browsing through the old philosophical texts until he discovered the early nineteenth-century *Book of the Covenant.* That Hebrew work, an explanation of Kant's philosophy, stated that with the power of pure reason one could prove that there is no God as easily as one could prove that there is a God; that man possessed free will as well as that he did not possess free will; that he is mortal and has no soul as clearly as that he has an immortal soul which is part of the divine spirit. In that case, Tsemakh reflected, all the rabbinic authorities were right when they wrote that belief in the existence of God was totally dependent on heartfelt faith. "Where then does one get this heartfelt faith, which even sinful Adam possessed and by virtue of which he became a penitent?" Tsemakh shrieked bitterly behind closed lips, afraid that if he opened his mouth and let the sounds fly out, the recluse who slept in the women's gallery would realize that the visitor in the dark beth medresh was wrestling with the problem of the existence of God.

4

REB SHLOMO-MOTTE THE HEBREW TEACHER SAT at home with his son, explaining why he should become an artisan. "You see the results of depending on others. You'll never be able to repay the tobacco merchant. Reb Menakhem-Mendl is doing you a favor, and the congregants who sit around the beth medresh stove are bickering about whether you're worthy of becoming a scholar, as though you had no parents to look after you. But if you earn your own living, nobody will tell you what to do. They'll only respect you for helping your mother bear her life's heavy burdens."

While father and son were talking, Tsemakh Atlas stood in Vella's fruit shop, trying to persuade her to send Chaikl to his yeshiva in Valkenik. "It's a small town three stations from Vilna, only two hours away by train. Every week wagoners come to buy merchandise in Vilna for the town shopkeepers, and you'll be able to send your son food packages with them. Reb Menakhem-Mendl is going too. So your son will continue with the same teacher and won't have to be dependent on the good graces of a drunkard."

At first Vella was bewildered. How could she let her one and only little boy leave her? But she soon consoled herself: three train stations away was not the other side of the sea, and there were Jews everywhere. She looked up at the young rabbi whose face radiated the Divine Presence and said, "It certainly won't hurt Chaikl to learn to be independent. Since you protected my son from the drunken tobacco merchant, you certainly won't let any harm come to Chaikl in Valkenik either. But I don't know whether my husband will agree, and whether it's right for Chaikl to leave his ailing father in his old age."

"The son's studying Torah will make his father well. Tell your husband that you don't want to see your son smoking on the Sabbath and discarding his tefillin."

"One can be an artisan and still be religious," the fruit peddler said, trying to defend her husband's view.

"If you can show me ten young artisans on your street who put on tefillin and don't smoke on the Sabbath," Reb Tsemakh countered with a smile, "I'm prepared to remove my rabbinic gaberdine and become an artisan myself."

The rabbi's clever response and his brotherly way of speaking to her moved Vella to tears. "Don't think I'm not constantly afraid that Chaikl will befriend the union workers who carry red flags against the government. Many mothers bewail their bitter fate—children imprisoned, and not for robbery either, God forbid. I promise to talk this over with my husband. Then as soon as my son comes here, I'll send him to the beth medresh to talk to you."

His mother's remarks and her buoyant mood told Chaikl that she had already decided to send him to the yeshiva. This both angered and amazed him. The whole street could hear her shouting, "Watch the horses. Look out for the cars!" as he crossed the street; and he always felt embarrassed at his mother's treating him like a little boy. Now she had suddenly agreed to let him leave home.

"Won't you miss me?" he asked her.

"And what if I will? How long can you hold on to my apron strings?" his mother said, watching him as he left for Reb Shaulke's beth medresh. What had the Valkenik rosh yeshiva seen in him, she wondered—his impudence toward older people? But on the other hand, the tobacco merchant wasn't as decent a man as he should be. If he could humiliate Mindl so cruelly in the presence of a whole congregation, no wonder his previous wife had run away from him.

Reb Tsemakh and Chaikl paced back and forth in the beth medresh, deep in conversation. Chaikl was pleased that the Valkenik rosh yeshiva used the yeshiva custom of calling him after the name of his home town.

"Reb Menakhem-Mendl tells me that you're talented, Vilner, so I want to ask you something. Our sages of blessed memory say, 'Woe unto the wicked man and woe unto his neighbor.' But what happens when a righteous person lives next to a wicked man? Who is the good man and who is the bad one?"

Chaikl responded immediately: "It depends on who is stronger. If the righteous man is stronger, then all will be well for him and for his wicked neighbor. But if the wicked man is stronger, than woe unto him and woe unto his righteous neighbor."

"You're very sensible," Tsemakh said. "But since you understand the matter of the righteous man and the wicked man, Vilner, why don't you understand that nowadays one cannot stay faithful to the Torah without an environment of good friends in a yeshiva? Do you think you're the sort of righteous person who's immune to the street's bad influence?"

"I didn't say I was righteous," Chaikl flared, annoyed that the rosh yeshiva wanted to catch him in a contradiction.

Tsemakh Atlas, his black gaberdine billowing as he walked, stopped in mid-stride and looked at him sharply: "You don't consider yourself righteous, but you don't consider yourself wicked either, right? And you certainly won't compare yourself to the likes of the tobacco merchant. You can't imagine yourself shedding tears of drunkenness and slavering with desire that burns your insides even more than liquor. You can't imagine yourself rolling about half-naked in a beth medresh and begging the Torah in the Holy Ark to return to you an abomination of a wife who has slipped through your fingers. That you'd be able to sink so low, Vilner, and tear your clothes off and howl with desire—that you can't imagine yourself doing. But our sages indeed feared such temptation and suspected themselves of succumbing to the worst transgressions. The Talmud tells us that the greater the man the greater his *yetzer ha-ra,* even in small desires."

Tsemakh spoke feverishly, and Chaikl's face burned like fire. He looked about, apprehensive that latecomers might be listening to their conversation. He imagined that the Valkenik rosh yeshiva knew of his sinful thoughts about Vova's wife, that beautiful witch who still drove her former husband crazy. But Chaikl plucked up his courage and looked the rosh yeshiva right in the eye.

"Would Reb Menakhem-Mendl be capable of doing what Vova Barbitoler has done?"

"Reb Menakhem-Mendl?" Tsemakh asked, flustered by the unexpected question. "Perhaps not. Certainly not! But another

Torah scholar might indeed have the character of a Vova Barbitoler. He could be a rosh yeshiva, a rabbi, a respectable Jew, a refined
Jew who never touches a drop of whisky; yet in essence he could
still be a Vova Barbitoler."

"If a Torah scholar can be a Vova Barbitoler, then what's the
good of going to study at a yeshiva?" Chaikl asked.

"Studying Talmud is not enough. One must study Musar and be
constantly on guard to prevent the Vova Barbitoler within us from
developing and thriving." The yeshiva principal pointed his finger
at the floor where the tobacco merchant had lain.

Tsemakh sat down on a bench, pressed his forehead to a prayer
stand, and fell silent. He knew that the question of Chaikl's
studying at the yeshiva should be settled. But his own remarks had
ignited a suppressed fire in him. Scattered memories flew about in
his mind like sparks; they buzzed and bit like angry flies. He drew
the Vilner close to him, put his arm around his shoulders, and
spoke with deep sorrow in his voice: "The Talmud tells us about
Rabbi Eleazer . . ."

The men who had come late for the Morning Service—each had
gone off to a corner and murmured the prayers softly to himself—
were already folding their prayer shawls and reciting some concluding passages. One worshiper, eyes still shut, whipped his head
from side to side, saying, "Remember what Amalek has done unto
you." Another bobbed up and down on his toes reciting the
Thirteen Articles of Faith. A third quickly chanted the Psalms for
that day. Then they rushed out of the beth medresh heading for
work. Tsemakh and Chaikl remained alone. The September sun,
the golden, autumnal light of late Tishrei, sent rays like sheaves of
wheat through the windows. But Tsemakh thrust the sunbeams
aside with the coal-black nocturnal glitter of his beard and eyes.

"Only the student of Musar sees all the buried lusts hidden in
him as if through a magnifying glass. And if a man discovers a bad
aspect in himself, he can uproot it from within him," Tsemakh
concluded the moral of the Rabbi Eleazar story.

Chaikl listened and longed to go to Valkenik and work to
improve his character until he too became a Navaredker Musarnik
like Reb Tsemakh.

"There's my father!" he cried.

His father's excited expression indicated that his mother had already spoken to him about the yeshiva. Tsemakh looked at the newcomer with obvious amazement. He had not expected the fruit peddler's husband to be a broad-shouldered man with a trimmed, rectangular beard and young, flashing eyes. Hat atilt and holding a heavy cane with an ivory knob, Reb Shlomo-Motte didn't look like a sick old Hebrew teacher without a cheder. He sat down on the bench next to the white-tiled stove and summoned his son.

"Don't even think about going to the yeshiva. You're going to learn a trade."

"Mama wants me to go," Chaikl muttered.

"You're not going!" his father yelled.

"I will go!" Chaikl ran to the door, ready to flee, but his father's warning cry—"But if you go against my will, don't bother saying Kaddish for me when I'm gone"—caught him and riveted him to his place.

"If your son doesn't become a ben Torah, he won't say Kaddish for you anyway," Reb Tsemakh said, walking toward the teacher from his place at the eastern wall. "Why are you against his going? We'll find him a good place to live. During the week he'll eat in the yeshiva kitchen with all the other students, and on the Sabbath he'll have his meals at a fine home."

Reb Shlomo-Motte rose slowly, leaned on his cane, and shouted to his son, "What are you standing there for? Go! I'll talk to you later."

Chaikl ran out of the beth medresh, his eyes brimming with tears, and Reb Shlomo-Motte shouted even louder at the rosh yeshiva: "I don't want my son to grow up to be a religious functionary, a mindless pietist, and an ignorant boor in secular matters. If I were still strong and could earn a living, I'd send my son to a school where they teach both Torah and secular subjects. But since I'm sick and poor, and a broken old man now, my son should become a worker who earns his bread, and not one who eats at strangers' tables. A person who doesn't support himself has to kowtow to those who give him bread; he has to be a flatterer and a hypocrite, or he becomes embittered and hates the entire world."

Tsemakh had held himself in check because Chaikl was present. Now he sprayed forth a torrent of words: "The greatest rabbis and the most prominent householders were once guests at other people's tables. Did they grow up to be any worse or more submissive than those who didn't eat that way? When a Jew gives a Torah scholar a meal, he offers it wholeheartedly. If by chance you run across a congregant who has no respect for a ben Torah, the boy knows that he has to have absolute contempt for such a lout."

Reb Shlomo-Motte sat down again and shrugged his shoulders. "Having contempt for a man who feeds you—that's the impudence of a beggar. If a person gets used to eating the bread of charity in his youth, he remains a cripple all his life."

Tsemakh went to the eastern wall, put on his coat, and stopped beside the teacher on his way to the door.

"You know who remains a cripple? The person who is taught from his youth to reckon with what this one thinks and that one says. When that drunkard humiliated your son and wanted to beat him too, you said nothing. But when I want to take him to a yeshiva where he'll grow in Torah learning among friends who are his equals, the maskil in you awakened to say that Torah and secular learning should go hand in hand. And I'm not so sure that you meant Torah, either. Nowadays Torah and secular learning do not go hand in hand. Neither do Torah and learning a trade. Nowadays one is either a ben Torah or totally irreligious," Tsemakh said, and with a wave of his hand he left the beth medresh.

At home that evening Reb Shlomo-Motte realized that he would not have his way.

"Why do you begrudge me a son who is a Torah scholar?" Vella asked her husband. "Don't I suffer enough? And what good does Chaikl do us staying at home? Does he shop for produce with me at the market? Does he help me call customers to the store?" But above all, Vella couldn't forgive her husband for his threat about the Kaddish. "One never knows whose day will come first," the fruit peddler said. "It could be me."

Reb Shlomo-Motte waved his hand as if to say: Do what you wish with your darling. Throughout the evening all three remained silent, and Vella wandered about bent over, suddenly aged.

Just before they went to sleep, when Reb Shlomo-Motte was out for a moment and Vella was preparing his bed, she quickly whispered to her son, "You little silly, you think your father doesn't want you to go study? He loves you and doesn't want to be alone in his old age."

Then she quickly wiped the tears from her eyes so that her husband wouldn't know she'd been crying.

5

ON BUTCHERS STREET, Zelda's big fruit store was continually crowded with customers. But if a woman wanted to shop elsewhere too, Zelda's daughters dashed outside like hungry wolverines and dragged the woman back to their store. On the other side of the lane, Vella the fruit peddler was afraid to say a word lest she feel the tongue-lashings of those loudmouthed women, those arrogant Sennacheribs. Vella, who knew the women's Yiddish Pentateuch, would say, "King Sennacherib arrogantly boasted that it was forbidden to say his name without washing, and Zelda and her daughters set the world afire with their big mouths."

Zelda's husband, Kasrielke the tinsmith, drank more than he worked; most of the time he simply loafed around. When he felt hunger pangs, he came to his wife's shop. Zelda and her youngest daughter handled the baskets of fruit; the middle daughter sold all kinds of greens; and the eldest daughter, the biggest shrieker of the lot, stood guard over the boxes of dried fish, the barrel of schmaltz herring, and the jars of sour pickles. The store was packed with customers, and the tinsmith pretended to help sell the merchandise. "Auntie, do you need apples?" He filled a paper bag with little apples. "Uncle, how about a herring?" And he fished out the largest schmaltz herring and wrapped it in thick paper. The daughters knew what their father was up to and chased him from the store. "Look at that—he's buddy-buddy with everybody! Go! Go on! We'll get along without you!" Kasrielke jumped out of the store with the bag of apples in one hand and the schmaltz herring in the other, like a cat that nabs a piece of meat from the soaking tub and jumps over a fence. His daughters yelled after him, "Parasite!" and his wife hoped that someday she'd get a message that her husband had fallen off a roof in a drunken stupor.

The family's pride and joy was little Melechke, Zelda's youngest child and only son. When his mother and sisters saw him coming into the store, they left all their customers. They surrounded him and kissed him; they delighted in him; they set aright the little scarf on his throat so that he wouldn't catch cold, God forbid.

"Melechke, God bless you! May we suffer all your ills. What did you learn in cheder today?" his mother and sisters chorused. Just then they saw Vova Barbitoler passing by. Since he had given Melechke his ritual fringes, their mouths—normally crackling with curses—suddenly became full of milk and honey.

"Good morning, rabbi. Our Melechke is wearing your ritual fringes. Yes, he's wearing them!"

But Kasrielke the tinsmith made fun of the women. "What sort of rabbi is he, that Vova Barbitoler, if he has one wife in Vilna and another in Argentina, and he guzzles even more whisky than me?"

To which Zelda replied, "Don't rack your brain over it. What if Reb Vova does have two wives! He's got a beard, hasn't he? And he gave Melechke ritual fringes, didn't he? So he's a rabbi."

Melechke was already studying one of the chapters in the Talmudic tractate *Baba Metzia*. Every evening he went up to Reb Shaulke's beth medresh to review what he had studied in cheder. Melechke was a soft-as-satin lad with a rosy little face and tender cheeks. He loved to have old congregants test him and praise his ability. But if someone said an unkind word to him, his dark blue eyes would mist over with tears.

Tsemakh Atlas watched the little lad praying behind the prayer stand with the large Talmud. He went up to the boy and asked him, "How old are you? Where are you studying? Who are your parents? Do you have brothers and friends?"

Melechke answered the questions sedately and in order: "I'm eleven and I study at the Yavneh Cheder." He pointed to the window. "That's where my mother and sisters have their fruit store. I have no brothers and no friends. The boys in the street are wild bullies and are always fighting."

"And what do you intend to do when you grow up?" the head of the yeshiva asked.

"I'm going to be a rabbi, a gaon, and a saint," Melechke replied, his face glowing and eyes triumphantly agleam, as though he had guessed in which of two outstretched fists a coin was hidden. For his clever and pious answer he expected the tall man to pinch his cheek, listen to him recite a chapter of the Talmud, wax ecstatic over his knowledge, embrace him, and say, "You're some little boy, you're some little scholar!"

Instead, however, the tall man shouted at him, "If you're going to stay in Vilna and roam around Butchers Street, you're going to grow up to be a fresh punk, not a scholar!"

Only when Melechke's dark blue eyes misted over with tears did Reb Tsemakh stroke his face and tell him a story: "Once upon a time, someone asked the Vilna Gaon how one becomes a gaon. He replied, 'Will it, and you'll be one.' If you really and truly want to grow up to be a great scholar, you must go to a yeshiva. So go tell your parents that the Valkenik rosh yeshiva wants you to come with him."

The fruit store was crowded with customers until late in the evening. Zelda's daughters always suspected that Vella across the way begrudged them their good business and might even cast an evil eye at them. "Here's salt in your eyes and pepper in your nose," they yelled to her. Moreover, they bragged to their customers for Vella to hear, "Our little Melechke is going to a yeshiva to become a rabbi, a gaon, and a saint."

Vella stood in her empty, half-dark little shop and wondered how they could let a little boy, no bigger than a thimble, go away from home. And besides, such contentious shrews weren't worthy of having a Torah scholar in the family. She shouted back at the Sennacheribs, "I'm not so sure your Melechke will make such a name for himself when he grows up. I'll be happy if my Chaikl knows a bit of Talmud and becomes a good Jew."

"How can you compare your ox to our Melechke?" the women ranted, their faces bursting with health.

Vella didn't say a word. A pauper is better off not being born, she mused. If she owned a store with three open shutters that faced the street, and had a warehouse full of merchandise and luck with customers, she would give herself airs too. Her Shlomo-Motte had been the finest Hebrew teacher in town, while the tinsmith, poor fellow, was a drunkard. Nevertheless, the tinsmith's wife and daughters had better luck than she did with people and even with

God. Those harridans attracted customers not because of their better merchandise but because of their quick tongues and ready invective. Customers loved to shop where it was crowded, where they were neglected, and where they were treated like dirt. But on the other hand, perhaps it was a sin to think like that. Zelda too was a mother; she too had felt birth pangs, and she too wants her son to be a Torah scholar.

But Melechke's father didn't like this at all, and at home in the evening he raged, "If the father's a tinsmith, the son should be a tinsmith too. What do you want to make out of Melechke, a Vilna rabbi?"

Zelda and her daughters clasped their aprons. "Why not? Why should a Torah scholar grow up only in the house of that seller of rotten apples?"

The next morning Reb Tsemakh stood in the big fruit store and talked about the holy Torah. "Valkenik is a fine little town," he said, "and I'll take care of Melechke." Zelda and her daughters listened piously, as they did to the woman who repeated the cantor's prayers for the women's section on Rosh Hashana. They blew their noses, wiped the tears from their eyes, and consented to Melechke's going. But as soon as the rabbi left the store, Zelda's three daughters exchanged glances, and wanton smiles gleamed in their sly little eyes. They combed their disheveled hair with dampened fingers and said, "First time we've seen such a good-looking, well-built rabbi. The young bums around Butchers Street don't even come up to his shoetops."

Tsemakh returned to Reb Shaulke's beth medresh and told Chaikl, "I was able to convince the fruit-store women to let me have their eleven-year-old boy, but I can't seem to convince you to bring Hertzke Barbitoler here for a talk. Doesn't it bother you at all, Vilner, to leave that lad in the hands of such a brutal father?"

But the Vilner was stubborn. "I don't want to start anything with Vova again," he said. Then, to his distress, he revealed something he hadn't wanted to divulge. "The boys at the cheder say that Hertzke helps himself to food, pencils, and notebooks from the students' schoolbags. He even pickpockets coin purses. And if he's caught, he laughs it off and says it was only a joke."

Tsemakh was bewildered and somewhat alarmed. But he soon

recovered and pleaded with Chaikl again. "Who knows how much Hertzke has to suffer at home? Perhaps he's even starving. During the years of revolution in Russia, when hunger and atheism reigned in the land, young Navaredkers risked their lives smuggling youngsters across the border to Poland to save them for the Torah and to keep them from growing up to be Bolsheviks and commissars. If you, Vilner, want to become a true Navaredker Musarnik, don't be scared of the tobacco merchant."

Chaikl waited for Hertzke in front of the Yavneh Cheder and told him that the head of the Valkenik yeshiva wanted to see him. Curious to meet the Samson who had shaken his father like a lulav, Hertzke, who was carrying a bottle, let himself be led to the inn on Zavalne Street.

Before he and Chaikl separated at the entrance Chaikl asked him, "Why are you lugging that big empty bottle along with your schoolbag?"

"I want to fill it up with flies," Hertzke answered.

"You're crazy! Where will you find so many flies in the fall? And anyway, how can you catch enough flies to fill up the bottle even in the summer?" Chaikl called, just managing to jump back as Vova Barbitoler's son smashed the bottle onto the cobblestones. The bottle burst into hundreds of slivers and Hertzke dashed up the steps, laughing gleefully at having frightened Chaikl and all the passers-by.

In the corridor of the inn, which had a religious clientele, Hertzke saw Jews with strange beards and gaberdines. He giggled even more and entered the yeshiva principal's little room. Tsemakh gazed at Hertzke, whose face was rigid and distorted, as if made up like a clown's. He was wearing a short windbreaker, and his pants were tucked into large, leather-strapped shoes. A square hat with earflaps and a stiff narrow visor was perched on his small, pointed head. He does look like a moron and a street urchin, Tsemakh thought. "Would you like to go to the yeshiva?" he asked the boy.

Hertzke nodded and grinned. "My father won't let me. If I go he won't have anybody to beat up. But I'm going to run away, just like my older stepbrother and stepsister ran away. One day when my father wasn't home, they picked up their things and went off to live somewhere else."

"And why does your father hit you?"

"He says it's because I don't put on ritual fringes."

"And why don't you put them on?"

"He'd hit me anyway because my mother ran away from him." A grimace came over Hertzke's thin face, and he flinched as if seeing his father's upraised fist hovering over him. "And what am I going to do in that town? Studying all the time is boring. Here I have a sled, and I go sledding in the winter."

"You'll have fun in Valkenik too. I'll talk to your father and ask him to let you go. Running away is no good. He could come to Valkenik and take you away."

"Then I'll run away to another town. He won't let me go on his own," Hertzke said gloomily. Then he perked up again. On a chair stood an open suitcase filled with underwear, clothes, and a few religious books. "Look!" he called, grabbing a belt and stretching it out with both hands as if measuring the suitcase.

"You can have it. But if something catches your fancy in Valkenik, don't take it. Tell me and I'll get it for you." Tsemakh pointed to the frugal meal on his table: half a small loaf of bread, a cut-up herring on a plate, and two hard-boiled eggs in a saucer. "Would you like something to eat?"

"No. I want this penknife." Hertzke grabbed the knife on the table and from its brown handle pulled out a little saw, a scissors, and a corkscrew.

"You can have it, too. Tell your father I'll come to see him tonight. Where do you live?"

"Seven Rudnitsky Street, by the gate, on the right-hand side." Hertzke put the penknife in his pocket and wrapped the belt around the palm of his hand.

"If my father won't let me go, I'll run away."

After Hertzke's departure Tsemakh sat in his room, frowning. No doubt about it, the boy was a half-wit and had no compunction about stealing, as Chaikl Vilner had declared. By all rights he should certainly be taken from his father, but on the other hand, Hertzke's behavior might be a bad influence on the other students. Tsemakh decided to visit the tobacco merchant and talk matters over with him. If the merchant wouldn't agree, Tsemakh would be spared the trouble of pondering whether or not to take Hertzke to the yeshiva. Nevertheless, he postponed the meeting with Vova Barbitoler from hour to hour. Finally, late that night he walked to Rudnitsky Street. A mesh-covered bulb hung from the vaulted gate entrance. The yellowish circle of light looked like the web of a huge dead spider. Tsemakh walked up the dimly lit wooden steps; they creaked underfoot, groaning with a dull pain. The weird silence of a morgue wafted over him.

In the main room, Vova Barbitoler sat at the head of a long table, busy with his ledger. He erased and wrote, humming serenely to himself, hardly glancing at the visitor, as though he were a familiar guest. Mindl stood at the doorway of an inner room, a kerchief draped around her shoulders, looking anxiously at her husband, as though expecting him to send her away. Hertzke sat on a bench by the wall, also gaping at his father. They didn't dare look at the visitor for fear of angering their master, who calmly wrote in his ledger as though he were setting down a judgment of life or death.

"Sit down," Vova growled at Tsemakh and waved his family away. Mindl immediately disappeared, and Hertzke followed quickly, hunched over as if not daring to lose a moment straightening his shoulders. Tsemakh felt the veins in his temples go numb. He sat down facing Vova, examining him to see whether the merchant's wife and son always trembled before him or whether today was an exception. Vova smiled dourly with all the wrinkles of his hairy face, as though delighted that he could make others fear him. He scratched his chin under his matted beard and looked like a man who had crawled out of a forest cave.

"In other words, you want to take my Hertzke to your yeshiva. You know, I didn't think you'd have the gall. First you grabbed me by the lapels and called me a wicked Haman, and now you want me to give you my son."

"I wasn't the first to call someone who lifts his hand against his neighbor wicked. Moses was the first when he said: 'Wicked one! Why do you strike your fellow man?'" Tsemakh said through clenched teeth, as if now too he took pleasure in calling Vova wicked. "And the way you treated your wife in public is inhuman."

"Are you going to tell me how to treat my wife? Do you feed her and put a roof over her head?" Vova responded with murderous fury. The dark glow of his eyes reminded Tsemakh of the yellowish shine of the bulb above the gate. "And do you have any notion of my suffering?"

"Even if you do suffer, does this mean you can humiliate your wife because you feed her?" Tsemakh spoke more softly than Vova Barbitoler, and his eyes, too, gleamed coldly. "And you don't treat your son any better than your wife—perhaps even worse. But no matter how much you beat him, he won't wear the ritual fringes. I won't even have to remind him; he'll surely put them on."

"I'm not Shlomo-Motte the Hebrew teacher. You won't be able to take *my* son away against my will." Vova smiled again with all his sullen wrinkles, like a wild beast sunning his face. From the drawer he removed the belt and the penknife and threw them on the table. "My little bastard showed me these toys you've given him so that I can see what a good man you are and let him go with you. So I gave him such a beating with your belt that he won't forget it the rest of his life. Take back your presents and don't butt into my life."

Tsemakh looked at the bench where Hertzke had been sitting and now realized why the boy's back had been bent when he'd run out behind his stepmother. The brute had beaten him so severely he couldn't straighten up. That fiend was even more inhuman sober than drunk. Tsemakh rose, while Vova remained sitting with half-closed eyes.

"I'm sure you're capable of stabbing your son in the heart with this knife too, except that you're afraid they'll hang you. But maybe you're not even afraid of being sentenced as a murderer. A brutal monster like you usually thinks: I'll take him with me! But you feel it'd be a pity to kill the boy; you want to stretch out the revenge because his mother ran away from you." Tsemakh slipped the belt and the penknife into his coat and waited for an answer.

Vova Barbitoler did not reply. He just nodded, agreeing with Tsemakh's appraisal of him. They exchanged malice-ridden glances, like enemies who know that if they meet again one of them will be trampled in the dust. Tsemakh went down the stairs, then felt a sudden blow on his head. While he had been with the tobacco merchant, the house porter had locked the main gate and left open only a small narrow door, which he had bumped into. Tsemakh felt both pain and pleasure; the blow on his skull had snapped him out of his apathy. He straightened his battered hat and went out in the street. Even if the world turned upside down, he had to save that tormented boy from his cruel father.

6

REB MENAKHEM-MENDL SEGAL BROUGHT his friend good tidings before morning prayers in Reb Shaulke's beth medresh. But Tsemakh's face still glowered darkly as if all the shadows of Vova Barbitoler's apartment had stuck to him.

"My wife has agreed," Reb Menakhem-Mendl told Tsemakh. "She realizes that although I'm not a very good businessman, an inaptitude for business doesn't mean an inaptitude for Torah. I will certainly be able to teach students. We decided that after I leave she'll sell out the remaining stock and close the shop. With a child to take care of, she can't run the store without help. My wages will support them until, with God's help, I set up an apartment and bring them to Valkenik."

After the Morning Service Tsemakh sat in a corner with Reb Menakhem-Mendl and Chaikl and described the awful experience he had had at Vova's apartment. "We must save the boy!" At which Chaikl added excitedly, "I'll help you," incensed at the tobacco merchant's brutal belt-lashing of Hertzke. Reb Menakhem-Mendl, however, was annoyed that his pupil was becoming a Navaredker activist even before he had spent a term at the yeshiva. And the idea of taking Hertzke without his father's permission annoyed him even more.

"The yeshiva isn't a place of refuge for persecuted boys," he whispered.

"Wrong! If the Temple altar and the towns where the Levites lived were ordained as places of refuge for the persecuted, then the yeshiva too can be such a haven, especially a yeshiva where Musar is taught," Tsemakh answered quickly. But he realized that a quarrel would be a bad beginning for two principals, two rosh yeshivas who would be directing one yeshiva. So he added mildly, "I'll take the entire responsibility upon myself."

Reb Menakhem-Mendl was a quiet man, but he was quietly stubborn, too. He tapped his blond little beard and the flaring nostrils of his short nose and answered with a grieved smile, "I don't want to evade the responsibility; I just wanted to tell you how I view the situation. But I still haven't changed my mind." Reb Menakhem-Mendl folded his tallis and tefillin into his bag and went to the door. Chaikl, following him with his glance, thought: He slipped out of the beth medresh as modestly as a timid little boy and left behind a pious silence.

But Tsemakh didn't let Chaikl daydream for long. "Vilner, wake up! It's time to do God's work. Go find Hertzke Barbitoler and tell him that I agree to his leaving without his father's knowledge. Today is Tuesday. I want him to pack his clothes into his schoolbag no later than tomorrow night, and, instead of going to the Yavneh Cheder on Thursday morning, he is to come see me at the inn. I'll take him to the Valkenik wagoners who cart merchandise to and from town, and toward evening he'll leave with them. The rest of us will take the train Friday morning. We'll arrive in Valkenik before sundown, just after Hertzke."

"What's going to happen when his father finds out?" Chaikl asked.

"He'll probably come to Valkenik to take him back, but we won't let Vova have him," the rosh yeshiva answered and accompanied Chaikl to the door. "Go, and good luck."

That same Tuesday evening Tsemakh Atlas told Melechke to get ready for the Friday journey. On Wednesday Melechke's mother and sisters were despondent. If a customer in their fruit store tried to bargain, the saleswomen yelled at him, "Our Melechke is leaving us for the entire winter to study Torah and we won't see him until Passover, and you're standing here bargaining with us over a kilo of apples." Just then they saw the tobacco merchant who had given Melechke his ritual fringes. Zelda told Vova about her joy and sorrow: "The Valkenik rabbi is rushing us as though with a whip. My little boy has to leave Friday morning. But how can you let a little child like that go off into the wind? He's still a tot, and the snows in the villages are as high as a man's head. He might even freeze there, God forbid."

"Give him warm clothes and he won't freeze. Since your little boy wants to go to study, you ought to be very happy," Vova Barbitoler grumbled and waddled away on his crooked legs.

At first he was glad to be getting rid of Reb Tsemakh, but then he became apprehensive. That wild Jew didn't look like the sort who would easily abandon his plans. So why had he abandoned his plan to take Hertzke? The tobacco merchant roamed around the little streets in a daze, only half-hearing his customers' remarks as he delivered their orders to them. In the evening, disgusted with himself, he dragged himself home with a chill, sober sadness in his heart; he felt as if his shoes were full of autumn mud. During supper he became aware of the empty chairs his elder son and daughter had used. Hertzke breathed with difficulty, as if his father's blows had damaged his lungs. The red freckles on his pale skin and sunken cheeks made him look ill. Vova was killing his wife and son with his silence, and Mindl felt as if she were sinking into icy, torpid waters. She bustled about her husband, ready to serve him whenever he wished, but he disregarded her. He slurped the soup, chewed the meat, licked his mouth at the fruit compote, and gazed at Hertzke from under his somber brows. Although Hertzke was sitting quietly, hunched over and eyes lowered, his father wanted to grab him and pummel him till his stubbornness broke.

After supper Vova smoked a cigar. The blue smoke gathered in his tangled beard, but, unlike a mist that seeps through cracks and holes, it couldn't escape his hairy face. Mindl cleared the empty plates from the table and went to the kitchen to wash the dishes.

"The Valkenik yeshiva principal is about to leave, and he's taking Chaikl and Melechke the tinsmith's son," Vova announced suddenly. From Hertzke's shudder he realized that his bloody bastard was already aware of this. The father didn't say another word to his son, but began humming a tune, as he usually did when a murderous rage came over him.

Hertzke had always slept in the room with his stepbrother, but since the older boy's departure Hertzke slept alone. At midnight he crept out of bed and thought about Chaikl's telling him to pack his winter clothes. But Hertzke figured he could pack his winter things later. First he had to sneak into the kitchen and take out a few sweets from Mindl's cupboard. He took his books out of his schoolbag and stuffed them under the mattress so his father wouldn't discover the next morning that he hadn't gone to school. Then, with the empty bag in his hand, he left the room barefoot, wearing only his nightshirt. He stopped in the dining room and put his ear to the closed bedroom door. His father usually snored, but now he didn't hear a sound. Hertzke suspected nothing and slipped into the kitchen. Pale blue moonlight streamed in from the window. It illuminated the stove, the threshold, a corner door, and the white cabinets that had been built into the wall near the ceiling.

He clambered up on a chair swiftly and quietly, stood on tiptoe, and opened one of the cabinet doors. Not tall enough to see inside, he groped his way blindly, hands outstretched, until he pulled out a flat, wide cardboard box filled with lump sugar. Hertzke removed the whole top layer of sugar pieces and replaced the box. Then he climbed down from the chair, placed the sugar in his schoolbag, and popped one piece in his mouth. While sucking greedily—and careful not to gnaw—he looked up at the other wide cabinet that stretched across part of the wall. A table was right beneath it, seemingly prepared for him so that he wouldn't need the chair. The cabinet doors, however, were tightly closed. When he opened them, they squeaked so loudly he actually felt a pain, as though a scab had been torn off a wound. But after opening the doors he found a treasure of large and small jars filled with preserves. He took down a quart jar, tore off the linen cover, and plucked out a few sugared cherries. They were already somewhat sour with age, but Hertzke liked them. In the meantime he left the jar on the middle shelf and looked up into the topmost shelf.

None of Hertzke's friends were as nimble as he when it came to jumping over a garden fence and nabbing fruit from trees. Now, nimble and quick as a monkey, first with one hand, then the other, he grabbed hold of the shelf and began to chin himself up. He saw strings of dried apples and pears for use in compotes. By now Hertzke was oblivious to the fear that had been picking at the back of his neck like an iron beak. Elbows pressed into the corners of the shelf and head and shoulders in the cabinet, he tore open a string of dried pears with his fingers. He had planned to take a dozen or so pieces and tie up the rest, but a careless movement of his elbow caused the pears to roll down. Afraid of the noise, he tried to catch the falling fruit—and himself fell down to the table, rolling over and tumbling to the floor. There he remained, not daring to budge, as if this would somehow stop the noise from reaching the other rooms. Then he had the sudden idea of fleeing the apartment in his nightshirt and running to Reb Tsemakh Atlas' inn. In his imagination he was trying to flee from the bare feet that were already shuffling in the dining room. Moments later, his father stood in the kitchen in his long underwear, smoking calmly. His smoking and his silence made Hertzke apathetically calm at once. He realized that his father hadn't been asleep and had heard everything.

Vova bent down to see what he had stepped on and picked up two dried pears. From Hertzke's bag he removed a handful of lumps of sugar. Vova laughed softly and sat down in a chair. Barefoot, beard disheveled, in his long underwear, and bathed with the blue sheen of the incoming light, he looked like a corpse from the cemetery. He didn't put on the light, but smoked calmly as he looked down at Confrada's bastard lying on the floor, twisted like a bagel.

"Why did you have to steal? If you'd asked me, I'd have given you what you wanted and as much as you wanted," Vova sighed.

Hertzke didn't reply. His father was lying, he thought. Vova had always begrudged him sweets with the excuse that it wasn't stinginess, it was just that he couldn't stand seeing in Hertzke his darling mother's character. She too had a sweet tooth. And if his stepmother gave him an occasional apple, pear, or piece of honey cake, she was always careful to do so without Vova's knowledge.

"And you weren't at all afraid of what would happen when I discovered your thievery?" Vova proceeded calmly with his investigation. "Perhaps you weren't afraid because you were getting ready to run away."

Hertzke coolly reckoned that before the beating his father should know the truth so that it would hurt him more. "Yes, I planned to run away," Hertzke answered, "to the Valkenik yeshiva."

"A yeshiva student a thief?" Vova wondered. One might have thought he was addressing not the black smear that was his son lying on the blue-lit floor, but his own shadow. "And the head of the Valkenik yeshiva knew that you wanted to run away? Did he talk you into it?"

Hertzke wanted his father to know that everyone was against

him. "Yes," he said, enjoying his sweet revenge, "he talked me into running away, and even Chaikl talked me into it."

But Vova wouldn't give Hertzke the pleasure of knowing that his response had come as a surprise. Vova began chuckling. "I knew Confrada's bastard would run away. Your mother ran away. Why shouldn't you run away? I also knew that that wild Jew from Valkenik would try to talk you into it and help you." Vova rose from his chair and kicked his son, signaling him to stand.

Hertzke stood but felt no pain in his bruised limbs—until his father's cold hand seized his neck. He shuddered. Frightened, he sniveled, about to cry, but Vova's iron fingers clamped tighter behind his ears. "Shut up! Don't wake Mindl." Hertzke fell silent and let himself be pushed forward. He was waiting for the blows to begin, whereupon he would raise such a clamor that everybody on the courtyard would assemble in the middle of the night. But this time his father didn't lift a finger to him. He led him through the dining room and stopped at a narrow corridor in front of a little windowless pantry. This dark, unheated room contained sacks of potatoes, an overturned table, broken chairs, and, on a shelf, the covered, straw-wrapped Passover dishes.

"I'm going to let you sleep and freeze here as long as I please. Maybe I'll feed you like a thief in jail, or maybe I'll just let you starve. But if you scream, I'll tie your hands and feet and gag you."

Vova pushed Hertzke, barefoot and wearing only his nightshirt, into the little pantry and locked the door with the rusty key in the large lock. Vova returned to his bedroom and lay down, shivering with cold. He didn't know whether Mindl was sleeping and had heard nothing, or had heard everything and was only pretending to be asleep. In any case, now he could have a restful night. He wouldn't let Hertzke out until that wild Jew and his gang left town. He still felt chilly under the warm blanket and thought of his son freezing in that dark room without a pillow or blanket. No matter if he froze there for a night. People like him survived everything.

7

THURSDAY MORNING CHAIKL sat in Tsemakh Atlas' room at
the inn, where both awaited Hertzke Barbitoler. Tsemakh ate
slowly, recited the Grace After Meals slowly, perused a sacred
text, and chatted for a while with his pupil. Then he became
anxious and said, "We have to find the tobacco merchant's son. If
he's not at the Yavneh Cheder, we'll have to look for him at home
when his father's not there."

Chaikl didn't display any great desire or courage for the new
mission, and Tsemakh pointed a long index finger at him.

"A man has to plan ahead, to avoid feeling guilty later because he
could have saved a friend but left him stranded in his anguish."

Chaikl went to the Yavneh Cheder. During the recess the boys
told him that Hertzke Barbitoler had not been in class. But Chaikl
was afraid to go up to Hertzke's apartment lest he meet the old bear
there. He felt hungry and returned home.

Vella was in her fruit store, gloomily pensive at her son's
departure the following day, when suddenly Chaikl burst in with a
cry like a wholesaler claiming a debt: "Mama, I'm hungry!"

Her smile accented Vella's high, angular cheekbones. "And
whom will you ask for food in Valkenik?" Then she turned
melancholy again and began lecturing her son. "Why are you
running around the day before you leave and not sitting with your
father? Strangers have more respect for him than you. Just now the
tobacco merchant came to see your father and invited him to the
tavern for a drink. And he assured me that he was going to bring
my husband back sober. Reb Vova was in such a festive mood
today, he even wished me *mazel tov* on your going to the yeshiva."

Chaikl immediately thought that the best time to dash into
Vova's house to get news of Hertzke was while Vova Barbitoler

was at the tavern. From Vova's wife he had nothing to fear—Mindl
was a good-natured soul.

"Where are you running to?" Vella shouted after her son. "Don't
you want to eat?" But Chaikl was already well on his way to
Rudnitsky Street. Vova's door wasn't locked and no one was in the
outer room. Chaikl heard a scream and dashed in.

"Let me out! Let me out!" Hertzke pounded his fists on the
locked door.

Mindl stood by the pantry, trying to calm him down. "Your
father said he'll let you out when the rosh yeshiva leaves town.
Meanwhile, eat the food he's given you."

At this Hertzke intensified his pounding on the door and yelled,
"I won't eat. I'd rather starve. You let me out. I want to go to the
yeshiva."

"Don't yell so loud," Mindl begged him. "I can't let you out. Your
father has the key."

Chaikl, astonished and frightened, stood behind Mindl. She
wasn't aware of his presence until he shyly touched her elbow, like
a little boy, as if she were his mother. Mindl turned, and at seeing
Vella's son her mouth dropped open in surprise.

Chaikl went up to the pantry door and called to Hertzke, "It's
me! Chaikl! Why did your father lock you up?"

"Chaikl!" Hertzke yelled happily and then burst into tears.
"Break the door down. Go tell the rabbi to get me out of here. My
father locked me up because he doesn't want me to go. But I don't
want to stay here. I hate him."

"His father caught him stealing food from the cupboard last
night," Mindl whispered to Chaikl out of the captive's earshot. "Go
away, son, before my husband comes. He'll do you harm, and he
won't spare me either for forgetting to lock the front door."

Mindl sobbed as if suffering had made her so weak that she no
longer had the strength to cry. Her words cut Chaikl to the quick
and he immediately slipped out of the apartment. Once outside, he
ran without a stop until he reached Reb Tsemakh's inn, where he
told him everything in one breath. The news that Hertzke had
wanted to steal from his father upset Tsemakh. But he soon shook
himself as though to get rid of all his doubts and resolutely put on
his coat.

"You say he's at the tavern now with your father? Show me the way there and I'll demand the key to the pantry room. It's even better that he's at the tavern now. There are probably other Jews there, too. . . . Let's hurry before he has a chance to leave."

Chaikl could hardly keep up with Tsemakh, who strode along swiftly, saying, "No wonder Hertzke wanted to steal from his father. It wouldn't surprise me if he wanted to revenge himself upon his father in a worse way."

They stopped at a corner. Chaikl pointed out the tavern in the distance and asked, "Should I come along?"

Tsemakh caught his breath from the quick pace and said, "You'll be no help to me at the tavern. It'll be better if your father, who is there now with Vova, doesn't know of your role in this."

Tsemakh turned abruptly and walked up Butchers Street.

After three in the afternoon the big tavern gradually filled up. It was still light outside, but inside the lamps burned darkly and murkily, wrapped in knots of steam. Dodya the innkeeper, without a jacket and with sleeves rolled up, carried glasses and bottles of beer between the fingers of his right hand. His outstretched left hand confidently balanced platters filled with jellied calves' feet, marinated herring, chopped liver, and sweet-and-sour fish. Dodya's head, with its stiff, closely cropped gray hair, shook slightly, but his neck and cheeks still gleamed with good health. He served the customers and joined all their conversations.

At two tables pushed together sat a group who made their living by attending public pawnshop auctions. Brothers and cousins all, they resembled one another: tall, sturdy men with thinning hair cleverly combed to conceal the bald spots. They were dandies who wore trousers with razor-sharp creases and jackets with narrow lapels, broad in the shoulders and fitted in the waist. Their dark brown shoes had hand-stitched vamps. They smoked thin cigarettes and drank foamy mugs of beer; and their mouths, too, foamed with arrogant remarks about their bloody enemies, competitors in the auction field. But Dodya the innkeeper wanted to incite them even more.

"Well, what's new, fellas? How's business, fellas? You're six feet under, huh? The jig is up and the battle's over, huh? Wild beasts are after you, lions and leopards! They're working with brass knuckles, pistols, and knives. For them to shove a knife into you and wipe it clean is like spitting for you guys. Just watch yourselves, fellas, because before you bat an eye you'll end up stretched out in the morgue."

"You jailbird, whose leg are you pulling? Give us five," one of the youths said, asking the innkeeper to shake his hand. Dodya did, and their eyes flashed as at a card game as they swore, "Our competitors will be six feet under, and only we'll be left to go to all the public auctions."

At the other tables sat wagoners whose wide carts delivered sets of furniture and trainloads of flour. They wore fur coats, shirts, stiff aprons, knee-high boots, leather-brimmed hats, and trousers with knee patches and leather inner flanks. Their unshaven, weatherbeaten faces, full of warts, scars, and pimples, were broad and hard as chiseled stones, and their foreheads and brows as close as beams. Their smoking eyes seethed with whisky, with piercing anger, with good-natured mockery. One carter, his head thrown back and his legs outspread, was beating his chest and shouting to a pal, "You don't understand me. May I drop dead if you understand me!"

His friend laughed in his face. "There's nothing to understand here. You're just a big bag of wind!"

Another carter held his pal by the lapels and shook him. "I knocked off three water glasses of whisky. May they take three glasses of blood from me if I didn't knock off three glasses! Don't you believe me?"

His friend let himself be shaken as he nodded drunkenly and foolishly. "I believe you. Why shouldn't I believe you?"

The customers slapped the bottoms of bottles with their broad palms and sent the corks flying. They drank whisky from large glasses. "*L'chayim!* Here's to good health! Bottoms up!" Then they banged the empty water glasses down on the table, grimaced, and sniffed at rye bread to drive away the bitter aftertaste, the burning, the nausea.

In a corner sat Reb Shlomo-Motte the Hebrew teacher and the tobacco merchant. Vova Barbitoler had ordered a pint and a snack—cold buckwheat pudding, marinated herring, and dry sugar cookies. Right after his first tumbler he began talking about Confrada. "She ruined my life. Because of the scandals I had on account of her, my first wife's older son grew up to be an embittered man, a grumbler who hardly says a word. Because he hates me, he doesn't even go to shul on Yom Kippur. My first wife's daughter hasn't married either—she was ashamed to bring prospective grooms into the house. And because of Confrada I make my longsuffering, good-natured, quiet Mindl miserable. Mindl is a saint. I know it well. Nobody has to tell me that. But nevertheless I'm still crazy for that bitch, that whore with the beautiful, impudent face. I want to put her out of my mind but I can't. I want to pluck her out of my heart and I don't know how. But you, Reb Shlomo-Motte, you're an intelligent man, a learned Jew. You've also had a hard life. Maybe you can advise me how to get rid of that piece of corruption."

The teacher listened and smiled sadly under his mustache. He was being asked to give advice; he was considered a smart man. But with all his wisdom he had accomplished nothing in his life. Reb Shlomo-Motte broke off a piece of a cooky, chewed, and thought: If the tobacco merchant is still in a dither over that good-looking woman with the impudent face, he really shouldn't have married a woman he didn't like.

"What you should do, Reb Vova, is to send your wife in Argentina a divorce. Then you'd be able to hold your head up like everybody else."

"You too? Now you sound like the Vilna rabbis and the congregants of Reb Shaulke's beth medresh." The tobacco merchant poured himself another glass. His hand shook and he spilled liquor on his beard. "You expect me to roam around like a frozen dog with its guts hanging out and send her a divorce so as to free her of the sin of adultery hanging over her? I didn't expect such an answer from you, Reb Shlomo-Motte! You too have fought fanatics all your life, and to this very day the congregants needle you for being a maskil."

The teacher responded calmly, "My quarrel concerned another trend in Judaism. I had another path in life, but I must admit that my time is gone. Reb Vova, you too have to understand that times change and a man along in years has to look at events from another perspective. As you yourself say, that woman in Argentina has a frivolous character and doesn't have a strong imagination. That is, she's a woman who can't imagine the outcome of her thoughtless deeds. People generally aren't so bad, but occasionally they do bad deeds because they don't consider the results of their talk and actions. Thus Confrada, too, married on an impulse and only later realized it wasn't a good match. From afar she couldn't imagine how much suffering she caused her abandoned husband, because by nature that sort of person doesn't think much. But she has remained a friend, and surely doesn't want you to suffer on account of her. So if you won't think of her as the worst shrew and still consider her your friend, then it won't be so terribly difficult for you to send her a divorce and also divorce her in your heart."

"A friend, you say? She's still my friend?" Vova Barbitoler's forehead broke out in thick drops of perspiration, and the capillaries in his yellowish, bloodshot eyes began to swell. "Now I see, Reb Shlomo-Motte, that you're a clever man indeed. You never saw her and yet you know her character well. That's the way those gangster brothers of hers spoke to me when they came demanding a divorce in her name. 'What do you want of her?' they pleaded. 'She writes us that she's still your friend. Your very best friend.' And that's just it, the fact that she's still a friend—that's what's driving me to the grave. That tells me she doesn't even feel guilty about marrying a wretched man, a widower with two orphans, and then chucking him and leaving him with a third child on his hands. If she'd remained an enemy, I could think Confrada hated me because her conscience bothers her that she's broken my life. But that piece of corruption shrugs her shoulders and laughs in amazement, like during those days when she was still with me. 'Ha, ha, ha,' she laughs. 'What does he want from me? Ha, ha, ha,' she bares her teeth. 'After all, I'm his friend.'"

Vova Barbitoler, his red, blotchy face angry and perspiring, imitated Confrada's laugh, revealing a mouthful of crooked yellow teeth. Reb Shlomo-Motte listened gloomily. Instead of meeting old friends and talking about old times, instead of arguing about the meaning of a word in the Bible or about some grammatical point, he was sitting in a smoke-filled tavern with a monomaniac, a man beset by a dybbuk. The tobacco merchant thinks no one has greater troubles than he. He can't even imagine that there are unseen troubles that cannot be yelled and raged away. The teacher wanted to go back home to his bed, but he pitied Vova and tried once more to reason with him.

"Confrada is living quietly in Argentina with her husband and children without your divorce—while you're torturing yourself to death and taking revenge upon yourself."

"No, I'm taking revenge upon her and her bastard. That little bastard bares his teeth just like his mother. 'Ha, ha, ha,' he laughs, but he's in my hands." In a festive mood, as if at a celebration, Vova poured himself another tumbler. "Will you have another glass? No? I know you're not allowed to because of your kidneys. *L'chayim,* Reb Shlomo-Motte, *l'chayim.* I still haven't told you everything. Listen, Confrada's brothers told me recently that she says if I send her a divorce she'll take Hertzke to Argentina. Get it? Now that sly slut is suddenly yearning for her little baby. But she doesn't want me to know this. She realizes that that's just what I'm waiting for—for her to burst like I'm bursting. So she pretends she's doing me a favor by taking back her fifteen-year-old son. Her children from her Argentinian husband are bastards, bastards until the end of time. Even God can't help to unbastardize them, and with this alone I've already had the pleasure of my revenge. But I've had an even bigger revenge. That whore is yearning for her little bastard. She's longing for him, she's dying to see him—but I won't send him. That wild Jew who looks like the Angel of Death, that rosh yeshiva, and your Chaikl have talked Hertzke into running away to Valkenik. But I sensed this and watched him until I caught him trying to steal from me last night. Now he's lying there locked up in a little room like a dog and here's the key." Vova Barbitoler took the big rusty key out of his pocket and placed it on the table as a witness. "What do you say now, Reb Shlomo-Motte? Have I had my revenge or not?"

"Jews don't do such things. You didn't handle the affair intelligently or decently." Reb Shlomo-Motte stood up quickly and began looking for his cane, which had slipped to the floor.

"There he is!" Vova shouted involuntarily, at seeing Tsemakh Atlas, who was standing by the bar talking to the innkeeper. A couple of the patrons looked on with curiosity. The newcomer's rabbinic garb indicated that he wasn't a habitué of taverns.

Tsemakh strode toward the tobacco merchant. "Cutthroat! Hand over the key to the room where you locked up your son."

There was a sudden silence. Everyone turned his head. For a second, Vova Barbitoler stood immobile. Suddenly he grabbed the rusty key from the table. "Here, you scurvy Jew, here's the key!"

he said. Then he suddenly raised his fists over Tsemakh's head, but Reb Shlomo-Motte was quick enough to seize his arm. At the same instant Tsemakh snatched the key from Vova with one hand and pushed him forcefully to the floor with the other. Spotting Reb Shlomo-Motte's ivory-headed cane, Vova seized it and sprang back up. A couple of youths intervened and shoved him back again.

"Were you going to hit a rabbi?"

Tsemakh held the key high and shouted to the crowd, "The tobacco merchant is a murderer! Because he's angry at his wife who ran away from him, he's torturing her son. Last night he locked the boy, clad only in a nightshirt, in a cold pantry room just because he wants to go study in a yeshiva."

Dodya the innkeeper spat. "Damn him! Such an old man and he's still howling over a runaway female."

One of the men laughed loudly. "I know Confrada's brothers, and I knew her too. Once upon a time she was really some gal, but now she's probably an old hunk of wrinkled shoe leather. She's no bargain any more."

A third member of the group suddenly assumed a pious demeanor, as if he were at the funeral of a close friend, and shouted at the tobacco merchant, "You ought to kiss the rabbi's hands for wanting to teach your scamp some Torah."

The auction-goers hooted and jeered: "That old heathen! Beat him to a pulp!"

Frightened and crestfallen because everyone was against him, Vova pushed his way to Tsemakh Atlas and cried, his voice rattling, "Give me back the key. He's my son. What do you want of me?"

"Neighbors, don't let him out of here until I free the lad. There's no greater mitzva than saving a boy from such a father," Tsemakh shouted and left the tavern.

Vova lunged forward to run after him, but the youths thrust him back as though playing with a ball. "Easy now. What's the rush?"

Vova fell back on a chair, buried his face in his hands, and began whimpering, "My son, my son!"

Silence reigned in the tavern. The patrons scratched their necks, sorry that they had interfered. Reb Shlomo-Motte, downcast and exhausted, bent over the tobacco merchant and patted his back, attempting to bring him back to reality. "Hertzke's not going to

Argentina," he consoled him. "He's only going to Valkenik, a small town near Vilna."

Vova lifted his tear-stained face. "Not to Argentina, you say, not to her?"

Reb Shlomo-Motte's milk-white beard trembled. "Not to her, not to her," he repeated, and he too wept out of pity for the tobacco merchant. Without the hope of revenge, the teacher mused, Vova was weaker than a child. But addressing his rational faculty was a waste of time—because above all Vova was afraid of ridding himself of his torments.

8

"WHAT DO YOU WANT?" Mindl kept asking Tsemakh from behind the locked door.

To which Tsemakh responded again and again, "Your husband gave me the key to free Hertzke."

Mindl finally opened the door and saw the key in his hand. Reassured now, she led the way to the locked room. Since Vova had given his son some clothes before leaving the house, Hertzke didn't spring out of the dark pantry naked and frozen, as Tsemakh had expected him to. He was only disheveled and bleary-eyed.

"Collect your things and come," Tsemakh said quickly, then turned to Mindl. "Your husband has given Hertzke permission to go to the yeshiva."

"If you say he's given his permission, I have faith in you that this won't bring calamity down on me," Mindl answered submissively and left with Hertzke to help him pack.

Tsemakh went into the main room and sat down at the table where he had recently spoken with Vova. He was pale now and his thoughts were whirling. He sensed a cramp in his knees and elbows. He stretched his legs, dropped his hands, and sat there listlessly. Mindl's trust paralyzed him. For the sake of taking the boy away, did he have the right to bring misfortune down upon a kindhearted, downtrodden woman?

Mindl and Hertzke came into the room, the latter carrying a packed valise. "Where's my husband?" Mindl asked anxiously. The rabbi's appearance made her suspect that something was fishy. Tsemakh attempted to move his dangling hands and to bend his petrified legs. Again he felt the painful cramp in his knees and elbows, as though his ailing conscience were squatting there.

"I lied to you. Your husband didn't give me the key. I took it from him by force."

The stepmother fell upon Hertzke's neck. "Woe is me! I'm ruined. Your father will kill me." Hertzke tore himself out of her grip and pulled Tsemakh Atlas by the sleeves. "Let's go, rabbi! Let's go! My father's going to come soon and lock me in the pantry again."

Mindl pleaded with Hertzke, wringing her hands, "Son, I've always protected and defended you. Why do you have to bring such a calamity down on me?"

Tsemakh listened mutely, as if it were a judgment on him. He would have liked to run to the farthest corner of the world, but he knew he dared not flee the misfortune that he himself had brought on. Hertzke stamped his feet and yelled, "I don't want to stay here. I hate my father. I hate him. I hate him!"

"I know you hate me," said Vova Barbitoler at the doorway. Hertzke was dumbstruck, and Mindl's whole body trembled.

"Vova, it's not my fault! At first the rabbi told me that you gave him the key." She put her hands on her heart. "He didn't tell me the truth until just a couple of minutes ago."

"Don't be scared, Mindl. I know it's not your fault." Vova was panting. He spoke with difficulty. "Go look for a bigger suitcase to pack all of Hertzke's things. All of them. And give him a box of lump sugar as well. And a jar of preserves and the dried fruit. Everything he wanted to steal last night. For if he's going, then let him go in style. The Jews of that town don't have to know that Hertzke hates his father and that he wanted to run away. Go and do what I tell you to," Vova yelled at his wife, who couldn't believe her ears. Mindl and Hertzke went into the inner rooms.

"Welcome." Vova Barbitoler turned to Tsemakh with outspread hands, as though greeting an important guest, but his face was contorted with hate and mockery. "You got scared, scared at the last minute, huh? Afraid that I might run after you to Valkenik and stir up the local Jews against you?" He wiped the perspiration from his forehead and sat down at the table facing Tsemakh Atlas. "And is it possible that at the last minute you realized you were committing a theft?"

Tsemakh was amazed that the tobacco merchant didn't assault him, and he couldn't believe that the brute would let his son go. Perhaps he had planned something and meanwhile was enjoying his wicked scheme.

Tsemakh looked Vova right in the eye. Not a muscle moved on Tsemakh's face as he said, "I'm not frightened and I haven't changed my mind. To save a boy from a father like you, I'm ready to sacrifice myself. But I was afraid you might vent your anger toward the boy on your wife, just as you constantly took revenge on him because his mother ran away."

"And you think she was right in running away?" Vova asked.

"I think that a woman who abandons a baby is inhuman, but you must not take revenge upon her son," Tsemakh answered, unaware how important it was to Vova that Tsemakh agree with him on the main issue that Confrada should not have fled.

"And what would you say if you knew that she wanted to take Hertzke? Do you think she has more right to him than I do?"

"I would strongly oppose a mother having a son in whom she has shown no interest all along, especially if she bore children with another man while still a married woman."

"Well, for your information, his mother wants to take him back. Her brothers who live here came to talk to me in her name. That's why I'm afraid to let him go, for fear his uncles will kidnap him."

"I hope you understand that I have no intention of taking your son with me to the yeshiva only to send him off to Argentina, a land where they keep neither the Sabbath nor the laws of kashrut." Tsemakh breathed easier. He saw that the tobacco merchant was indeed ready to submit and that everything would end peacefully. "His uncles can see him more frequently and persuade him more easily if he stays here in Vilna than if he's in Valkenik. And besides, I promise you I'll be on guard that his mother's family has no contact with him, and if something happens, I'll notify you immediately."

"He'd be better off under my care, but I have no choice. You butted into my life and talked him into running away, so now he shouts it out loud that he hates me." Vova took his wallet out of his pocket. "Here are fifty zlotys for his expenses until he's set up with a room and a place to eat and everything else. You can keep him as long as you like and do with him what you want. If he grows up to be a scholar, it'll be a miracle; and if he stays a thief, that's not my fault either. He has his mother's blood, her character, her gestures. He also resembles his uncles, those gangsters. So remember your promise to protect him from his mother's brothers."

Hertzke came in carrying a square, metal-banded wicker basket with a lock. Mindl held a linen bag packed with sweets taken from the cabinets.

Vova turned his back on his son and spoke to the wall. "Go! You don't say good-bye to a father you hate."

Tsemakh gathered that Vova Barbitoler didn't wish to bid him farewell either. He took the heavy basket from Hertzke's hand, said good night, and left the apartment first. Hertzke grabbed the bag of sweets from Mindl's hand and ran after the rabbi. Vova turned his head quickly and managed to see his son bare his teeth at him before he ran out.

Mindl stood with outstretched hands. She wanted to run after her ward, to kiss him and wish him well, but she was afraid of her husband. Vova burst into laughter.

"What a bastard! Fine, so he hates me! But you always stood up for him and tried to stop me from hitting him, and he didn't even say good night to you."

"Vova, it's not my fault." Mindl began trembling again, afraid that her husband might pour out his entire bitterness on her.

But Vova calmed her as he had before. "I know it's not your fault. I know you're a good soul, a quiet dove. I know it." Vova remained sitting, his head sunk to his chest. Oh, how I wish Mindl weren't so good and quiet, he said to himself. How I wish she were a little bit like that slut and could torment me and laugh at me and cry crocodile tears and bring me to the point where I'd be scared she'd run away, too. Then I'd be able to forget that other one, for the new troubles would drive away the old.

Vova yearned to doze off and sleep for a long time. Confrada's brothers, he continued thinking, will probably write to her that Hertzke went off to a yeshiva, and the shock will well-nigh kill her. She's not that stupid. She understands that a son who is a Torah scholar will be ashamed of her and won't want to know her. That's when I'll *really* have the sweetest revenge. . . .

He pried his eyes open and looked at Mindl. She was standing over him with folded hands, nodding as though she had heard his thoughts.

"The house is empty. First the older children went away and now the youngest one. Desolation everywhere." Vova moved his tongue with great difficulty, and his head slowly sank down to his chest.

9

THAT SAME NIGHT VELLA the fruit peddler had a discussion with her husband. Reb Shlomo-Motte had returned home, sick and agitated. He described the scene at the tavern and said, "Reb Tsemakh Atlas is a wild man—I've never seen the like of him. Chaikl won't learn either Torah or good behavior from him."

Vella was so angry at Vova for locking his son half-naked in a cold dark room that she angrily replied to her husband, "I consider the rabbi a saint and a hero. I have nothing against Chaikl for talking Hertzke into running away to the yeshiva."

Early Friday morning Vella rose feeling heavy-hearted because of the words she'd had with her husband on the eve of their son's departure. Then Mindl came in and said, "My Vova finally agreed to let Hertzke go, so I came to say good-bye to your son and to ask him to take care of Hertzke like a brother. Vova is all broken up.

He's not going to the train station and he won't let me go either."
Mindl burst into tears and Vella wept with her. Both women stood
in the hall in the gray dawn, each gazing into the other's tear-filled
eyes, looking like two lonely birds left alone on a late autumn
meadow after all the other birds have flown away.

Chaikl wondered why his father had put on his sunglasses in the
half-dark room. When he said good-bye, Chaikl pressed his lips to
his father's cheek and felt it wet with tears. His father had donned
the glasses to conceal them, but they rolled from under the glasses
onto his white beard. Vella stood nearby wearing her black
Sabbath shawl, prepared to accompany her son. Her face glowed
with the festive gloom of the Eve of Yom Kippur when she said
good-bye to her husband before he went to the beth medresh.

Melechke's entire family accompanied him to the station. His
mother and sisters wore high galoshes over felt boots, aprons
around their hips, and woolen kerchiefs on their heads, as though it
were already midwinter. Melechke's father was in the train order-
ing the three yeshiva lads around, telling them how to set up the
baggage on the shelves under the seats.

Kasrielke had been drinking on an empty stomach. He shouted
to Tsemakh Atlas, "I still haven't changed my mind! If the father is
a tinsmith, the son should be a tinsmith too. But my brood here
wants Melechke to grow up to be a rabbi, a gaon, and a saint."
Then Kasrielke shouted to Reb Menakhem-Mendl, "You're lucky!
You're leaving your woman behind and setting out for the big wide
world. I wish I could leave my brood and make my way out into
the great big world."

Reb Menakhem-Mendl smiled sadly. His wife hadn't been able
to come to the train station to bid him farewell because she had no
one to take care of the baby.

The locomotive whistled and the car began to move. The
tinsmith rushed to the doorway as nimbly as he climbed onto a
roof. All three students pressed themselves to the window.

Hertzke scrutinized the conductor. He had a large mustache and
a protruding paunch, and he wore a uniform with shiny buttons.
After a wide-mouthed, lazy yawn, he checked the time on his
round, big-bellied pocket watch. Melechke's mother and sisters
waved their hands, faces beaming with joy and wet with tears.

Kasrielke ran along the entire length of the platform yelling, "Melechke, be a good boy! Don't be a bench warmer with piles." But his remarks weren't heard through the thick glass and the clatter of the wheels. Chaikl didn't take his eyes off his mother. She stood with hands lowered, and the edges of her black Sabbath shawl fluttered in the wind.

Melechke wore a little cap with warm earflaps and a pair of knitted woolen gloves attached to a string drawn through his sleeves. "Look at that baby," Hertzke ridiculed the eleven-year-old. "His mother still has to pull his gloves through his sleeves so he won't lose them."

Melechke's cheeks became beet-red; his eyes filled with tears. But he kept himself from crying so as not to be called a baby. "My mother gave me a wooden box full of smoked whitefish."

Hertzke laughed at the little show-off and said, "And I have an album with stamps from all the far-off tropical lands. Just wait and I'll show you."

Amazed and envious, Melechke looked at a postmarked stamp with a picture of a bulky, short-legged rhinoceros with a gaping maw and huge incisors. "This stamp is from Africa," Hertzke bragged, "where the black people live. They go around naked, just like people in the bathhouse, and clang cymbals like at a wedding." He displayed another stamp, a deer with long, twisted horns. "If we could use this horn as a shofar on Rosh Hashana," Hertzke said, "the sounds would be heard all over town."

Now it was Melechke's turn to deride him. "You boor! Don't you know that a shofar comes from a ram's horn and not from a deer? About a deer the Talmud says, 'Quick as a deer,' but you don't know that either, you boor. See? I know more Torah than you!"

Hertzke giggled. "What do I care if I don't know Torah!" Then he showed a stamp with an animal that stood up on its hind legs and had an open pouch on its belly to carry its young. Melechke had seen gypsies carrying their little ones on their shoulders. He had also seen a cat carrying its blind, newborn kitten in its mouth. But he had never before seen a creature with pointy ears which held its little one in its pocket.

"A lot you know," Hertzke mocked him and pointed to a stamp with a woman holding a torch in her upraised hand. "It's from

America. Before the ship arrives you pass this stone woman with the fire pot on her head!"

Flustered and red-faced, Melechke asked for a stamp from Ur, the birthplace of Father Abraham.

Vova Barbitoler's son laughed mockingly once again. "You're a fool! Ur is in a Bible story, and I have stamps from real lands." Finally, he displayed a stamp of a little man with sideburns, epaulettes on his shoulders and medals on his chest, standing in the middle of a red wheel.

"It's a general from Argentina, where my mother lives. Soon she's going to come and take me and I'll go to Argentina. So what do you say now? Foo on you!" Hertzke stuck his tongue out at Melechke and replaced the stamp album in his basket.

The two yeshiva teachers sat in a corner, deep in conversation. Longing to have his cheek pinched and to hear words of praise, Melechke approached them and said, "Hertzke has stamps from all over the world, but he doesn't have a stamp from Ur, that boor! And he says the city of Ur is only in a Bible story and isn't a real place. And he also says that he's going to go to his mother in Argentina."

Reb Menakhem-Mendl tugged at his little beard with a worried look, and Tsemakh glared at Hertzke Barbitoler with such fiery eyes that he shuddered. A feel of hatred for Melechke came over Hertzke and he decided to pay him back. He would tell all the boys in Valkenik that besides being a show-off Melechke was also a snitcher, and that his mother, Zelda the tinsmith's wife, and her daughters were nicknamed the Sennacheribs.

Chaikl wasn't in the mood to chatter with the other youngsters and didn't even talk with the principals. He looked out the window and watched as telegraph poles, barren fields, bare trees, a roadside well, and a peasant in a cart all rushed by. But before his eyes he saw his father in the sunglasses he had put on to hide his tears, and the edges of his mother's black Sabbath shawl still fluttering in the air like a big, tired bird flying over the ocean with no place at all to rest.

PART IV

1

VALKENIK'S WOODEN shul, on the hillside facing the synagogue courtyard between the beth medresh and the rabbi's house, overlooked all the squat little houses in town. The shul entryway had side doors as well as a main entrance, wooden turrets at both corners of its western wall, and a round window under the long, narrow roof. The shul itself, with its huge square windows, rose from under another roof. A triangular window sidled out of a third roof, and a fourth little roof soared up like a yarmulke on the head of an old man with a mossy beard and silver eyebrows.

When Chaikl Vilner arrived in the town on Friday afternoon, he entered the shul for the Evening Service and was immediately captivated by its majesty. Large thick pillars supported the ceiling. Worshipers passed finely carved and decorated arches to get to the pulpit. An open circular staircase led up to a balcony that hung overhead. From the ceiling and in all corners hung bronze lamps, silver menorahs, and copper trays that reflected and enhanced the gaslight. All kinds of prayers, warnings, and exhortations, written with gallnut ink in Torah script, were pasted on boards affixed to doors, walls, and pillars. That same Friday evening a Valkenik lad confided to Chaikl Vilner, "You know, there isn't one iron nail in the entire wooden shul and there are parchment amulets hidden in the walls as a charm against a fire in the holy place."

After the Sabbath morning prayers, Chaikl saw the perpetual calendar operated by a concealed clock in the doors of the Holy Ark. The beadle of the shul, an old man with laugh wrinkles around his eyes, showed him a piece of gold-and-silver-embroidered cloth that pictured drums, trumpets, banners, and cannon on low wheels. Amidst all these weapons were two Latin words: "Gloria Patria."

"When Napoleon of France passed through Valkenik on his way to Moscow," the old man told Chaikl, "he was so impressed by this wooden shul built on a hill that he cut off a piece of the luxurious cloth that covered his horse and presented it to the synagogue as a curtain for the Holy Ark."

After that Saturday in mid-Cheshvan, or November, the shul, known as the Cold Shul, was closed for the entire winter. But it imbedded itself in Chaikl's soul and beamed into his mind. A secret legend spun in his imagination, joining the locked shul and the cemetery on the other side of the river. In the height of autumn, the town, only three stations away from Vilna and eight kilometers from the train, looked as though it were forgotten by the world. Because of the poor, muddy roads, village peasants were too lazy to come to the market, and the Valkenik wagoners stopped going to Vilna for merchandise. Chaikl's lively, homely Butchers Street sank in his memory as if under piles of withered pine needles from Valkenik's evergreen forests. The shadow of the old wooden synagogue spread over his face. He stopped laughing out loud, talked little, prayed piously, and studied hard.

Reb Tsemakh Atlas had persuaded the yeshiva supporters in town not to try to get a room and eating days for every student. Instead, the younger pupils would sleep in the wayfarers' guest house, and all the students, young and old alike, would eat at a central kitchen on weekdays. Women promised to collect bread and challas, barley and dairy foods. The butchers agreed to provide meat several times a week. A widow nicknamed Pockmarked Gitl was to be the cook. Townspeople said she hadn't accepted the job for the few zlotys, and certainly not for the sake of the mitzva. Blind in one eye, with her good one Gitl was on the lookout for bridegrooms for her two daughters, Rokhtshe and Leitshe. Pronouncing their names, she stretched the vowels in the Polish fashion to show that they were as dear to her as her good eye.

The widow had her own little house. It had a small foyer with a stove and two other rooms. The three oldest Torah scholars and the more mature, advanced students from nearby small towns ate in the nicer of the two rooms. The advanced students had gentle eyes and wrinkled, scholarly brows; while strolling along the lanes, they tucked their long earlocks behind their ears and their hands into their sleeves behind their backs. The younger students ate in the other room, along with the older, slower students from surrounding Jewish villages. The latter were tanned, thick-lipped, robust youths who wore their hats pulled down over their unruly hair. Their loud, rough voices were as crude as a pair of work boots. Next to these tall, broad-shouldered youngsters, Reb Menakhem-Mendl Segal looked like a kitten beside overgrown mice. Pock-marked Gitl served the older students, and her two daughters attended the younger group.

Rokhtshe, the elder sister, a hefty girl with a round face, had round eyes that were a bit too large and little tuft of black hair above her puffy lips. She always went about with a shy smile, as though she were at her engagement party and the groom's kin were sizing her up with knowing glances. But Leitshe, the younger sister, wasn't at all scared of men. She didn't even hesitate to appear with half-naked arms in the presence of the yeshiva students. Leitshe had a habit of paddling with her hard elbows, throwing back her head with its short-cropped hair, and showing what she could do with her lanky body and sturdy, well-sculpted legs. First she would twist her head and torso to the left, right hand on right hip, then she would shift legs and bend to the right, left hand on left hip. She turned thus without a stop as though dancing a quadrille. Telling her girl friends that she hated dunderheads, with her hard elbows she thrust aside the Valkenik youths who ran after her. From among the Torah scholars there was no one to choose either. Most were still youngsters with the first fuzz on their cheeks. The three oldest students looked like fanatics to her. Terribly bored and longing to tease someone just for the fun of it, Leitshe cast her eye upon the sixteen-year-old Chaikl Vilner.

That ox isn't as gentle and pious as he pretends to be, and he likes girls, the young cook thought, swaying her hips each time Chaikl entered. He looked at her dreamy-eyed, and grunted as if warning her to stay away—which made the game more attractive to her.

Once she stepped on his foot. Chaikl blushed, jumped up, and ran off in the middle of the meal. He stayed away for a day, as though he'd declared a self-imposed fast. Afterwards, he sat in the dining room with such a stern expression that Leitshe was afraid to start anything with him.

Chaikl was always among the last to come to the kitchen. He knew that the village lads were apt to gobble up everything and leave nothing for him, but he was trying to strengthen his faith and not worry about being deprived of a bit of worldly pleasure. One morning after prayers, when all the pupils had gone to eat breakfast, he remained in the beth medresh, next to a window of the eastern wall, gazing out at the closed Cold Shul on the hill opposite. In his imagination he saw the Holy Ark and the carved lions that supported the Torah crown with their paws. Above the Holy Ark, Mount Sinai smoked. Beneath the balcony an eagle fluttered, holding in its claws a lulav and an esrog while the royal crown rested on its head. Chaikl turned and saw fat black crows perching on the low roofs of the little houses. They flew down to the snow, burrowing and searching for food in the refuse, and returned to the roofs. Then Chaikl remembered that he still hadn't eaten breakfast.

Besides bolstering his faith, Chaikl was also attempting to uproot the bad trait of pride. In the kitchen he sat with the younger students, although according to his age and level of learning he could have eaten with the older group. His fellow townsman Melechke Vilner, however, was furious at being placed with the younger students. "I know more Torah than those dummies from Dekshne and Leipun," he complained, picking at a piece of herring with his delicate fingers. Hertzke Barbitoler, sitting next to him, poked Melechke with his elbow and grabbed what he could from the platter. Meanwhile Leitshe the cook came and spread some white cheese on a piece of black bread for Melechke. "Eat, Melechke, eat. Do you want your tea with granulated or lump sugar?" The way Leitshe bent over the little boy, Chaikl couldn't help seeing how her tight blouse stretched across her protruding breasts.

"That teeny-weeny baby has to be spoonfed," Hertzke said, laughing at Melechke, who seethed with anger. Leitshe scolded Hertzke and pampered the rosy-cheeked little boy even more tenderly. In so doing she turned her profile to Chaikl, as if wanting to show off her hips and bulging buttocks. "The Ox," as the cook called Chaikl Vilner behind his back, grew angrier and perspired profusely. He hastily ate a tiny piece of bread, took a few sips of tea, said grace quickly, and stormed out of the kitchen. Most of his portion was left over for the ever ravenous Hertzke Barbitoler.

Chaikl returned to the beth medresh, pushed his prayer stand to the eastern wall, and continued studying. From time to time he gazed out at the locked Cold Shul, and his fever cooled. Suddenly he stopped, terrified. It seemed to him that he was standing on the steps of the shul's anteroom, looking down at the entire sanctuary. He saw that someone had fallen asleep for the winter on a bench along the eastern wall—and the sleeper was he himself. Chaikl anxiously looked about the beth medresh to see if anyone else was aware of his crazy fantasies. His glance fell on the marble slab over the pulpit, inscribed with the biblical verse, "I have set the Lord before me always." Chaikl had once read in a little Kabbalistic tract that concentrating on that biblical verse was a proven charm against sinful thoughts. Wrinkling his brow, he gazed intently at the letters, so that they would enter his mind like the parchment amulets that had been put into the walls of the shul as a charm against fire.

2

THE THREE OLDEST SCHOLARS enhanced the Valkenik yeshiva's reputation. The first was the prodigy Sheeya Lipnishker. His crossed eyes were black and sullen, and he had loose, curly earlocks, and a sparse little beard that seemed pasted on with pitch. Sheeya Lipnishker didn't like the big yeshivas where everyone had to study the same Talmudic tractate and had to attend the rosh yeshiva's lectures. He had no regard either for those hairsplitters who wondered if the hat was on the head or the head beneath the hat. Sheeya had settled in Valkenik a year ago. He burrowed into a corner of the beth medresh and studied an entire Talmudic tractate every week. The town provided him with a room and with Sabbath meals in the home of a prominent congregant. In mid-week, pious women brought food to him at the beth medresh. Lipnishker slurped up the soup straight from the pot and chomped on a piece of black bread. Not once did he remove his eyes from the holy book before him. Having eaten and quickly said grace—he didn't even thank the women—he rushed back with renewed strength to the thicket of the Talmud and its commentaries.

When the town agreed to support the little yeshiva, one of the problems had been what to do with Sheeya Lipnishker. Reb Tsemakh Atlas suggested that the prodigy become part of the yeshiva. He could continue studying on his own in the manner that suited him best, but he might also play a useful role in discussing Torah with the younger pupils. Yet when a youngster approached him with a problem, Lipnishker, enraged at being disturbed, would screw his little finger into the youngster's ear so forcefully the boy's head would shake. "Well, what do you want?" he would mutter angrily. The youngster, who had only wanted to glean some Torah knowledge from the prodigy, would outline his problem. Then Sheeya would cast pages of the Talmud at him, gesturing with his thumb and shouting, "You lunkhead, you nitwit." One couldn't imagine his answering without flaring up. If the questioner attempted to argue with Sheeya, he would grab the boy by the jacket and pull off a button. "You're also one of these hairsplitters who can't give a straight answer?" Seeing that the prodigy was destroying his only suit, the questioner would slip out of his grasp and flee. But Sheeya Lipnishker had been known to give chase among the prayer stands and run around the pulpit until he seized the boy's arm, pinching and tweaking it.

In the kitchen, impatient to be served, Sheeya couldn't sit still. Instead of wearing a shirt with a tie, he wore a little white towel around his neck. He was infested with vermin, which was all the more visible on his snow-white neckerchief. One of the wags joked that all this was alluded to in the Psalms: "There are many bugs without number, living creatures great and small." Whenever he entered and left the kitchen, Sheeya Lipnishker would meet Leitshe and stare at her with his sullen crossed eyes. The young cook would immediately begin swinging her hips and paddling her elbows. She did so out of habit, without intending to make herself attractive to him. She couldn't even understand how a man with dirty hands could be a great scholar. Sheeya Lipnishker disgusted her.

The oldest ben Torah in the yeshiva was Yoel Uzder, a thirty-five-year-old bachelor with a large round face, a low forehead, and eyebrows that grew together. Yoel Uzder had previously studied in Kletzk, where he'd been called "the Sedate Mind." Not a speck of dust or a wrinkle appeared on his clothes. He wore his hat puffed out and round, the brim turned up. Before sitting down to study, he donned a skullcap and carefully held the hat by the brim until he found a secure place where it wouldn't get dusty or crushed. In his room in Kletzk, the housemistress had known that she had to be careful in passing by Yoel Uzder's bed. He himself made the bed, carefully tucking the blanket under to make it absolutely smooth. Before lying down he eyed the bed suspiciously, wondering if anybody had touched the cover. If he thought someone had indeed touched it, he slept poorly that night. With another yeshiva student he shared a subscription to the religious paper published in Warsaw, but Yoel's condition was that he had to read the paper first. If the paper was wrinkled, he had no joy in reading it.

On summer evenings, when the Torah scholars took walks in groups, Uzder strolled along all alone, cane in hand. Head thrown back, he walked with a taut, measured stride, like a soldier on parade. The yeshiva people and passers-by wondered how he could walk so mechanically: he always lifted the cane and threw his elbow out in the same fashion, like a machine or an automated golem. He spoke loudly—but very slowly. When asked a question, his first reply was, "Wait, wait! Don't rush, don't talk so quickly." Hence no one was amazed that "the Sedate Mind" had remained an old bachelor. He had thought and pondered too long. He had in fact been engaged once, but two weeks later returned to the Kletzk yeshiva, declaring that he had broken the engagement because nothing good comes out of haste.

Yoel Uzder was extremely careful not to have any dealings with the younger students. If he saw a group of youngsters during his walk, he stopped and waited for the group to pass by, lest an outsider assume he was one of those just beginning to study independently. Only once, after breaking his engagement, did he pour out his bitter heart to a younger lad from his home town. "My fiancée was a bit deaf," he said. "It's true, they warned me about this even before writing the engagement contract. But since she heard what I said to her, I thought to myself: Never mind what people say. But after the engagement ceremony I noticed that the girl heard me while I was close to her because of my habit of talking loud. From far off she didn't even hear me when I yelled. And that's why I broke the engagement."

Afterwards Yoel greatly regretted that he had confided in the boy from his home town. The latter blabbed it to others, and the yeshiva lads began making fun of him.

"What's all the fuss about, Reb Yoel? So what if the bride's a bit deaf? We've heard of perfectly righteous men who looked for a deaf-mute wife so that she wouldn't be able to hear or speak slander." Yoel Uzder decided then and there to leave Kletzk. He wanted to escape all the ridicule.

But there was another reason too. As a youth, Yoel had been left an orphan and raised in a filthy orphanage, dressed in rags. So he grew up with a desire for a clean bed and neat clothes and with a lust for money. He skimped on himself and put away a fortune. The yeshiva people at Kletzk always approached the Uzder for loans. They knew that a down-slanting frown indicated refusal; an up-slant, however, implied consent. At first his brows would always bunch downward, but after a while they would move up. Still, he constantly feared he wouldn't be paid back. This was the other reason for his departing the Kletzk yeshiva—henceforth he wouldn't have to lend money any more. He wasn't known in Valkenik, and he was glad that no one knew about his fortune.

But Yoel himself broke the news, anyway. He knew by heart all the Talmudic sayings on money and loved to quote proverbs about its importance. While so doing he would rub his thumb and forefinger as though counting coins. The first to discover that Yoel Uzder had a bundle was Yosef Varshever.

In the yeshivas of Mir and Radun there were students from Hasidic Poland, children of rich fathers who wanted their sons to be scholars in the Lithuanian manner. These Hasidic youths wore shiny boots and brand new gaberdines made of the choicest Polish cloth. Silk belts girded their waists, and little caps were perched on their heads. Among the poor, short-jacketed Lithuanian students the Polish youths stood out with their fine garb, imposing appearance, and Hasidic fervor. But there was nothing Polish about Yosef Varshever's clothes, demeanor, or manner of speaking. Thin and rather short, he had white hands, a pale, delicate face, a round chin, and a small, chiseled mouth. He had light gray eyes, long lashes, and thin brows. He wore pince-nez half-glasses but would frequently remove them. The spring of the pince-nez had notched two V-shaped little blue veins on the bridge of his nose, and this gave him an even more delicate and fragile appearance.

Yosef Varshever had a light, dainty stride, which made him look as if he were walking on water. His pressed, well-tailored suit looked as if it had just come from the shop. Even during the muddy season he wore shiny black lacquered galoshes lined with red felt. He couldn't stand overcoats lined with heavy cotton ticking; he always wore a light coat that had a fake handkerchief pocket and a narrow velvet collar. Coming in from the street he would shiver slightly, huddle into his coat, and gently rub his jaw on the raised velvet collar. He was smoothly shaven—he didn't miss a hair. In the beth medresh he scrupulously washed his delicate white hands in the water basin, then dried them with a thin, transparent silk handkerchief instead of the sour communal towel. Studying Talmud by himself, he would chant softly and sweetly, one leg crossed over the other. Occasionally he would give a little cough, lift his soft cap, and run his fingers through his dark blond hair, as if fearing it might fall out because of his scholarly zeal.

It was known that the Varshever had already attended all the great yeshivas. He spent one semester at one school and three months at another until it occurred to him to study for a while in a Lithuanian town.

By asking for a small loan of two zlotys, Yosef Varshever discovered that Yoel Uzder had a bundle of cash.

"What gave you the idea of asking me and not someone else?" Yoel replied, afraid that people in Valkenik were already aware that he had money. But not wanting to say no, he offered the Varshever one zloty. The latter didn't even bother refusing; he merely returned to his prayer stand and sat down to study, his legs crossed. Yoel, in his corner, began chanting loudly over his

Talmud to show that he didn't care. But actually he was troubled over having refused his friend a loan.

Irritated, he removed his skullcap and put on his hat. Hands behind his back and belly out, Yoel Uzder approached Yosef Varshever and said resolutely, "I'll lend you a zloty and a half, not a penny more, and on condition that you pay it back in about a week."

Yoel immediately turned to leave, but at that instant Yosef Varshever put out his narrow white hand and said, "Let's have it."

Later on, the younger students too began coming to the Uzder for loans. At first he refused, but later he offered them half or a quarter of their request. Soon Gitl the cook and her two daughters learned that the bachelor was a rich man. Once when he entered the kitchen to wash his hands, Leitshe prepared the large two-handled copper pitcher on the bench for him. She knew that the pious young man would not take the pitcher directly from her hands. Yoel rolled up his sleeves and prepared to wash. The young cook then suddenly burst into laughter and asked him, "How come you're so stingy when your friends ask you for a few pennies' loan?"

Infuriated by this false accusation, Yoel stared at her in surprise. "I don't give loans? On the contrary! Whom did I refuse? It's just that it takes a lot of nerve for a young man to ask for a whole zloty. A zloty is made up of two fifty-cent pieces, five twenties, ten tenners, fifty two-penny pieces, and a hundred one-penny coins. So I lend the youngster half a zloty, which is five tenners, twenty-five twopence coins, and fifty full-sized pennies."

Leitshe immediately sensed that the old bachelor wasn't a bad chap, just a fool. He wasn't the right piece of goods for her. Let her older sister Rokhtshe take up with him if she liked him. Leitshe had her heart set on Yosef Varshever. True, he was a head shorter than she, but he was handsome and well dressed and wasn't afraid of looking at a girl. Her first conversation with him concerned Yoel Uzder: "I notice that the old bachelor doesn't talk with the younger students. Tell me why."

Yosef smiled. "The Uzder himself still has the mentality of a child. He doesn't talk to the young ones because he's afraid he might be considered a youngster himself."

Bewitched by this clever answer, Leitshe concluded that the

Lipnishker prodigy was crazy; Yoel Uzder was foolish; but Yosef Varshever was clever and as beautiful as an angel. Leitshe wondered why she hadn't noticed this before.

Yosef, aware that the young cook wanted him to like her, once remarked in passing, "The only foods Lithuanians know are herring and potatoes." Leitshe blushed to her ears and Varshever said not another word about food. He simply came in to eat lunch after all the other students had gone. In Yosef's honor the table was decked with a white cloth, and warming in a separate pot on the range was the best cut of meat, which the cook had saved from the yeshiva kettle. On a day when the meal was meager, Leitshe's mother would shop on credit and prepare a rich man's feast for Yosef.

At first, word spread in town and then in the yeshiva that Yosef Varshever was going to become engaged to Leitshe the cook. The yeshiva boys wished him *mazel tov*. Yosef, however, glared at them in cold silence.

One afternoon, when Yosef was away from the beth medresh, Yoel Uzder told his friends, "As for the bride, I wouldn't be in such a rush even if she were as clever and beautiful as the Queen of Sheba. And as for the dowry, who knows whether the dowry that Yosef Varshever will get will even be enough to pay back the one and a half zlotys he borrowed from me and still hasn't paid back?"

3

REB HIRSHE GORDON the textile merchant had once been the Valkenik rabbi's son-in-law. His first wife, the rabbi's daughter, had died two years after the wedding and left him with a son. Although Reb Hirshe had remarried and had a grown daughter from his second wife, he was still known as the rabbi's son-in-law and was the most respected man in town. Poor brides entrusted him with their dowries. Families that had squabbled over an inheritance chose him as an arbitrator. Vilna textile merchants gave him yard goods without promissory notes. Peasants from the surrounding villages trusted him on his word alone. Everyone knew that Reb Hirshe Gordon didn't fleece his customers and didn't give short measure. In fact, his honesty and piety made him lose customers. He would scold a poor girl for selecting an expensive cloth. Once he chased a young woman from the store because from the yardage she ordered he realized she was about to make a short, sleeveless dress with a low neck.

Reb Hirshe had a square black beard sprinkled with gray. He looked everyone straight in the eye with his dark, fiery eyes. He spoke loudly and to the point; he couldn't stand secrets. He spared neither the rich nor the poor. His motto was "Don't favor the poor in your judgment. A pauper has no special privilege when he's wrong." People in town said he was a better Torah scholar than his former father-in-law, the Valkenik rabbi, but Reb Hirshe wasn't the least bit arrogant toward the unlearned. He didn't even don the garb of the Torah scholar in honor of the Sabbath. He always wore boots and a felt fedora. When he strolled with his friends in the outskirts of town he carried a tree branch instead of a cane. He constantly reiterated one theme: We must avoid friendship with the freethinkers and even with religious Jews who live in peace with freethinkers. And in order to keep an old custom from being discarded, he was prepared to fight and to suffer humiliation.

Every Friday evening a poor boy would go through town summoning the people to shul for prayers. One day, however, Valkenik was left without a town crier, for the boy had gotten a job at the cardboard factory on the other side of the forest. Reb Hirshe then reminded the communal council several times to find another lad for this task.

"Don't worry about it," the community leaders replied. "Valkenik Jews know when to come to shul without a town crier."

The next Friday Reb Hirshe himself went through the lanes and streets before sunset, chanting loudly, "Jews, come to shul! Come to shul for Friday evening prayers."

That evening the matter was discussed at dining tables all over town. In the beth medresh on Sabbath morning the rabbi publicly reproved his former son-in-law: "Your action was beneath your dignity and beneath that of your family and all of Valkenik."

After the services, Reb Hirshe went up to the pulpit and announced, "I shall do exactly the same thing next Friday. An old Jewish custom must not be abrogated."

The trustees of the community then undertook a search until they found an elderly Jew to assume the task.

The Valkenik rabbi, Reb Yaakov Hacohen Lev, had occupied the rabbinic chair for fifty-one years. One day he surprised the congregation by announcing that he and his wife were going to settle in Palestine. Hearing that a rabbinic position would be open, rabbis flocked to Valkenik from far and near—and every candidate appealed to a different faction in town. Basically, the town was divided into a camp that looked for an old-fashioned rabbi and a camp that wanted a rabbi to have a secular education too. Finally the two embattled sides compromised and offered the rabbinic post to the rabbi's son-in-law. The enlightened side agreed to having Reb Hirshe Gordon and good-naturedly joked with him: "We may have to quarrel with you. Still, we admit that Valkenik can't hope to have a finer rabbi than you."

But Reb Hirshe declined: "A rabbi is dependent upon others' opinions, and I don't want to be dependent upon anyone."

Meanwhile, late autumn approached with its first frost and the plague of mud. Because of his advanced age the rabbi postponed his journey to the Land of Israel until the following summer. Those who sought the forthcoming rabbinic post were too lazy to come to Valkenik during the bad weather. They didn't feel like taking a trip by train and then by horse and wagon on the slim chance of getting the job. The town devoted itself to the task of providing for the yeshiva students and setting weekly dues among the congregants for the wages of the two teachers. The argument about the rabbi lay dormant for a while.

Tsemakh Atlas would not easily have persuaded the Valkenik residents to accept the yeshiva if Reb Hirshe Gordon had not been the first to proclaim his support. So great was the respect for the rabbi's son-in-law that everyone wanted to follow his lead. Since Reb Hirshe was the most important man in town, the Sabbath meals at his home were reserved for Chaikl Vilner, because he was a diligent student and worked hard on the improvement of his character.

"You see, if you're a good ben Torah you never lose out," Reb Menakhem-Mendl told his student in the Navaredker manner.

Chaikl had expected the rabbi's son-in-law to question him on the Talmudic tractate he was learning. All week long he had studied various texts and prepared his commentary. Reb Hirshe Gordon, however, welcomed him amiably but hardly spoke. Reb Hirshe was concerned that his guest should not be ashamed to eat, but he himself was immersed in Midrash texts in preparation for his own lesson. During the wintry Friday nights, after supper and a short nap, the old Valkenik rabbi would usually teach the weekly Torah portion to the congregation. Of late, however, the old man had become more feeble and his former son-in-law substituted for him. Therefore Reb Hirshe perused his books at the table and talked to no one.

Reb Hirshe's son by his first wife was away from home, studying at the Kamienitz yeshiva. At the table with Reb Hirshe were his second wife and their sixteen-year-old daughter. Tsharne was rather chubby, clumsy, and not yet developed. But she had a pair of smiling light green eyes, dark brown hair with a reddish sheen combed into two long thick braids, and cherry-red lips so fresh they looked as if she'd just been weaned. The mother resembled the daughter but was taller and broader. Both women wore large, red-flowered blue shawls around their shoulders; both gazed with constant admiration at the master of the house.

"After Sabbath, Papa, I'm going to pluck out the gray hairs from your beard. A beard is nice all black or all white," Tsharne said with a sudden laugh. She looked at Chaikl with an expression at once childishly capricious and proudly domineering, as if wanting him to be charmed with her papa too.

Reb Hirshe raised his head from his book and looked resentfully at his daughter for having no shame before a visiting ben Torah. But his daughter's bright, merry eyes melted his angry look, and he immediately buried his head in the volume by Alshikh, a hidden smile playing behind his mustache. His wife smiled too, her cheeks glowing and rosy. Chaikl felt a twitch in his heart and anguish in

his breast. He imagined Tsharne stroking her father's beard when
no one was looking. But he couldn't understand what she and her
blushing mother saw in Reb Hirshe's bearded face. He waited
impatiently for the supper to finally end, but when it was over and
he went outside he regretted that he couldn't stay longer and watch
the daughter gaping at her papa.

Tsharne spent all of the next day at the Valkenik rabbi's house.
Although she was Reb Hirshe's daughter by his second wife, the
rabbi and his rebbetsin loved her as if she were a flesh-and-blood
granddaughter. Chaikl Vilner sat dolefully through the Sabbath
cholent lunch and the supper as well. Without Tsharne's presence
her parents seemed to him as gray and boring as the late autumn
outside. The rest of the week Chaikl saw in his imagination the
reddish tint of the girl's hair blending with the flaming gold light of
the candles in the tall candelabra. The Friday night repose at the
textile merchant's house, the table decked with a white cloth, the
large bookcase, the mistress of the house with her serene face, and
Reb Hirshe's pitch-black beard with its silver threads—everything
trembled in a quiet, chiaroscuro dance around Tsharne's image,
until she seemed to become Shulamith of the Song of Songs.

Chaikl gave a Musar interpretation to the fiery remark of Reb
Israel Salanter: "A man is free in his imagination but a prisoner of
his intelligence." How could he compare Reb Hirshe Gordon's
daughter with the heroine of the Song of Songs, which is the Holy
of Holies, a love song between the People of Israel and the Holy
One Blessed Be He? He felt that for him the girl was more spirit
than flesh. She didn't warm his body as much as she befuddled his
thoughts. The transgression, then, was even greater. How could
she become spirit for him when he still had a long road of Torah
and Musar before him?

All week long Chaikl Vilner sought Tsharne in the Valkenik
lanes to prove to himself that she was indeed flesh and blood, like
any other human being made from a putrefying drop! But he didn't
meet her, and in his imagination the red-flowered blue shawl on her
shoulders became the Holy Ark's curtain. He decorated her with
carved deer and lions until in his eyes she became the Holy Ark in
the locked Cold Shul. Tsharne had also woven herself into the
chant he used for Talmud study. Chaikl saw that he couldn't get rid

of her. He would have to talk to the head of the yeshiva, Reb Tsemakh Atlas, and ask him how he could subdue the *yetzer ha-ra* which had disguised itself as a Holy Ark.

4

REB LIPPA-YOSSE WAS Valkenik's ritual slaughterer and *baal-tefilla*. He was an old man in his seventies, and although he still sometimes led the congregation in prayer he no longer slaughtered animals. His place had been taken by his elder son-in-law, Yudel. Everyone called Yudel by his wife's name; hence he was known as Yudel Hannah-Leah's. His wife, however, called him "my shlimazel." Yudel had cold, fishy eyes, a yellowish face, and an ashen gray beard. He always trembled with fear because he knew nothing perfectly. He read the Torah in shul but he made mistakes in the chant, even in the reading. The worshipers would look into their Pentateuchs and call out corrections. This flustered Yudel even more; he began perspiring and made greater blunders. When he stood by the prayer stand and saw a congregant grimacing, Yudel assumed that his singing didn't please him or that he was in a rush to get home for the Kiddush. So Yudel began praying hastily. But this very same worshiper later complained to him, "Why were you in such a rush?"

When Yudel slaughtered a cow in the presence of the butchers he was scared to death. Because of his fear, his slaughtering was declared unkosher, and the cost of the animal was later deducted from his salary. Yudel also performed circumcisions, but the townspeople had more confidence in the Tatar from a nearby village than in Yudel Hannah-Leah's. So he waited for his wife to be confined and give birth to a male child which he would circumcise. But his wife was always delivered of girls. There wasn't a single boy in his family of females. Hannah-Leah, short, sallow-cheeked, and big-nosed, had a puffy belly even when she wasn't pregnant. She was always ailing because of her frequent births. Whenever she became pregnant she went to her neighbors and sighed anxiously, "Pray to God for me that I give birth to a girl." She would rather have had another daughter than a son whom her shlimazel would circumcise.

The old ritual slaughterer also had no joy from his younger son-in-law, Azriel Weinstock. He was a competent man with a fine income, but he was never at home except for Passover and Sukkos. Azriel traveled all over the world collecting money for a yeshiva. No one knew precisely for which yeshiva he was collecting. They only knew that he went to London and Amsterdam every year, and rumor had it that he wasn't exactly weaving prayer shawls out there.

In Valkenik, Azriel Weinstock was nicknamed "the Throat." When he talked, he would push out his belly, lean on his cane with his left hand, and with his right stroke his fat, well-nourished white throat. People in town didn't like him because he was secretive about the mysterious yeshiva he represented and because of his arrogance. They had heard he was a wonderful preacher; nevertheless, they couldn't persuade him to give a sermon in the Valkenik beth medresh. His father-in-law despised him even more than Yudel, the shlimazel who was only good for fathering girls. Azriel was away for most of the year. When he came home for one of the festivals, he sat at the table with head thrown back, stroking his fat throat and smiling sweetly, as though musing over the marvelous days he had spent abroad.

His wife, Ronya, the ritual slaughterer's younger daughter, was thin and wispy, with a firm body and high shoulders. Although thirty and the mother of two little boys, she still blushed like a young girl, and when she laughed two dimples appeared in her cheeks. No one in town knew whether Ronya was as naïve as she seemed to be or whether it was just a clever pretense. In any case, everyone liked her and considered her good-natured and amiable. While the worry-laden Hannah-Leah complained about her shlimazel, her younger sister said not a word about the husband who was never at home. When a friend once asked Ronya where Azriel was, she had seized one of her boys and one of her sister's girls and laughed and played with the children without saying a word. Her friends were certain that she herself didn't know her husband's whereabouts and was ashamed to admit it.

Reb Lippa-Yosse's house was large and neglected; it had many side rooms. Since the whole family lived and ate together, the old slaughterer gladly took in the two rosh yeshivas, Reb Tsemakh Atlas and Reb Menakhem-Mendl Segal. Ronya's two neatly dressed and well-washed boys and Hannah-Leah's dowdy and unkempt girls, sallow-cheeked and big-nosed like their mother, always created an uproar at mealtime. Reb Lippa-Yosse sat at the head of the table. His shouts quieted the grandchildren and he ordered his daughters about; he didn't even look at his son-in-law, who was more afraid of Reb Lippa-Yosse than of the butchers and the skin flayers.

Reb Menakhem-Mendl sat at the table with half-closed eyes, like a sick chicken. The bustle in the house distressed him. He dreamed of the time when he could bring his wife and child to Valkenik and have his own place. Tsemakh, however, smiled and displayed a lively interest in the large family and its commotion, as if he had never seen such a household.

Ronya gave him an occasional sidelong glance, the color rising lightly in her face and neck. She laughed softly to herself and addressed her sons in a thin, singing voice, her head turning to and fro like that of a dove picking seeds. Her barrette became loose and two small braids tumbled down over her shoulders. She beamed with a festive joy, as if her husband had suddenly returned sooner than expected. In the hubbub around the crowded table no one saw the way she looked at the yeshiva principal or the change in her face when he stood up to leave. As soon as Tsemakh rose his warm smile vanished. A bitter wrinkle came into the corners of his compressed lips and he quickly left the house. Ronya ceased feeding her children and remained sitting with her hands dangling at her sides.

Tsemakh envied even Yudel. True, Yudel wasn't held in esteem by his family, but nevertheless he was surrounded by his own and didn't sit at a stranger's table. When Tsemakh left Lomzhe he hadn't imagined how difficult it would be to become a recluse. Tsemakh remained in the beth medresh wrestling with his thoughts until late at night. He returned to his quarters at Reb Lippa-Yosse's when all the rooms were dark, and he lay down to sleep hungry. The next morning Reb Lippa-Yosse rebuked him for not coming to supper.

"My daughter Hannah-Leah cooks and cleans all day long. At night she falls into bed dead tired. She can't get up after midnight to warm your meal."

"God forbid!" Tsemakh answered. "I'm not asking her to do that."

Tsemakh didn't want to sit at Reb Lippa-Yosse's big family table and suffer pangs of envy. However, he was prepared to come for supper to avoid any complaints against him. But that evening Reb Yisroel the tailor, a yeshiva volunteer, asked Tsemakh to join him at a meeting of the community council. "I want you to help me demand wood for the guest house. The students are freezing there." Tsemakh accompanied Reb Yisroel to the meeting, where the chairman and the councilmen replied, "The townsmen who support the yeshiva kitchen and invite students and other guests for the Sabbath also have to pay the rosh yeshivas' wages. They have to pay the cooks and the women who have the older students as boarders. So where will we get the money to buy wood for the guest house? Valkenik also has to raise money for its own charitable institutions."

When Tsemakh left the council meeting a snowstorm was raging outside, and the wind whistled as though laughing at him: He had torn himself from the business world in Lomzhe in order to inculcate his young pupils with spiritual values, but he had completely forgotten that he would have to depend upon business-men for material support so that his students wouldn't starve or freeze.

Back in Reb Lippa-Yosse's house, Tsemakh crossed the large, dim dining room and noticed a white cloth on his side of the table. He saw sliced bread in a little wicker basket and two covered plates. One contained stuffed cabbage and the other clear beef broth. He was very distressed that the hard-working Hannah-Leah had to get out of bed to warm up his meal, but he thought: Well, never mind. This time I'll eat so that her efforts won't have been in vain. However, he would ask her not to do this again. To enter the kitchen to wash his hands, Tsemakh had to pass through a dark corridor. As soon as he entered this passageway he bumped into Reb Lippa-Yosse's younger daughter.

"Go and eat," Ronya whispered.

For a while Tsemakh was tongue-tied. He knew it was forbidden to stand in the darkness with a strange woman. Nevertheless, he didn't move, and the woman opposite him didn't budge either.

"Thank you, but don't do this again," he murmured.

"I'll do this again tomorrow. I'll do this every day." Ronya laughed blissfully and disappeared without another word.

5

RONYA AVOIDED looking at Tsemakh at breakfast; he didn't take his eyes off her. From her restless fluttering he realized that her family knew nothing about the meal she had prepared for him. Then their eyes met and he saw in her glance the fear that he might have discovered her secret. A moment later her cheeks turned crimson. She began playing with her two sons and with her sister's girls, who even at this early hour were already dirty and tear-stained. Radiant and happy, she looked out the window at the snow and laughed to the whole family as though it were already the dawn of spring, but she avoided looking at the lodger and at her old father.

That evening Tsemakh came for the family supper. Ronya sat at the table looking sad and lifeless. Her sons, who had inherited fat white goose necks from their father, were demanding something from her. She apparently had not heard them, for Reb Lippa-Yosse shouted, "Didn't you have enough sleep? The kids want to eat."

Ronya shuddered and quickly began feeding her children. Tsemakh in his turn was so immersed in staring at her that he didn't hear Reb Menakhem-Mendl talking to him about a yeshiva matter. He realized that Ronya was gloomy because he had taken away from her the pleasure of preparing his meal. Poor woman, he thought. She's miserable. She's humiliated because her husband is never at home. He noticed that she now avoided his glance, as though he had done her some harm.

The next day he again came in after midnight and found his meal prepared as it had been two nights earlier. Tsemakh told himself that he was doing this for Ronya's sake; he didn't want her to feel hurt because he was rejecting her solicitude. Sometimes a person can be helped more by taking than by giving. But when Tsemakh entered the dark little corridor and didn't find Ronya there, he was disappointed. On his way back from the kitchen after washing his hands he was still expecting her to suddenly block his path. But she didn't appear, and he entered the dining room feeling contempt for himself: He was a fine Musarnik! He was supposedly doing her a favor by eating, yet he wanted her to be there too.

Most of the large dining room was in shadow. Tsemakh chewed without appetite and wondered why Ronya was preparing supper for him. He glanced across the table where she always sat with her sons. In the mirror he saw a woman holding a child in her arms. He shivered and looked again at the mirror on the opposite wall to see if he had only imagined it. He saw the reflection of the kerosene lamp over the table, two chairs, and a half-open door in the background where Ronya stood holding her son. Tsemakh chewed slowly, careful not to move lest Ronya guess that he saw her. Why didn't she want to be noticed, and why did she stand there holding her child? Probably he had cried and she had picked him up to rock him to sleep. Perhaps she had brought the child as a sort of protector. Tsemakh rose slowly to give Ronya enough time to disappear. At once her image in the mirror melted away.

He went to his little room, undressed, and lay down in bed. He fell asleep at once, as if the black depths of unconsciousness had come to the rescue of his exhausted thoughts. Suddenly he saw Slava bending over him with a cold, beautiful smile on her face. "Is it good to be alone?" her eyes asked. Once again Tsemakh found himself in the half-dark dining room, and in the mirror he saw Slava sitting on the sofa in their room in Lomzhe. A corner of his mind was still awake, as at twilight when a patch of sky still glows with the last red streaks of sunset. How could his wife and his Lomzhe room be in Reb Lippa-Yosse's house in Valkenik, he wondered—and immediately saw an angry grimace on Slava's face. She had surely noticed Ronya and her child standing behind his

back by the half-open door. Now Slava would spit in his face. He
had left home to become a recluse, but instead he was involved with
another man's wife. Tsemakh felt his heart churning with pity for
Ronya, who yearned to serve someone, to care for someone. But he
also pitied his wife. He saw Slava rising from the sofa in their
Lomzhe apartment and approaching him in the slaughterer's house.
Soon she would shatter the mirror and cut herself on the glass
splinters. He wanted to shout, Careful! but then the mirror
vanished along with Slava.

The door behind him was still half open. Darkness surrounded
him. Although he didn't turn around to look, he knew that Ronya
was no longer behind him. Now someone else stood there: his first
fiancée, Dvorele Namiot of Amdur, looking at him through
tear-filled eyes, as on the day he had entered her store and quickly
told her he was leaving. She had gazed at him with a despairing
smile and her lips had trembled. Her cheeks had turned cold,
white. She had said two words: "All right." He hadn't known then
he would never return to Amdur, but she had known. He now
realized that her smile had shown that she sensed he was
leaving for good. Dvorele still stands there at the doorway of her
shop just the way he left her, and from her pale, tear-stained smile
he imagined how long she sobs softly into her pillow.

The memories in Tsemakh's mind faded. He felt himself being
dragged down by the feet, as if one gravedigger standing deep in a
grave held a corpse by his wrapped legs, while the other, at the
edge of the grave, held him by the head. He heard a woman crying
and didn't know who it was. He wanted to cry too but could not.
The sand on his chest stopped him from drawing his breath. He
felt his head and body already covered with earth, but his ears were
still outside the grave, like two fully grown leaves with a network of
small red veins. The nightmare stormed a long time in his mind,
teasing and burning, until he sank into a pitch-black sleep which
dammed up all his senses as if with clay.

The next morning he couldn't recall the dream precisely but felt
the mist-wrapped nocturnal creatures still wandering about in his
mind. As soon as he went out into the blinding wintry brightness,
his tallis bag under his arm, he recalled Slava's cold, beautiful smile
as he had seen it in his sleep. He looked at the squat houses, the
snow-covered roofs that hung over the windows like fur caps worn

down to the eyes, and remembered that just a year ago he had become a frequent visitor at the Stupels'. Would Slava ever have thought of preparing a supper for a lodger? Tsemakh quickly stepped across the beth medresh threshold, realizing that in his thoughts he was trying to step across the truth that Ronya wasn't catering to him just for the sake of a mitzva.

The pupils were already waiting for him. As soon as he put on his tallis and tefillin, they began their prayers. He heard the youngsters praying piously; their voices pierced him. Was he a rosh yeshiva, a principal? No, he was a demon in disguise! Tsemakh swayed and clapped his hands and said every word of the Shema, the Hear O Israel, loudly and clearly. Rising for the Silent Devotion, he drew his tallis over his head and covered his eyes. But when everyone was immersed in the Silent Devotion, the door of Dvorele Namiot's store in Amdur opened in the rear room of his mind. In one's sleep, he thought, one tells the truth one fears to say while awake. He had committed a grave injustice against Dvorele Namiot. Nevertheless, he hadn't thought about the injustice, but merely that she would not have been a suitable wife. His anguish and regret at having humiliated her came to the surface only in his dreams. What had become of her? He hadn't even bothered to find out whether she had married.

Ronya was late for breakfast. Tsemakh waited impatiently for her. She came in bright and fresh. Her barrette, full of little combs, stood high on her head, like the erect, colorful comb of a bird. She led her two little boys by the hand and smiled at Hannah-Leah's girls. She threw a gay, playful glance at Tsemakh but was astonished when he looked at her anxiously, as if both of them had a sinful secret to conceal.

"How did you like last night's warm supper?" she sang out in her resonant, childish voice, looking at him mockingly for standing there with an open mouth like a golem. The usual noise of the children effervesced about the table, and nobody paid any attention to Ronya's remark. Finally Tsemakh mumbled his thanks, but she was already in her seat across the table and couldn't hear him.

Their eyes met again. Ronya was serving her children, and her sly smile, mixed with maternal kindliness, pleaded with him not to be angry like a little boy. She'd had to say something about his supper. Her sister would notice that the meal was gone, or a member of the family might see him eating there at night. Tsemakh felt the heat of a steaming pot in his intestines, and the flame beneath the pot surged over his body up to his temples. He moved his long legs under the table like a stallion banging his hoofs on the ground. He looked at the mirror on the opposite wall and saw a man with a beard and earlocks. But sullen wrinkles were etched from the nostrils to the corners of his mouth, and hellfire burned in his eyes. He ate with lowered head so that the others would not notice what was happening within him. Ronya sat in frightened wifely submissiveness, as though sensing his seething desire and already prepared to submit to him.

Tsemakh paced back and forth in the beth medresh all day, talking to himself: With a married woman? They wouldn't even have to look too long for a hiding place. He came home late at night and she waited for him in the dark corridor. They both had their own rooms. Perhaps she wasn't thinking that far; perhaps she only intended to play a bit. But whether she intended this or that, she was ready. Her behavior showed that she was hiding more than she revealed. Under no circumstances should he return to sleep at the house. However, spending the night in the beth medresh was no good either. Congregants or some of the yeshiva people might see him and wonder why he hadn't returned to his quarters. He decided to spend the night in the attic, in the Musar meditation room.

6

THE MUSAR room, accessible by a long, winding outside staircase, was like a high, narrow tower facing the broad, square, tin-roofed beth medresh. During the summer the community-owned building below housed visitors: a famous itinerant preacher, an emissary from a yeshiva, or a once prosperous townsman who was now traveling from place to place seeking a dowry for a daughter. None of these prominent Jews could be asked to spend the night at the community guest house with the beggars and wanderers. Tsemakh had been successful in persuading the community to set up the attic as a Musar room, but during the winter the room wasn't heated and the students didn't go up there to study. The straw mattress had been removed to the guest house, leaving the wooden bed bare. Next to the only window stood a table and chair. A kerosene lamp hung from the ceiling. On a bench by the entrance were a clay pitcher and a bowl for washing.

Tsemakh went up after evening prayers, lit the kerosene lamp, and said, "Here is your grave." He would stay all night even if he froze. He sat down on the hard boards of the bed and buried his face in his hands: His entry into the secular world had commenced with a slammed door that reverberated through all of Navaredok. And his return to Torah had come after a scandal with his wife's family. He had dreamed of running a large beth medresh and delivering profound Musar talks. But his only accomplishment was a little yeshiva, hardly a cheder—and he, its principal, was being tempted by a married woman. Suddenly Tsemakh heard footsteps on the stairs. He was astonished, for he knew that none of his students secluded themselves in the unheated Musar room.

Chaikl Vilner didn't know how to discuss his temptation with Tsemakh Atlas without telling him about Reb Hirshe Gordon's daughter. Hence he postponed his talk from day to day. On Thursday, however, he became frightened. The following day he would have to return once more for his Sabbath meals at the Gordons'. He watched Tsemakh pacing back and forth in the beth medresh and envied him: A Musarnik like him could tear the *yetzer ha-ra* from himself with one swoop. Reb Tsemakh paced about so energetically and with such an intense look that Chaikl didn't dare interrupt him. But when Reb Tsemakh left the beth medresh his pupil followed him outside and saw him going up to the Musar room. Chaikl was glad; in the attic he and his principal would be able to talk without being disturbed. For a while he stood in the synagogue courtyard wondering how to begin, and then he went up the stairs.

The rosh yeshiva, somewhat surprised, asked Chaikl to be seated on the only chair, while he sat on the bare wooden bed. He supposed that the Vilner had come up to complain about some lack of comfort. Some of the students didn't want to sleep in the guest house and demanded regular rooms. Others preferred eating days in local homes rather than herring and black bread in the kitchen.

Chaikl, however, was concerned with matters of the spirit. "I've come to talk about my promise to study diligently, be pious, and do good deeds for friends. But it's difficult, very difficult . . ."

"Of course it's difficult. It's very difficult," Tsemakh murmured to himself.

Chaikl twisted impatiently on the chair. "I don't mean that studying diligently is difficult, or that putting on tefillin every day is difficult, or that doing a friend a favor without reckoning benefits for oneself is difficult. I can help a friend without thinking of honor or repayment simply because he once helped me. But what's much more difficult than doing good deeds with pure intent is—not doing bad deeds. I mean, a man can actually stop himself from doing bad deeds, but how does he manage not to have an evil intent and thoughts of sin? That's what I've come to ask you."

Tsemakh stared wide-eyed at his pupil. When he had gone to Navaredok as a youngster of Chaikl Vilner's age, he too had realized that uprooting unclean desires from oneself was more difficult than doing good deeds.

In the glow of the kerosene lamp Tsemakh's face seemed to have the dry, yellowish skin of a recluse who fasted regularly. Chaikl looked at his teacher's furrowed brow and bent shoulders. He wondered why the rosh yeshiva breathed so heavily, spoke with a choked voice, and groaned and gagged on his own words.

"You know, Vilner, how often our sages of blessed memory remind us that the *yetzer ha-ra* is made of fire and that man, who is flesh and blood, cannot withstand the *yetzer ha-ra* unless he has divine help. Man possesses free will only to start the struggle against the *yetzer ha-ra*, but not to win it. To win it he must have divine help. But the question is: Where and how should man begin this battle with the evil spirit in him? The answer is that one must begin from a point of truth. No matter how high the eagle can fly, his feet have to take off from a certain point to enable him to start his flight. Similarly, man must begin from a point of truth. However, someone can admit to the truth that he is a swine—and then continue to burrow in the filth. At the same time, a person like that is quite proud of his courage in telling himself the swinish truth. Admitting the truth means that after a man recognizes the lie, he is in a rush to get away from it and can no longer tolerate it. Only then does someone have the foundation from which to begin the war with the *yetzer ha-ra*."

"But what if the lie has disguised itself in a point of truth? What if the *yetzer ha-ra* masquerades as a Holy Ark, and the one who is tempted doesn't know whether it is really the *yetzer ha-ra* or the Holy Ark?" Chaikl addressed the floor to avoid looking the principal in the eye. "To rid oneself of the doubt, there is an answer: Smash the carved Holy Ark. But who knows whether this will help? Philosophers say that man doesn't have free will. No matter how much man struggles with himself, he can only do what he must do."

A bright smile lit up Tsemakh's face for a moment. He liked the image about the *yetzer ha-ra* that had masqueraded as a Holy Ark. He had noticed that the Vilner often spoke in fine metaphors. But then Tsemakh's face became furrowed again. No matter how much he had suffered from temptations, he had never once doubted that man can prevail over himself.

"Philosophers say that man doesn't have free will? It's right here, Vilner, that you can see the difference between a Musarnik with Torah and a philosopher without it. The Musarnik tells himself the truth: If he can't overcome the *yetzer ha-ra*, it's his own fault. But the philosopher without Torah generalizes out of his particular situation. Since he can't overcome it, no one can. Nevertheless, the thinkers who disparage free will admit that man can be partly guided by his rational mind, which can distinguish between truth and falsehood; or by his feeling of compassion, which can distinguish between good and evil; or by his aesthetic sensibility, which can distinguish between beauty and ugliness.

"But all this is an absolute lie!" Tsemakh suddenly raged with the anger of a sick man who hears his neighbors singing and dancing while he is in pain. "How can one's sense of beauty prevent evil, if ever since the beginning of time there have been wicked men who have prostrated themselves before beauty? Moreover, without Torah the feeling of compassion too vanishes like smoke when the ostensibly compassionate man doesn't get what he wants. And as far as the rational mind is concerned, it's the most deceptive mirage there is. Man's mind is a small, smoky lamp, and when lust blows through his nostrils it extinguishes all rationality. Man is by nature a compromiser. He's expedient, he's lukewarm, he's a fence-straddler, a fool who picks his own pockets. And his rational mind is that night lamp which shows him how to deceive himself, how to sin. The man of truth, however, must shout to his rational mind: 'Thief, watch where you're going!'" Tsemakh shouted up at the night lamp hanging from the ceiling, then sat with lowered head. He had not forgotten how his two old yeshiva friends, Zundl Konotoper and Duber Lifschitz, had come to Lomzhe to bring him back to the right path and he had driven them away with his talk about the perfect state of man's intellect.

"Man can overcome only with the strength of the Torah and the strength of his own will," Tsemakh said, swaying with his eyes closed. "Even the cleverest scheme can't help man overcome his own sickness of soul if he doesn't ultimately tell himself: 'This is the way I want it.' After all the reckoning and after sweating out the entire truth according to the Torah, man's essential strength is still in his own decisive will: 'I want it this way and no other.' There is no idea under the sun that can't be interpreted in diametrically opposite ways. Take death, for example. The Holy Scriptures and our sages of blessed memory constantly remind man about the day of death and the need to repent. We know of Musarniks who slept in cemeteries or sat in the purification chambers so that they might see what the end of man is and become more pious. Nevertheless, we know that in wartime soldiers do as they please because they aren't sure they'll survive. And the prophet Isaiah has stated that evil men shout, 'Let us eat and drink for tomorrow we shall die!' So we see clearly that the fear of death, which prompts the man of heightened religious sensibility to reflect upon repentance, brings the seeker of worldly pleasure to the opposite state—enjoy yourself while you can. We conclude, then, that basically man doesn't choose his path according to reckoning but through an inner decision: 'I want it this way and no other!'"

Chaikl was gloomily silent, and for a while Tsemakh was still too. Something is bothering Chaikl Vilner, but he's too ashamed to articulate it, Tsemakh thought. He continued, "Sometimes a student is homesick for the place where he lived free from care. He interprets this feeling by saying that he's tormented by his inability to honor his mother and father. That too is a *yetzer ha-ra* that has masqueraded as a Holy Ark."

"That's not it," Chaikl grumbled peevishly.

"Then are you dissatisfied with the meals in the kitchen?" the principal asked.

"No. My mother sends me food packages with the carters from Vilna. I've got something else on my mind, but I find it hard to talk about. It's very cold here in the Musar room. I'll go back to the guest house, even though it's not heated either."

As soon as Chaikl rose, Tsemakh followed suit, not wanting his student to wonder why he wasn't going to his room. Both went down the stairs and stood outside as though bewitched by the mysterious silence. The sky glowed frosty blue in the distance, more remote than usual. The hunched, snow-covered little houses seemed taller. The Cold Shul and its turreted roofs cast a shadow that shrouded all of the synagogue courtyard.

"Are you pleased with your Sabbath meals?" Tsemakh inquired of his student.

"I'm pleased with my Sabbath," Chaikl muttered quickly, and hurried down the hill to the guest house on the river bank. He even forgot to say good night, fearing that he might blurt out to his teacher that indeed it was on the Sabbath that the *yetzer ha-ra* had masqueraded as a Holy Ark.

7

A SLANTING RAY OF LIGHT from the beth medresh fell on Tsemakh. He hadn't known where to turn. He couldn't bear the cold, the hunger, the loneliness in the attic. But the ray of light brought him joy, as if it were a heavenly sign showing him the way. Someone had evidently remained in the beth medresh for a bout of nighttime study. He would study till the morning too, he decided.

He couldn't continue this way much longer. He would have to find a way out. But for tonight it was a salvation.

He approached the beth medresh and looked in through a low window of the illuminated side room. A little boy sat bent over the table, his head pressed against the open Talmud. Tsemakh saw that it was Melechke Vilner, fast asleep. The principal tugged at his beard as though it were pasted on and he was already sick of the disguise. If the entire town had known of his forbidden lusts and had cast stones at him, the humiliation couldn't have been greater. How could he concern himself with the problem of his pupils freezing in the guest house when he was busy thinking of a married woman?

Through the dark anteroom of the beth medresh Tsemakh entered the side room and watched the sleeping boy. He touched his shoulder lightly. One cheek pressed against the open Talmud, Melechke breathed quietly and didn't awake. Tsemakh carefully lifted him, wrapped him in his broad rabbinic coat, held him with both hands, and went outside. He took two steps and stopped. Where could he put him to sleep? The guest house was cold. He decided to take him home to his own bed. He wouldn't drop Melechke in the middle of the street in the snow and sleet just because Ronya was waiting for him in the dark little corridor. He hadn't looked for an excuse to return to his quarters; Divine Providence had ordained it. He was carrying a living Torah scroll in his hands and the Torah would protect him. Last night Ronya too had stood with her sleeping son in her hands as though wanting the child to protect her. What a boy Melechke was! Wasn't he afraid to stay by himself at night in the beth medresh?

In the dining room the white tablecloth gleamed beneath the covered plates of Tsemakh's warmed supper. He looked up and saw Ronya waiting again in the dark corridor, without her son. Tsemakh stopped at the half-open door, and Ronya immediately left her hiding place as if in forced obedience to his mute command.

"It's Melechke Vilner, the youngest boy in the yeshiva. I found him in the beth medresh asleep over a Talmud. I want to put him in my bed. It's too cold in the guest house." Tsemakh spoke in a low, hostile voice because Ronya was blocking the way to his room.

Ronya's initial fright passed. Motherly joy flashed in her eyes.

"Give him to me. I'll put him to sleep with my children." She took Melechke into her arms. Tsemakh watched her straining under the sweet heavy burden as she went softly and carefully to her bedroom. . . . Soon it would be too late. Soon she would return and tell him she had placed the lad with her children and he would seize her and embrace her. She would become tongue-tied and breathless. She would shiver with fright, but nevertheless expect him to carry her as quickly as possible to his little room. She had purposely placed Melechke with her children and not on his bed as he had requested. Tsemakh saw his shadow on the wall: it had broad shoulders and a large head—a hairy creature, half beast and half man, with a wild, overgrown beard, an evil spirit who emerged out of the nether depths of hell to satisfy his lusts. He looked to the doorway, prepared to flee . . . but remained. He heard her soft steps, and his heart stopped within him.

"Your little student is sleeping like an angel. He didn't even wake up for a second. You'd make a good father," Ronya whispered. By the light of the lamp he saw her smiling sadly. She pointed to the table, indicating that he should sit down to eat.

"Don't prepare suppers for me any more. People will find out," he murmured, his lips trembling and his body shivering with the suppressed storm.

Ronya shrugged. "What will they find out? That I'm warming up supper for our lodger? Is that what they'll find out? I'll tell them myself in the morning that I put your pupil to sleep with my children."

Her sober remarks made Tsemakh realize that she was teaching him how to behave. She had seen fear in his eyes and laughed at him.

"Are you afraid?" she asked.

"Yes, I'm afraid to stand near you," he rasped, and a string of fire ran down his spine from his scalp, like a flame that singes a tree trunk and suddenly leaps to the branches.

"But I'm not afraid," she answered like a Lilith of deminight. "I've heard that your wife is a beauty from a wealthy house. Do you love her? Is she really as beautiful as they say?"

"Who says that?" He looked at the mirror where he had seen Slava sitting in last night's dream.

"Leitshe, the cook at the yeshiva, told me that your wife is a beauty," Ronya replied. "Leitshe heard it from her fiancé, Yosef Varshever."

Ronya's effusiveness cooled Tsemakh's fever, a fever woven with silence and the mystery of night. Her mention of Yosef Varshever sobered him even more. He didn't like the youth and was disgruntled that this wanderer from yeshiva to yeshiva knew so much about his family life.

But Ronya continued chattering. "A wife shouldn't be left alone." She saw Tsemakh looking at her in confusion and a look of annoyance came into her eyes. Her voice became shriller, as though she were recalling her husband, who traipsed about all over the world. "Don't you hear me? I said a wife shouldn't be left alone."

"I hear you. It's true. You're right." He turned to the doorway as if immediately prepared to run and find the young and beautiful wife he had left alone.

Ronya blocked his path and whispered, frightened, "Where are you off to so late at night? Finish eating and go to sleep."

Tsemakh spoke quickly and feverishly. "No, no. I won't eat and I won't lie down to sleep. I'm going back to the beth medresh."

Ronya grabbed his arm but quickly withdrew her hand. "What's the matter with you? Are you forgetting that your pupil is sleeping with my children? Tomorrow morning everyone in the house will know that you brought him and they won't understand why you left," she said angrily and with astonishment, as though suddenly realizing that an immature man stood before her. Her chin trembled convulsively; a mocking grimace contorted her face. "And if you leave now, will you stop being sorry you left your wife alone?"

"It's too late now," he persisted stubbornly. "This time I'll eat and spend the night here. But tomorrow or the day after I'll find another room and move out."

Ronya gave him a stern, apprehensive glance and warned him in a weary voice, "If you move out so suddenly, my sister and perhaps even my father might suspect that something happened here. I promise I won't warm up your meals any more."

"And you won't stand behind the door," Tsemakh added.

"I won't stand behind the door," Ronya repeated and looked at him with pained surprise, as if incredulous that he could be so hard and crude. Ronya moved her fingers over her forehead and eyes as though wiping away a dream. Then she left the dining room and closed the corridor door slowly and firmly, as if forever.

8

FRIDAY EVENING Chaikl again sat in Reb Hirshe Gordon's house, casting sidelong glances at Tsharne. She was bringing in the food from the kitchen: steaming gefilte fish, chicken soup with islets of fat swimming in it, and stewed chicken, sweet and sticky. Tsharne's mother, distributing the servings, seemed to him prettier and more efficient than the daughter with her short hands and chunky legs. Chaikl noticed that Tsharne carried the dishes sulkily and was afraid to say a word lest the laden tray fall from her hands. He also noticed a little black ribbon dangling from beneath her dress; it shook like a clock pendulum. Her stockings were wrinkled, not drawn on tight, which so distressed the young student that he lost his appetite for the rich Sabbath foods. He was also angry at the master of the house for not talking to him. Wearing a simple fedora and a short jacket, as though it were mid-week, Reb Hirshe didn't lift his eyes from his Pentateuch and commentaries.

The meal passed in silence. When Tsharne brought in plates of cold plum compote and glasses of hot tea, Eltzik Bloch, Reb Hirshe's former brother-in-law and the elder son-in-law of the Valkenik rabbi, came in with a hearty *"Gut shabbes!"*

Eltzik Bloch, a man with a trimmed gray beard who owned his own stone house and fancy goods shop, was a councilman of the community and the chief spokesman for the enlightened pious Jews of Valkenik. Nevertheless, unlike Reb Hirshe Gordon, he was not called "the rabbi's son-in-law." People said that Eltzik Bloch bickered with his wife because her father, Rabbi Yaakov Hacohen

Lev, considered his former son-in-law more important than he. Rumor had it that when Valkenik had offered Reb Hirshe the rabbinic chair, Eltzik Bloch demanded of his wife that her father not permit his former son-in-law to be his replacement. The old rabbi had supposedly replied that Eltzik shouldn't grieve; Hirshe wouldn't accept the post. Yet he hoped Hirshe would accept, for then Valkenik would have fewer disputes. These remarks were bruited about in the rabbi's name. His prediction was right: whichever candidate Eltzik and his side supported, Reb Hirshe opposed.

In public the two brothers-in-law treated each other politely. After a squabble at a meeting or at the beth medresh Eltzik always came to his brother-in-law for a friendly conversation. On Friday nights he came to hear Reb Hirshe explain the weekly Torah portion. Now he had come to accompany Reb Hirshe to the beth medresh. He spoke familiarly with all the members of the family, and Tsharne brought some fruit and tea for her uncle. As soon as she sat down, Tsharne again seemed to Chaikl to be a princess. Her cheeks, forehead, and chin gleamed richly, like the skin of a juicy, winy fruit.

Eltzik Bloch peeled an apple with a small knife, chewed the slices, and told Reb Hirshe, "The rabbi of Miadle has arrived and will preach tomorrow. People say he's a keen scholar and knows Polish too. But in your eyes he has one defect. He belongs to the Mizrachi."

"It's a defect indeed," Reb Hirshe said without removing his eyes from the Pentateuch.

"Perhaps you'll change your mind after all and accept the post. That way we can avoid quarreling. All sides agree on you," said Eltzik Bloch.

"Don't worry, Uncle. Papa won't become a rabbi in Valkenik," Tsharne said, laughing. Eltzik, somewhat flustered, laughed too. "Don't misunderstand me. I'd be the first to vote for him."

Tsharne, as happy as a child who has outsmarted a grownup, was about to add something, but her father's sharp glance warned her to be still.

"If your mind is definitely made up not to be the Valkenik rabbi," Eltzik continued, "why don't you say who your candidate is? The rabbi from Misagoleh, for instance, is considered one of the shining lights of our generation. What's more, for the ultrareligious of Valkenik he has the additional virtue of not knowing Polish. He doesn't even read the Agudah party newspapers. Nevertheless, even the enlightened group would also support the Misagoleh rabbi because he's an old-fashioned rabbi who doesn't meddle in politics. So why don't you want to support him, Reb Hirshe?"

"A rabbi *should* meddle in politics," Reb Hirshe answered dryly.

"If you think so," Eltzik Bloch wondered, "then you should be a rabid supporter of the Zhetle rabbi. He's a declared Agudahnik who pours fire and brimstone on the Mizrachi people."

"He's not enough of a scholar," Reb Hirshe grunted, his face darkening.

But his brother-in-law shrugged and a sly smile gleamed in his eyes. "Isn't there a single living sage in the house of Israel worthy of taking up the rabbinic post of Valkenik?"

His lips compressed, Reb Hirshe remained silent—a silence that pierced Eltzik like pin pricks. He turned to the women and began berating the yeshiva of the Navaredker Musarniks. "I can't see how such wild creatures are let into a respectable town. I've been to their services a few times and I've seen how they throw themselves around and yell: 'Ay-ay-ay! Oy-oy-oy!'" Then he lashed out at Chaikl, "You think you're scholars? You're madmen!"

"When Papa prays, he doesn't sway back and forth and doesn't shout 'Ay-ay-ay.'" Tsharne laughed, and her laughter made Chaikl's throat dry.

Eltzik Bloch became even more furious. "In the beth medresh the Musarniks break all the benches and prayer stands. They've made a pigsty out of the guest house. They were given new straw mattresses which they ripped, covering the floor with scattered straw. Straw comes out of the Musarniks' sleeves and even their ears."

"Are they that careless?" Tsharne threw a glance at Chaikl as though looking for wisps of straw in his ears. Eltzik was pleased that he'd been able to draw Tsharne, at least, into the conversation. He pushed his winter hat back and derided the students even more: "And the way they scratch! And no wonder! If you don't change your underwear, you sit with the Talmud and scratch."

"The children are away from home, far from their parents, studying Torah, so there's no one to take care of them." Hirshe Gordon's wife smiled at Chaikl to assuage his humiliation.

"And if children are away from home, far away from their parents, studying Torah, can't they go to the bath on Friday to boil out their shirts and long underwear?" Eltzik Bloch grimaced. "There's a washtub in the guest house, but the Musarniks wash only their fingertips in the morning. They walk around with clods of mud stuck on their hands and necks; filthy, ragged and tattered. But the Zionist pioneers, children from respectable homes, go out to training camps and wash their own laundry. They're not afraid of cold water. These pioneers who are preparing to settle in our Holy Land aren't even afraid of fire."

"Well, it's time to say grace." Hirshe closed his book as though he hadn't heard a word of his brother-in-law's babbling about the pioneers.

Chaikl said grace with lowered head. Before his eyes he saw Friday night at his parents' home. The thin candles in the copper candlesticks had burned down and the kerosene in the lamp was used up too. Only the wick flickered and twitched, surging toward the ceiling, wanting but unable to leap out of the glass, like a little animal in a deep pit. His father sat between the bed and the table, sadly contemplating his bookcase. In the dark room his milk-white beard looked even whiter. His mother, exhausted and nearly frozen from the week's work, had dozed off before finishing grace. Her hands were on the table, her twisted fingers cracked by cold and wind. He had left his parents and gone off to a yeshiva to become a better Torah scholar, and a small-town girl had come along and agitated his thoughts. He deserved to be humiliated.

As soon as Chaikl had finished grace and left the house, he began to revile Tsharne in his mind. Was she really Shulamith of the Song of Songs? The latter was described as tall and slim, a pillar of smoke, while the Valkenik girl, with her shrill, childish voice, was short, lazy, and capricious. Her mother was incomparably prettier and, moreover, good-natured, radiant, and warm. Even Leitshe the cook had a better figure than Reb Hirshe's daughter. And though Leitshe had work-worn hands and a perspiring face, and was frequently dirty from the kitchen stove, she could carry dozens of plates and glasses in both hands. But Tsharne was a clumsy creature, a little sloven on calf's legs! Chaikl poured out his wrath at her at length until he felt better; then he went off to the beth medresh to study, to make up for the week's work lost in following his fantasies.

Reb Tsemakh Atlas too had a distressing Friday night. At the slaughterer's house, Ronya lay sick in her room. Hannah-Leah brought her food several times but returned each time with the full tray. Ronya, she declared, had a splitting headache and didn't want to eat. Reb Lippa-Yosse couldn't bear for any member of his household to be late or not come to the table, so he took advantage of Ronya's absence to speak his mind about Azriel Weinstock: "He runs around all over the world and cares nothing about his wife and little children."

Tsemakh listened and felt like a sneak thief. He had no doubt that it was his harsh words and his rejection of her care that had prompted Ronya's illness. But he'd had no other choice. Perhaps it would have sufficed for her to be like a sister to him; for him it could not suffice.

Tsemakh waited impatiently for the meal to end and left at once for the beth medresh. He went into the side room where he had found Melechke sleeping the previous night and sat down at the table under the cold light of a small electric lamp. But as soon as he opened a book he once again stood with Ronya in the dark dining room at midnight. Why had she repeated that one ought not to leave a wife alone? Was she thinking of her own husband? Or was Ronya thinking that his wife was no better than she and that he shouldn't feel guilty? All his forbidden lusts melted away at once when he thought of that. Surely his wife too would find herself similarly tempted and would be even more readily amenable than Ronya. Slava had already had one man before her marriage, and now she was angry with him because he had fought with her family and gone away. And if he moved to other quarters, would this guarantee no further temptations? The only solution was to reconcile with his wife and bring her to Valkenik. Tsemakh felt a buzzing in his head and had to press his back to the wall. Since he had been living in Valkenik and running the yeshiva, it had become even more clear to him that Slava was not suitable to be a rebbetsin and would not want to be one. Perhaps she had counted on his inability to bear loneliness, as well as on other obstacles. But he would be able to bear it all. He wouldn't return to Lomzhe to become a merchant at his brothers-in-law's store. He would remain in Valkenik and guard himself scrupulously so as not to stumble, neither with a woman nor with any new controversy.

Chaikl Vilner came into the room looking upset. Seeing his rosh yeshiva, he became even more excited. He was in a rage at Reb Tsemakh, at Reb Menakhem-Mendl, and at everyone who had urged upon him the magnificent Sabbaths at the home of Reb Hirshe Gordon.

"Last night you asked me if I was satisfied with my Sabbath at Reb Hirshe Gordon's. I don't want to go there any more. Not even for tomorrow's lunch," Chaikl said curtly. He told Tsemakh how Eltzik Bloch had humiliated him, ending with, "And Reb Hirshe's family looked at me to see if I too wasn't as dirty as the other yeshiva boys who sleep in the guest house."

"So why didn't you give it back to him? You know how," the principal wondered. "I didn't think you were the sort to hold your tongue."

Chaikl sank into an angry silence. He would rather have the rosh yeshiva consider him a coward than admit that a provincial girl had made him tongue-tied and that she had been the *yetzer ha-ra* masquerading as a Holy Ark.

He had to listen silently to the rest of the principal's rebuke. "If Eltzik Bloch hadn't seen you becoming embarrassed at being a poor ben Torah, he wouldn't have spoken to you so impudently, and the Gordon family too would have had more respect for you. Nevertheless, don't let a little shopkeeper's insult bother you. As it turns out, it's even better that you controlled your temper and didn't answer. But for God's sake don't dream of not returning to Reb Hirshe Gordon's house tomorrow for the Sabbath meal. He might even become a bitter enemy of the yeshiva, and that could lead to catastrophic consequences."

Chaikl looked at Tsemakh Atlas in amazement. Since when had Reb Tsemakh Atlas been afraid of controversy? He too was now shivering with fear over a quarrel, just like Reb Menakhem-Mendl Segal.

9

FOR THE SABBATH LUNCH the old slaughterer was in a worse mood than on Friday night. Ronya was still sick in her room. Moreover, during the Morning Service at the beth medresh he had had an argument with Eltzik Bloch.

Therefore Reb Lippa-Yosse sat at the table, ranting. *"Mazel tov!* We've had peace and quiet for a long time. Congregants are already taking sides for and against our visitor in town, the rabbi from Miadle. A little cobbler from Liade can offer his opinion as to whom he wants as a rabbi, but *I* have to bite my tongue and keep still because I work for the community, even though a rabbi and a slaughterer are as close as a hook and eye. Because Eltzik Bloch is furious that the town's leading citizens oppose the Miadle rabbi and side with Reb Hirshe Gordon, Eltzik is slandering the yeshiva students and its principals. But Hirshe Gordon is dissatisfied with the yeshiva too. He says that he was the first to permit the Navaredker Musarniks to come to town. He thought they would wage a holy war here as they always did everywhere. Now, he says, he realizes he made a mistake."

Reb Menakhem-Mendl listened gloomily. Had he known earlier that controversy over a rabbinic chair was seething in Valkenik, he would have thought it over ten times before agreeing to come to the yeshiva. One couldn't study in tranquility in a town beset by quarrels. He had no livelihood here either, and was in no position to bring his wife and child to Valkenik. The Valkenik townsfolk weren't overcommitted to caring for the yeshiva students and teachers. His friend Reb Tsemakh had forgotten to tell him in Vilna about the local squabble, or perhaps he purposely hadn't mentioned it.

"The yeshiva mustn't meddle in the fight between the two

brothers-in-law and their factions," Reb Menakhem-Mendl said. He looked at Tsemakh with trepidation, wondering if he would stand on the sidelines in the controversy. To his astonishment Reb Tsemakh remained silent, and it even appeared that he agreed.

"The Miadle rabbi somehow looks familiar. And is that young chap going to be the Valkenik rabbi?" old Reb Lippa-Yosse fumed. "I was polite and nice to Eltzik Bloch. I didn't raise my voice. After all, he's the rabbi's son-in-law and a community leader. I said to him, 'Reb Eltzik, what do you want? Do you want the yeshiva boys to give their opinion as to which rabbi they prefer? They're only children and they have to sit and study.' So then Eltzik opened up his big mouth: 'You're siding with the Musarniks because their rosh yeshivas are your lodgers, and you too,' Eltzik shouted at me, 'you too are getting community wages for nothing. You're not doing any slaughtering. Your hands shake. And you can't lead prayers because you're as hoarse as the wall. And your son-in-law is just a downright cripple'!" Reb Lippa-Yosse screamed at his son-in-law, Yudel the slaughterer, who huddled into himself in fright.

"Your lodgers aren't getting mixed up in this, so don't you butt in either," Hannah-Leah yelled at her father.

"I'm not butting in, I'm not butting in." With his handkerchief Reb Lippa-Yosse wiped some beans, bits of meat, and strands of noodles off his beard; then he ordered his grandchildren to join him in singing the psalm that precedes the grace.

Hannah-Leah's girls would always sing with him, having inherited the ability from a long line of cantors, and Ronya's boys would stand on the bench waving their hands. Reb Lippa-Yosse's two daughters usually joined in too. But this time Ronya's boys sat still, feeling bereft without their mother, and one of Hannah-Leah's daughters scratched her little sister just before grace. The girl began crying and the grandfather shouted at her to quiet down. The granddaughter blubbered even more bitterly, and Reb Lippa-Yosse yelled, "Hannah-Leah, take this whining child away from the table."

Yudel, unable to bear his lack of control over members of his own family, sighed to his crying daughter, "Don't leave. You're sitting at your father's table."

Reb Lippa-Yosse was stunned at his son-in-law's impudence,

and Hannah-Leah shrieked at her husband, "Don't you butt in either!"

Yudel's cadaverous nose became even paler. He sighed more intensely. This time they said grace without singing. The old slaughterer rose from the head of the table with a groan. He wanted to take a nap before going to the beth medresh for the Afternoon Service and the visiting rabbi's sermon.

Because of the short winter Sabbath, the Miadle rabbi spoke before the Afternoon Service to enable the congregation to eat the third Sabbath meal at home and then return in time for the Evening Service. That week's Torah reading was the final portion of Genesis, and the visiting preacher began auspiciously. "Scripture says: Jacob lived in the land of Egypt seventeen years. This means that he truly came to life in the land of Egypt. All the previous years he had spent mourning his son Joseph—one cannot call this living." The congregation liked this interpretation, and the older Jews groaned, "Ah, joy from children!"

The eastern wall was occupied by well-to-do householders with combed beards and fleshy noses who wore soft leather boots and stiff derbies. The power of these well-established pillars of Valkenik, owners of shops in the market place, surged from their faces. From time to time they yawned, belched from the noodle pudding, and bent an ear to hear what the Miadle rabbi had to say. With eyes still rheumy from their Sabbath afternoon nap, they looked angrily at the rebels, the young folk who wanted to choose their own rabbi, someone who knew Polish.

Sitting in the first row, opposite the Holy Ark, were old men in high fedoras, their parchment-dry faces overgrown with hair almost into their ears. They loved to complete the biblical verse that the preacher began. On the farthermost benches—from the rear up to the pulpit—sat the artisans, with bent fingers, hunched backs, and dejected faces. The town's bakers, with their cloudy eyes and doughy faces, jutted out from among the artisans like long, dried sticks. Standing all night by the bread troughs, they never had enough sleep and always fought off drowsiness while eating, praying, or listening to an itinerant preacher. Around the tables at the rear and next to the stove against the western wall sat the carters from Vilna, wearing their high felt boots and caps with earflaps. They had brought merchandise for the local shopkeepers and still felt the frost in their bones and the strain of riding from Thursday night till Friday morning with a heavily laden wagon. Hence they liked to sit in the beth medresh amid the Sabbath congregation and warm themselves with a Jewish word.

When the Miadle rabbi came to the verse in which Jacob adjures his son Joseph not to bury him in Egypt, the aged Valkenik rabbi, Reb Yaakov Hacohen Lev, began to moan and groan. Since he had decided to go to the Land of Israel, he meditated upon repentance, his deceased daughter, and the children he would leave behind. He hoped that he would not die while on his journey, God forbid, before arriving in the Holy Land. The Valkenik rabbinic post no longer interested him, but he knew he would have to part amicably with all sides. For this reason he sat by the Holy Ark and listened to every candidate, nodding into his sparse yellowish beard and enjoying all the sermons. But the congregants never knew which rabbi he preferred.

On the same bench sat Reb Lippa-Yosse. He was staring intently at the Miadle rabbi, as he had during the Morning Service. Now he could hardly restrain himself from shouting out. He had finally recognized the young speaker. He was ready to swear that this wandering preacher was from Ishishok, that he was Shmuel-Itche the spice merchant's son. He had known him as a youth; even earlier, as a lad; and even earlier than that, when he lay in his cradle and he, Lippa-Yosse, had been his mohel and had circumcised him. The old slaughterer became red with rage: I was his mohel—so don't tell me he's going to be my rabbi! He's going to lord it over me and decide for me what's kosher and what isn't?

In conclusion, the preacher came to the verse in which Jacob blesses his sons. He quoted the verse, "Joseph is a fruitful bough," and spoke about the righteous Joseph whose brothers made his life miserable. "But this was not only because of jealousy. Joseph and his brothers had differing paths in Judaism. Leah's children, of noble stock, didn't want to befriend the children of the maids. But the attitude of Joseph the righteous was that the maids' children must not be rejected. He even befriended the prisoners in jail. And that's why he was worthy of being second to the King of Egypt and of having the privilege of saving not only the entire house of Jacob, but the whole world as well during the seven years of famine. Only much later did his brothers realize and admit that Joseph's way had been the correct one."

The town's leading citizens understood that the Miadle rabbi was speaking out against the Agudah people who didn't want to befriend the freethinkers. Since the rabbi was a member of Mizrachi, his attitude was like Joseph's: the freethinking Zionists should be befriended. The congregants smiled. They considered this interpretation of reasons why Joseph was sold too simplistic. And Eltzik Bloch had assured them that the Miadle rabbi was a sophisticated, wordly man. Eltzik Bloch stood at the eastern wall in a rage. The guest rabbi was not his candidate either, but he was from the Mizrachi, and when a Mizrachi candidate failed, Eltzik Bloch saw in it his own failure. And, to make matters worse, his former brother-in-law, Hirshe Gordon, was sitting next to the Holy Ark and snoring with gusto, as if he were under a quilt.

Reb Hirshe did not like itinerant preachers. He usually left the beth medresh before the rabbinic candidates stood up to speak and returned just in time for the Evening Service after they had finished. But during the Miadle rabbi's sermon he remained sitting, bent over an open Talmud. A few minutes later his head and hands sank down toward the prayer stand and he fell asleep, whistling through his nose and hissing through his lips like a wagoner halting his horses. When the preacher stopped to catch his breath, the congregation heard Reb Hirshe snoring. Eltzik Bloch would gladly have poked him to stop his rasping, but Eltzik was afraid of a scene, a scandal.

The Miadle rabbi also heard the snoring. He looked all around until he saw a man sleeping over an open Talmud near the Holy Ark. When the rabbi bent over the balustrade and addressed the snorer, the latter honked even louder. For a full minute the rabbi stood on the steps of the Holy Ark at a loss for words. Since this was his first visit to Valkenik, he felt that he was standing before these unknown Jews like a naked person in the presence of those fully dressed. But he overcame his confusion and continued speaking.

The icy sheen of the wintry world outside illuminated the preacher's pale, delicate face and his dark blond beard. His kind eyes glowed with youth behind his gold-rimmed glasses. Nervousness made him wave his hands more than necessary, and the congregation noted his long white fingers and soft, clean sleeves. The artisans in the rear rows and the wagoners around the tables looked at the rabbi with curiosity and affection, but the merchants and scholars in the crowd remained cool. The visitor sensed that he hadn't impressed the men at the eastern wall; and the thought that he would have to cut short his sermon because of the short winter's day flustered him even more. He ended hastily with the verse in which before his death Joseph adjures his brethren to take his bones with them upon leaving Egypt. The aged Valkenik rabbi once again groaned aloud, hoping that he would be worthy of living to see the Land of Israel. Then the preacher quickly concluded with: "And the redeemer shall come to Zion and let us all say, Amen." The congregation responded with such a loud "Amen" that Reb Hirshe was startled out of his sleep, neither dead nor alive, as though he had heard the blowing of the messianic shofar.

During the Afternoon Service, when the young rabbi stood praying by the eastern wall, the old slaughterer sidled up to him and asked, "Aren't you from Ishishok, Shmuel-Itche the spice merchant's son?"

Seeing the old man delighted the Miadle rabbi no less than finding a close relative. "Of course I'm Reb Shmuel-Itche's son, and I still remember you from the time you used to come to Ishishok."

But Reb Lippa-Yosse backed away angrily and muttered to himself, "Couldn't fool me; it's him all right!"

Following the Afternoon Service, the congregation waited for the departure of the visiting preacher and his host, the Valkenik rabbi, who had invited him for the third Sabbath meal. Then the congregants sitting by the eastern wall began leaving too. They surrounded Reb Hirshe and asked him how he had liked the sermon.

Gordon looked at them in amazement. "How should I know? I dozed off."

At this Eltzik Bloch burst out, "That's sheer cruelty! Plain murder! And if the Miadle rabbi doesn't suit your taste, isn't he a Jew? Isn't he a scholar? Can one squeeze the life blood out of him and snore away during his sermon?"

But Reb Hirshe merely shrugged. "It's a false accusation. I was studying my daily page of the Talmud and didn't have enough time to leave before the sermon because the rabbi started preaching very early. And since it didn't seem proper to leave while he was speaking, I stayed to hear him, fighting with sleep as with a cutthroat. But I couldn't overcome the drowsy feeling. A terrible fatigue came over me. So what's all the fuss about?"

Eltzik Bloch was once again made aware that his brother-in-law had a devilish power in him. As soon as Reb Hirshe left the beth medresh the congregants began running after him, like Hasidim after their rebbe. The only ones who remained around the pulpit were a group of wags and a couple of old men, senile and weak-legged, who still had not reached the exit.

One brazen fellow clapped his hand familiarly on Eltzik's shoulder and said, "Don't be so downhearted, Eltzik. Reb Hirshe Gordon's a smart chap. That's why he doesn't want to slander the visiting rabbi. Anyway, everyone has seen that this Miadler is a softy. He's like a little chick. He's no good for Valkenik. Come and eat, Eltzik."

"Since when am I Eltzik to you? Did we work in the same pigpen?" Eltzik shouted at the backslapper. "My former brother-in-law's name is Zvi-Hirsh, so why do they call him Reb Hirshe with an 'e' at the end? Unless that's their way of saying there's no greater scholar than Reb Hirshe, no greater saint than Reb Hirshe, and if Reb Hirshe snores away during somebody's sermon, there's some hidden wit and wisdom there too. Since when are the Valkenik dunderheads such connoisseurs of Torah scholars?"

"Can we help it if your name is Eltzik and Bloch is such a short family name?" The wag sighed sympathetically. "It's really no one's fault that we can't stretch your name out like your brother-in-law's, Reb Hir-she Gor-don."

Eltzik Bloch saw that he had made a fool of himself and was being ridiculed. People might even suspect him of being envious of his brother-in-law. Meanwhile, old Reb Lippa-Yosse was slowly making his way from the eastern wall. He listened with obvious delight as they derided the community leader who had berated him early that morning.

"Are you also offering opinions as to who should be the Valkenik rabbi?" Eltzik Bloch shouted at him.

"I'm not mixing in," Reb Lippa-Yosse answered in a fright.

Nevertheless, chagrined that Eltzik Bloch had scolded him like a child, the old man forgot that he wasn't interfering and yelled, "I still remember the Miadle rabbi when he was a youth, a boy, a babe in the cradle. He's from Ishishok, Shmuel-Itche the spice merchant's son. It was I who circumcised him! I!" The slaughterer displayed his fingers with his shiny large nails as witness to the truth of his remarks. "I was his mohel—don't tell me he's going to be my rabbi!"

"I don't understand. If you circumcised him, isn't he allowed to be your rabbi?" Eltzik Bloch gaped at him.

"I was his mohel—don't tell me he's going to be my rabbi!" Reb Lippa-Yosse couldn't understand what it was that Eltzik Bloch didn't understand.

The young people were doubled over with laughter, transported with delight. The old dotards asked Reb Lippa-Yosse again and again if it was indeed true that he had circumcised the Miadle rabbi, and then they shouted, "If you really did snip the young rabbi, then he certainly won't become the rabbi of Valkenik. Over our dead bodies!" The old men smacked their toothless gums.

Eltzik's head was splitting; the world had gone mad. He stood there in a daze. Reb Lippa-Yosse too fell into an apprehensive silence, realizing that Bloch would now become his enemy and persecute him.

The unsuccessful Miadle rabbi was forgotten at once, but the quarrel between the slaughterer and Eltzik Bloch was spread throughout the town by the young wits. All week long, whenever a group gathered at the market place or in a shop, some pranksters stood in their midst, putting on a show. One would imitate the slaughterer, while the other mimicked Eltzik Bloch.

At home, Hannah-Leah yelled at her father, "I told you not to butt in."

"I didn't butt in. But think of it, Hannah-Leah. I was his mohel—don't tell me he's going to be my rabbi!"

10

ON THE SATURDAY NIGHT of the uproar in the beth medresh over the Miadle rabbi, Yosef Varshever, Leitshe the cook's fiancé, quietly became engaged to Gedalya Zondak's daughter. Gedalya Zondak was a grain and hide merchant and provided butchers with cows and calves. His eldest daughter, Nekhoma, was a pudgy girl with a thick, milk-white neck. To camouflage her big body she wore broad, loose clothing like a pregnant woman. She didn't associate with the local youths. Nevertheless, they all were confident that Nekhoma would marry a merchant.

When they heard the news, the market shopkeepers congratulated Gedalya Zondak and asked him, "How did your daughter happen to choose a yeshiva scholar, especially one of these Polish types?"

Zondak shrugged as if he were amazed too. "How should I know? Yosef lives with us and eats with us on the Sabbath. My wife and daughter like him very much. So if my daughter's happy, I'm happy. I'm going to take him into my business. I'm also giving him a dowry, and a couple of years' free board in my house, and two rooms as well. Besides, a scholar is no worse than some local ox."

"True," the shopkeepers agreed. "A scholar is no worse than some local ox. He's got brains, that Polish chap. He latched onto a gravy train. But why such a quick and quiet engagement? And how come good friends weren't invited for a drink?"

Zondak shrugged again. "How should I know? My son-in-law-to-be says he hates a fuss."

All of Valkenik had congratulated the Zondak family, but the cooks, Pockmarked Gitl and her daughters, still couldn't believe the news. Yosef had never even mentioned his lodgings. But when he stopped coming to the kitchen to eat, Gitl quickly threw a kerchief around her shoulders and went to the beth medresh. Yosef Varshever was always off in a corner, studying alone. The students peered over their prayer stands, watching the cook say something to him and get a calm response. She stood there dumbstruck while he continued swaying calmly over his Talmud. Then the woman pulled the kerchief over her head and mournfully left the beth medresh.

Gitl went from house to house pouring out her bitter heart to the women of the town. While Gitl complained, the women thought: I never believed that elegantly dressed scholar would marry a poor kitchen maid. But they told the cook, "Don't keep silent. Go stir up the town!"

The widow then went to Eltzik Bloch, who shouted at her, "Go see Reb Hirshe Gordon. After all, my brother-in-law was all for bringing those dirty Musarniks into Valkenik."

"That's not the trouble! Yosef isn't dirty. He's neat and has a doll's face. That's why my Leitshe lost her head over him," Gitl grumbled and went to Reb Hirshe Gordon's textile shop.

Reb Hirshe heard her out, elbows on the counter and eyes immersed in a text. He answered slowly, still not removing his eyes from the book: "I'm not getting involved. My advice to you is: Don't run around from house to house. By doing this you're lowering your daughter's prestige in the eyes of other prospective suitors. You should talk to the Zondaks themselves and to the yeshiva principal, Reb Tsemakh Atlas."

The cook plucked up her courage and opened the door to the Zondaks' residence, but Zondak's big wife pushed her out immediately.

"You're making a pretty penny by feeding the students," she screamed. "You and your girls take the best cuts of meat for yourselves from the pot, while the yeshiva students get shoe leather and prune pits."

"My miserable widow's lot I wish on you," Gitl told the fat woman and returned to her kitchen, cursing that rogue from Warsaw.

Rokhtshe, her elder daughter, left the house. She was ashamed for the students to see her younger sister, the rejected bride, wander around the rooms in a daze, with shiny, flushed, tear-stained cheeks. Going about sloppily dressed, bleary-eyed, and smiling pathetically didn't bother Leitshe at all; it almost looked as if she liked to have people pity her.

As Gitl served the students, she fulminated with street invective, "That snake in the grass likes Zondak's girl better. That Warsaw scoundrel wants to have a full bed of stinking meat."

The yeshiva students sat silently with lowered heads; they had no appetite for the food. Only when they returned to the beth medresh did Yoel Uzder say what was on his mind: "The Varshever is no obscure Talmudic passage for me. He still hasn't repaid me the one and a half zlotys he owes me, so I'm not surprised he fooled a widow and her daughter."

The womenfolk incited their husbands. A simple boor like Gedalya Zondak, they said, had enough sense to snatch a Torah student; but they, clever fathers and respectable Jews, didn't think of looking for a scholar for their daughters. The husbands then stopped the prospective father-in-law and told Zondak straight to his face, "You've robbed a widow and an orphan."

Gedalya Zondak shrieked in a rage, "For all I care, all of Valkenik can go to hell. That pockmarked cook and her daughter were just dreaming."

Everyone knew, of course, that Zondak was lying. The proof was the quiet engagement. However, no one wanted to get into a fight with him. But when Reb Yisroel, the yeshiva supporter, reminded the men about the condition of the students, they responded, "All of Valkenik is now burning mad at the yeshiva."

"What good's the burning? The pupils in the guest house are freezing. Big deal—a youth has broken an engagement. So how are the boys to blame?" Reb Yisroel argued.

Reb Yisroel the tailor had the dignified bearing of a pious, tranquil man who was an artist at his trade, a recognized master at sewing gaberdines for Torah scholars. Valkenik respected his long white beard and his ability to get along with people. It had been his mitzva to find home hospitality for visitors to Valkenik. Since the yeshiva had settled in Valkenik, Reb Yisroel had become its patron, and the townsfolk didn't dare refuse him. But after the Yosef Varshever affair, he went about humiliated, and the basket in which he gathered food for the yeshiva kitchen remained half empty. He heard the same song from the smiths behind the bridge,

the artisans on Synagogue Street, and the carters who lived in the
hovels on the river bank: "Would a local scoundrel have had the
nerve to fool a widow and her daughter the way that bench warmer
did?"

One man told the tailor that he wasn't obliged to tear the bit of
food from his children's mouths and give it to a stranger. Another
man gave one fewer herring to the yeshiva kitchen than he had the
previous time, grunting, "It's money down the drain anyway. A
poor man could never get a Torah scholar for a son-in-law."

A third, a carter, gave generously and shouted into the yeshiva
patron's ear, "Yosef Varshever befriended housemaids just like the
biblical Joseph befriended the children of his father's maids, as the
Miadle rabbi mentioned in his sermon. But marrying a housemaid
is another story. That's beneath his dignity, that righteous saint.
But when he sees a rich man's daughter, he doesn't run away.
Gedalya Zondak's girl has really twisted that Varshever around her
little finger."

Reb Yisroel reported all this to the yeshiva principals. Reb
Menakhem-Mendl's face turned waxen. "Reb Tsemakh, you talk to
Varshever. The yeshiva may crumble away." Tsemakh, who had
never liked the youth with the cold, neat appearance, had avoided
him even more since Ronya had told him that Yosef Varshever had
spoken about his wife. Tsemakh realized that this wanderer from
yeshiva to yeshiva knew too much about his family life in Lomzhe.
Lecturing him would do no good. An opportunist like Varshever
wouldn't care if he was causing harm to a group of students.

Gitl the cook, however, was still demanding justice. She remembered that Reb Hirshe Gordon had suggested she talk with Reb
Tsemakh Atlas. Therefore she went to see Reb Lippa-Yosse one
weekday evening when everyone was gathered at the supper table.
Hannah-Leah amiably asked her to be seated.

The cook remained standing, her kerchief about her head.
"Everybody knows why I've come, so I don't want to waste any
time and disturb your meal." She went on softly and submissively,
"Yosef is saying that he never promised me or my daughter that
he'd marry her. He says they never even discussed it. It's true it
wasn't discussed. But he knew that everyone considered him
Leitshe's fiancé, and he never denied that. He always came into the
kitchen when all the other students had gone and let himself be

served separately. I didn't want to feed him the meager rations the students eat, so I went out of my way. I bought on credit from the shopkeepers and prepared all sorts of fine dishes for him. He knew I was a poor widow and couldn't afford to do this just for the sake of a mitzva."

Gitl burst into tears, and the ever-despondent Hannah-Leah stood wringing her hands. Reb Lippa-Yosse sadly shook his head, while Yudel looked at his daughters in fright, as if thinking that they too might become orphans. Reb Menakhem-Mendl shrank into himself, and Tsemakh, from under his knitted brows, saw Ronya staring at him with a hard, penetrating glance.

Hannah-Leah had long since noticed the change in her sister. She had suddenly become ill and had lain in her room without eating. Since her return to the table she had looked depressed and avoided Reb Tsemakh's glances. He too avoided hers—but his way of not looking differed by far from that of a pious Jew who averts his eyes from a strange woman. Previously, Tsemakh had indeed looked at Ronya, and how he had looked. Ronya was dying for trouble and now she'd found it, Hannah-Leah thought. As soon as Gitl the cook departed, she was the first to attack the principal.

"Appearances are deceiving. Frequently one can't imagine what sort of a rotten character a Torah scholar can have," Hannah-Leah said loudly, and her husband added, "If I were a rosh yeshiva I would have dragged Yosef Varshever by the hair up to the pulpit in the beth medresh and forced him to admit he's a bastard."

Reb Lippa-Yosse, who had lost his mighty roar since his feud with Eltzik Bloch, groaned. "I don't know what's become of Valkenik. In the old days the fiancé would have been fined and Gedalya Zondak would have been ashamed to show his face in the street."

"I'll talk with Yosef Varshever," Tsemakh grumbled. Through clouded eyes he saw Ronya's faint, mocking smile—she seemed to know he was afraid of Yosef Varshever.

The next morning in the beth medresh Tsemakh told Gedalya Zondak's future son-in-law, "I want to talk something over with you."

Yosef quietly followed him to the side room. As soon as Tsemakh closed the door he lashed out at Yosef, as though wanting to crush him: "You charlatan! The sages say that people like you are the worst kind of thieves because you deceive people. You knew the widow considered you her daughter's fiancé. Everyone in town and all the people at the yeshiva felt this way and you didn't deny it."

"Do I have to account to everyone?" Yosef stepped back as though fearing a slap. "Even if I did consider becoming engaged to the cook at first, I could have changed my mind when I found out that she had no dowry, no house, no money for wedding expenses, and no trousseau for herself. And especially since we never talked about marriage and never publicly signed an engagement contract."

Yosef drew closer to the principal. His pale face angry and contorted, he spoke in a low, secretive voice, "I know of a Navaredker Musarnik who was engaged to a girl in Amdur. But this girl, who was an orphan too, had a dowry and her own house, and her father had promised the groom free board. The engagement contract was signed. Nevertheless, the fiancé broke the engagement with the Amdur girl and married a girl in Lomzhe because she was prettier and richer."

Yosef Varshever left the room.

Tsemakh sank down on the bench and sat there as if turned to stone. He heard the anteroom door opening and closing, but it seemed to him that the creaking sound came from the other end of the world. From the window he saw a woman with a basket making her way down the hill to the rabbi's house, no doubt going to ask if her chicken was kosher. Or perhaps she was going to the rebbetsin to buy yeast for the challa, Tsemakh mused, and immediately forgot about the matter. A crow settled on the sill outside. It beat its wings a few times and stayed there, hunched over. It was an old crow, tattered and wet. It kept opening and closing its beak as though unable to caw. Tsemakh imagined that he and the crow were the only surviving creatures on earth after another Deluge. Yosef Varshever passed by the window. He looked toward the side room several times, as though realizing the state in which he had left his principal. Tsemakh watched his footprints form in the snow and felt no hatred toward him. Yosef Varshever didn't know everything. He still didn't know that he, the Navaredker Musarnik, had just avoided being tempted by a married woman.

11

POCKMARKED GITL saw that Reb Hirshe Gordon was right. She shouldn't go weeping from door to door as though her daughter were a piece of rejected merchandise. So she took the opposite approach and stated, "Wait till you see the gem of a groom that Leitshe's going to end up with!" Leitshe too put on a happy face so that everyone could see that she didn't give a damn about Yosef Varshever. But her mother's public outcry during the first few days now rebounded with a tenfold echo. The town youths picked up Gedalya Zondak's remark that the cooks had been dreaming and made straight for Gitl's window, where they sang, "A dream, a dream, a dream, you dreamed a dream!" The town youths hadn't forgotten how Leitshe would slap the hands of anyone who wanted to put an arm around her waist. Now they had their revenge. When she went shopping at the market a couple of chaps would materialize, seemingly out of thin air, and converse loudly as though she weren't there: "Well, what do you say about Leitshe! She dreamed a dream she was going to marry a rabbi and become a rebbetsin. Hey, look! There she is, the rebbetsin!"

Leitshe cried to her mother, "I can't take it any longer. I'm going to put an end to myself."

On Sabbath morning, when the men of Reb Lippa-Yosse's household went to the beth medresh, Gitl the cook visited his daughters again. "I'm not going to cook for the yeshiva students any more. It's not enough that the town wags are drinking Leitshe's blood in the market place, but now one of the yeshiva boys is doing it in my house. He's one of those Vilna rascals and his name is Hertzke Barbitoler. All week long he eats in the kitchen, and on the Sabbath he's over at Sroleyzer the bricklayer's house. This Hertzke looks more like a street urchin than a yeshiva boy. He always jumps into the little entry by the kitchen, pretending he wants a drink of water, then sings right into Leitshe's ear, 'A dream, you've dreamed a dream!'"

The Sabbath afternoon tranquility at the slaughterer's house was shattered as it had been a week earlier.

"You ought to be ashamed of yourselves for having a student who spends the Sabbath with the most disreputable person in town," Hannah-Leah shouted at the yeshiva principals. "That's where he's learned that ditty which pokes fun at the poor cooks."

"One can learn more important things than a little ditty from Sroleyzer and his gang," Yudel added.

"Everybody knows that Sroleyzer makes most of his money from being a fence," Reb Lippa-Yosse said in amazement. "If somebody steals a cow or a pair of horses from a barn or if a shop is stripped clean in the market place, everyone knows that Sroleyzer will retrieve the stolen goods for a neat bundle of cash. Why was a yeshiva boy sent to him?"

"Perhaps," Yudel answered, "the fence asked for a student for the Sabbath, and Reb Yisroel the tailor was afraid to refuse him. Who wants to start trouble with Sroleyzer?"

"Everyone is afraid of the bricklayer," Reb Lippa-Yosse told his lodgers. "When he hears of a townsman who wants to build a house or a new stove, Sroleyzer tells the man that he'll do it, and the other bricklayers are afraid to compete with him. But he hates to work. Being a fence is a much easier livelihood, so he hires an artisan to work for him. And when it comes to paying, he chops off a quarter or a third of the promised wage. The robbed mason runs to the rabbi—but Sroleyzer laughs at rabbinic judgments, and the rabbi himself doesn't want to defy him. Every Saturday evening his gang gathers at his place. They begin smoking before the Sabbath is out, and boys dance with girls till late at night. While all this fun is going on, he and his group plan the week's robberies. Even the butchers are afraid of him. He could very easily spill the beans and tell the authorities that besides slaughtering at the slaughterhouse they also do it on the sly in the stalls."

Reb Menakhem-Mendl looked at the principal and silently reminded him of his warning in Vilna not to take the tobacco merchant's son to the yeshiva. Tsemakh met Ronya's glance and saw that she too was gazing at him, in astonishment and pain, as though finally realizing that he wasn't a strong person, that he didn't notice what was happening around him.

"Where does this Sroleyzer live?" Tsemakh asked.

"Near the bathhouse—that's where the saint lives," Yudel answered.

Before the Evening Service, the congregation in the beth medresh recited psalms and the yeshiva boys in the side room studied Musar by heart in the semidarkness. Tsemakh slipped outside and went down the hill to the bathhouse on the river bank. All the crooked little houses on both sides of the lane were dark. The women there were waiting for the lights in the beth medresh to be lit before they lit their own lamps. But at the end of the lane a red-flecked light poured from a window and seemingly stained the snow piled high around the house. Tsemakh moved along the wall to the window and looked in. A table stood in a corner and couples were dancing in the middle of the room. Young people sat on benches along the walls, clapping their hands and stamping their feet in rhythm with the dancers. Tsemakh moved to the other window and immediately saw the person he was seeking. Hertzke Barbitoler, wearing a coat, was sitting on a bench, chewing something and watching the turning couples. Tsemakh entered a dark foyer, and before he opened the low door of the smoky room, a thought flashed: Serves me right. Because he had fought with Vova Barbitoler over this rascal in a Vilna tavern, now in Valkenik he had to fight with a thief because of him.

Hertzke was holding a handful of sunflower seeds. He shelled them quickly and skillfully, spitting out the husks with the tip of his tongue. When he saw the principal he was dumfounded. A glassy haze came over his eyes. The dancing couples stopped and looked with curiosity at the unexpected visitor. By the benches along the wall, girls with steaming faces and high bosoms gaped at him, as did the young men with their low, hard foreheads, broad, flat noses, and thick, protruding lips like unplaned boards.

Tsemakh strode over to Vova Barbitoler's boy and seized him by the shoulders, but Sroleyzer quickly intervened. He was cool and composed, his large head and broad shoulders bent slightly to the side. Hands behind his back and belly thrust forward, he blocked the path of the uninvited guest, indicating that he shouldn't try to lord it over anyone in another man's house.

"A good week to you, rabbi. What an honor to have you drop in on us. Your little yeshiva boy has no complaints against me. He eats here, drinks here, and has loads of fun here."

"You're a Haman!" Tsemakh bent his head forward and the two heads nearly collided like brass trays. "A Jew with compassion in his heart would have chased a wayward yeshiva lad back to the beth medresh and not taught him how to go off on the wrong path."

With the experienced eye of a roughneck, Sroleyzer sized up Tsemakh Atlas' broad shoulders and thought: I've seen stronger chaps, but I've never seen a rabbi with such a sharp, pale face, glaring eyes, and wild look. He coolly reckoned that he had more important things to do than get into a fight with the yeshiva principal.

"Your bench warmers are no concern of mine," he said, laughing sarcastically. "Take your brat away and flay him like a dog for all I care."

Tsemakh turned to the underworld types and lectured them: "What good does it do you Jewish youths to make fun of a poor Jewish family and, what's more, to teach that ugly little song to a yeshiva student? The cooks have stopped feeding the yeshiva students and they'll have to go hungry now."

Hearing this, the bricklayer raged at Hertzke: "I feed you, and now, on account of you, people are badmouthing me and saying you've learned terrible things here in my house!" Then he turned to his gang and began shouting even louder, with the sham anger of a thug who sides with the underdog: "You blockheads! Damn you! Don't you have anything better to do than embarrass a widow and her daughters?"

One of the young men clapped his hands to his heart and swore, "May I drop dead in the Christian quarter if I so much as said a word!"

A second youth slapped his own cheek in astonishment. "Boy, what a liar that Leitshe is!"

A third scratched the back of his head. "How was I to know? I just meant it for a joke."

One of the girl dancers shook off the elbow of a tall youth who had leaned on her as if she were a chest of drawers. "Move your foot, you oaf! If Leitshe were a rich man's daughter, would you have made fun of her?"

Tsemakh quickly left the house, dragging Hertzke Barbitoler by the hand. Once outside, he shook him with both hands as he had shaken his father in Vilna.

"If you behave like this again I'll tie you up and send you back to your father. He'll beat the life out of you and lock you in the pantry. And nobody is going to let you out."

"My mother will come to let me out," Hertzke grunted, but Tsemakh had not heard.

The incident impressed all of Valkenik: "The head of the yeshiva wasn't afraid of creeping into the lion's den, and the lion himself, Sroleyzer, was frightened."

In Reb Lippa-Yosse's house they were amazed, too. Ronya's cheeks glowed crimson once again. At the table she sought to catch Tsemakh's eye with her pleasant, radiant smile. But she saw his face clouding over; he couldn't understand her behavior. Her conduct didn't please Hannah-Leah, either. But Ronya no longer suppressed her pride and joy that their lodger was bold and strong and not a broken man, as of late he had seemed to be. Still, when Tsemakh went into the kitchen to wash his hands and met Ronya there, she immediately fled. If both of them happened to be alone in the dining room, she called her sons and her nieces.

Touched by Reb Tsemakh's defending her daughter's honor, Gitl immediately began warming up the pot for the yeshiva students. Hertzke brazenly came to the kitchen to eat, as though nothing at all had happened, but he didn't show up in the beth medresh to study. Tsemakh found out from Melechke that Hertzke sat on his bed all day, turning the pages of his stamp album. Soon, Hertzke boasted, all the other boys would be jealous of him. "But why should we be jealous of that blockhead?" Melechke asked. "The oaf still doesn't even know the first page of the Tractate *Nedarim* he's been studying all winter long."

Once Hertzke came into the beth medresh and began jumping around among the benches. The students had always considered him a good-for-nothing and paid no attention to him now. But Reb Tsemakh bent over his prayer stand and said angrily, "You cause us only trouble and embarrassment. I'm not going to let you go to the bricklayer again for the Sabbath, and no other member of the congregation will invite you to his house."

Hertzke lifted up his left foot and inspected the sole of his shoe. "Don't worry about me. My mother's coming from Vilna tomorrow, and she'll take me to Argentina."

As rude as he had been before, he still hadn't dared to stand in the presence of Reb Tsemakh with his foot in the air. The students turned from their Talmuds and looked at the scamp. Tsemakh thought the lad was showing signs of madness. His remarks seemed even wilder than his behavior.

"Your mother? From Argentina? Does your father know your mother is coming?"

"My father knows. My mother came from Argentina and talked to him about letting me go there. But he said no. So my mother is coming here and my father is following her." Hertzke dropped his left foot and raised his right, as if inspecting his soles to see if they were sturdy enough for the long journey.

12

CONFRADA STAYED at the Valkenik inn and Vova Barbitoler rented a room next to hers. He didn't leave his undivorced wife for a moment and was present during her first meeting with Hertzke. Confrada fainted, wailed, and kissed her son, while the disheveled Vova constantly muttered, "He's my son, my son." Hertzke let himself be caressed and wept over by his mother, but he held himself like a man. He didn't kiss her and didn't cry; he didn't even glance at his father. Though Vova pleaded with him, "But it was I who raised you," Hertzke backed away from him and roared like a wild beast that won't let itself be tamed, "I hate you and I'm going to Argentina."

Valkenik was in an uproar. People refused to believe that a mother had abandoned her babe at the breast, and that her husband, a pious Jew, had refused her a divorce for fifteen years. Sroleyzer's gang added their own juicy morsels and spread the news. But these sweet chaps felt cheated. They had thought that Sroleyzer had become a penitent in his old age. They had assumed that it was his desire to latch on to God's good graces that had made him snuggle up to a yeshiva lad, let him stuff himself for free every Sabbath, and even shout at the boy, "Shove it in—don't just whinny like a horse." But it turned out that the old scoundrel hadn't done this for the sake of a mitzva. Where there were two, he would be the third in divvying up the spoils. Hearing the brat report that his mother was planning to come and take him, Sroleyzer had gathered that it would be to his advantage to have a hand in the matter. During the winter he had gone to Vilna a few times and met with Hertzke's uncles. This brood lived up in the Novogorod quarter of town and were called "the Order Keepers." They were the roughnecks' arbiters. The Order Keepers agreed with Sroleyzer that he should keep an eye on the brat lest his father kidnap him and disappear. And upon the arrival of his mother, that Argentinian piece of goods, he'd be handsomely rewarded.

The bricklayer's pals swore that they didn't envy the old thief's earnings; still, why should a Jew be a swine? The local townsfolk asked Sroleyzer, "Is it true what your gang is saying about you?"

"It's true," he replied coldly. "I felt sorry for the living orphan. So what do I deserve for that? Perhaps a crown of thorns on my head like Jesus?"

Confrada's room at the inn was open to everyone, and curiosity seekers crowded in all day long. Chaikl Vilner was there too. In all the excitement he had forgotten that it was beneath a ben Torah's dignity to be in such company and that he had to be wary lest he meet the tobacco merchant face to face. Chaikl was burning with curiosity to see the woman with the beautiful face and the blond braids who was so devilishly enchanting that her jilted husband longed for her fifteen years in a row. But when Chaikl pushed his way into the room with all the other townsfolk and saw Hertzke's mother, he stood there transfixed and open-mouthed. Was *that* the one? Was *that* the way she looked?

In the middle of the room sat a woman with rolls of fat bulging on her neck, and legs like chunks of wood that made her high-heeled shoes lopsided. The short, tight sleeves of her brown wool dress revealed a pair of muscular arms, and its low-cut neck displayed a part of her wrinkled bosom. Her soft, faded cheeks were smeared with rouge, and her lips gleamed with a thick layer of lipstick. Heat wafted out of her face as if she'd just stepped out of a hot bath. Her eyes still shone bright and clear, and she still had her own teeth. But instead of the long blond flaxen braids that Chaikl had heard so much about from Vova Barbitoler, he saw a reddish-brown elflock that looked like rust on a burned pot.

Confrada spoke with the clear, authoritative voice of a community do-gooder and reckoned on her fingers: "His first wife he drove to the grave while she was still young. And by this first wife which he drove to the grave while she was still young he had two children. A boy and a girl. It was I who raised them. Fine kids, good kids. The way I hear it, they couldn't stand being with him so they ran away from home. So, dear brothers and sisters, when he was rid of the first wife, he started chasing me. He blackened his beard, curled his mustache, and convinced me I'd be a princess in his home. I wouldn't have to put a finger in cold water. I'd step into a palace filled with so much food, even the dogs would lick their chops. And I, innocent lamb that I was, I let myself be talked into it. But when I settled in—well, that's when hell began for me. That cutthroat didn't let me out of the house for a minute. He watched my every step. He sucked my blood. Then I had a bright idea. It was a godsend. I pleaded with him to let me visit my oldest brother in Argentina. And that's when I got rid of him, all praise and thanks to Him who lives forever."

She pulled a handkerchief out of the large black handbag on her knees and began wiping her tears. "Don't ask, dear brothers and sisters, how much I suffered at his hands. And my little son suffered even more. But the one most to be pitied, dear brothers and sisters, is his third wife. After all, he married again even though he didn't send me a divorce. I heard that his third wife is good and gentle, a quiet and pious woman. Her only fault, people tell me, is that she doesn't have her own hair, poor thing, and that's why she always wears a wig. So he humiliates her publicly and spills her blood by the bucketful. One shouldn't fool around with the likes of him, dear brothers and sisters," Confrada concluded in a singsong voice. The people in the room exchanged glances: One shouldn't fool around with the likes of her, either.

"Confrada, have a heart." Vova Barbitoler edged out of a corner where he had been standing all along. "You left me with a little baby and told me you were only going for a couple of months to see your brother. And I've been waiting for you for years. For years."

"I understand you, I understand." The woman nodded as though sympathizing with his grief. "I'm not surprised you waited for me. Where in the world could an old skirt-chaser like you have found a beautiful young wife like me? Who would've wanted to suffer as much at your hands as I suffered? Sure, sure, I should have thrown over my kindhearted, handsome young husband in Argentina and my little children, may they live and be well, and run back pell-mell to an old Jew with a beard full of lice. Ha, ha, ha!" Confrada bared her teeth, and Hertzke, who stood by the window with an expressionless face, bared his teeth too, as though to show how much he resembled his mother.

Vova Barbitoler couldn't get used to the thought that he had tormented himself for fifteen long years over a fat-fleshed woman with faded dyed hair. His lust for her had suddenly vanished, along with his deep-rooted hatred. Ashamed, he regretted fighting with half the world because of a self-induced mania. All he wanted to do was plead with her to let Hertzke stay with him, so he wouldn't be left alone in his old age. But Confrada's impudent, venomous little laugh kindled his hatred for her once more. He was angry to the marrow of his bones, and his eyes seemed to start from their sockets.

"You whore!" he shouted, stamping his feet. "You haven't changed. You're old and ugly now, but you still laugh that slutty, teasing little laugh of yours, like you used to when you'd come home in the middle of the night from your lovers. My guts turned over in me and you just laughed: 'Ha, ha, ha.' I hope your life goes to pieces the way you made my life go to pieces!"

"Jews have law and a rabbi," a man with a trimmed beard and a goatish voice interrupted. "You go to the rabbi and ask him for a decision or a compromise. Why should you throw mud at each other and make a laughingstock of yourselves in public?"

"To the rabbi, to the rabbi." Vova lunged toward Confrada. But she pertly put both her fists on her hips and, unafraid, laughed in his face.

"I'd be in a pretty pickle if I'd waited for the rabbis to let me remarry. I'd have been under a tombstone in Argentina or in a grave in Vilna long ago, just like you drove your first wife to her death. But since you ran to pray every day, since you peeked into my pots to see if I was keeping kosher, why didn't you obey the rabbis and send me a divorce? Yet you yourself remarried without a divorce. And now you want me to go to the rabbi with you!"

Vova sighed, tired of fighting. "I'll give you a divorce. If Hertzke stays with me, I'll give you a divorce. He's my son. I raised him."

"You're an old man already and you'll die soon, so why do I need your divorce? You tell me, why do I need your divorce?" Confrada looked at him pityingly and addressed him as sweetly as she could. "And why are you asking me? Why don't you ask him? Speak up, sonny boy, do you want to stay with your father?" she said, beaming with joy at the thought that everyone in the room would hear Hertzke's answer.

"I want to go to Argentina, and from there I'll go see other countries on my stamps." Hertzke turned to Chaikl. "See? I'm going to cross the ocean and you're going to warm the bench. So who's on top now?"

In the crowd, the tobacco merchant spotted Reb Shlomo-Motte the Hebrew teacher's son. For an instant a sly, thievish glee flashed in Vova's eyes. He raised both hands and burst into laughter. "Chaikl is here too? It was you and your rabbi, the rosh yeshiva with the eyes of the Angel of Death, who dragged him here. Both of you can drop dead along with that whore!"

Chaikl began retreating slowly, intending to leave—but he couldn't push his way through the tightly pressed throng. Confrada looked amiably at the youth whom Vova had cursed.

"The people who saved him from your hands for even a couple of months have done a great mitzva." She sighed and gazed at Hertzke for a long time. Then she turned to the crowd with a worried face. "He's sixteen but he still acts like a little boy. Blast his father for giving him such an upbringing! He beat him so long he made him slightly daft. Go now, good people, go in good health. Look for better entertainment and enjoy someone else's troubles."

The crowd pushed its way out, and Chaikl departed with them.

"Damn her!" someone said, and spat. "I'll bet in Argentina she's a madam in a whorehouse."

"What an actress!" another man said excitedly. "She ought to sell tickets so people can see how she eats his guts out."

"What a bitch!" a third man groaned. "But her husband is no better. He's a Jewish murderer."

The Valkenik folk went back to their homes, to the market place, to the shops—and Chaikl returned to the beth medresh. Nevertheless, he looked back several times as if afraid that Vova Barbitoler might be following him, stick in hand.

13

THE SCENES at the inn stirred up the whole village. The townspeople shrugged and said, "Couldn't the yeshiva principal pick a fight with a better sort than Vova? And he wanted to make a Torah scholar out of a brat like Hertzke?" And in the back lanes people laughed. "One can't make a yarmulke out of a pig's tail. And this was the lout that Reb Tsemakh brought down here for us to support?" But Tsemakh no longer paid attention to what was being said of him in town. He waited for his meeting with the tobacco merchant as if it were the sentence of a court—and he didn't wait in vain.

Vova Barbitoler left Confrada at the inn with Hertzke for a while and asked where the yeshiva principal lived. He came in the morning and found everyone at breakfast. Dead silence reigned in the room. Hannah-Leah looked anxiously at her old father, and Ronya, fear-stricken, looked at the principal. Tsemakh's face turned ashen. But Vova didn't make a scandal, as he had been expected to. He sat in a chair next to the window, and his bloodshot eyes wandered from person to person around the table. His glance rested on Reb Lippa-Yosse, and he gave a soft little laugh, like a madman.

"I begged that rosh yeshiva of yours not to butt into my life. I've got enough troubles without him. But he fought with me until he got my little boy. I warned him that Hertzke's mother in Argentina and her brothers in Vilna wanted to kidnap him out of here. So he convinced me he would watch him with a thousand eyes. Now I find out that my son was the house guest of a thief, the worst man in town. And this crook arranged with Hertzke's uncles for his mother to come from Argentina and take him away. That's the way your rosh yeshiva watched him."

Reb Lippa-Yosse and his family awaited Reb Tsemakh's reply. But Tsemakh looked as if he couldn't possibly remember what had so engrossed him that he forgot to watch the lad and see whom he made friends with. Ronya looked at Tsemakh apprehensively, as though pleading with him not to remember what had engaged his thoughts.

But it was the soft-spoken Reb Menakhem-Mendl who answered. "Even if the boy had been watched with a thousand eyes, nothing could have prevented his mother's coming from Argentina to take him. The very same thing could have happened in Vilna."

"She wouldn't have found him in Vilna. If he had stayed in Vilna I would've known she was coming for him and she'd never have found him." Vova Barbitoler wiped the thick drops of perspiration from his face and his matted beard. "It's not your fault, Reb Menakhem-Mendl. It's your friend's fault. God sent him to bring trouble down on me, and he's fulfilled his mission."

The tobacco merchant rose and swayed toward the door. When his hand was already on the latch he turned again and addressed the old slaughterer. "By rights I should stay in town and bring things to the point where he'd have to run away from here. I don't have anything to go home to anyway. My house is empty and desolate. But even though respectable people shy away from me, I don't want to destroy the yeshiva the way he destroyed my life, and the way he destroys, it seems, everything he touches."

Vova Barbitoler departed. The silence in the room was so profound that the family at the table heard the drip-drip of the kitchen faucet. Ronya gazed wide-eyed at Tsemakh and a shudder ran over her body, as though the cold drops from the faucet were dripping on her head.

Around noontime Tsemakh came into the beth medresh. The younger students stood by the windows looking out. Seeing their principal enter, they returned to their Talmuds but continued glancing at the street in suspense. Tsemakh sat down in the corner behind the pulpit and buried his head in a sacred text. An excited and perspiring yeshiva boy ran in with a cry, "They're leaving!" and the students from Valkenik surged outside. They still considered the yeshiva something of a small-town cheder, with little discipline. But the Torah scholars from other towns, both young and old, remained in their places. Melechke Vilner, however, couldn't restrain himself. With the haste of a child chasing a runaway ball, he dashed outside after the group of local youths. Tsemakh and Chaikl raised their heads over their prayer stands, and the two responsible for Hertzke's coming to Valkenik exchanged glances.

A sleigh came through Synagogue Street with Confrada and her son on the back seat. Confrada wore a hat with a feather, a caracul coat, and two large silver-fox furs around her shoulders. Vova Barbitoler and Sroleyzer the bricklayer followed the sleigh. Behind them came a sleigh with no passengers. Vova Barbitoler had hired it to take him to the Valkenik railway station so he could return to Vilna with Hertzke and Confrada, but instead the father followed Confrada's sleigh on foot through the village, pleading and begging all the way. Men, women, and children stood on their porches watching the scene.

"He's my son!" Vova seized Confrada's sleigh with both hands.

"My, do I feel sorry for his wife!" The Argentinian woman turned and looked at the crowd standing on both sides of Synagogue Street. "My sonny boy and I have already overcome him, but his third wife is in a terrible fix. Oh my, do I feel sorry for her!"

Sroleyzer the bricklayer was apparently pleased with the reward he had received for his help, for he amiably slapped the tobacco merchant on the shoulder and told him, "Be a man! You're a father, it's true, but a calf runs after the cow, not the ox."

Vova raced forward and blocked the sleigh's path. The driver barely managed to stop the horses.

"Confrada, I'll give you a divorce, but don't take Hertzke away from me." He stood with outspread hands and feet to prevent the sleigh from moving.

"You tell me, why do I need your divorce? You're an old man already and you're going to die soon," she mocked him as she had done at the inn.

Sroleyzer felt ill at ease because everyone was looking at him as the chief architect of this filthy business. He shouted to the driver, "Don't sit there gaping like a loon! Give that old croaker a taste of your whip and move on."

The driver turned to Sroleyzer with uplifted whip. "But I'm not you. I'm not going to run over anybody. And I'm not getting rich from this trip, either." Then the driver guided his horses around Vova Barbitoler, who now remained standing behind.

Hertzke was sick and tired of his parents' fighting, and uninterested in the onlookers' stares. But he wanted the yeshiva students to see him going away. When the sleigh passed the beth medresh, he saw the group of yeshiva boys, Melechke among them. Overjoyed, he jumped up from his seat and stuck out his tongue at them, and thumbed his nose with both hands at Melechke.

Vova Barbitoler was still wandering around in the snow between the two sleighs and yelling, "My son, my son!" when the sleighs passed the market place on the way to the train station. There, new spectators emerged from the houses. The local people on Synagogue Street began to disperse, shaking their heads, groaning and spitting in disgust.

Melechke returned to the beth medresh and approached Tsemakh Atlas. "Rabbi, don't be upset that Hertzke is leaving. He's a boor and a wicked boy. He always teased me about the time you found me sleeping over the Talmud and carried me in your hands like a bundle." Melechke's eyes burned with rage. And then the little boy related an incident that had happened in the guest house: "Last night Hertzke came to take his packed basket from under his bed. He told me, 'Here, you can have my big basket if you give me your little suitcase.' So I told Hertzke, 'My suitcase is new. My mother bought it for me before I left for the yeshiva. But if you'll give me your stamp album, we'll swap.' So Hertzke said, 'Nuts to you; I'm not going to throw in the stamp album. But if you want to swap, I'll give you my tefillin and my ritual fringes. So I said to

Hertzke, 'What do I need your tefillin for? I'm not even Bar Mitzva. And anyway, how can you give me your tefillin and ritual fringes? What will you pray with, and what will you use to make the blessing, you nitwit, you goy?' Then Hertzke burst out laughing and said, 'They don't pray in Argentina, and they don't put on tefillin there. And I'm never going to make the blessing with the ritual fringes again, because my father always beat me to make me put them on and because the rabbi dragged me out of Sroleyzer's house.' So I didn't swap with Hertzke. But Hertzke left his tefillin and ritual fringes here anyway. They're on the window in the guest house."

Tsemakh hadn't expected Confrada's son to become his enemy too. Seeing his rosh yeshiva sitting in melancholy silence, Melechke began to console him again. "It's good that Hertzke went away. He was saying bad things to the boys in the guest house, things he'd learned during his Sabbath stay at his host's place. And you know what he said to me? 'My Sabbath is a sunny one and yours is full of gloom.'"

"Why is your Sabbath gloomy?" Tsemakh asked through taut lips.

Melechke lowered his head, regretting that he had revealed his secret. Tsemakh suddenly became tense and alert. He hadn't known what kind of people Vova's son had been associating with, and he didn't know what had been happening to Melechke, despite his promise to the boy's family to watch him as if he were the apple of his eye.

"Tell me, where do you have your Sabbath meals?" he asked, and Melechke decided he had better tell him.

"I eat my Sabbath meals at Reb Zalmen Kaletzky the peddler's house. Reb Zalmen is a widower and he has no children. On Friday night he makes Kiddush over two little black challas, and the two of us share a herring."

"Why didn't you tell me or Reb Yisroel the tailor to get you another Sabbath host so you wouldn't have to go hungry?" Reb Tsemakh asked.

"I'm not going hungry," Melechke answered. "Reb Zalmen Kaletzky just doesn't have time to prepare the cholent because he comes home late on Friday afternoon from his village rounds. So for Sabbath lunch we eat chopped radishes and chicken fat or cold chicken fat with bread sprinkled with salt. For the third Sabbath meal we eat the hard-boiled eggs that Reb Zalmen brings from the village. Reb Zalmen also fills up my pockets with apples for me to eat during the week. And when I leave, Reb Zalmen always asks me not to go eat anywhere else, for sitting alone at the Sabbath table will make him sad, and he doesn't want people to know he's poor. He pats me and tells me that he loves me as though I were his only child," Melechke said, finally revealing the secret of why he had become so attached to the peddler.

Melechke's earlocks were already thick and the four fringes dangled from under his jacket; nevertheless, he still yearned for someone to caress him. He looked at Tsemakh, trembling like a young fawn with bright eyes and thin, unsteady legs. Tsemakh felt a warmth in his ice-cold limbs and put his arm around Melechke. The little boy was waiting for this and at once thrust himself between Tsemakh's knees. The principal patted him, thinking of the poor peddler who ate cold, frugal meals but in whose house tranquility reigned. He too would gladly have moved into such a house and eaten bread and salt, on Sabbath and weekdays, as long as tranquility, sadness and tranquility, surrounded him.

14

THE SNOW FELL far and wide without letup and lay for days on end, festively neat and bright but causing weariness and desolation. It was the middle of Shvat, or February, and the winter still had a long way to go. The townspeople went about feeling bored, a gnawing sadness in their hearts. The quiet roared in their minds, and the silence of far-off places numbed their senses. During the long winter nights the stillness of the surrounding forests pierced their ears, which seemed plugged with clay. People lay open-eyed in their beds, bathed in perspiration; they sensed their bones breaking and a dull paralysis in their heads. The darkness was oppressive, like a quilt on a feverish person who can't flee his nightmares. During the day, the town stared blankly through opaque windows at doorsteps piled high with drifts. Dusted with snow, the shopkeepers stood in their stores, hands tucked into their sleeves, gaping as though they had forgotten human speech.

In the beth medresh, prayers and studies dragged on lazily, sleepily. The young students became more pious and sedate. The many pages of the Talmud that they had mastered piled up in their heads. Their earlocks grew long and they didn't trim their growing beards. The only things that bloomed in midwinter on these devout, hairy faces were the pimples of their adolescent desire.

Chaikl Vilner no longer thought of Tsharne. He stuffed his mind with the formidable Aramaic terms of the Tractate *Nedarim*. One Thursday he was swaying over a Talmud, reciting a passage aloud to himself. Tired of sitting on the bench, he began pacing back and forth in the beth medresh. Deep in thought, he didn't notice that he had walked out into the anteroom, where he continued gesticulating to himself until he bumped into a woman.

At the entrance of the beth medresh stood a young woman. She had on a full black fur coat with a semicircular white collar and her hands were in a muff. A round, flat fur cap fluttered like a bird over her blond hair. Covered with snowflakes, her shiny fur coat glistened with a wet, bluish sheen. Her hair, eyebrows, and nose were covered with the tiny star-shaped flakes.

"May I see the rosh yeshiva, Tsemakh Atlas?" the woman asked Chaikl. "Tell him his wife is waiting outside for him."

Chaikl Vilner thought he was dreaming. He had scarcely stammered, "He's teaching the younger students now," when the woman smiled, revealing two rows of white teeth behind her freshly painted lips.

"Are you one of my husband's pupils too?"

Chaikl nodded and went into the side room. Tsemakh sat at the head of a long, narrow table listening to the youngsters discussing a Talmudic passage. Looking as if he himself didn't believe the news, Chaikl whispered the message to the principal. Tsemakh gazed at him incredulously, flustered and alarmed. He removed his skullcap, put on his hat, and went outside.

The woman smiled at Tsemakh, her large, shining eyes brimming with a blue radiance. It *is* his wife! Chaikl shouted to himself, but he evidently lingered too long because the principal murmured, "Thank you," and waited for him to leave. Chaikl returned to the beth medresh with dreamy eyes. He saw a scudding golden sun, a silver fountain spraying. He was so surprised that he told none of the students about the woman outside, as if looking at her were his secret, a stroke of good luck which only he'd been worthy of.

"I'm in the midst of a lesson with my students," Tsemakh muttered, disconcerted.

"And you can't interrupt it?" Slava asked.

"Of course I can." He winced. "I mean, I didn't expect you. You didn't write that you were coming. True, I didn't write myself. Where are you staying?"

"At the town inn," Slava said, then added dryly, "Since you didn't send for me, why did I have to write that I was coming?" Then Slava gave a sudden laugh. "Tsemakh, you already have the long beard and earlocks of a full-fledged rabbi."

"Please wait a minute till I put my coat on and tell my students that the lesson is over for today."

While she waited for him her face became angry and stern. He looked at me so impassively; he's become more cold than ever, she thought.

Tsemakh stood next to her in his long rabbinic coat. Her silk-gloved hand slipped easily into his arm. As they were about to go down the steps, Sheeya Lipnishker stormed out of the beth medresh. The prodigy with the bobbing earlocks and sparse little beard wore his towel around his neck instead of a shirt; his long, stained ritual fringes hung down below his short jacket. He was rushing to the toilet with the rage of a prodigy who was all head and in whom the Torah seethed. To save precious time, he had already unbuttoned his coat, loosened the belt of his trousers, and begun searching all his pockets for tissue paper. On the steps he noticed the rosh yeshiva standing with a female wrapped in the fur of some wild beast of prey, and the female was holding the rosh yeshiva by the arm. Sheeya's huge black cross-eyes bulged. The pupils contracted and the popping whites quivered. That beauty in fur seemed to be a she-demon; he saw a smile on her forbidden lips. The prodigy was so befuddled that he raced down the steps as if he'd leaped over the threshold of hell. Slava choked with laughter for a moment, then a grimace of disgust froze in the corners of her mouth.

Valkenik residents had seen the woman on her way to the beth medresh. When they learned from the innkeeper that she was Tsemakh Atlas' wife, they fell into an astonished silence. It was the silence of a meadow at dawn, before the birds awake and the summer sun shows its golden finger. Coming back from the beth medresh with Tsemakh, Slava noticed people staring at her through the frost-misted windows. This pleased her, but she thought it odd that Tsemakh walked at her side so stiff and tense, not even daring to turn his head. So she also held his arm with her other hand, as though unable to extricate herself from the deep snow. Slava walked with measured little steps, and Tsemakh too avoided walking quickly, lest it appear he was pulling away from her and she was running after him. He couldn't bring himself to tell Slava that her way of holding on to him was not befitting the wife of a rosh yeshiva, so he inched along sluggishly. Synagogue Street was so long today it seemed it would never end. Instead of speaking, Tsemakh coughed several times, and his coughs echoed along the quiet streets. Slava looked up at the sky, down at her fur-trimmed boots, and smiled left and right to the half-hidden faces of the kerchiefed women who emerged from everywhere to peer at her. She cast a sidelong glance at her bearded husband and thought: He's a stranger. But she maintained her affectionate smile and adjusted her fur cap.

The innkeeper approached them in a dither. He didn't know to whom to turn first. "Rebbetsin, would you like to have some sour cream and cheese, or perhaps a couple of new-laid eggs? My wife just finished whipping up fresh butter, and I'll bring you some cakes the baker made. Or do you prefer homemade bread?"

The rebbetsin answered good-naturedly, "I'm not hungry." And as soon as the innkeeper left she burst out laughing. "Me, a rebbetsin?"

Slava waited for her husband to take off his coat and show how happy he was at her arrival. But he stood there dispirited, gazing with a strange dread at the two beds by the windows. Not wanting to be overcome by the same feeling toward him, she pressed close to him and threw her head back with an intoxicated smile on her face. She was curious about what sensations she'd have in kissing this bearded man when they hadn't touched each other for so long.

She waited a moment, then immediately retreated. "You don't even want to kiss me?"

"I do. Why shouldn't I?" But the petulant expression of a misunderstood deaf-mute flashed on his face. "There are laws . . ."

He did not finish. She fixed her eyes on him until she understood what he meant. He's become a bench warmer, a fanatic, a mindless religious, she thought, removing her coat. Her gray wool dress, tight at the waist, revealed her narrow shoulders and her now fuller hips. Slava sat down at the table, rolled up her sleeves, and rubbed the full length of her arms, as if her skin had become stiff with cold.

Seeing her pouting—her usual gesture when upset—Tsemakh realized that she felt grossly insulted. He sat down opposite her and said, "I've missed you very much. Perhaps I didn't want to admit this, so I didn't write to you . . . but you know I'm not two-faced. I can't violate what the Torah bids us and what I teach my students. According to the law, as long as a woman doesn't immerse herself in the ritual bath, the mikva, or in a river, her husband may not touch her."

Once again Slava smiled with her blue eyes, her teeth, and the corners of her mouth. She wasn't benign enough to forgive and forget so readily, but now she felt she had to push her anger into some far-off corner of her mind. Tsemakh appeared to be much more tender than before; he didn't want to hurt her. Even his eyes have become pious, she thought.

"And how is it living here?" she asked.

"I live," he answered grudgingly and looked at her transparent ears, visible beneath her well-combed hair. Her long white neck, finely chiseled nose, and round firm jaw had not changed. Her cheeks, made lean as if by an inner fire, and her wan smile added to her sage look. Tsemakh gazed at her as if incredulous that she was his wife, that she had come to see him. At that moment he couldn't understand how he could have abandoned such a woman to go and suffer torments away from home. His sensual lips jutted out from under his thick mustache; his nostrils pinched.

Slava saw that his eyes weren't pious any longer. A wild desire was coming over him, just as in old times. She had always known that he was an ascetic by nature and despised himself for his passions. He couldn't love a woman and didn't feel the joy of loving. She saw now that he hadn't changed. His face quivered with passion and rage. He was furious with himself for wanting her. She too was now kindled, but only with anger. At that moment she loathed him for his vulgar male desires, for his beard and earlocks, for his wrinkled, scowling brow. She was disgusted by his hooked nose, like that of a hawk that pulls a fish onto a stone and devours it alive. Soon he would cry out, "I can't wait any longer!"

Slava set a pair of wicked eyes on him and laughed. "And is lusting after a wife who doesn't go to the ritual bath permitted?"

He remained silent, amazed at her unexpectedly harsh tone and vicious, mocking glance. She became even more incensed and went on ridiculing him. "On the one hand, you never stopped being a yeshiva student. You went around in the house without a hat, humming that melancholy melody of the Musarniks. On the other hand, I had no faith in your piety even when you began going to the beth medresh. You didn't ask then if my kitchen was kosher or if I was kosher. But now, at our very first meeting, you want to know if I dunk myself in a ritual bath. It seems you can only be kind and gentle to downtrodden people like a pregnant maid."

"Was Stasya found?" Tsemakh was no longer paying attention to his wife's complaints. With anxiety in his voice he asked quickly, "Where is she? Has she had her baby?"

"I don't know," Slava said indifferently.

Tsemakh became even more anxious. Astounded, he said softly, "What do you mean you don't know?"

Slava saw that his desire for her had vanished in an instant. He was pale, and fear was in his eyes.

"My sister-in-law Hannah knows where the girl is," Slava told him. "Don't worry. Stasya is working in a Jewish house somewhere in a village or a town."

"So her whereabouts *are* known. Then you could easily have found out more about her. How is she being treated? And what's going to become of her when she has a baby on her hands and can't work?" he murmured in a pleading voice.

"Knowing that she was found, that she didn't commit suicide, is enough for me. That's all I know and that's all I care to know." His wife bent her head to him across the table, like a beautiful angry beast thrusting its head through the bars of a cage.

She lacks compassion, Tsemakh thought with heavy heart. He stood and said serenely, "I live in the house of the local slaughterer. They're a respectable family, so I have to let them know that you've come. I also have to spend some time in the yeshiva. Afterwards I'll come back here and we'll eat supper together at the inn." Slava saw that he weighed his every word, careful not to anger her. But his eyes had a dry, hard sheen and his lips were drawn.

15

THE RABBI from Misagoleh, Reb Aryeh-Leyb Miadovnik, had been in Valkenik the previous summer and appealed greatly to the religious element. The enlightened group too liked his Torah learning and wisdom and his avoidance of Agudah party politics; but he was a bit too old-fashioned and knew no Polish. But when Eltzik Bloch and his faction realized that the religious element wouldn't let them choose a town rabbi who appealed solely to them, both sides agreed to invite the Misagoleh rabbi for the Sabbath when the Song of Moses was read.

Since his downfall with the Miadle rabbi, Eltzik Bloch no longer spared his brother-in-law and loudly spoke his mind for everyone to hear: "Reb Aryeh-Leyb Miadovnik isn't going to skip to Hirshe Gordon's pipe."

The visiting rabbi stayed at the Valkenik inn and Eltzik Bloch danced attendance on him. Friday morning, when Tsemakh went to see Slava, Eltzik Bloch met him in the corridor and, face beaming, stretched out his hand.

"A hearty welcome to your guest! When a Talmud scholar has a bright and beautiful wife it's an honor for the Torah. Please come and greet the rabbi from Misagoleh."

Tsemakh realized that he dare not refuse Eltzik Bloch, who had all along been an opponent of the yeshiva and now wanted to make peace. He walked with Eltzik to the rabbi's room.

Reb Aryeh-Leyb Miadovnik had removed his gaberdine and wore only his long woolen ritual fringes over his shirt. He was lying on a low sofa and considering his situation: The Valkenik wages won't suffice for livelihood, nor for doctors and prescriptions for his sick wife. And besides, the local rabbi wants a lot of money for his house—and in cash, too—to cover the cost of his journey to the Land of Israel. Where would he get so much cash to buy the house? The town of Misagoleh didn't want him to leave and wouldn't give him a loan.

Just then the rabbi saw two men entering. He rose from the sofa and got into his gaberdine. Reb Aryeh-Leyb Miadovnik was a head taller than Reb Tsemakh Atlas; his face was bordered by long curly earlocks and a disheveled white beard. The big eyes beneath his bushy brows welcomed the entering men amiably and sadly.

"What are the students learning now?" he asked Tsemakh Atlas. "And does the village support you decently?" During the conversation his face remained clouded over with worries, and Tsemakh looked troubled too. Only Eltzik Bloch beamed with joy. He had undergone a complete change; he praised the students, the yeshiva principal, and Reb Tsemakh's wife.

"Valkenik is in a turmoil. Yesterday Reb Tsemakh's wife came to town. I tell you, she has the face of a princess. Everyone in town is delighted that the rosh yeshiva won't have to be alone any longer."

"Well then, *mazel tov*." The elder rabbi turned to Reb Tsemakh, and the two parted with warm farewells, each preoccupied with the complexities of his own life.

After the Friday night candles were lit in the beth medresh, not a sign of gloom could be seen on Reb Aryeh-Leyb Miadovnik. His wide, fleshy face glowed red after his Sabbath eve immersion in the hot mikva. The congregation couldn't take its eyes off the man whose every move and gesture signaled self-assurance. The scholars at the eastern wall told one another that the rabbi from Misagoleh literally radiated common sense. That he was not a hairsplitter was readily apparent. Though he wouldn't close his eyes to something forbidden, he wasn't strict and pedantic. Even the malcontents who perpetually complained liked him. He was the sort of man who wouldn't hesitate to proclaim unkosher the meat of a butcher who charged exorbitant prices. The poorer Jews from the rear benches thought they would have a friend in the rabbi; he would listen to them attentively and advise them in times of stress. After the Kabolas Shabbes prayers, the congregation looked on as the Misagoleh rabbi conversed with the Valkenik rabbi. As the two men sat in a corner near the Holy Ark, the silver of both their beards was webbed into one. They were whispering about something, and their faces beamed like those of old friends who meet when they are along in years and exchange stories about the joy of having grandchildren.

When the visiting rabbi stood for the Evening Service, revealing his full height, the congregation beheld a mighty Cedar of Lebanon. For the Silent Devotion the beth medresh glowed with quiet joy and ecstasy, like an orchard full of ripe red apples. Only Reb Hirshe Gordon prayed loudly, in everyday fashion, as though he were hurrying to get to a local fair. He even gestured to Yudel the cantor to make it quick. But this time Gordon's brother-in-law, Eltzik, sitting with him by the eastern wall, didn't mind. On the contrary, he didn't care if Hirshe pulled his tricks; he'd see that it wouldn't do him any good. Everyone was agreed upon the rabbi from Misagoleh.

In honor of the important guest, the yeshiva people also prayed with the congregants in the large beth medresh. The young pupils looked respectfully and enviously at Reb Aryeh-Leyb Miadovnik. What a gaon! What a famous rabbi! Only the rosh yeshiva, Reb Tsemakh, stood off in a corner by himself, looking like a poor wayfarer in town whom nobody had invited for the Sabbath. After the Evening Service, Tsemakh saw the entire congregation surging forward to wish the two rabbis a *gut shabbes*; he also saw Reb Hirshe Gordon pushing against the crowd toward the exit. He heard Gordon telling him, "For your information, the rabbi from Misagoleh is an opponent of Musar. Now you can't stay neutral." But Hirshe's angry words came to him from far off, like a sound wafting across a river in a fog.

Tsemakh, the last to leave the beth medresh, walked along slowly until Synagogue Street was empty. He was alone now with the cold, starry sky, the deep snow, and the violet shadows around

the porches. Filtered through the frost-covered windows, the
candles glowed more faintly than in the houses themselves. He
stopped in front of his lodging and looked over the bridge toward
the forest. When Tsemakh had come into the house, the slaughterer's family expressed joy at his wife's arrival. "Now don't forget to
bring her for the Sabbath," Reb Lippa-Yosse directed. Tsemakh,
however, felt like leaving the house and crossing the bridge into the
dark forest and walking day and night without stopping, until he
was in another world where there was no Valkenik and no conflict
over a rabbi, a place where he was not yet married and would not
have to dine at the same table with his wife and Ronya.

He stepped behind the porch for a moment, eyes closed, wanting
to blend with the stillness of the night. But the nocturnal peace of
the turquoise snow, the silent woods nearby, and the secret sparkle
of the green stars neither attracted nor calmed him. He felt drawn
to the homely warmth of a beth medresh full of Jews. On Friday
night the electric lamps and the lit candles on the lectern flamed
with a tremulous gold that was completely different from the light
of midweek; but the heavens did not change, the stars in the sky did
not shine any differently in honor of the Sabbath. Even Maimonides, Tsemakh thought, admits that the infinity of stars was not
created for the benefit of earth or man. But in this world and in our
holy place of worship the quiet joy of praying glowed on everyone's
face—on the scholar's and on the rich man's by the eastern wall, as
well as on the pauper's and on the common workman's sitting
behind the pulpit. Praying revealed something dormant within
everyone. It manifested itself clearly after a secret life deep within,
as if the worshiper had shouted down into a deep well and heard his
bizarre echo resounding from the depths. If the worshiper was a
man of heightened piety, the prayer overwhelmed his body and
spirit, his life and soul. All his limbs trembled with ecstatic joy.
But even when the worshiper was a simple sort who prayed for
health and livelihood, for his wife and children—such a man
derived joy from the prayer itself. After the service he felt purified,
like the sky cleared of rain clouds. But he, Tsemakh mused, was
not like that. He had never even really wept at prayers, for he
considered weeping a kind of passion—he was disgusted by the
man who indulged himself with tears of self-pity. From his lips
came no songs of praise or thanksgiving. He knew only one

melody, the melancholy Musar melody, which cut pieces of flesh
from one's body. Instead of feeling joy of soul at prayers, he
tormented himself with analysis of soul. He often felt that his soul
also yearned and trembled to worship God with joy. But his soul
was suffocated as if by prison walls, with his constant admonition
of himself and others. While he chastised his pupils, he also envied
their daily singing at morning prayers, "With abounding love hast
thou loved us, O Lord our God . . ."

Tsemakh opened his eyes and looked once more at the nearby
woods. He wished he were a petrified tree among the snow-clad
pines. Unlike all the other Jews in town, he had never chanted the
Song of Songs on Friday evenings before the Kabolas Shabbes
service. He did not want to lie to himself. As if it were not enough
to disagree with the Kabbala that the Song of Songs is a song of love
that the soul sings to the Creator, he didn't even have enough of the
basic feeling of love for his own wife to sing the Song of Songs to
her. Suddenly Tsemakh started. Why was he standing here? Slava
and the old slaughterer and his family were waiting for him with
the Kiddush.

He sat at the table between Reb Lippa-Yosse and Yudel, but still
saw before his eyes the silent snow-covered forest behind the town.
Slava and Ronya were at the other end of the table.

"I see from your room that they treat you like a prince here,"
Slava said. Her eyes sparkled with the cleverness of a woman who
makes herself at home wherever she goes. She wore a black woolen
skirt and a white blouse, lace-embroidered at the sleeves and
around the neck. So as not to sit bareheaded at the Friday night
table she had covered her head lightly with a white silk kerchief.
Ronya wore a long dark blue dress, as though wanting to appear
older and more sedate. But her every movement quivered with
youth, like a thin tree that flutters and glistens with pale green
leaves.

After the Kiddush Ronya quickly told Slava, "Now you can
remove the kerchief." But Slava replied just as quickly, "It doesn't
bother me."

Along the wall sat Hannah-Leah's sallow-faced, long-nosed little
girls, eying the visitor with morose resentment. Hannah-Leah,
who was serving, looked very worried. She was troubled and
frightened because her younger sister was so agitated. The princi-

pal's wife seemed to be a very clever woman—as suited to be a rebbetsin as she herself was to be a doctor.

One of Ronya's sons, who was sitting next to Slava, boasted, "When Papa comes he's going to bring me a sailor suit with brass buttons and a round hat with a tassel as long as a squirrel's tail."

"Papa's going to bring me a sailor suit too," his brother out-shouted him, "with a big white collar, and the tassel on my hat is going to be even longer."

Ronya seemed pleased that her sons remembered their father. She turned to Slava. "My husband went abroad and promised to bring the children sailor suits. Have you ever been abroad?" Ronya asked, breathing hotly.

"No, not yet," Slava answered and glanced quickly at Tsemakh, who was looking uneasy. He snapped awake at Slava's glance as though a needle had pricked him, and began listening to the conversation at the table.

"Eltzik Bloch is trying to make peace with all his opponents," Reb Lippa-Yosse was saying, "to strengthen his group. He also gave me a hearty '*gut shabbes*' and told me, 'Don't worry, Reb Lippa-Yosse. Our future rabbi is a gaon and a righteous man. He's not a wild man and he won't deprive anyone of his livelihood. Your son-in-law will be our ritual slaughterer for life, and you're going to lead us in the Musaf prayers till you're a hundred and twenty. Your children and grandchildren now sit at your table and you'll live to have great-grandchildren, just as the Psalm says: "Your children are like olive trees around your table."' Since Eltzik Bloch wanted to make up with me, I joked good-naturedly: 'But the first part of the verse says: "Your wife is like a fruitful vine." To have joy from children one has to have a wife at one's side.' But I was afraid to tell him that I too support the Misagoleh rabbi lest Reb Hirshe Gordon become my bitter enemy."

Even though Reb Menakhem-Mendl didn't look at strange women, he was tempted to look at Reb Tsemakh's rebbetsin. Back in Vilna he had heard that she came from a rich and nonobservant family. Indeed, he saw that an aura of wealth hovered about her, and it was obvious that she didn't cover her hair at home. In that case he ought to thank God that he hadn't fallen into the hands of a modern woman. He was distressed, however, that his wife, may she live and be well, hadn't been able to visit him in the middle of the term. His meager earnings just barely sufficed to support her and their child in Vilna. Like a pious lad who holds his ritual fringes to keep demons from harming him, Reb Menakhem-Mendl tugged at his little beard to free himself from the envy that had insinuated itself into his heart.

"I don't understand," Reb Menakhem-Mendl murmured, "why Reb Hirshe Gordon opposes him. Valkenik has no need to look for a better rabbi than the one from Misagoleh. He's a well-known scholar and preacher, resolute in his opinions. And I have no doubt that he will support the yeshiva."

"If the rabbi from Misagoleh weren't a well-known scholar and preacher, resolute in his opinions, then Reb Hirshe Gordon would surely have supported him," Reb Tsemakh interrupted heatedly, like a tongue of fire suddenly bursting through a flaming oven door.

"The yeshiva should not get involved," Reb Menakhem-Mendl sang his old song, wary that his friend might again be heading for a fight. Ronya also shuddered in fear. Slava looked at her husband with a smile, as though enjoying the fact that he was getting excited.

But Tsemakh calmed down as quickly as he had flared up. "Reb Menakhem-Mendl is right. The yeshiva should not get involved," he muttered and scowled at the bench by the window, the bench where Vova Barbitoler had recently sat and asserted that everything Tsemakh touched he destroyed.

16

THE QUARREL between the two brothers-in-law intensified before the Sabbath Morning Service. As frosty sunlight came in through the beth medresh windows, the artisans warmed their backs by the hot dry bricks of the stove at the western wall and turned their still sleepy faces to the sun rays that tickled their hairy noses and ears. By the eastern wall the more affluent congregants donned their prayer shawls and began the morning blessings.

Suddenly, from the front of the shul Eltzik Bloch was heard shouting at his brother-in-law, "I took money from the rabbi of Misagoleh to help him become the Valkenik rabbi? I took a bribe?"

"I didn't say that." Reb Hirshe didn't lift his eyes from the Talmud on his prayer stand.

"But you just said that since the enlightened faction first opposed the rabbi and now supports him, it's a sign that they took money!" Eltzik shouted louder.

"I didn't say that. I said that if the freethinkers like the rabbi from Misagoleh, he's not suitable for the religious element," Reb Hirshe answered calmly, raising his voice so that the surrounding congregants would hear every word.

The early morning quarrel at the beth medresh reverberated in Reb Lippa-Yosse's house at lunch. The Torah reader, Yudel the slaughterer, had chanted worse than usual that morning, and, of all places, he kept stumbling during the Song of Moses, when the entire congregation was standing. The worshipers corrected him and banged their prayer stands, shouting, "Are you blind? Get glasses!" Even more muddled, Yudel had begun to make reading mistakes in addition to his faulty cantillation.

At the table, Reb Lippa-Yosse complained to Hannah-Leah, "The congregants yelled, 'If Yudel mangles cows the way he mangles the Torah text, we haven't been eating kosher meat.' Where does he keep his head? Even cheder boys know the Hebrew and the melody for the Song of Moses. After all, it's in the prayer book, and we say it every morning."

Yudel, still panting with fright as he had on the pulpit, said in self-defense, "It was Reb Hirshe Gordon who mixed me up. Last night, at the pulpit, he told me to speed it up."

Hannah-Leah, humiliated and angry at having Tsemakh Atlas' wife see that Yudel was a shlimazel, scolded him: "How come last night's remark frightened you this morning? Nobody said *you* took money from the Misagoleh rabbi."

The children were squabbling too. In honor of Tu Bishvat, Arbor Day, they had received hard, dry pieces of carob, and each child thought the others had gotten bigger pieces. To quiet them down, their grandfather said, "Today it's a mitzva to feed the birds."

The grandchildren ran to the back yard with bread crumbs. The men remained at the table, and Ronya invited Slava into her room, where they drank tea, ate fruit, and chatted. Slava talked about her brothers and Ronya about her women friends. Suddenly she blushed and said with childish fervor, "Why don't you move in with us? I have two big rooms, and I can give you one of them."

Slava looked pleased, as though delighted by the suggestion. "But won't it be crowded? Isn't your husband coming home soon?"

Ronya gave a pathetic, guilty smile. "My husband only comes home for the holidays."

From the window the women saw the men leaving for the beth medresh. Old Reb Lippa-Yosse took small steps in the snow and Yudel followed lazily. Reb Menakhem-Mendl huddled into his short coat, but Tsemakh, wearing his broad rabbinic hat and a long black overcoat, appeared taller than the snow-covered Valkenik houses. Slava watched him with misty eyes.

His wife loves him very much; she's proud of him, Ronya thought, and wanted to like Slava in order not to hate her. Her Azriel, too, was tall and broad-shouldered, but he had a red beard. Azriel would not have brought home a pupil who had fallen asleep over his Talmud, she thought. He doesn't even care that he doesn't see his own children for six months at a time.

"I have an idea." Slava took Ronya by the hand. "Let's go hear the new rabbi. I'm curious to see the people in your town."

In the long, low-ceilinged, half-dark women's gallery, elderly women stood by the narrow window that looked down into the beth medresh. The rabbi was already speaking and the other women didn't notice the two newcomers. Slava and Ronya moved up to an unoccupied window and watched. Opposite them, by the eastern wall, stood Tsemakh. He leaned against a prayer stand and listened, his head turned to the preacher. Reb Menakhem-Mendl sat on the adjoining bench. The preacher, standing next to the Holy Ark, was not visible because of the many men crowded into the high pulpit in the center of the beth medresh. His melodic chant, however, could be heard clearly.

"Because our Father Abraham split logs for the sacrifice of his only son, the tribes were adjudged worthy of having the Red Sea split for them," the rabbi from Misagoleh said. "But the sea didn't part until the Jews were in water over their necks, so that they might learn to have faith in the Almighty. And when the Israelites crossed the sea and sang the Song of Moses, children on their mothers' bosoms sang with them because everyone had seen the Divine Presence. And that prompted the custom of feeding birds on the Sabbath of the Song of Moses, because at that time all God's creatures sang about the miracle of the Exodus from Egypt. Others claim that the custom was begun to remind us that just as the winged creatures find their little seeds everywhere, the Holy One Blessed Be He fed the Jews in the desert."

Heads appeared in the little windows of the women's gallery. They all wore marriage wigs and old-fashioned hats decorated with feathers and resembled a row of birds perched on a fence.

Soon the rabbi ceased chanting and commenced an involved interpretation of Tu Bishvat. "The school of Shammai says that the new year for trees is the first day of the month of Shvat, but the school of Hillel says that it falls on the fifteenth of Shvat, or Tu Bishvat."

When the rabbi quoted Talmudic words and phrases the women were completely lost. The heads that had peeked out of the little windows withdrew into the women's gallery, as birds on a fence fly off when the sun slips behind a cloud.

Suddenly Slava heard a sharp voice shrieking from the pulpit, interrupting the rabbi's sermon.

When the heckler finished, the rabbi calmly repeated, "In the third and sixth year after the sabbatical year, one sets aside the first tithe and the poor man's tithe. During subsequent years, one sets aside the first tithe and the second tithe."

But the man on the pulpit interrupted again: "You're not telling us anything new."

The rabbi's voice gradually grew weaker. Whenever he tried to reply, the other man would interrupt. Slava saw that the worshipers behind the pulpit didn't understand the argument either, because they were asking one another what the bickering was all about. Those sitting along the eastern wall cried out, "Impudence! For shame! Let the rabbi speak!" But the group that surrounded the interlocutor on the pulpit outshouted them: "Let the rabbi's son-in-law speak. Reb Hirshe knows more Talmud than a dozen rabbis." The beth medresh rocked and seethed. A broad swath of sunlight came in through the window and cut across the hairy, angry faces like a scythe, covering them with the copper tinge of sunset.

Slava saw that Tsemakh had moved from his place. He made his way forward and looked scathingly at the man disturbing the rabbi's sermon. But Reb Menakhem-Mendl stood next to him, tugging at his sleeve.

"Your husband shouldn't get into this," Ronya cried out.

Slava did not reply. A smile of triumph trembled in the corners of her mouth. She longed for Tsemakh's madness, for his wild courage and strength. She wanted him to jump into the fire and be burned. Only then would he return to her and live solely for her.

Eltzik Bloch ran up to the two rosh yeshivas, thrust Reb Menakhem-Mendl aside, and began pulling Reb Tsemakh's sleeve, urging him to intervene. Tsemakh let himself be drawn forward until he stood by the pulpit steps. Sroleyzer the bricklayer blocked his path. Now Sroleyzer could present himself as a respectable congregant and at the same time square accounts with the yeshiva principal who had dragged Hertzke Barbitoler from his house.

"You aren't by any chance planning to drag the rabbi's son-in-law off the pulpit, are you?" Sroleyzer loudly trumpeted for the entire beth medresh to hear. "You're a stranger here, and you're not going to lord it over us in our town."

From all sides people shouted at the bricklayer, "Thief! Fence!" Tsemakh advanced toward him as if he were a low-hanging gray cloud shaped like a man. Ronya moaned aloud, completely forgetting that Tsemakh's wife stood at her side.

Reb Hirshe Gordon pounded the pulpit desk with both hands until silence reigned for a moment. Then he bent over the pulpit railing and pointed a finger at Tsemakh. "Nowadays one can't be a rabbi or a rosh yeshiva and stay on the sidelines. Whoever doesn't speak out against the sinners of Israel helps them. The rabbi from Misagoleh is neutral in the holy war that the pious wage against the freethinkers. And you, a Navaredker Musarnik and a rosh yeshiva, you also have your reasons for not publicly opposing those heretics."

From the floor Eltzik Bloch waved his fists up at his brother-in-law and shouted with all his might, "You troublemaker!"

The crowd eyed the principal, awaiting his reply, but he merely stared at Reb Hirshe Gordon and said nothing. Slava wanted Tsemakh to lunge at the loudmouthed heckler, as he had lunged at the customers in their store and at her brothers, and as he had fought with her and ruined their marriage because of a maid. But Tsemakh didn't lunge at the man with the unkempt beard. He was afraid of him. He was afraid of having to leave the town and return home.

Slava moved away from the little window and told Ronya bitterly, "I've had enough. I'm tired of this. I'm going back to my inn to rest. You stay if you want to see more."

Slava left quickly. Was it any concern of hers if provincial Jews squabbled over a rabbi? Let Ronya delight in her lodger, Tsemakh Atlas . . .

Seeing that the principal wasn't responding, Reb Hirshe Gordon bent over the railing and shouted, "Reb Yosef-Yoizl Hurwitz of Navaredok always persecuted every rabbi if he suspected him of not being a fire-and-brimstone opponent of the maskils. And if you're not a fanatic, then you're not Reb Yosef-Yoizl's disciple. You're not a true Navaredker Musarnik!"

Tsemakh, not budging from his place, still maintained his silence, as though waiting for Reb Hirshe to revile him even more. And only when Reb Hirshe turned away from him did Tsemakh return to his seat next to Reb Menakhem-Mendl, who was amazed and awed by his friend's restraint.

Hirshe Gordon and his followers left the pulpit and pushed their way outside. A sudden stillness came over the beth medresh. Eltzik Bloch ran to the Holy Ark and shouted up to the preacher in a pleading and angry tone, "Please continue, rabbi, please continue!"

The rabbi resumed his sermon but his voice was weak. He concluded his interrupted analysis and returned to the weekly Torah portion, but his words echoed as though in empty space. The congregants looked at the empty pulpit, and the silence in the beth medresh thickened as if mourners were sitting dejectedly on the benches.

After the Havdola ceremony at the conclusion of the Sabbath, Tsemakh went to the inn. Although Slava's room was dark, the glow from the snow outside illuminated the table, the green wall, and the two brass knobs of the bed where she lay awake, huddled into herself. Hearing his heavy breathing, she turned and saw him sitting on a chair.

Tsemakh grated his teeth and spoke into the darkness. "My guts were turning over at not answering that loudmouth. I still have a knot in my stomach. But I had no choice. I had to keep quiet. Hirshe Gordon is dangerous because he convinces others, and himself as well, that his battles are for the sake of heaven. A plaster saint like him can destroy the world."

Slava sat up quickly. For a moment her legs swayed back and forth at the edge of the bed, then suddenly she jumped up. She put on the light, stood in front of the mirror, and touched her right cheek, red and wrinkled from the pillow. She combed her disheveled hair and addressed the mirror.

"I noticed your restraint in the beth medresh today. They spat in your face and you didn't say a word. But you waged war with me and my brothers because you looked for an excuse to leave home."

"You're talking like a child." She heard his weary voice behind her back. "You yourself saw how afraid Reb Menakhem-Mendl was of our meddling in this quarrel. He closed his little shop in Vilna and left his family to come and teach at the yeshiva. I'm responsible for him, for his wife and child, and for all the students and their parents who sent them here. How can I possibly destroy the yeshiva for the sake of a quarrel with a community leader? Your brothers didn't close up their flour store because of me."

Someone knocked on the door. Eltzik Bloch came in, exhausted and agitated. He wiped the perspiration from his forehead and began talking about his brother-in-law.

"I've known Reb Hirshe Gordon all these years, but only today did I first realize that I don't know him at all. But his father-in-law knows him very well. The old Valkenik rabbi told the Misagoleh rabbi that he didn't feel well and couldn't come to hear his sermon. It's clear now that the old rabbi realized what Hirshe Gordon was up to and didn't want to be present. After Havdola we were supposed to meet with the rest of the congregation and discuss the terms of a rabbinic contract with Reb Aryeh-Leyb Miadovnik. But after the fight in the beth medresh every congregant came up with a different excuse for not coming to the meeting. That Hirshe Gordon has a hellish power in him. Everyone quakes in fear of him." Eltzik Bloch sighed and winced. "What am I babbling about? The rabbi from Misagoleh would like to see you. Console him, Reb Tsemakh. Tell him he'll be the Valkenik rabbi yet."

Reb Aryeh-Leyb Miadovnik was pacing back and forth in his room and didn't break his stride when the two men entered. His gaberdine open and his hands behind his back, he spat out the words like daggers: "Everything that God does is for the good. There are several reasons why I shouldn't exchange Misagoleh for Valkenik. And that's why I've decided that, with God's help, I'm going to leave this town tomorrow morning."

"There's no way of preventing a fresh punk from shooting off his mouth," Eltzik Bloch croaked. "People even bickered with Moses. Everyone says you're not only a gaon, you're also not fazed by anyone. So are you now going to be fazed by a troublemaker?"

Reb Aryeh-Leyb Miadovnik gestured impatiently and said, "I am firm in my opinion when I have to stand up for the honor of the Torah. But others"—he turned to Tsemakh Atlas—"should have stood up to defend *my* honor. You'll probably reply that you don't dare fight with the congregation so as not to ruin the yeshiva. But I ask you: Why should your students want to grow up to be Torah scholars if they see their teacher stand idly by at the humiliation of an old rabbi who's spent his entire life toiling at Torah? I don't want to hear your answer. For having seen my humiliation and remained silent, I forgive you. But for having seen the humiliation of the Torah and not involved yourself, you won't be forgiven."

Reb Eltzik Bloch was mute and frightened, as though certain that the rabbi's curse would soon come true. But Reb Tsemakh Atlas clenched his jaw and went out without a word.

Slava was standing in her room looking apprehensive as if expecting bad news.

"The rabbi from Misagoleh just cursed me because I didn't stand up for his honor. His curse doesn't frighten me. No matter where he goes he'll be a rabbi. But if the yeshiva falls apart, many of the students won't go anywhere else to study. That's why the students are more precious to me than the rabbi from Misagoleh and his rabbinic post." Tsemakh sprayed out the words with an angry laugh, his eyes burning with the mistrust of a seasoned Musarnik who suspected even a gaon—ostensibly furious over the Torah's honor—of being concerned about his own honor.

17

ON SUNDAY MORNING after breakfast, Leitshe the cook visited Slava at the inn. She wanted to look sophisticated; so though it was midwinter she was wearing a pleated black skirt, a white polka-dot blouse, and a short, straight summery jacket. She sat with legs crossed and talked nonstop, nibbling prunes and loudly sipping tea. She had already managed to tell Slava all about the big Warsaw scoundrel, her milksop-faced former fiancé Yosef Varshever, and about the little Vilna rascal, Hertzke Barbitoler. Slava shuddered at hearing how the tobacco merchant had followed Confrada's sleigh on foot, pleading with his wife for his son. Tsemakh sees only his own view, she thought, and is blind to happenings around him. But of late he had apparently begun to realize the troubles he caused by meddling in the affairs of others. That was why he didn't want to start a fight over the visiting rabbi. Slava felt she needed a respite from everything she had heard since early that morning. But Leitshe was still rattling the prune pits and her tongue.

"My ex-fiancé with the befouled face, pardon the expression, told me all about you even before anyone laid eyes on you here. May he and his bride live happily ever after if he said a word of truth about you and your husband. Your husband is a noble soul. He stood up for me like a sister. After what happened with the big scoundrel from Warsaw and the little rascal from Vilna, my mother quit managing the kitchen. But we didn't want your husband to be angry, so just for his sake we're cooking for the yeshiva students again. It won't be beneath your dignity to come see where your husband's students eat. After all, you're our rebbetsin. Everybody's jealous of you. Refined, good-looking men like your husband aren't around by the dozen, you know. Ronya's husband has a fat belly and a red beard. He comes home twice a year for the holidays. The rest of the year he's abroad, and folks say he doesn't sit in shul all day either, if you know what I mean. A man like that I'd kick out of the house head first. But since Ronya is a gentle woman, and a bit odd, she suffers in silence."

Slava pressed her temples and murmured, "I have to lie down. I woke up this morning with a headache."

Leitshe started. "Why am I sitting here chattering? I have to go marketing for the yeshiva's lunch." Like a proper housewife she gathered up her sucked-out prune pits and put them on the saucer. "I hear that that worthless trash Gedalya Zondak and his daughter, that hunk of meat with calf's eyes, have asked Yosef Varshever to invite Reb Tsemakh to recite the wedding benedictions before the wine drinking, may they drink poison! As far as I'm concerned, Reb Tsemakh can go to Yosef Varshever's first wedding and two years later to his second wedding and four years later to his third wedding," Leitshe concluded; and with one foot on the threshold she reminded Slava, "It won't be beneath your dignity, you know, to come see the house where your husband's students eat."

Slava felt her hair becoming damp with perspiration. She remembered that while she and Ronya sat side by side during the Sabbath meals Tsemakh had avoided looking in their direction, and that Ronya had trembled in the beth medresh for fear Tsemakh would get into a fight over the visiting rabbi. Ronya's husband was abroad all year and people said he had other women there. So Ronya could fall in love with her lodger whose wife was away.

Within an hour of the cook's departure another visitor knocked on the door—Yosef Varshever.

He walked in softly, an angry smile glinting in his beautiful cold eyes. While offering Slava one thin, elegant hand he lifted his hat with the other, after the fashion of the nonreligious, worldly Jews.

"I'm the one the cook just slandered, saying I deceived her," he said with a scornful expression, and he sat down at the table in his hat and striped coat with its upturned velvet collar. Seeing Slava's surprise at his knowing who had been to see her, he grimaced contemptuously and said, "One knows everything in a small town. Yet I'm the only one who knows that Reb Tsemakh Atlas was once engaged to a girl from Amdur but broke it off."

Slava, astonished at his insolence, asked him dryly, "What do you want?"

"What do I want?" Varshever's eyes glittered viciously through his small pince-nez. "I don't want a thing for myself." His voice shook with the rage of a truculent man who never forgives an insult. "But my father-in-law wants your husband to officiate at the wedding to show Valkenik that the yeshiva doesn't consider me a double-dealer. So pass this on to your husband and spare me the trouble of getting into a fight with him."

"What can you do to him? Tell everyone that my husband once broke off an engagement? Is that all?" Slava was even more astounded at the youth's insolence.

"I didn't sign an engagement contract with the cook, but your husband broke a written engagement contract with a girl from a respectable family." Yosef bit his nails. "And what's more, I didn't leave a wife six months after the wedding."

He spat out the last words as if through a thin glass tube. Slava felt her eyelids quivering. She would gladly have spit in his face and shouted, "Get out, you bastard!" But perhaps Tsemakh was indeed afraid of this despicable lout, so it was better not to antagonize him.

"As I understand it, you're very pleased with your current match." She smiled sweetly at him.

Varshever winced. "Pleased? My bride-to-be is quite pretty, but she's a small-town girl and her father is a low-class boor. Gedalya Zondak wants to know what I'll do after the wedding. He wouldn't even mind if I became a rabbi in some small town." Yosef rubbed his jaw and twisted his mouth in derision. "Becoming a rabbi just because I know the Talmud would be exactly the thing for me, right? Maybe I ought to be a cantor because I have a good voice?"

Slava saw that the young man was a bundle of nerves, so she purposely provoked him with sham amazement. "Indeed, why don't you become a slaughterer and a cantor, like the local slaughterer and cantor, Reb Lippa-Yosse, or his son-in-law?"

"Me become a small-town slaughterer? Me lead prayers in some wooden beth medresh?" Yosef trembled with rage and looked around to see if anyone was listening. "Since you're from a big town and not a fanatic, I know you'll tell me the truth. I'd like to travel around the world collecting money for a charitable institution, like Azriel Weinstock. The story goes that he really lives it up out there." The youth gave a peal of licentious laughter, then flared up once more. "If I hadn't landed in a hick town I could have gotten a rich and educated heiress, like all the others. I could even have married a college girl," Yosef Varshever remarked with anguish as he said good-bye and left for the cold outdoors, shivering with cold and anger in his thin coat.

What hurts that heartless lout is that he can't be even more heartless, Slava thought. Then she had a sudden realization. Since their wedding Tsemakh had never mentioned his first fiancée. All along Slava had assumed that Tsemakh cared as little about the Amdur girl as he did about her and her brothers. But now she realized that Tsemakh hadn't mentioned his ex-fiancée because of guilt feelings toward her.

Slava decided that she must make sure the cooks remained Tsemakh's friends and not give the local townspeople an opportunity to say that the rosh yeshiva's wife wasn't interested in seeing how the students lived. She pulled a dress, a blouse, and a petticoat and stockings out of her suitcases and prepared a little bundle. Leaving the inn she asked directions to the students' kitchen.

Gitl met the unexpected visitor holding a big wooden ladle in her hands. Her dirty, perspiring daughters stood before the steaming pots. Slava remarked pleasantly that she had come to meet Leitshe's mother and sister. But Rokhtshe, with the puffy cheeks and little black hairs above her lip, wasn't at all pleased with the visitor, and Leitshe's face was now unfriendly too. The earthen floor and foyer were soaking wet from the students' handwashing. On the kitchen table bits of lung and liver and potatoes lay on the flat, chipped plates.

"Today we happen to have a meager lunch," Gitl apologized, looking at the rebbetsin's unbuttoned fur coat and her soft woolen suit.

"I'm not an inspector. I realize you cook what they give you." Slava tried to be cordial to the cook. Seeing that she was in the way, she slipped out of the foyer—and landed in the older students' dining room.

Yoel Uzder and Sheeya Lipnishker were in the midst of a heated argument. The former was chanting aloud and the latter contradicting him, waving both hands. As the principal's wife entered, Yoel Uzder fell silent. Sheeya Lipnishker, a piece of meat between his teeth, rolled his crossed eyes and grumbled angrily, like a beast when a morsel is snatched from his mouth. Gitl entered with the meat portions. She had put on a white apron but served clumsily. She was ashamed of the filthy tablecloth, the chunks of black bread thrown on the table, and the chipped plates. The boys sat with lowered heads, chewing without appetite now. Their silence made Slava feel how strange she was to them. And she didn't like looking at their pale faces, some with beards and all overgrown with thick earlocks.

She went into the room where Gitl's daughters served the younger students. Here the tablecloth was even dirtier. Since there weren't enough plates, the young boys, wearing battered hats and tattered jackets, ate from earthenware dishes. The oldest boy in the group, Chaikl Vilner, didn't take his eyes off Slava. She recognized him as the one she had asked to take her to Tsemakh when she arrived. He too had long earlocks pushed back behind his ears, but he stared at her so intently that she felt his glances on her hands and feet, her throat and neck, on the hair beneath the silk hair net she wore instead of the traditional hat or kerchief. Slava flushed and smiled uneasily. She was uncomfortable but nevertheless interested to see that she had aroused the feelings of a young lad.

Melechke looked at her like a bright-eyed little rabbit; his face glowed. Leitshe constantly pleaded with the boy, who was fastidious by nature, to get him to eat from the earthenware crockery. Now he sat and waited to be coaxed, his little fist propping up his chin. But Leitshe wasn't in the mood to beg him; in fact she shouted, "You may be an only son at your mother's house, but you're not an only son here. You don't have to eat if you don't want to."

Melechke was furious, and to keep from crying he began to strum his fingers against his lips. One of the boys noticed this and laughed. "Look! Melechke Vilner is playing piano on his lips."

And Leitshe added, "That little fusspot wants to show his aristocratic background."

Slava waited until the students departed. Gitl wiped the soaked earthen floor of the foyer with a rag and her daughters cleaned up the tables.

"Melechke left without eating," Leitshe grumbled angrily. "Besides being an only son at his mother's, he's also a favorite of the principal and of the people in the slaughterer's house. One night Reb Tsemakh found him asleep over his Talmud in the beth medresh and carried him to his apartment for Ronya to put him to sleep with her children."

Again Ronya! Slava mused. But Leitshe interrupted her thoughts. "And what did my ex-fiancé, that Varshever scoundrel, want with you?"

Now Slava understood why the cooks had given her such a hostile reception. Valkenik was a small town, and within fifteen minutes everyone knew who had visited whom. And this was the muck Tsemakh wanted to drag her into?

"Yes, Yosef Varshever did come to see me," Slava answered. "He wanted me to persuade my husband to come to the wedding. But pay no attention, Leitshe. He doesn't make a good impression. No wife will be happy with him."

Gitl beamed and stretched her hands out to the principal's wife as though to an angel. "You took the words out of my mouth. I've been saying all along it's a miracle we got rid of him in time. But my daughter can't forget his handsome face."

"I can't forget his befouled face?" Leitshe angrily swooped the tablecloth from the table. Then she covered the bare wood with an oilcloth and laughed. "What do I care! Reb Tsemakh can go to Varshever's wedding and Varshever can go to hell. I don't care one bit."

Slava untied the package she had brought and asked Leitshe to take it. The girl looked greedily at the dress and blouse and was ready to try them on. Gitl wiped her eyes and said, "I hope you and your husband will grow old with honor and wealth. You can be sure that we won't give up the yeshiva kitchen because of that swine of an ex-fiancé."

But Rokhtshe's face flamed. She raised her usually downcast eyes to her younger sister and said, "I've been telling you all along not to even mention his name, and why do you have to take presents?"

"I don't mean to insult anyone," Slava said in self-defense. "Leitshe came to visit me, so I returned the visit and brought a little gift."

"Thank you, I'll take it. I'm not a conceited snob." Leitshe's eyes flashed at her sister.

Rokhtshe, afraid of her firebrand sister, stammered, "I'm not saying the things aren't any good. I just meant that Leitshe is taller and thinner. But if the dress and blouse are taken in at the waist and the hems let down, they'll fit her perfectly."

18

ON MONDAY MORNING, when Tsemakh came to see his wife, he saw Slava transferring her clothes from the closet into two empty suitcases. He sat down at the edge of the bed and muttered gloomily, "Are you really leaving?"

Slava, bent over a suitcase, continued packing and spoke more to herself than to him: "Weren't you expecting me to leave? It isn't like you to put on a false front."

"I'm not putting on a false front," Tsemakh said sadly. "The few days you've been in Valkenik have made me realize that you can get along with anyone you want to."

"You're mistaken," Slava said over her shoulder. "I could only keep up the saintly woman masquerade for a couple of days." Then she turned to him and said from the corner of the room, "You've exchanged a shoe for a wooden sandal. In Lomzhe you never had any dealings with people like the Vilna tobacco merchant, his son, or his mother from Argentina. The local community leader, Hirshe Gordon, is a thousand times worse than my brother Volodya. Volodya would never have dared prevent an old rabbi from speaking in a beth medresh. And this Yosef Varshever is much worse than my nephew Lolla. The Varshever is ready to do things far worse than seducing a maid, and you'll end up having to go to your student's wedding."

"I told you last night that I won't go to his wedding. What's more, he's not my student. Students have to be raised and tended from the time they're still children." Tsemakh sighed and his face clouded over with yearning. "My students are the boys I brought over the border from Russia and left behind in Nareva."

During the night Slava had come to the conclusion that if Tsemakh truly loved her he wouldn't suffer because of the broken engagement or worry that people might find out about it. "Aren't you at all afraid of Varshever's threats to tell everyone about your broken engagement?" She watched him carefully.

"Of course not. Neither his threats nor his slander," Tsemakh replied after a lengthy silence.

Slava again began to fuss with her suitcases. "If I had known that before, I wouldn't have been so patient with the fool. Still, I'm glad I got to know the local people from close up—I see they're not my sort. In fact you ought to be glad I'm leaving. The only proper wife for you would be one of the women who support your yeshiva."

Tsemakh jumped up. "If you made an effort, you could get along with the local women, just as I do with the men. The congregants here are perfectly aware that Hirshe Gordon has committed a grievous offense against the rabbi from Misagoleh. Nevertheless, they're even friendlier than before and even more respectful. In fact they're delighted to play the innocent with Gordon, to keep him from knowing what they think of him, or at least to prevent him from having any complaints against them. The congregants, you see, aren't in the least dependent on him. They're doing this because they see no sense in fighting with him. But all the years I've taught myself and others to speak only the truth are now taking their revenge on me—and keeping me quiet is costing me in blood. Nevertheless, I'm prepared to relent even more in order not to break up the yeshiva."

"But you didn't keep yourself from minding other people's business and breaking up our marriage," Slava replied, bringing up her old argument. "I'm still not sure whether you'll be able to force yourself to act differently in the future. I certainly couldn't force myself to. Sooner or later the local people would realize that they disgust me and then they would hate me. But you're a yeshiva principal and as such you shouldn't have a wife who is hated by those who pay him."

Slava held a lace-trimmed white silk slip and stroked it as if it were the warm fur of a living creature. "Come home with me and I'll conduct myself the way you want me to. I'll keep all the laws pertaining to women."

Tsemakh sighed wearily and sat down, his shoulders slack. He saw that his wife was preoccupied only with herself; she didn't want to understand anything that didn't appeal to her.

Slava smiled at herself. She was weary too; she had momentarily forgotten that she couldn't convince him of anything. She packed the frothy lace slip and turned back to him. "And where will you live, at the slaughterer's?"

"Well, yes. I've been living there all along with my friend Reb Menakhem-Mendl," he stammered in confusion.

"Your friend can stay there, but you shouldn't." Slava placed her hand on his shoulder. Her face shone with a pale light. "Ronya is a gentle soul. She's a good and perhaps even clever woman, but she can't hide her feelings. Because of her you may suffer humiliation and anguish."

Slava stated this as if it were an obvious fact, so that Tsemakh would make no attempt to deny it. His face told her she hadn't revealed a secret of which he was not aware. Her good-natured genial way of advising him in sisterly fashion had dispelled his fear that she knew about Ronya.

"I don't know what kind of excuse to give the slaughterer." Tsemakh groaned like a man with everyday worries. "And I have nowhere else to go."

"Where would both of us have lived if I had stayed here?" she asked.

"Reb Yisroel the tailor offered me half of his large apartment," Tsemakh answered. "He thought you'd stay longer and settle down here."

"When you're not a hero, you're a weak little man. Move into the tailor's and tell him I'll be coming back soon. You can always say I'm on the way back." She laughed hollowly.

Tsemakh, oblivious to her tone and mood, was glad she had thought of a way to free him from his entanglement. "I'll be home for Passover," he said suddenly.

Her eyes flashed blue fire. "And will you return to the yeshiva after Passover?" He said nothing and Slava laughed. "What a clever way out! I never even thought of it. Indeed, why shouldn't I help you get rid of your guilt feelings over leaving a wife? You'll come home for Passover like Ronya's husband and you'll have both a clear conscience and a wife in bed. And I, of course, will go to the mikva first so that you can use me. And then you'll come back for Sukkos while I walk around with a big belly. My belly will grow on me and your beard on you. Now go and let me finish packing." She pushed him out of the room and locked the door behind him. "Go!" she screamed after him, her voice so loud and wild that he left immediately, fearing that she might soon begin pounding her fists on the door.

Toward evening Slava went to the slaughterer's to say good-bye. Reb Lippa-Yosse sat alone at the dining-room table, scratching his mustache. The lights were already lit because of the short winter day. The old man raised his head and half-closed eyes against the light to see who had entered.

"Very nice, taking away our lodger," he said with mock anger.

Slava was amazed that Tsemakh had so quickly and unhesitatingly carried out her demand. He wanted her to see before she left that he and Ronya would no longer live under one roof. To smooth over Tsemakh's unexpected behavior, Slava began to confide in the old man as to a father. She liked the severe but good-natured head of the family, a friendly and simple man, more than the others in his household.

"You know, of course, that it's really no life when wife and husband live apart. So I asked my husband to move into the tailor's house right away. After all, others might want to have such nice rooms. But I don't know exactly when I'll come back. First I have to sell my share of the business and the house I inherited from my father in partnership with my brothers."

Reb Lippa-Yosse sighed. "Believe me, I know how bad it is for husband and wife not to live together. Even a blind man can see that my older son-in-law Yudel is a shlimazel. When Yudel is at the slaughterhouse I sit here shaking with fear lest that shlimazel has made an ox unkosher. But my younger son-in-law Azriel is not a shlimazel; in fact he's too clever a creature. So that playboy has fun abroad while his young wife fades and withers away. Is it any wonder, then, that Ronya has lately fallen ill for the second time? She stretches out on her bed with her head thrown back like a little calf that hasn't had a drop of water to drink. She doesn't let anyone call a doctor. She claims it's nothing. But after all, I'm her father, and I know that if you have a husband like that you can get emaciated and shriveled up like a dry wooden tub left out in the sun." Through his beard Reb Lippa-Yosse scratched a pimple on his chin as if it were the cause of all his troubles.

Hannah-Leah came into the room. All Sabbath long she had given Slava the cold shoulder, but now she began quite sweetly, "Reb Tsemakh has gotten the finest room in the house of the finest man in town. The tailor's grown children have their own apartments, so it's quiet there, as quiet as a mouse, and the tailor's wife cooks very well."

"But until Reb Tsemakh's wife returns, he can continue eating with us," Reb Lippa-Yosse told Hannah-Leah.

"You think Tsemakh is going to live at the tailor's and come running to eat here three times a day?" his daughter scolded him as if he were a child.

"I hear your sister isn't well. What's the matter with her?" Slava asked.

"I don't know and neither does she," Hannah-Leah flared.

"I'd like to see how Ronya is and say good-bye to her." Slava rose from the table. Hannah-Leah became even more disheartened but said nothing.

Ronya lay in bed undressed and covered with a quilt. As soon as Slava entered, Ronya sat up and said, "It's nothing. Just a headache and a bit of fever. Thanks for coming. Are you really leaving by yourself? I was sure your husband would go with you," she panted through her little mouth with its babyish fever-chapped lips.

"Did you really think in your wildest dreams that my husband would abandon the yeshiva and leave?" Slava laughed in sheer amazement.

"I thought Reb Menakhem-Mendl would stay to run the yeshiva and your husband would go home with you." Ronya laughed too and blushed. "But I see it was silly to think that. But why don't you stay in Valkenik? I told you, you could live with us, but it's really better at the tailor's house. They have large clean rooms and no children. Why should you leave?"

"I'll come back soon," Slava replied, her cold white face like porcelain. Her eyes glittered wickedly at the woman who wanted to take her place. But Ronya's eyes smiled back at her with mild reproach for not admitting that she wouldn't return to Valkenik.

Both women fell silent. Slava was certain that Ronya had become ill worrying over whether Tsemakh would leave. She was melancholy and had a weak character. Resentment had made her sick and driven her to depression. Neither the townspeople nor her family understood her; the only one who did was her irascible elder sister. Slava looked at Ronya's thin arms, crisscrossed with blue veins. Her collarbone protruded, her breasts looked sunken under her nightgown. Ronya's pale face and her lowered head with its barrette were like a narrow, crooked light burning dimly and gloomily in a cold, empty room. Her husband lived abroad while she faded away yearning for love, Slava thought, overcome by a wave of hatred toward her own husband. Tsemakh would bring her to the point where she too would look like Ronya. Since he'd abandoned his first fiancée, he was concerned for all suffering women except his own wife.

Ronya's sons bounded noisily into the room. One was dragging a little stuffed horse, the other pushing a little cart. Ronya's eyes shone as she stretched her hands out to the children and embraced them. Slava too was glad the boys had come in. Sitting there in silence, the two women had reached the point of either confiding in each other or quarreling. Slava watched Ronya kissing her children. She wouldn't let them leave her bedside, as if consoling herself and wanting to show that she had someone to love after all. Then Hannah-Leah came in to sniff out whether her sister hadn't said too much to the clever visitor.

The little boys were fighting over their toys. Hannah-Leah scolded them, impatient for the rosh yeshiva's wife to leave.

"Where can I buy carob and other fruits?" Slava asked. "Before I leave I want to take a Tu Bishvat present to Melechke. That's the boy my husband found dozing over a Talmud in the beth medresh and brought here to sleep."

"Melechke only slept here one night. He's a cute little youngster. Your husband likes him, Reb Menakhem-Mendl likes him, and I like him too." Ronya stroked her own children as if to say that nevertheless she liked them above all.

"It's very nice of you to be interested in your husband's students." Hannah-Leah finally said a friendly word. She told Slava which shop in the market had the best fruits. "I'm glad you'll be coming back soon," she added, then had no more to say. And since she couldn't play the hypocrite and despised the sly tactics of city people, she was astounded to see Ronya and the principal's wife parting as if they were sisters. Ronya looked at Slava with an odd, wan smile, as if afraid that Reb Tsemakh's wife might leave hating her—then the two women kissed good-bye.

19

SOYEH-ETL, the caretaker of the guest house, also tended the Valkenik cemetery. She sewed shrouds for dead women and washed them for burial. Once upon a time she'd been tall, but now she was bent almost double. The skin on her big, high forehead was like wrinkled yellow parchment and her hands were covered with a thick network of veins. The old woman had outlived her husband and all her children; she had no family or kin. The younger generation in town hardly knew her, but she knew the dead in the graveyard well. On the anniversary of someone's death, on Tisha B'Av, or on the eve of the Days of Awe, when a townsman would ask where a great-uncle was buried, Soyeh-Etl would point out the overgrown grave. She rarely spoke and had apparently forgotten how to think, as though her brain had been overrun by cemetery weeds. When she did speak she whispered like a bird, cackled like a hen, or gave the good-natured little laugh of a senile old woman. Although everyone in Valkenik considered her a kindly soul, people still kept away from her. They feared taking things from her hand, as though by doing so they were touching the Angel of Death. But old Soyeh-Etl didn't mind, for she lived among the tombstones. Wandering about in the cemetery, her face radiant, she smiled as if in silent conversation with the dead beneath the mounds of earth. When poor strangers spent the night in the guest house her eyes would light up with joy, but during the winter the cemetery was covered with snow and no wandering paupers were to be seen. Day after day Soyeh-Etl would stand at a window of the guest house, gazing across the river at the tombstones, as though consoling the dead from afar that she had not forgotten them.

A wooden wall divided the guest house in two. The bigger part was a dormitory for wayfarers and the smaller was the old caretaker's room. A large oven was built into the wall and its doors faced the old woman's quarters. Since the guest house had been occupied by the yeshiva boys, Soyeh-Etl had stopped looking out the window at the cemetery and begun peeking in at the students through the cracks between the boards of the partition. Every morning after the boys had left for prayers, Soyeh-Etl cleaned and swept their rooms and made their beds. Then she returned to her own apartment, waiting for the students to return at night. The diligent ones would sit down at the big, book-laden table to study, and from her hiding place the old woman watched them swaying over their texts and heard their sweet chanting.

Recently a boy had come in to ask for a pot of tea. Since then Soyeh-Etl always had ready a kettle of boiling water and earthenware cups. The yeshiva boys had no qualms at all about taking things from the cemetery caretaker's hands; they just weren't drawn to her treat. She had neither tea nor sugar, just hot water and chicory. Once a boy looked through the crevices in the wall and met her eye. The youngsters stood watch by the wall and discovered that the old woman was peeking in at them. Some of the boys didn't want an old woman to see them getting undressed; others just wanted to play a trick on her. The young lodgers stuffed the cracks with cotton, rags, and straw, assuming that Soyeh-Etl would pull out the rags while they were in the yeshiva. They would then repeat the process until they wore her out. And if that didn't work, they would cover up the crevices with wood.

That night the students found the room clean and the rags in the crevices untouched. Two boys went into Soyeh-Etl's room to ask for hot water, confident that now they would be driven out. This time, however, the old woman offered them freshly brewed tea and a quarter of a lump of sugar each. The boys returned to their friends, ashamed at having grieved the old woman. But the Musar seekers among them maintained that one shouldn't be bought off by a piece of sugar: It still wasn't proper for a woman to be looking into men's quarters. Melechke Vilner told Reb Tsemakh about this, and he immediately ordered all the cotton, rags, and straw to be removed from the cracks in the wall. "We can't deny her the pleasure of listening to students studying Torah," he said. And to those who complained that they were ashamed, the principal shouted, "The old woman could be your great-grandmother!"

"Melechke Vilner doesn't seem to mind if an old woman watches him," the boys told one another and removed the rags from the cracks as their principal had bidden.

But now that the winter frosts had come and Soyeh-Etl didn't have enough wood to heat the oven, the students stayed as long as they could in the warm beth medresh and stopped studying in the guest house. They returned there only to sleep. The old woman, longing for the sweet voices of the young scholars, had resumed gazing out the window at the snow-covered cemetery. On Tu Bishvat the cold subsided somewhat, and in honor of the new year for trees, the old caretaker was given a few bundles of wood to heat the oven. The normal schedule at the yeshiva was relaxed for the holiday. Hence the residents of the guest house came home earlier than usual.

Chaikl Vilner went to the old woman to ask for needle and thread. She nodded her emaciated head happily and gave him a needle and a spool of white thread. "I need black thread to fix a jacket, not white thread to sew a shroud," Chaikl shouted into her ear. Soyeh-Etl nodded good-naturedly again and gave him black thread. Chaikl went back and sat down at the table to mend his jacket. Since meeting the rosh yeshiva's wife he had begun paying attention to his clothes, and he was vexed with Reb Tsemakh Atlas, who totally disparaged the material world but himself wore beautiful clothes and had a lovely wife. No matter how often Chaikl told himself that this beautiful woman was ten or twelve years older than he and would someday become a blowsy harridan like Hertzke Barbitoler's mother, it was all in vain. He thought of her constantly, even though he knew that this sin was infinitely greater than thinking about Tsharne, Reb Hirshe Gordon's daughter; now he was sinning in his thoughts with a married woman.

Melechke Vilner sat opposite Chaikl, holding the Tractate *Nedarim* and counting the pages he had completed. Something was oppressing Melechke too. When he went to the Vilna wagoner to get his Friday food packet from home, the driver had replied that he had nothing for him this week. Melechke knew that his mother and sisters were busy selling fruit for Tu Bishvat. Hertzke Barbitoler's mother had come for him from across the sea, but his mother and sisters didn't even have time to bring a package from Butchers Street to Stefan Street, the Valkenik carters' station.

At the table there was also a boy from Aran, called the Araner, who was trimming his nails with a little knife. Some of the yeshiva lads lay on their beds looking into books or talking among themselves. The Podbrodzer, a strapping, pimply youth, scurried about in the narrow passageways between the beds studying Musar with a chant.

Suddenly the "ay-ay-ay" remained stuck in the Podbrodzer's throat. The Araner stopped slicing from the table the slivers of wood he would need to burn his nail parings, and the other boys scrambled off their beds. Melechke poked his head forward, like a rabbit that flares its damp nostrils and pricks up its ears at a rustle in the twigs. Only Chaikl saw nothing because he was so upset and so busy with his sewing. The more he patched his jacket, the more holes he found. The elbows and the cuffs were threadbare, the collar half torn off, and the buttons dangled on single threads. Only when he heard a bell-like woman's voice did he lift his head. The rosh yeshiva's wife stood there, handing Melechke a large paper bag.

"I've brought you and your friends some carob and fruits for Tu Bishvat."

Later Melechke had to defend his behavior in response to the entire group's criticism. For he forgot all courtesy and grabbed the proffered bag with both hands. "It's for you and your friends," Slava reprimanded him tenderly. He turned beet-red and took his hands off the paper bag. Some of the boys stood with their hands behind their backs and earlocks tucked behind their ears, smiling at Melechke's childish behavior. Chaikl sat holding the needle and thread in his hand, gaping like a golem. Long afterward his face burned with shame each time he recalled that the rosh yeshiva's wife had seen him with a tattered jacket on his knees, just like a patchwork tailor.

Slava looked at the two rows of beds along both walls, covered with wrinkled quilts and dirty pillows. Some pillows were bare and feathers seeped out of the red linings. Straw fallen from the mattresses lay scattered on the floor. The students' tefillin bags and canvas sacks hung on nails above the beds. "We have mice," the Podbrodzer youth announced to Slava lest she wonder why they didn't keep their belongings in boxes and suitcases.

Melechke had something even nicer to report, and let no one accuse him this time of slandering his friends. "Before we recite the bedtime Shema Yisroel we ask one another for forgiveness. We don't want anyone to go to sleep angry at a friend, so we beg one another's pardon."

His friends smiled indulgently again, like grownups, at Melechke's boasting. The principal's wife approached the oven and touched the bricks. "The oven is heated, but it's cold here. The holes have to be plugged up." She bent down and looked into the cracks through which light from the other side was filtering into the room. At once she jumped back, startled—she'd seen another pair of eyes opposite hers.

The Podbrodzer spoke up once more. "Don't be afraid, rebbetsin. It's the caretaker of the guest house. She has a habit of peeking in. But the rosh yeshiva told us not to plug up the holes because we can't deny the old woman the pleasure of listening to students studying Torah."

Slava returned to the boys sitting around the table.

"Good-bye, everyone. Keep well. I'm leaving tomorrow," she said, noticing the disappointment and sadness on their faces.

"When are you coming back?" Melechke cried out as though she had deceived him. Touched by the students' regret at her departure, she suddenly sensed a choking feeling in her throat. She didn't want to lie to the yeshiva boys as she had to the slaughterer's family.

"I don't know when I'll return, Melechke. I don't know." Slava made a motion to caress the lad, but restrained herself so as not to single him out. She graced Chaikl with a secret parting smile, full of seductive charm and pain, as if she understood the anguish in his heart and was suffering torments herself. Chaikl saw tears in her eyes. Her smile beamed in him a long time, like little golden flames through frost-covered windows, like green pine needles through the snow.

As soon as Slava left, the *yetzer ha-ra* assailed Melechke once more, and he grabbed the paper bag with both hands. "Carob! Figs! A whole box of figs! A string of dates!" he yelled.

The others were still depressed because the young and beautiful rebbetsin was leaving. They had no great desire to look into the bag of fruit.

Realizing he might be suspected of being a glutton, Melechke began explaining the reason for his behavior. "The truth is I was very cross because my family didn't send me a Tu Bishvat food package. So it was sent down to me from heaven. Providence sent the rosh yeshiva's wife to give me carob to teach me that, as Reb Menakhem-Mendl says, one never loses out by being a pious ben Torah, and the true path of life is the way of Navaredok. Pure and simple faith. Faith without lifting a finger. It's this moral lesson that made me so happy, not the carob itself."

Chaikl sat with hands dangling at his side, no longer in the mood to stitch his tattered jacket. Now he didn't care if he went about in rags. The other students looked silently at the cracks in the wooden wall. Henceforth only the warm, kindly, faithful eyes of old Soyeh-Etl would watch over them throughout the winter until they returned home for Passover.

PART V

1

A WEEK BEFORE PASSOVER, Chaikl went home to Vilna for
the holiday. Afraid of encountering Vova Barbitoler, he asked his
mother about him.

"It's better not to ask." Vella sighed as she sat on her low stool in
her little fruit shop and gazed down at her apron. "He's become an
embittered pauper. Because he was always drunk and fighting, he
lost his customers and is in debt to the wholesalers. Since his
ex-wife came from Argentina and took away their son, he's become
even more helpless and has completely neglected his tobacco
business. He's even stopped going to the tavern. Reb Vova has
begun to do business in prayer shawls and ritual fringes. You
remember, he used to give them away to orphans for the sake of a
mitzva. Now he pleads with the Talmud Torah trustees to buy
them from him. His wife Mindl says he's purposely trying to
debase himself before the people who knew him as a charitable
man. In fact Mindl says she wishes he'd drink and rage again like he
used to and not go around like a living corpse. His son and daughter
by his first wife want to help him now, but he told them to lead
their own lives and not think of him. He didn't even invite his
children to the Seder. It's as plain as day he wants to torture
himself. But I can't understand Hertzke's behavior. When he left
for Argentina he didn't even say good-bye to Mindl, even though

she, as his stepmother, had treated him better than his real mother and suffered a great deal for standing up for the boy. It's not for nothing, then, that people say the apple doesn't fall far from the tree. Hertzke really has somebody to take after. But I shouldn't talk like this . . ."

Vella looked out and stood up, agitated. "Zelda the tinsmith's wife is flooded with customers while I'm standing here chattering. The congregants at Reb Shaulke's beth medresh say that you too had a hand in Reb Vova's troubles because you helped Hertzke run away to Valkenik."

"And the very same congregants who now pretend to pity Vova persecuted him for years," Chaikl said angrily. "They would have burst with envy if Hertzke had grown up to be a Torah scholar. They also begrudge a poor fruit peddler a son who is a ben Torah because their children are ignorant boors and don't put on tefillin."

Vella looked at Chaikl in fear and murmured, "I thought you'd calm down during this half-year away from home. Now I can tell you the truth. I didn't expect you to last a full term in the yeshiva. I was afraid you'd get into a fight there, or something wouldn't please you, and you'd come back in the middle of the winter."

During the Passover Evening Service in Reb Shaulke's beth medresh, Chaikl slipped behind the pulpit and watched Vova Barbitoler standing by the bench along the eastern wall. A gold-embroidered curtain glittered on the Holy Ark. The glow of the candelabra and the electric lamps fluttered over the bookcases with awe-inspiring mystery. The faces of the congregants already radiated the royal repose of sitting at the Seder in their white robes. Eyes and cheeks shone and sparkled, as though even now under the influence of the four cups of dark red wine. But on Vova lay the gloom of a man on his way down who no longer had any pretensions. His beard matted and unkempt, he looked weary with workaday cares.

Chaikl wanted to be the first to leave the beth medresh after the Evening Service, but he had to wait for his father. It took a long time for Reb Shlomo-Motte to stand up, put on his coat, and, leaning on his cane, make his way to the door. Meanwhile the rest of the congregants had rushed out, and the last to drag himself after them was Vova Barbitoler. Reb Shlomo-Motte wished him a happy holiday and Vova responded with a nod.

Then Vova saw Chaikl and made a great effort to smile. "How is your rosh yeshiva, Reb Tsemakh Atlas? Has he gone home for Passover?"

Frightened and guilt-ridden, Chaikl quickly said, "Our rosh yeshiva didn't go home for Passover because his wife's family isn't religious. His wife came to Valkenik in the middle of the winter but left a couple of days later. People say she doesn't want to be a rebbetsin and she and her husband don't get along."

Reb Shlomo-Motte and Vova Barbitoler exchanged glances. Chaikl bit his tongue, regretting his remarks. But no sign of vengeful joy appeared on Vova's face. He stood there for a minute like a deaf man who sees the world but cannot hear any of its sounds.

"When Hertzke and his mother were already at the train station," Vova began in a whining voice, his eyes roving as if looking for his son, "I ran after him holding a little psalmbook. 'Take this and say a chapter for your unhappy father along the way,' I told him. And you know what my son said? He said, 'I left my tefillin and ritual fringes in the Valkenik guest house just to spite you and the rosh yeshiva and all the yeshiva students.' Then he burst out laughing, and his mother laughed with him, like a witch. God will repay the rosh yeshiva for what he has done. But it's my fault too. I shouldn't have married such a woman nor had a child by her. Have a happy holiday."

Vova wiped his tear-filled face with his palm and left the beth medresh, waddling on his crooked legs. Reb Shlomo-Motte choked back a sob and swallowed it.

"I always thought he couldn't live without his deep-rooted yearning for his wicked wife and without satisfying his lust for revenge. But still, I never dreamed he would become so broken," the old Hebrew teacher murmured as he walked to the anteroom steps. Chaikl followed and looked out the door in fright, imagining that perhaps Vova Barbitoler had quickly drunk a bottle of whisky, had hidden it in his pocket and was now waiting outside, empty bottle in hand, to get even with him. But there was no one by the exit. Chaikl breathed easier.

"Don't say a word to Mother about our conversation with Hertzke's father," Reb Shlomo-Motte told his son. "She'd cry all night long and it would spoil our Seder."

But their Seder was spoiled in any case. The old teacher chanted the Kiddush, sipped the wine, then suddenly felt ill. He looked despairingly at the Seder plate with the matzos and at his bookcase, as though already bidding them farewell. Vella too looked at the lit candles with a mute reproach to God, as if to ask why he was shaming her festival. She and her son helped the old man undress and lie down. Chaikl sat down again to continue the Seder but had scarcely managed to say, "This is the bread of affliction," when his mother dozed off, her head on the table. Reb Shlomo-Motte opened his eyes and gestured to Chaikl not to prolong the chanting of the Hagada, since Vella was dead tired from all the Passover preparations. Chaikl began reciting quickly and in a matter-of-fact voice. His mother woke up and said indignantly, "What's your hurry? I'm not asleep," then turned to her husband and said sternly, "No matter what, you're going to rent a room in Valkenik this summer."

When he came home for the Passover recess Chaikl had told his parents that Valkenik was surrounded with pine forests and people spent their summer vacations there. Vella had urged her husband to join their son in Valkenik and enjoy the fresh air, as the doctor had ordered. But her husband had replied, "The community supports the yeshiva students, while your fruit baskets support me. And what's more, I don't want to leave you alone, because when I'm in town I can at least come into the store and chase you home to eat. Who'll do that when I'm away?" Now, however, Reb Shlomo-Motte remained submissively silent; he realized he'd have to agree.

Vella didn't remember where she'd stopped in the Hagada when she dozed off, so she began again from "This is the bread of affliction that our ancestors ate."

2

MELECHKE RETURNED TO VILNA with Chaikl for Passover, but his family's holiday was spoiled too. Melechke still consented to kiss his parents, but he wouldn't let his sisters touch him; he treated them as strange women. During prayers in Reb Shaulke's beth medresh he dashed about among the benches, clapping his hands and studying Musar out loud. While the Silent Devotion was said, he swayed and rocked back and forth, shouting, "Ay–ay–ay." The congregation was astounded. Reb Senderl the kettlemaker asked him, "How come you're making such a racket during the Amen?"

Melechke Vilner cited a passage in the Talmud and translated it for him from Aramaic: "'Whoever answers amen with all his strength, for him the gates of Paradise are opened.' And Reb Israel Salanter teaches us that with shouting one rises into rapture."

Reb Senderl lowered his glasses to the tip of his nose and stared at the little boy who was already making advance preparations for the gates of Paradise to be opened for him.

"You pipsqueak! You're telling *me* about Reb Israel Salanter! I heard him in the Vilna synagogue courtyard before your loud-mouthed mother was born. The white-bearded Reb Israel Salanter of blessed memory was a great scholar and a fine human being. But you—you're no bigger than a fig and you're already pulling nasty tricks."

Melechke gazed contemptuously at the old man but left the beth medresh without a word, his hands behind his back.

Later, when his mother and sisters asked him if the people in the beth medresh had tested his ability in Talmud, Melechke gaped at them in astonishment. "Why should I let myself be tested by a simple congregant? What does he know about the struggle to perfect one's character?"

Zelda and her daughters looked at him, flustered; they didn't understand either his terminology or his behavior.

Zelda's husband, Kasrielke the tinsmith, worked in a matzo bakery between Purim and Passover. During these four weeks he didn't set foot in a tavern and he was more respected at home. After standing by the hot oven all day, he came home at night worn out and immediately lay down to sleep. Nevertheless, the night before the Seder he scattered bread crumbs on the window sills and then, holding a lit candle, a wooden spoon, and a goose feather, went to gather the crumbs and fulfill the mitzva of searching for leaven. Melechke, however, turned the house upside down and looked for leaven products in all the cabinets and drawers and under the beds. The next morning, before leaving for the bakery, his father had to run to the Vilna Gaon's beth medresh to sell the leaven. And Melechke, the little rabbi, rushed to the synagogue courtyard to burn the bread crumbs and wooden spoon bundled into a linen rag.

Before Zelda and her daughters went to their store to deal with the pre-holiday rush, they sat at a corner of the table to eat their last meal of bread. Melechke stood over them like a kashrut inspector, concerned lest a bread crumb fall to the floor, God forbid. His mother and sisters beamed with joy—their youngest was already a full-fledged rabbi—though at the same time his fanatical carryings-on irritated them a bit. But the real troubles began at the Seder.

Kasrielke stood by the bakery oven until evening and didn't have time to go to the bathhouse. He came home perspiring, dusted with flour, and starving. Zelda and her daughters also returned exhausted from their fruit store, hardly able to stand on their feet. Nevertheless, the family waited patiently for Melechke to finish swaying and praying in the corner so that they could begin the Seder.

But no sooner had they sat down than Melechke, eyes burning, reminded his father, "For the Seder you have to put on your white linen robe."

Kasrielke burst into laughter. "I don't even wear it for Yom Kippur, so why should I play the fool now?" He gathered up the chicken wing, the hard-boiled egg, the bitter herbs, and the other symbolic foods, and arranged them helter-skelter on the Seder plate.

But the little rabbi studied the model plate pictured in the Hagada with a pious face and rearranged everything. "The roasted chicken wing has to be on the right side of the plate. The hard-boiled egg has to be on the left. The bitter herbs have to be placed beneath the two, right in the middle."

At this the exasperated father snapped at his little zealot, "What's most important is to be a good man and not a louse. No matter where the horseradish is, it's still bitter."

Melechke sat in silence, however, his yarmulke on the back of his head and his lips pressed shut.

Kasrielke raised the wine cup, rushed through the Kiddush, guzzled the wine to the last drop, sighed with pleasure, and licked his lips.

Little Melechke jumped up. "According to Jewish law, you're supposed to lean on your left side and drink slowly."

"Well then, I'm not drinking according to the law," his father replied. Then he took a handful of green leaves, which tasted as bitter as his troubles, and after dipping them into salt water said the blessing over vegetables.

"No! First comes the hand washing!" Melechke shouted. "First you wash your hands without the blessing and then you dip the greens!"

"Damn you!" His father spat out the chewed green leaves. "Your fanaticism is bringing my gall up. Devils should have a Seder with you."

"Do what he tells you to!" the women shouted at the master of the house.

The tinsmith was used to having his wife and daughters, those Sennacheribs, silence him with their ranting and raving. But now he saw that even his eleven-year-old pietist had more say in his house than he. This stirred his wrath, and he began reviling all the bench warmers and all the sanctimonious fanatics hunched over their books.

Then his mother and sisters began shrieking at Melechke too: "You're spoiling the holiday we worked so hard for."

Melechke didn't say another word, but his silence and the jut of his shoulders expressed so much obstinance that it was perfectly obvious he would rather fast the whole of Passover than yield, at which the entire family suddenly gave in and submitted to all his demands.

On the third morning of the festival, a half-holiday, Zelda and her girls opened their store. It was immediately swamped with customers browsing among the baskets of fruit and boxes of smoked fish and barrels of shmaltz herring. After their rest during the first two holy days, the women, hungry for business, served their customers quickly, as if the merchandise were burning their hands.

Suddenly Melechke appeared in the shop, gazing at everything with an inspector's stern mien, and announced for all to hear, "Bread crumbs or other leaven may possibly have fallen into the merchandise, which means that nothing can be sold till after Passover, even if all the fruit goes rotten."

The customers exchanged glances and shrugged at the peculiar child. But his mother and sisters had had enough. Still dressed in their winter clothes, woolen kerchiefs and galoshes over felt boots, they ran out of the store into the street. They straddled the water-filled gutter and wailed in despair, "Help! The Musarniks have driven him crazy!"

The customers couldn't believe their eyes and ears. Look at that little saint! they thought. And who's responsible. The Vilna rabbis, of course!

"When hair grows here"—Zelda pointed to the palm of her hand—"that's when my little boy will go back to those Musarnik maniacs."

Melechke listened and sadly shook his head. Pure and absolute self-interest, he thought, using the Musar term. His mother and sisters were quite prepared to sell products undoubtedly contaminated by leaven as long as they could stuff themselves with money. Indeed, the entire world was leaven, and it had to be rejected like unwanted dirt.

He left the shop with his head high to show everyone that he wasn't a bit intimidated. Then, remembering that a Navaredker seeker must be exceedingly careful not to look at the world and its enticements face to face, he pulled the ritual fringes down from under his short jacket as a barrier between himself and the materialistic world of Butchers Street. Let them look at his ritual fringes and make fun of him. He didn't care. But to his great distress the preoccupied passers-by took no notice of him at all.

He was even more distressed that he didn't have a younger brother. He yearned to bring another student back to Valkenik so Reb Tsemakh would see how, as the Musarniks taught, he turned many to righteousness. Melechke began to wander about in the courtyards, lying in wait for a boy who might want to become a ben Torah.

In a small courtyard on Shavla Street, Yossele ran toward him wearing his father's worn-out boots and his elder brother's battered cap. Yossele had moist eyes, a split nose, and protruding ears, like a rabbit brought from village to town who emerges from his straw-lined box to gaze at the world around him.

Squat, patched little houses with crooked roofs were bidding good-bye to winter. A fog lay over the gray stone houses. The remaining snow, yellowed and melted in spots, gathered into muddy puddles. Yossele too was taking the air, free of the green mold of damp cellars, the cramped, dark rooms where he and his little sisters lived. He remembered Melechke from a year ago and sniffed. "How you doin'?"

Melechke said, "What have you done to go higher?"

"I climbed over a big stone wall today," said Yossele.

"A man has to know what his purpose is· in this world." Melechke patted his earlocks down on his cheeks. "You're telling me you climbed over a big stone wall today, but what have you done to go higher in spiritual matters?"

"Me and the kids from the courtyard climbed the big iron fence of the Rudnitsky Street church too. The caretaker chased us with a stick but he couldn't catch us." Yossele pointed to Melechke's ritual fringes and sniffed again. "How come you're wearing such long ones, just like the old men with gray beards? The boys in the street'll laugh at you."

Melechke turned away from Yossele in contempt. "Go away. You're still a boy, not a sensible man."

Melechke left to look for a sensible man who was worthy of becoming a yeshiva student. On the corner of Shavla and Butchers Street he saw Chaikl approaching. Fifteen minutes earlier, when Chaikl passed Zelda's fruit store, Zelda and her daughters had pointed at him and said, "Look, there goes that smarty who helped kidnap Hertzke and drive our Melechke crazy!" Then Zelda and her girls had renewed their oath that their little boy wouldn't return to the Musarnik maniacs.

"Did you find any new students for the yeshiva?" Melechke asked his older fellow townsman and fretfully reported, "I haven't succeeded in that mitzva yet."

"What sort of wild antics are you up to?" Chaikl asked angrily. "Your mother and sisters accused me of driving you crazy. And what's more, they say you're not going back to the yeshiva."

"And you pay attention to those women? Who's asking them?" he muttered, turning up his nose in disdain for his family. "With God's help, I'm going back to the yeshiva the morning after the holiday is over. When are you going?"

Chaikl didn't reply. Finding new students in Vilna for the yeshiva was the furthest thing from his mind. He knew he would have to bring his sick father to Valkenik for a rest cure, but he had no idea where to rent a room with meals for the few pennies his mother could afford.

3

FREYDA VOROBEY WAS SUPPORTED by her elder sister's monthly checks from America, but she still couldn't budget herself properly. Nicknamed "Freyda the American," she had a reputation in Valkenik as a spendthrift who loved sweets and expensive fruits. When the tall, skinny Freyda was seen dashing down the streets at breakneck speed in rain or shine, heat or snow, clad in her white kerchief and black socks, people snickered and said she was hurrying to the bakery to beg for ginger cakes, strudel, and honey *teiglakh*. But she could never extricate herself from debt, and shopkeepers became increasingly less generous with credit. If a kindhearted storekeeper was still to be found, people whispered that when "Freyda the American" got her ten or fifteen dollars and came to settle her debts, he presented her with a crooked bill.

Her son, Nokhemke, went about in rags and was always dirty, as though he'd grown up near a sewage ditch. But he was a quiet little boy and loved to roam about in the beth medresh. He helped the beadle sweep the floor, bring water for the washstand, and set up the prayer stands. While working he liked to sing. Chaikl had noticed his sweet voice, which sounded as if the carved wooden birds from the Cold Shul had come alive in his throat.

"How come you're always wandering around doing nothing and never open up a book?" Chaikl had asked him.

"I don't even know how to pray with a Siddur," Nokhemke had replied.

During the winter Chaikl had begun to teach him how to read. Both lads sat in a corner of the Valkenik beth medresh every evening and studied by the light of a candle set on the prayer stand. The congregation was amazed. It had never occurred to any of them to wonder if Freyda Vorobey's little darling knew how to read. The yeshiva people looked on and smiled. Instead of discussing Talmud with his friends, Chaikl Vilner was teaching the abc's. Chaikl hadn't forgotten the contempt the congregants of Reb Shaulke's beth medresh had for him and their skepticism about his ever becoming a ben Torah. That was one reason why he empathized with a poor lad whom everyone ignored.

Once Chaikl took a penknife out of his pocket and trimmed Nokhemke's dirty nails. The boy laughed wildly and screamed, "You're tickling me," as if he'd never had his nails cut. The next morning Freyda Vorobey came up to Chaikl's prayer stand and said with great deference, "For teaching my son I should really wash your feet and drink the water. Why be miserable in the guest house? Why don't you move into my place and you'll have a soft, clean bed?"

Chaikl had long since become sick of the guest house, so he dropped in on Nokhemke's mother to see if he'd want to live there. The cottage was roomy and a curtain covered the entrance to the alcove, but the plaster was peeling from the walls, and dried moss peeked out from between the boards. The front room contained two simple wooden sleeping benches, a tottering table, and an old, broken-down chest of drawers. In the small kitchen empty pots

gloomed mutely on the cold stove. Poverty shone from the clean
pans on a closet shelf. By the window Chaikl saw a sharp-featured
girl with coal-black eyes. Judging by the face, she was obviously his
prospective landlady's daughter. Chaikl wondered why the mother
was always wandering through the streets while her daughter,
Kreyndl, was never seen outside.

When Freyda resumed persuading him to move into their house
he asked, "Where will I sleep?" and went into the alcove to inspect
it too.

Kreyndl followed immediately. "This is my room. Move in with
us," she whispered quickly, as if she'd waited impatiently for the
moment to make the remark.

Kreyndl's hot whisper kindled Chaikl's imagination. Kreyndl's
little room looked as if it were prepared for a young couple: it had a
large wooden bed heaped with bedding, and a window facing a
fenced-off little yard piled high with snow. The girl was waiting for
an answer, proud and angry, her eyes feverish with longing.

To avoid giving an immediate reply Chaikl changed the subject.
"Your little brother will soon be Bar Mitzva and he still doesn't
know how to read."

"If you moved in here with us you could teach him. Do you want
to live here?" Kreyndl asked breathlessly.

"I'll think about it," Chaikl muttered and quickly left the house,
afraid of being tempted by the girl who seared him with her eyes.
But Freyda Vorobey, confident that the young student would
move in, told her friends. The news reached Reb Yisroel the tailor,
who then had a long talk with Chaikl Vilner.

"It's certainly a great mitzva to study Hebrew with a poor lad,
but living at the Vorobeys' doesn't befit a ben Torah. Freyda's
husband works at the cardboard factory beyond the forest. Everyone calls him Bentzye the Golem. Others call him Bentzye the
Apostate. Actually, he didn't convert. He just lives with a peasant
woman from a nearby village without rabbinic blessings. He gives
her his earnings, eats there, sleeps there, and gets drunk with the
other village peasants. Some of our people here have tried to
persuade him to come back home and live like a Jew. But he says he
doesn't want to work like a horse for a woman who squanders his
hard-earned money on sweets and only offers him a hunk of old
bread without chicken fat. The peasant woman, he says, gives him

boiled ham and cabbage. She mends his underwear and he sleeps on top of the warm stove. That simple oaf doesn't like Jews at all. He even helped Sroleyzer the bricklayer steal a cow from one of our townsmen's barn. When people found out where the cow was, Sroleyzer denied having any part in the affair. He put the entire blame on Bentzye the Golem, and Bentzye was nearly sent to prison. Out of anger at the bricklayer, Bentzye became even more estranged from Jews and from his wife and children. He lives with this gentile woman and tells the peasants that all Jews are thieves.

"Poor soul!" Reb Yisroel sighed and seemingly against his will smiled into his silvery beard. On the one hand he felt compassion for a Jew who'd lost his soul, but on the other he wanted to laugh at the wayward Bentzye the Golem's finding fault with others.

Now Chaikl understood why no one in the village paid any attention to Freyda Vorobey's son and why her daughter always stayed at home. Kreyndl was ashamed to show herself on the street because of her father's behavior. Although Chaikl no longer considered moving into their little house, he wanted to continue studying with Nokhemke. But the boy stopped coming to the beth medresh and even avoided Chaikl on the street.

Once, however, Chaikl caught Nokhemke by the hand to keep him from running away. "Why aren't you coming to study?"

Nokhemke averted his face. "My sister won't let me."

Chaikl laughed inwardly, pleased that he hadn't moved into the Vorobeys'. Kreyndl had no doubt assumed he would become her fiancé.

During these events of the past winter Chaikl hadn't dreamed that after Passover he would pray to God that the Vorobeys would take him and his father into their apartment. When he returned to Valkenik he spent days looking for a summer apartment, but the owners of houses near the forest had their steady tenants year after year, and nobody in town wanted to get involved with a poor sick man who sought room and board for a pittance. Chaikl went to see Nokhemke's mother, hoping that she too wouldn't refuse him, but seeing that Freyda wasn't there and that Kreyndl sat by the window as in months gone by, he grew even more despondent.

"How come I never see your little brother either in the beth medresh or outside?" Chaikl asked.

"He's gone to work in the cardboard factory like his father. And how come you didn't step into our house all winter long?" The girl singed him with her eyes. "I know why! People have been talking against us. They say it's not fitting for a yeshiva boy to live with the likes of us."

"During the winter I lived in the guest house," Chaikl explained, "so I didn't need any other quarters. But why didn't you let Nokhemke study with me?"

The girl answered with a crooked smile and the shrill voice of a night bird. "Since our place wasn't good enough for you, Nokhemke's studying with you wasn't good enough for me."

Just then Freyda Vorobey huffed in, laden with bags of food. Having received money from America that morning, she had paid off some of her old debts and incurred some new ones. She was in a good mood and was pleased with the visitor. Chaikl felt better too. Seeing that this weak-brained woman was basically a kindly soul, he told her why he had come.

"Your father will live here and eat with us," Freyda answered loudly, delighted that she'd be able to run from store to store shopping.

"And how much would it come to per week?" Chaikl asked anxiously.

"I don't know how much it'll come to per week. I won't make a profit on you," Freyda answered without a trace of resentment.

But her daughter made a face. "We're not thieves. But it's beneath your dignity to stay here, right?"

"I'll live here too, of course." Chaikl was silent for a while and then stammered out a request: "I . . . I don't want anyone to know about this until my father comes."

Freyda had the befuddled look of a suddenly awakened hen. She didn't understand why she couldn't tell anyone. But her daughter realized that the yeshiva student didn't want to be again talked out of moving into their house.

"She won't say a word," Kreyndl said, flashing an angry glance at her mother.

Chaikl reported everything in a letter to his parents, and one sunny, windy afternoon a local wagoner brought a passenger to the Vorobey household from the Valkenik train station. Heads covered with skullcaps peeped out of the houses on Synagogue Street and through the open windows of the beth medresh. The Valkenik residents saw a broad-shouldered man of average height slowly climbing down from the wagon and paying the driver. He had a square, trimmed white beard; his cap was tilted on his head and his coat draped over his shoulders. None of the townspeople knew the lodger of the "imperial family," as they called the Vorobeys.

Only the yeshiva principal recognized the Vilna Hebrew teacher, Reb Shlomo-Motte. Tsemakh wondered for a while why Chaikl hadn't mentioned his father's coming to town. Then he turned from the window back to his text. He shut his eyes and mused. He had failed with the tobacco merchant's son, and now he wasn't even sure whether the son of the old teacher and maskil would remain faithful to Torah and Musar.

4

AZRIEL WEINSTOCK HAD COME home for Passover and stayed longer than usual. He was involved in a financial dispute with the yeshiva for which he had been collecting abroad. Every day in the beth medresh Tsemakh looked at the broad-shouldered Azriel whose neck bulged with rolls of fat. Since moving into Reb Yisroel the tailor's house, Tsemakh had not visited his previous quarters, but he hadn't forgotten the woman who had tended him so solicitously and whose devotion he had so rudely rejected. And precisely because he hadn't seen Ronya again, her image reverberated even more delicately and gently in his memory. He wanted to remember her as a chaste and modest woman and held on to the thought that he was a temptation for her because she was always alone. Hence he had to do something to prevent her from remaining alone and yearning for someone to look after.

The next morning after prayers, as Azriel Weinstock was taking off his tallis with its gold-embroidered collar, Tsemakh Atlas, still in his tallis, came up to him and murmured, "I'd like to discuss a certain matter with you."

The emissary's gleaming, freckled face cooled immediately. He assumed that this brand-new Valkenik resident would ask him which yeshiva he was collecting for and what percent he earned. But, to his astonishment, instead of asking questions, the principal proposed that he give a Talmud course in the yeshiva for the middle-level students.

Whenever Azriel Weinstock had to restrain his laughter or suppress his rage, his carefully tended white neck turned red and the roots of the hairs beneath his chin pricked him like wires. To remain in town and give lessons to students seemed like a big joke to him. Nevertheless, he didn't burst out laughing. He tilted his head back and fingered the prickly hair roots.

"Well, and what about livelihood? Where will I get money to support my wife and little children?" He looked worried, as if traveling around abroad were sheer torture for him.

"The local residents here pay me and Reb Menakhem-Mendl a weekly salary. You've probably heard from your father-in-law about his lodger, our assistant rosh yeshiva Reb Menakhem-Mendl Segal. He went home for Passover before you came. I'm sure that he too will be pleased to have a third teacher. We'll ask the local residents to increase their weekly contributions, and I'll go to Vilna to the Yeshiva Council to request funds for our school."

"I have strong doubts that the Valkenik residents will increase their contributions for a third teacher. And, furthermore, the Yeshiva Council in Vilna supports only the large yeshivas with older students, not these tiny small-town yeshivas." Azriel Weinstock took a stiff hairbrush from his vest pocket and combed his mustache. "How much do you get a week?"

"The weekly wages haven't been properly set as yet," Tsemakh replied, vexed that Azriel's first questions concerned salary. "Reb Menakhem-Mendl and I get fifteen, sometimes twenty zlotys a week."

"Pay like that wouldn't even keep me in potatoes," the emissary said over his shoulder, the corners of his mouth curling with boredom and contempt. "Even my brother-in-law Yudel the slaughterer earns more."

Black as pitch and pale as the white stripes of his black-and-white tallis, Tsemakh the small-town rosh yeshiva looked at the globe-girdling emissary's trimmed red beard, the coppery yellow whites of his eyes, and his thick protruding lips—and was suddenly struck by the thought that Ronya wasn't particularly attached to her husband. Perhaps she didn't love him at all. In that case, she should certainly not be left alone for the whole summer.

"In addition to the weekly wages that the congregants pay and the support I hope to get from the Yeshiva Council, I'm prepared to give you half of my own wages."

"Really? And why are you doing all this?" Weinstock yawned.

"Last winter the yeshiva had students at four different levels," Tsemakh answered, "but Reb Menakhem-Mendl and I couldn't give that many lessons. So younger and older students had to sit together and couldn't make proper progress in their studies. We're expecting more students for the summer term. Those who went home for the holiday will be returning with friends. You see, the yeshiva has earned a reputation among Jews in the surrounding villages and now they'll be sending their children. So we'll need a third teacher as surely as a Jew needs a pair of tefillin." A note of increasing irritation had crept into Tsemakh's voice. His eyes blazed as if he wanted to use another tone and say something entirely different.

The sober, seasoned emissary had concluded that it didn't pay to get too deeply involved with the Navaredker Musarnik, so he coldly rebuffed the offer. "No, I have no intention of becoming a yeshiva teacher." He removed a round snuffbox with a green cover from his right vest pocket, put some snuff into his left nostril, and sneezed with great pleasure. Then he snuffed some into his right nostril and sneezed resoundingly once more. His face perspired as though he had drunk hot tea with raspberries after a hot bath. "I have a cold," he announced, wiping his face, neck, and throat with a handkerchief, and offered the snuffbox to Reb Tsemakh.

"Thanks, I don't use snuff," Tsemakh said. He looked at the hefty man's protruding paunch and felt sorry for Ronya.

Weinstock's serenity during his talk with the principal was actually a pretense. When he returned home from prayers, a red streak of rage suffused his throat and neck. He suspected his father-in-law, that old fool, of having incited the Musarnik to persuade him to remain in town, but in order not to disturb his breakfast, Azriel Weinstock began telling about his conversation with Reb Tsemakh only after he had finished eating.

"Where did your former lodger get such a wild idea?" he asked, cleaning his teeth with a wooden toothpick and rolling the yellowish whites of his eyes.

"Why are you looking at me?" Reb Lippa-Yosse shouted. "I didn't ask Reb Tsemakh to talk you into staying here. I'm not that stupid yet. I know full well that even if you'd been offered the post of Valkenik rabbi you wouldn't stay in town."

"If a man offers me half his own wages as a bonus to stay in town and give Talmud lessons in a little yeshiva, he must have some ulterior motive!" With the tip of his tongue Ronya's husband searched for food particles in his gums.

While the prosperous Azriel Weinstock was at home, Yudel the slaughterer sat at the table even more depressed than usual. Hannah-Leah was more irascible than ever, vexed with her shlimazel and loathing her brother-in-law, who would leave her sister and the children alone again when the holiday was over.

But fearing that that double-dealer and skirt-chaser might suspect something, Hannah-Leah now spoke to Azriel quite amicably, in contrast to her usual manner. "Tsemakh Atlas has a rich wife—at home he can have anything his heart desires, even pigeon's milk. But nevertheless he denies himself all the creature comforts to run a yeshiva. No wonder he's ready to give away half his wages to enable the students to have another teacher. He's a Musarnik, after all," Hannah-Leah concluded, throwing a sidelong glance at Ronya to warn her not to say a word, God forbid.

"It's amazing that nowadays you can find a girl, and a rich one at that, who'll take such a queer duck for a husband." Weinstock lazily dribbled the comment out of the edge of his mouth. The Musarnik no longer interested him.

Ronya, sitting between her two sons at the other side of the table, looked at her husband. He sat where Tsemakh had sat during the winter. Since Tsemakh had moved out and never visited, the painful thought that he had forgotten her had cut deep into Ronya's heart. Now she realized that Tsemakh wanted her husband to stay in town so that she wouldn't be alone. He was concerned for her, but he himself hadn't even gone home for Passover. The tailor's wife had told her that he ate little and was always distracted.

Ronya was ready to jump up and run to find out how he was, at least to look at him, but for the sake of her two sons she forced herself to remain calmly in her place. As she watched her husband picking his teeth, belching, and hiccuping, a triumphant little smile stole into the corners of her mouth. It gave her pleasure to deceive her husband, if only in her heart and thoughts, and she was happy that Tsemakh had not persuaded him to remain at home.

5

TSEMAKH'S AQUILINE NOSE PROTRUDED ever more sharply from his haggard face, like a hawk's beak through dense foliage. His beard grew wild, like spreading moss; his thick mustache covered his lips; and his bushy brows hung over his eyes. He looked like a hermit, but he knew deep down that he still felt no joy in putting on tefillin and wearing the ritual fringes, just as they had given him no joy when he was younger. It became clear to him that all his temptations stemmed from one root cause: he lacked faith.

Tsemakh now lived in a quiet apartment where he had a sunny, spacious room. His new landlord, Reb Yisroel the tailor, had been married for more than fifty years, and he and his wife had nothing more to say to each other. When he spoke she looked at him anxiously, concerned lest he use up his remaining strength. And when she spoke he listened solicitously until the echo of her voice dimmed like the clatter of a grandmother's porcelain dishes whose painted decorations had faded. Only rarely did the old couple's children and boisterous grandchildren come to visit. Consequently, no one disturbed Tsemakh as he sat in solitude in his room for days at a time.

Reb Yisroel didn't ask him when his wife would settle in Valkenik. The townspeople finally realized that there was an undercurrent of discord between the yeshiva principal and his wife. Her look and demeanor had made it clear that she didn't want to be a rebbetsin.

With the beginning of warmer weather Tsemakh began once again to go up to the attic Musar room. He felt more alone in the attic, with its hard bench and bare table, than in the tailor's large room, which had two big windows and two wide beds with clean linen. During the spring days after Passover, Tsemakh's thoughts cast an autumnal gloom over him, making him feel like a bare tree in the wind.

Yes, he was a recluse—but unwillingly and without joy. He thought of Reb Israel Salanter, the founder of the Musar movement. Reb Israel's big, innocent, melancholy eyes had seen hell, and he wanted to save Jews from its torments. Hence he wrote in his Musar Epistle: "Man will be whipped in hell. He will have to give an account of his deeds in the next world." Contemporary Musarniks too, as well as every faithful ben Torah, believed in reward and punishment, even though they said little or nothing about the concept. They discussed fear of heaven and fear of sin because these were loftier than fear of punishment. But he, Tsemakh Atlas, had never given a thought to that otherworldly punishment, as if hell were just a fantasy. He believed in the perfect man, and he himself wanted to become a heavenly man— but his heaven was empty, without a God, like a Holy Ark without Torahs. Even had he agreed with the philosophers who, via logic, proved the existence of God, he still wouldn't have been a true believer. The true believer felt God in his heart and in all his senses and went to sleep and awoke knowing that there was a Creator. But if he, Tsemakh, wasn't sure of the First Principle, he was not only a hypocrite masquerading in beard and earlocks, he was also a thoroughgoing fool, a blithering idiot. Why should he torment himself by being a recluse when he still possessed all his strength?

Even when Tsemakh stood in the beth medresh among his pupils, praying with his tallis over his head, he was still haunted by his passion for probing into himself, by his mania for constantly rebuking himself. He had left the worldly hedonists because they had no Torah. But the Torah was considered the highest and most profound form of wisdom only by those who believed that it was given at Mount Sinai. Those who didn't believe in Divine Revelation considered man's rational faculty more divine than the Torah laws, the reasons for which no one knew. Tsemakh looked out the beth medresh window and imagined a black fire coming from the blinding rising sun that ignited his beard and earlocks and the tallis on his head, leaving him standing naked, a burned, blackened trunk. A thought roared in his mind, then crumbled like thunder: He hungered and thirsted for a world of virtue, not a world of starry-eyed piety.

The first Sunday morning of Iyar, or May, he looked out of his attic room and saw people converging upon the Valkenik rabbi's house from all sides. The yeshiva crowd came from the beth medresh up on the hill, and the congregation approached from the lanes around the synagogue courtyard. Wagoners and artisans arrived from their little houses at the river's edge, and village Jews strode along the sandy paths from Dekshne and Leipun. All of Valkenik and the farmers from the surrounding countryside had come to accompany the old rabbi and his wife, who had been waiting for the blessed day of their journey to the Land of Israel. The morning was sunny and clear. A sudden wind brought clouds, but they too had apparently come to bid the old rabbi farewell.

Azriel Weinstock and Yosef Varshever emerged from Synagogue Street. Bored at having to stay in town because of the financial dispute with his yeshiva, Azriel had condescended to let Yosef cultivate him. Fawning and flattering, Yosef danced attendance on the yeshiva fund raiser who traveled around the world; he looked Azriel in the eye with envy and pleading.

"Maybe you can do something for me so that I won't rot away in this town. It's not even a month after my wedding and my father-in-law, Gedalya Zondak, is already spreading the word that I'm a lazy bum. I don't get up in time for prayers and I waste days on end taking walks and chatting instead of sitting and studying. But I don't want to be a religious functionary, and I don't want to be a merchant or a shopkeeper."

Tsemakh saw them from his attic room and laughed. "Birds of a feather flock together." An Azriel Weinstock and a Yosef Varshever always find each other. And that red-bearded, potbellied collector undoubtedly believes in the God of Israel. He has concocted for himself a God of Israel who doesn't forbid him to be either money-hungry or a sinner. Chances are he has amassed a treasure trove of verses and rabbinic epigrams to support the contention that his every deed is done according to law and for the sake of heaven.

Tsemakh withdrew from the window with the bitter smile of a man who no longer pretends to hope for good fortune but still envies every fortunate man. And he considered Azriel Weinstock a very fortunate man indeed. If only that creature were more considerate of his wife and little children, Ronya would be devoted to him heart and soul. Ronya wasn't Slava.

After Purim, Tsemakh had written Slava that he wanted to go to Lomzhe for Passover, but she hadn't bothered to reply. She probably thought that by going home for Passover he'd fulfill his obligations to her and be rid of his pangs of conscience as well, as she had told him in Valkenik. She didn't want him to have a clear conscience toward her. But on the other hand, she didn't want to come to him and adjust to his way of life either. Ronya, however, didn't chase away her husband who came home every six months. Had her husband treated her tenderly and asked her to come, she would have taken the children and traveled everywhere with him, as Dvorele Namiot from Amdur, too, would have done. . . .

Tsemakh considered his having to go bid the old rabbi farewell an act of salvation. He no longer had the strength to bear his self-imposed solitude and endless self-rebuke.

A substantial crowd was standing around the rabbi's house. Harnessed wagons were waiting for the older congregants who would accompany the rabbi for the eight-kilometer trip to the train station. The rabbi's front hall was filled with large, well-stuffed sacks, suitcases, hand baskets, and square wooden crates packed with books. Surrounding the rebbetsin were women kinfolk and local housewives. Two women were busily sewing into a sack the bed linens that the rebbetsin and her husband had used during their last night in Valkenik. The old rabbi, Reb Yaakov Hacohen Lev, sat at the head of the table in his big rabbinic courtroom with its empty bookshelves, as if he might still have to hand down one last decision before leaving Valkenik. The town's venerable men sat on both sides of the table, and behind them stood the yeshiva people. Reb Tsemakh Atlas headed for a corner, inhaling the all-pervasive atmosphere of tears and grieving silence. Chaikl Vilner stood among the Torah students, amazed, silent, and almost frightened. He had never seen an entire community of Jews in a cloudburst of tears over their old rabbi's departure.

Foremost among the weepers was the rabbi himself. Looking out the window at the beth medresh where he had prayed and taught for more than fifty years, he broke into sobs. The gray-haired townsmen around him began crying too, thinking of the weary burdens of bygone years, of the back-bending old age that had come upon them unexpectedly, and of their meager livelihood. They also shed tears because troubles were intensifying for Jews and because the young generation was becoming increasingly estranged from Jewishness. The rabbi calmed down for a few minutes, and the people around him sat immobile and with lowered heads. Then he glanced again at the empty bookshelves and renewed his weeping. The old men then recalled how often they had sat in this room for meetings, for a rabbinic judgment, to take counsel, or just to be social with their rabbi over a glass of tea—and they too burst into tears again.

Eltzik Bloch tugged at his little gray beard but couldn't squeeze out a tear. He stood there sadly, however, musing that the verse, "Jacob departed from Beersheba," was now applicable to him. In his biblical commentary, Rashi states, "When a righteous man leaves a town, its light and beauty depart with him." Now his father-in-law, Reb Yaakov Hacohen Lev, was departing, and so Eltzik Bloch's prestige would depart too.

Old Reb Lippa-Yosse was even gloomier. He and the rabbi had known each other since their youth. If not for Lippa-Yosse's old friend, Yudel would have been dismissed as slaughterer, and they wouldn't have let him, Lippa-Yosse, lead the prayers, because, as his enemies would have it, he was too old and hoarse. Reb Lippa-Yosse struggled mightily to hold back his sobs. His lips puffed out and perspiration covered his red, steaming face. With murder in his eyes he looked around for Azriel, but in vain. His hapless son-in-law Yudel sat at the table, but Azriel Weinstock hadn't even deigned to enter the rabbi's house to say good-bye.

That smart-aleck was parading around outside. Furious now, Reb Lippa-Yosse could no longer control his desire to burst into tears, and he gave a thin, shrill peep that sounded like a lame blast from a ram's horn.

The rabbi started out of his pensive reverie and began crying anew.

"Save your strength, rabbi," people begged him.

"Fifty-one years! I've been rabbi here over fifty-one years," the old man sobbed.

Reb Hirshe Gordon stood pressed against the wall next to Beynush, his son by his first wife, the old rabbi's daughter who had died while still a young woman. Beynush, a thin seventeen-year-old who was too tall for his age, had come home for Passover from the yeshiva in Kamienitz and stayed on until his grandfather's departure. Holding a twig into whose fresh bark he had carved a series of rings, he looked at everyone hesitantly, somewhat flustered.

The crowd knew that the real weeping and wailing would begin at the railroad station, when the rabbi and his wife would have to part from their late daughter's only son. But Reb Yaakov didn't want to wait for the farewell at the station.

"Come here, Beynush, stand next to me," he called, his long ash-gray beard trembling.

Beynush's father, Reb Hirshe Gordon, stood erect and silent. Large hot tears—they actually gave off heat—rolled down from under his glasses into his beard, but, teeth clenched, he remained silent.

Seeing the behavior of the orphan's father, the other congregants didn't dare let out a sob. Only Sroleyzer the bricklayer blubbered and whined in his broad voice, "Easy, rabbi, easy now. God'll be with you." And he rubbed his tear-stained cheeks with the palms of his hands.

Crammed in among the throng, Tsemakh regarded Sroleyzer the bricklayer and thought: That thief and informer is a weeper and talks with God too. But his God of Israel doesn't forbid him to be a thief and an informer. Even if Sroleyzer realized that he did forbidden things, he was confident that with his thievish Sroleyzer-ish mitzvas he'd be able to buy his way out of hell. The Valkenik Jews and all other pious Jews assumed that they had the same God, the same Torah, and the same hell. But in truth each man had his own God, his own Torah, and his own hell.

6

ON LAG B'OMER, a week after having seen the old rabbi off to the Land of Israel, Valkenik welcomed its new rabbi and arbiter, Reb Mordekhai-Aaron Shapiro from Shishlevitz.

The rabbi had first visited Valkenik the Sabbath before Purim without being invited. He was on his way to Vilna, he said, to buy books and see a doctor. But while waiting at the Valkenik train station he had mused: Why not stay in a Jewish town for Sabbath and deliver a sermon? Since no faction in town had sent for him, no one opposed him. Reb Mordekhai-Aaron Shapiro, then, preached with everyone's approval and appealed to everyone with his homiletic epigrams. He also remembered to say a good word about the old rabbi, who sat in the beth medresh during the sermon.

"Our prophet par excellence pleaded with God: 'Let me cross the Jordan and see the good land on the other side of the river,' but Moses' prayer wasn't answered. Your rabbi too, my distinguished congregants, prayed that he might cross the Jordan. He said, 'I've been Valkenik's mentor and guide for fifty-one years; now let me into our Holy Land.' Your rabbi's prayer, however, *was* answered. Soon, my distinguished congregants, your rabbi, with the help of God, will be going to the Land of Israel."

The phrase "Let me cross the Jordan" appealed to the simple worshipers and even to the more affluent householders. It was true that the visitor didn't seem to be good-natured and patient. He had the small, stormy eyes of an irascible man, and when he wasn't addressing the audience in his mellifluous sermonic tones, his voice was shrill and screechy. But Eltzik Bloch and his group of enlightened Jews understood that the rabbi from Shishlevitz was

too clever to be an Agudah party member. And Reb Hirshe
Gordon and his zealots realized that the rabbi from Shishlevitz was
too smart to follow the Mizrachi crowd. So both sides asked him if
he wanted to become the Valkenik rabbi.

His rounded shoulders sagging modestly, Reb Mordekhai-Aaron
replied, "Well, if you wish it. Actually, I've been offered a post in
the Grodno rabbinic court, and Grodno, as you know, is about
twenty or thirty times bigger than Valkenik. But there I would
only be a rabbi for one street and one beth medresh. So I prefer
being in a small town where I'll be the town rabbi. You can make
Kiddush over a small challa as long as it's whole, but not over a big
one that's already been cut."

The rabbi's two sons-in-law were especially pleased that Reb
Mordekhai-Aaron Shapiro was prepared to buy the old Valkenik
rabbi's house and pay cash for it. As much as Eltzik Bloch and Reb
Hirshe Gordon had bickered over the rabbinic candidates, both
were concerned that the old couple should have enough money for
their journey and for settling in the Holy Land. The biggest sum
had to be realized on the sale of the rabbi's house, and until the
arrival of the Shishlevitz rabbi no candidate for the Valkenik
rabbinic post had been able to pay cash for it. Both brothers-in-law
agreed on him; the other congregants, exhausted by the long
controversy, concurred.

Lag B'Omer morning Valkenik awoke to the pounding of a bass
drum and the blare of trumpets. The fire brigade's brass band
began the day with marches in honor of the festival. The young
people had been upset because the old rabbi departed during the
Omer days when no music was permitted and they couldn't see
him off with the band. Now they doubled their efforts in honor of
the new rabbi. The congregants grumbled, "Trumpets all of a
sudden," but the young folk didn't ask the old people's opinion and
brought the band to the synagogue courtyard. Since the musicians
were firemen, they wore copper helmets, blue uniforms with
shoulder straps and wide leather belts, and shiny high boots. The
horns and tubas were twisted like snakes around their necks. The
bandmaster conducted, and the musicians, using all their buttons
and keys, boomed forth with their brass instruments.

In honor of the new rabbi they had built in the middle of the synagogue courtyard a wooden tower on which was hung a linen sign with large letters: "This is the gate of God; the righteous shall enter in it." The wagoners unharnessed their horses and rode them. The horses' manes were decorated with garlands of greens. Little bells were tied to their necks so that everyone would hear of the new rabbi's arrival in town, as the Torah says of the High Priest: "And his voice was heard when he entered the sanctuary." The nags, famished and sleepy, with toilworn flanks and sagging bellies, stood with drooping, melancholy heads. But the wagoners sat straight in their saddles, as though they were riding prancing cavalry horses with steaming nostrils, impatient to charge into the battlefield.

Sroleyzer the bricklayer moved up to the head of the troop of horsemen. Although no longer young, he still sat his horse well, his hat tilted to the side, in command of the Valkenik riders as though they were a band of Cossacks in high fur hats. "No wonder," the townspeople joked, "Sroleyzer has great skill and practice in leading horses out of other people's stables."

The Hebrew teachers and their pupils also gathered in the synagogue courtyard. The cheder lads didn't carry the traditional Lag B'Omer bows and arrows, but as on Simkhas Torah they carried aloft banners inscribed "Long live our rabbi!"

The owners of the Valkenik cardboard factory, Jewish manufacturers from Vilna, had lent their carriage with its hand-decorated harness to bring the important guest from the train station. Ten of the leading citizens had set out in another carriage to welcome their new rabbi at the station. All of Valkenik left the synagogue courtyard for the market place and then proceeded to the open road behind the town to await the arrival of the rabbi and his retinue. The brass band led the way, bass drum booming, cymbals clashing, and all its horns blowing at full force, while the musicians' eyes popped with the strain. The brass instruments, the helmets, and the jacket buttons sparkled, gleaming and glittering in the sun. Behind the band the riders pranced on the bell-bedecked horses, and after them marched the cheder children holding up the banners "Long live our rabbi!" And then, finally, came the entire village: the well-to-do congregants in their derbies and tail coats; the artisans in their peaked cloth caps; elderly women in their Sabbath marriage wigs and younger ones in white silk shawls; and then a crowd of youngsters, boys and girls together. The yeshiva people ambled along quietly beside the local throng, pleased with the honor being accorded the Torah. A number of the younger students thought that they too, with God's help, would become great scholars and enter a town with great pomp and ceremony.

In the beth medresh there remained only weak-legged old people who betimes had grabbed good seats next to the Holy Ark so as to hear the rabbi's sermon better. But one person remained in the attic room—Reb Tsemakh Atlas. The sudden silence in the synagogue courtyard hammered at his temples even more than the previous pounding of the bass drum. He saw a breeze soughing through the weeds around the beth medresh and thought he heard the grass whispering: We know why you haven't gone to greet the new rabbi.

Reb Mordekhai-Aaron Shapiro's son and son-in-law had been yeshiva friends of Tsemakh Lomzher's in Navaredok. They had studied together during the war years in Homel, in White Russia. After their return to Poland, both young men had married and become principals of small-town yeshivas, under the auspices of the great yeshiva in Nareva, where Tsemakh had studied when he was a bachelor. Tsemakh knew that his friends had no faith in his repentance and that they still hadn't forgiven him for going out into the secular world. Hitherto not one of these keen-witted Navaredker Musarniks had chanced into Valkenik. But with the coming of the rabbi of Shishlevitz to Valkenik, his son and son-in-law would surely visit him during the summer. For secular-minded or even pious householders Tsemakh could have shown contempt; but with old friends who had never strayed from the path, he knew he would feel crestfallen. Moreover, the rabbi's son and son-in-law might tell the Valkenik congregants that in Nareva, Tsemakh Atlas hadn't been considered suitable to teach even young yeshiva students.

The happy uproar of the crowd approached from the market place. The synagogue courtyard, the big anteroom, and the beth medresh were quickly filled with people. From all sides came shouts, "Make way, make way!" and the rabbi was carried into the beth medresh on the shoulders of two youths. Thin as a needle, he had a large gray beard and tightly curled earlocks that looked like two weights of a grandfather clock. Reb Mordekhai-Aaron Sha-

piro, sitting on the broad shoulders of the two young men, seemed
bewildered and touched by the royal honor being accorded him.
But he was anxious to come down from their shoulders with all his
bones intact.

Dusty yellow rays streamed in through the beth medresh
windows and crisscrossed with the beams of light from the lamps lit
in honor of the festive occasion. Faces and heads swam in the fog
created by the sunlight and the sparkle of electric lights. The
joyous celebration prompted men and women to mingle in the beth
medresh. The women's gallery was full of men who thought they
might see and hear better upstairs, and women pushed their way
into the beth medresh down below. Reb Mordekhai-Aaron Shapiro
stood on the steps of the Holy Ark. Opposite him on the pulpit
stood Reb Hirshe Gordon, surrounded by community officials.
Before the rabbi began his sermon, Hirshe Gordon was supposed
to read aloud the rabbinic contract, but the brass band was still
deafening the crowds outside with its incessant playing. The
people in the beth medresh made a commotion: "Pipe down! This
isn't a village blowout!" The musicians stopped playing and Reb
Hirshe Gordon began to read the rabbinic contract:

"Whereas on this day there have come together the princes and
masters, the elders and rulers, the councilmen and leaders of the
holy community of Valkenik . . ." Reb Hirshe's face was flaming,
his voice shrill and hoarse. As he read on, his voice became even
shriller and hoarser. In high-flown, hyperbolic Hebrew and a
pastiche of biblical verses, the rabbinic document asserted that the
holy congregation of Valkenik had long sought a mentor and guide
who would lead them along the path of righteousness and seal up
the cracks in the divided house of Israel. "The mighty ones of our
congregation wandered in thirst to find the wellspring of light and
wisdom. Finally, God in heaven felt compassion for us because
unto Him we directed our prayers. Heaven led us on the correct
path, and even from a distance our eyes beheld the famous and
illustrious gaon, the sun that illuminates the earth and the inhabi-
tants thereof, the Sinai and uprooter of mountains, who is of course
our teacher and rabbi, that pillar of wisdom and fountain of glory,
whose name is honored far and wide, and he is none other
than . . ."

Just then Reb Hirshe Gordon began weeping, his voice rasping and reproachful, as though he were infuriated at himself for bawling like a woman. It was obvious that he was exerting all his strength to suppress his sobs. He coughed once, twice, a third time, but the tears choked him and prevented him from reading further.

At first a pall fell over the congregation. Everyone was silent. Later, whispers rustled through the crowd; then came a rising murmur of resentment against Reb Hirshe for spoiling the celebration. The newly welcomed rabbi stood on the steps of the Holy Ark, hunched over and trembling. He looked to the pulpit with fear in his eyes, as though the reading of the document, which had broken off at the point where his name and his father's name were to be mentioned, were a bad omen for the future. Suddenly someone shouted, "*Mazel tov!*" The deathly stillness was punctured, and the entire congregation began to shout, "*Mazel tov, rabbi! Mazel tov—*" The crowd outside caught the spirit of the merry tumult, and the orchestra in the synagogue courtyard began pounding away so lustily that the windows of the beth medresh shook and the hanging lamps swayed and clanged against one another: *Mazel tov, mazel tov!*

Weeks later the Valkenik residents were still debating and analyzing why Reb Hirshe Gordon had burst into tears as he read the rabbinic contract. Friends and thoughtful congregants held that the tears that tore their way out of him were those he had suppressed when the old rabbi, the grandfather of his orphaned son, Beynush, left for the Land of Israel. But wags and cranks asserted that Reb Hirshe couldn't bear to see another man becoming the Valkenik rabbi, and furthermore couldn't bear to be the one who had to read the other man's rabbinic contract, with its catalogue of flourishes and praises.

7

THE FIRST SUMMER RESIDENT had arrived at the cottage in the green courtyard of the abandoned pitch factory, at the edge of the pine forest. He had come in a peasant's cart that bypassed the town and proceeded along a side road that led from the railway station through the fields. On top of the tall white chimney of the old factory the storks, steady summer visitors, began fanning and beating their dry wings, welcoming their neighbor of many years. On the hill near the courtyard an enormous tree with protruding roots also swayed its long branches and transmitted the glad tidings to the woods. The pines in the depths of the forest shook and trembled, overjoyed that their old friend—who frequently strolled at dawn with a tallis over his head—had already arrived. The rustle, swish, and whisper of the pine trees went deeper and deeper, until the thick forest ended and a plain of cornfields, meadows, and gardens began. Here the greenery was new and didn't know the regular summer resident of the cottage. But nevertheless, even the new greenery piously swayed along with the old shrubs and trees as though it too knew of the visitor's prominence.

From the sown fields the sounds reached the other side of the bridge where a Jewish blacksmith lived, and he brought the news to the first morning minyan at the beth medresh. The congregants were still in a daze from the brass band, still in a tipsy, jolly mood from the celebration in honor of the new rabbi. But news of the visitor transformed the midweek mood into one of Sabbath holiness: "If he, long life to him, has already arrived, it must indeed be summer," said the worshipers at the first minyan.

"Who's come?" one man asked his neighbor.

"The author of the famous book, *The Vision of Avraham.*"

Reb Avraham-Shaye Kosover did not sign his name to his books. Nevertheless, everyone knew that this humble man whose wife ran a little textile shop in Vilna had written *The Vision of Avraham on Tractate Eruvin* and *The Vision of Avraham on Tractate Sabbath*. Scholars spoke of him with great awe, but occasionally a religious functionary would tug at his beard and argue angrily: "He doesn't want to be either a rabbi or a rosh yeshiva. And he certainly doesn't involve himself with worldly affairs. If a man sits and studies all his life, what great accomplishment is it if he becomes a gaon?"

"Thank God we too have immersed ourselves in Torah study," another scholar would say, smiling to show that the great rabbi's learning didn't intimidate him—but he still couldn't hide his envy. "What's known everyone knows; and what isn't known no one knows—so what's his contribution?"

His intimates talked about him in a low voice, as though his request to remain unnoticed had forced them to speak of him in a whisper. They said that Reb Avraham-Shaye had once been urged to give a Talmud lesson in a yeshiva for young married men but had replied that even saying grace in the company of two other Jews was a hardship for him. People frightened him. Nevertheless, as much as he tried to hide from people, his fame grew like a tree: slowly, quietly sun-drenched, and full of secret joy.

He was always the first of the summer vacationers to arrive in Valkenik; he came right after Lag B'Omer and was the last to leave on the Eve of Rosh Hashana. The first summer, a delegation of the town's leading citizens, headed by Reb Hirshe Gordon, had gone to pay him a visit. Reb Hirshe, as was his wont, reviled the Zionists; and Reb Avraham-Shaye, as was *his* wont, remained silent. When one of the visitors told a joke, his burst of boyish laughter astounded the visitors. Then he fell silent again and sat with lowered eyes until the men realized it was time to leave. But curiosity to know what sort of person he was brought the Valkenik residents back once more. This time there was a purpose to their visit: They wanted him to intervene in a quarrel between the religious and enlightened factions. But Reb Avraham-Shaye, literally trembling with fear and vexation, said, "I don't want to get involved in any quarrel."

Later Reb Hirshe Gordon had fumed in the presence of Valkenik's religious Jews, "A scholar carries the responsibility for his entire generation, and it certainly is his duty to get involved."

Reb Hirshe Gordon stopped visiting the summer guest at the edge of the pine forest. Other congregants came to see him two or three times during the summer but didn't find him at home. Members of his family said that he had gone for a walk in the woods or to bathe in the river.

When the congregants reported this to Reb Hirshe, he laughed at them. "Don't you realize he's hiding from you? He's not normal; he's a wild man!"

People more moderate than Reb Hirshe Gordon, however, came to the defense of this man of solitude: "It's hard for him to receive visitors because, poor soul, he's a sick man." The Valkenik congregants had heard that Reb Avraham-Shaye had had heart trouble since his childhood. People would find him resting on an iron cot in his forest cottage, holding a little Talmud in his hand, or lying stretched out on a wooden bench by the long table in the middle of the grassy courtyard.

Reb Yisroel the tailor, the old yeshiva patron, came from Smargon. He said that when he had lived in Smargon and was already a father, Reb Avraham-Shaye was a young pupil at the local beth medresh. Nobody noticed anything special about him. He was a gentle boy, extremely diligent in his studies. Day and night he stood by his prayer stand, his back to the congregation, studying. Then one morning after prayers a recluse in the Smargon beth medresh heard loud crying. The recluse looked around and discovered Avraham-Shaye in tears, praying before the open Holy Ark. No one else was in the beth medresh at the time, and the recluse sat in a corner between the stove and the western wall. Avraham-Shaye didn't see him and prayed, "Master of the Universe, open my eyes that I may behold wondrous things from your Torah. I promise to study Torah all my life, just for the sake of study. Solely for the sake of study. Only for the sake of Torah. I am but a stranger on the earth; hide not your commandments from me." The eavesdropper quickly slipped out of the beth medresh lest the young scholar see him and feel embarrassed or frightened. "And I myself heard the recluse tell this to a gathering of congregants in the beth medresh of Smargon," Reb Yisroel the tailor bore witness.

The story gave the Valkenik Jews the chills. A Bar Mitzva youth had wept before an open Holy Ark and said he was a stranger on the earth. It was obvious, then, that he had been ill even as a youngster and hadn't believed he would live.

The pious summer residents prayed in a little forest cottage next to the cardboard factory. Reb Avraham-Shaye also prayed there and rarely came to town, except for an occasional Sabbath After-noon Service, or on Tisha B'Av to stroll around the cemetery and on the Sunday morning before Rosh Hashana for the first of the Penitential Prayers. He would also visit the old Valkenik rabbi, Reb Yaakov Hacohen Lev, upon his arrival and departure. And since Reb Yaakov Lev was taciturn too, they would sit mute for fifteen minutes or half an hour and then bid one another farewell.

Once when the Valkenik rabbi had to adjudicate a difficult case between two forest merchants, he sent a wagoner and the beadle to Reb Avraham-Shaye inviting his assistance. But both returned with a refusal. The rabbi then went in person to ask for help, but Reb Avraham-Shaye declined again. His pleas that such requests should not be made of him were so heartfelt that Reb Yaakov Hacohen Lev insisted no longer. Instead, he just withdrew from the case because he could come to no decision. The incident annoyed the Valkenik rabbi, but another time Reb Avraham-Shaye Kosover irritated him even more.

One cloudy Thursday morning a butcher came running to Reb Avraham-Shaye. "I slaughtered an ox," he said, "and found an adhesion in the intestines. Would that make the meat unkosher? The Valkenik rabbi is leaning toward saying it's kosher, but he's afraid to say so on his own unless you agree, too."

Reb Avraham-Shaye saw that the butcher was panting breath-lessly from running and that his hands and feet were trembling because of the financial loss he might suffer. So he replied at once, "I'm coming." But before he put on his coat and found his walking stick, it had begun to rain.

"Perhaps we should wait till the rain ends?" the butcher asked.

"We'll walk under the trees," the rabbi answered, "and we won't get wet. It's only a drizzle and it'll soon stop." The two men walked awhile without saying a word. When the rain ceased as suddenly as it had begun, Reb Avraham-Shaye told the anxious butcher, "You see, a man must have faith. The sun is shining already, and by the time we come to town our clothes will have dried too."

The Valkenik rabbi was incredulous when he saw Reb Avraham-Shaye coming, and on foot too. With his chin resting on the handle of his cane, Reb Avraham-Shaye sat in silence for a few minutes and heard the rabbi's discourse on the animal's adhesion.

"Kosher," he whispered as though answering amen to someone's benediction. Reb Yaakov Hacohen Lev had assumed that Reb Avraham-Shaye would delve into holy texts with him, immerse himself in involved analyses pertaining to the problem, and search for a way out—and here he was giving his decision crisply and bluntly without any hesitation.

"A Jew's money is precious to me too, especially a poor man's, but you still haven't heard all my doubts. I don't want to feed unkosher meat to an entire community," the old Valkenik rabbi flared.

Reb Avraham-Shaye stood up and replied serenely. His voice, however, was somewhat louder than usual, as though he were afraid that the venerable rabbi didn't hear very well. "You can surely rely solely on your own opinion even in more difficult cases. But since you said you had doubts, accept my concurrence in your decision that the animal is absolutely kosher."

Overjoyed that he was saved from a great loss, the butcher accompanied Reb Avraham-Shaye through town and asked him to wait a moment until he could find a wagoner to take him back to his house. "Before I left for the forest, the Valkenik rabbi told me, 'Go, try your luck. As far as I know he won't involve himself.' So I went to you practically without any hope. That's why I didn't take a wagoner with me. So at least let me get you someone to take you back."

Reb Avraham-Shaye smiled broadly, and when he smiled his mustache and cheeks and the corners of his mouth shook. "What I'm doing now isn't because of saintliness or pride. We must learn from our patriarchs and prophets how to conduct ourselves. The prophet Samuel made the Jews swear and bear testimony: 'Whose ox have I taken and whose donkey have I taken?'—meaning that he had taken neither ox nor donkey from anyone in Israel. Do you think the prophet Samuel wanted people to sing his praises for not

breaking into a barn at night and stealing an ox or a donkey?" Reb
Avraham-Shaye's gay laugh resounded. "The answer is that the
prophet Samuel probably had to decide questions concerning
adhesions quite frequently, but after one of his adjudications he
didn't let anyone harness a donkey and give him a ride back home."
The rabbi then thanked the butcher for accompanying him and
left. His heavy arms dangling at his sides, the butcher followed Reb
Avraham-Shaye with his eyes until he vanished among the trees,
leaving the path of golden sand desolate in the sunny silence.

8

BECAUSE THE STUDENTS at the yeshiva were spending their
first summer in the village, they had not yet met the author of *The
Vision of Avraham*. But they thought: So what? He has nothing to
discuss with simple congregants, but certainly he will spend some
time with Torah scholars.

The first person who wanted to meet him was Sheeya Lipnishker. Sheeya turned over all the books in the beth medresh and
couldn't find one of Reb Avraham-Shaye's volumes. So he immediately propounded a conundrum: "If in a place of study one finds the
Babylonian Talmud, the Jerusalem Talmud, the works of Maimonides, Rabbi Yaakov's *Arba Turim*, and Joseph Caro's *Shulchan
Aruch*, but can discover nothing by Reb Avraham-Shaye, it's a sign
that students can do without him. So how come he's considered a
latter-day decider of law and has taken the world by storm?"

The young prodigy ran out of the beth medresh into the market
place and dashed into Reb Hirshe Gordon's store with a cry: "Do
you have any of Reb Avraham-Shaye's books?"

Reb Hirshe Gordon too had once wanted to know the reason for
Reb Avraham-Shaye Kosover's greatness, and when he went to

Vilna to buy textiles he had bought the scholar's books. Sheeya Lipnishker, holding the packet of borrowed texts, went to the beth medresh to burrow into them. For twenty-four hours he thumbed through the tomes, turning pages—then rushed out through the town to the forest. With his crooked, yellowish teeth he bit his lips, waved his hands and reviled himself: "You lummox! You clunk!" His mind seethed with twenty responses for one problem and twenty questions for one answer. He rebutted all of Reb Avraham-Shaye's ideas, refuted everything, disproved all his interpretations, made naught of them all, until he got lost in the thick woods. He tripped over stumps and became entangled in overgrown roots. Finally, however, more by his scholar's intuition than his big crossed eyes, he found the rabbi's cottage and stormed into the courtyard.

He ran back into the beth medresh, his excitement undiminished, and shouted to the students who surrounded him, "I talked to him ten minutes, twenty minutes, twenty-five minutes. I refuted his interpretations of the Talmud, of Maimonides, of the entire *Shulchan Aruch.* He heard me out, said nothing for a long while, then answered as follows: 'Perhaps you're right. I don't remember by heart what the Talmud says; I don't even remember what I've written. In general, it's difficult for me to discuss Torah matters.'"

While the students stood there amazed and baffled, Yoel Uzder laughed to himself. Reb Avraham-Shaye is a clever man, he thought. He doesn't want to deal with madmen. "But he'll spend some time studying with me," Yoel whispered to the younger boys.

Yoel went to the rabbi's cottage as dressed up as when he had visited his prospective bride. He grasped the middle of his walking stick and held it away from his body, as one holds a lulav and esrog. He strolled slowly, careful not to get his shoes dusty. Meanwhile he calmly pondered his queries and his replies, as was befitting a sedate young adult. He returned in the same fashion to the beth medresh. Not a speck of dust was on his suit; not a wrinkle or a fleck marked his hat. However, his forehead was perspiring heavily. Just as Yoel Uzder couldn't turn his head without moving his entire body, he couldn't concoct a lie. Yoel told the whole truth: "Reb Avraham-Shaye let me speak until I was finished. He told me the same thing he told Sheeya Lipnishker: 'I don't remember by heart what the Talmud says; I don't even remember what I myself have written in my own books.' But nevertheless, he didn't just sit there in silence; he also talked about secular matters. He asked me how long I had studied in Kletzk, why I left, and how long I intend to remain in Valkenik. But since I can read between the lines, I knew exactly what he was driving at," Uzder said loudly.

"Maybe he wanted to borrow a couple of zlotys from you," the yeshiva boys joked.

"He wanted to know why I'm not married yet." The old bachelor put a finger to his temple and wrinkled his brow as he did when deliberating whether to give a friend a loan.

The third visitor to the pitch factory was Reb Menakhem-Mendl Segal, who had returned to Valkenik late in the semester, after Lag B'Omer. He had heard much about Reb Avraham-Shaye in Vilna and had seen him several times but had never spoken to him. Now Reb Menakhem-Mendl hadn't come to speak about Torah matters but to ask advice.

Beneath the tall pine trees the short assistant rosh yeshiva looked even smaller, almost like a midget. Deeper in the forest, soft blue shadows covered the dark green blanket of pine needles, as though night still lurked there. Wherever Reb Menakhem-Mendl turned, the sun-baked trunks exuded a pungent odor of balsam in the stifling heat. The sandy path, smelling of dry dust, stretched along the forest where whitewashed peasant huts gleamed, surrounded by little green gardens. In an empty lot filled with lumber a peasant was banging nails into the roof of his hut. The sharp blows rang out proudly, as if to snap the surrounding region out of its drowsy noonday doldrums. The freshly stripped logs of the new hut smelled sweet and sparkled in the sun.

But as Reb Menakhem-Mendl ambled along the footpath, he heard nothing and saw nothing. Even if someone had stopped to tell him of a newly discovered continent peopled by outlandish creatures he would have sighed: "Why tell me? It's a waste of time from Torah learning. The world of the Talmud is enough for me." And since Reb Menakhem-Mendl was worried about his own situation, he certainly wasn't in the mood for forest, path, or peasant huts.

A big table flanked by two long benches stood in the middle of the courtyard. Reb Avraham-Shaye was lying on one of the benches with his face to the sun. No book was on the table. The rabbi's eyes were shut. Only the vaulted, wrinkled brow and the radiant smile bore witness that he was concentrating on a Torah matter. When he sensed a shadow blocking his sunlight, he opened his eyes and saw his diminutive visitor, who sidled up to him timidly, like a sparrow to proffered crumbs. A momentary flicker of impatience passed over Reb Avraham-Shaye's face. He sighed in exasperation and stood up to greet the visitor.

As the men stood facing each other, Reb Menakhem-Mendl introduced himself. He told the rabbi where he had studied as a youth, then added, "After my wedding I was miserable because I had to sell shoemakers' accessories. Then my old friend from Navaredok, Reb Tsemakh Atlas, came to my rescue and brought me to Valkenik to teach Talmud in the local yeshiva. But my wages during the winter didn't suffice for me here, nor for my wife and child in Vilna. It goes without saying that I couldn't bring my family here as Reb Tsemakh said I'd be able to do. When I went home for Passover, my wife asked me to stay in Vilna and become a shopkeeper once more. But we had already closed my little store at the beginning of the winter, and that meant I'd have to buy a new supply of accessories or look for a brand-new business. But you see, first of all, I'm a bad businessman. Second, I had no money to start all over again. Third, I really didn't want to be in business again and not be able to take a couple of hours off during the day to study Torah. So after long discussions I finally convinced my wife that the situation in the yeshiva might improve during the summer and I'd be able to bring her and the child to Valkenik. So she finally agreed to my coming back. That's why I came back so late in the term, after Lag B'Omer. But I found the situation in the yeshiva even worse than during the winter. On the one hand there were new students, both young and old. But on the other hand the local townspeople are now paying less of an allowance for both the students and the yeshiva teachers. So I don't know what to do—whether to stay in Valkenik or to go back to Vilna."

During Reb Menakhem-Mendl's sad, prosaic murmuring, which sounded like a plaintive morning prayer, Reb Avraham-Shaye listened attentively, his large, kindly, sky-blue eyes wide open.

Then he stretched out on the bench once more, pressed his chin against the edge of the table, and motioned to his visitor to sit down on the other bench.

"If you returned to Vilna, could someone else give the Talmud lectures in the yeshiva in your place?"

Reb Menakhem-Mendl had gone to ask for advice, true—but in his heart he had expected the noted gaon to lecture him about his doubts and encourage him to remain with Torah. But instead he'd merely asked him if a substitute was available in case he returned to business in Vilna.

"Just now I don't know of anyone who could replace me. The truth is, we really need a third teacher—but since Valkenik cannot, or doesn't want to, support two teachers, how can we think of a third one?"

"I've heard that the local yeshiva follows the Navaredker tradition, and I know that the larger Navaredker yeshivas send their older students out to teach in smaller schools. Why hasn't someone from one of the centers come to help you here?"

"Our principal, Reb Tsemakh Atlas, isn't on good terms with the main center in Nareva, where he studied. So they don't send any young scholars to help us," Reb Menakhem-Mendl answered and thought: Since Reb Avraham-Shaye solves difficult problems of the law, his questions are straight to the point.

"And why isn't the principal on good terms with the center in Nareva?"

Reb Menakhem-Mendl was hesitant about replying, but finally said, "Reb Tsemakh Atlas married into a freethinking family and was uprooted from Musar for a while. Because of this the Navaredker yeshiva has a grudge against him, even though he later left his rich home and made Valkenik a place of Torah learning."

Reb Menakhem-Mendl realized that he hadn't given Reb Avraham-Shaye a satisfactory explanation. The problem was a difficult one for him too: Musarniks not forgive a penitent? Why didn't Nareva want to make peace with Reb Tsemakh Atlas?

"I know that Valkenik has long been split by the quarrel over choosing a rabbi. Didn't this divert students from their Torah studies?" Reb Avraham-Shaye asked.

Reb Menakhem-Mendl was once again amazed at how quickly Reb Avraham-Shaye grasped a situation. He began to unburden his heart: "During the winter, some of the yeshiva boys were indeed diverted from their Torah studies. They ran to hear the sermons of the rabbinic candidates. Even the diligent students couldn't find a quiet spot in the beth medresh; in every corner congregants stood arguing about a rabbi. Perhaps it was a mistake to establish a yeshiva in a town split by controversy." Reb Menakhem-Mendl sighed. Angry with Tsemakh Atlas for making him give up his business and dragging him off to a small town, he added in irritation, "Even in establishing the yeshiva the rosh yeshiva showed that he isn't very responsible."

"I'm going to town tomorrow to visit the new rabbi, so I'll come to the yeshiva too." Reb Avraham-Shaye rose from the bench and said, "Please excuse me for not sitting up. I've been used to stretching out this way for many years now. I find it easier to breathe lying down." Hands folded on his chest and head thrown back, he accompanied his guest to the courtyard gate.

"Do you hear my neighbors sharpening their beaks and fluttering their wings? They have no worries." The rabbi pointed up to the nest of storks on the tall white chimney of the one-time factory and laughed gaily. Reb Menakhem-Mendl's sad eyes gazed at him in astonishment. "Incredible!" he said to himself. "Thinking of storks!" But to his question—whether to return to Vilna or remain in Valkenik—the author of *The Vision of Avraham* had given no response.

9

"REB AVRAHAM-SHAYE WILL COME to the beth medresh tomorrow and will probably give a Talmud lecture. The Valkenik Jews will then have greater respect for the yeshiva and perhaps they'll increase their support, or at least pay on time." Reb Menakhem-Mendl announced the good tidings to the principal.

Reb Tsemakh, however, scowled and answered irritably, "I don't care whether their learning impresses him or not. And I don't think the Valkenik shopkeepers will increase their support by as much as a penny because a great scholar has come to visit the yeshiva. I'm more concerned about the students, both young and old, running to this summer resident to pilpulize with him, as if that were the most important thing."

"What *should* be the most important thing for the yeshiva boys, if not to study Torah and discuss Torah matters?" asked the amazed Reb Menakhem-Mendl.

"The most important thing for them is to work and toil at becoming men of noble and upright character. Bahya ibn Pakuda, author of *The Duties of the Heart,* and Luzzatto, author of *The Path of the Upright,* were also opposed to these empty pilpuls." Tsemakh exploded with rage. "Ever since your youth in Navaredok, Reb Menakhem-Mendl, you've been naïvely pious! But in the battle with one's *yetzer ha-ra* one has to be sharp. You know what the Musarniks say: 'A monk is pious.' I still belong to the generation of Navaredker Musarniks who would kill themselves to perfect their character. And I haven't given up a normal home life just so my students can display their virtuosity with clever interpretations."

Reb Menakhem-Mendl's hands trembled angrily at hearing Reb Tsemakh talk with such contempt about Torah study and Torah scholars. He wanted to tell him, "It's envy speaking! You're vexed that you didn't grow as a scholar and that you can't even give a Talmud lesson to older students in a little yeshiva." Reb Menakhem-Mendl also wanted to ask, "Why is it that so many years of studying Musar and all that Navaredker fervor didn't save you from the swinish desire to marry a beauty from a rich and freethinking family?" But it was the naïvely pious Reb Menakhem-Mendl, as Tsemakh called him, who could suppress his anger better than all the veteran Musarniks and not blurt out everything on his mind. As it was, he spoke with more bitterness and rancor than was usual for him.

"I still haven't seen any proof of your students' and seekers' kindness and higher achievements. In any case, you know that ever since we studied together in Navaredok, as you yourself just said, *I* have insisted on toiling day and night over the Talmud and its commentaries. Nowadays the great Navaredker yeshivas of Nareva,

Mezritch, and Pinsk also insist on sitting and studying. If your way is different, you shouldn't have brought me to your beth medresh. And since we're on the subject, I might as well tell you that you had no right whatsoever to talk me into closing my store and coming here if you weren't sure I'd be able to bring my family. Which *Code of Law* told you that you could throw my wife and child to the winds because you needed an assistant rosh yeshiva?"

"I was sure the people in town would keep their promise to take care of the rosh yeshivas—that's why I persuaded you to come," Tsemakh answered heatedly. He added with a crooked smile, "It's also possible that had you run to consult Reb Avraham-Shaye earlier, he would have advised you not to become a teacher. Since *he* keeps all his Torah learning to himself, it's quite likely he would have told you to do the same."

"Is that the way you talk about a saintly gaon?" Reb Menakhem-Mendl replied, even more incensed. "You say that Reb Avraham-Shaye keeps his Torah learning to himself? What about his books? Everyone can learn from *them*. And he doesn't earn a penny from them. If a customer sends him more than the cost of the book, he sends the extra money back immediately. What's more, he doesn't look for honor. None of his books bear his name."

"But everyone knows who the author is anyway, so his honor isn't diminished at all because his name isn't on them. On the contrary, in addition to getting honor for his brilliance, he's also praised for his modesty." Tsemakh laughed angrily. "Books are not students, Reb Menakhem-Mendl. For students one pours out one's heart and soul. A student can never learn as much from a book as he can from a teacher. And let me ask you this: Do you think a man is modest if he calls his book *The Vision of Avraham* while he himself is called Avraham and lets people refer to him as the author of *The Vision of Avraham?* Does this Reb Avraham-Shaye Kosover really believe that he has grasped the truth of the Torah in his *Vision* as clearly as our father Abraham discerned the Divine Presence in *his* vision?"

The two principals were talking in the beth medresh pulpit. Reb Menakhem-Mendl had been leaning his left elbow on the pulpit railing so long that it had begun to hurt him. But he couldn't take his eyes off his friend; he looked at Tsemakh terror-stricken, as though he were suddenly standing before the gates of hell.

Tsemakh shifted his weight on his long legs until his rage dissipated; he had spewed out what he could not contain, and now he regretted his indiscreet remarks.

"But on the other hand," he said, "I don't have anything against Reb Avraham-Shaye's visiting the yeshiva. All the students have to be told to be in the beth medresh tomorrow so that he can see the entire group. Perhaps, as you said, even some benefit can come from it." Tsemakh bit his lips with self-hatred for having to talk so ingratiatingly. "And as far as your family is concerned, I can't do a thing to make the local residents keep their word. But I'll gladly give you half my wages, so you can have more to send home to your wife and child. I don't have to send any money home. Half will suffice me."

"God forbid: I won't take a penny from you," Reb Menakhem-Mendl said, shuddering, and the two friends separated with a feeling of estrangement.

The news that Reb Avraham-Shaye was coming to the yeshiva brought a festive mood to a mundane weekday. All the benches were occupied. Hats, skullcaps, and caps were swaying over the Talmuds. Yoel Uzder relaxed for this once his rule of having nothing to do with younger students. He stood in front of two adjoining prayer stands, one foot resting on each bottom plank, waving his hands like a bear attacked by a pack of dogs. The young students assailed him with Talmudic questions, but Yoel out-shouted them: "Your supposition is wrong from the start!" Sheeya Lipnishker scurried about over the length and breadth of the beth medresh, talking to himself and gesticulating with his thumb. "The interpretation is exactly the opposite of that offered by Reb Avraham-Shaye. So he offers an interpretation! Big deal!" Melech-ke Vilner trailed Reb Menakhem-Mendl, asking dozens of questions, very much chagrined that his teacher wasn't responding. But Reb Menakhem-Mendl had no patience for the boy at the moment. He was bustling about from one end of the beth medresh to the other, like an in-law on the even of the wedding, occasionally casting a triumphant glance toward the principal's corner: Let Reb Tsemakh see how fervently the yeshiva boys study when they expect a great Talmud scholar.

Sitting behind his prayer stand, Tsemakh felt a frozen smile in the corners of his mouth as one feels icicles on his mustache. Besides yeshiva students, he also saw older Valkenik Jews sitting around the table at the western wall waiting for Reb Avraham-Shaye. Having heard during morning prayers that the author of *The Vision of Avraham* was coming to the yeshiva, the congregants had left their shops to be present when he discussed Torah with the yeshiva students. Reb Avraham-Shaye was a man who hid from the world, but the world ran after him. Was that why Tsemakh lived a miserable life away from home—so that his students should kowtow before an author of new books as if the old ones no longer sufficed? In Lomzhe, Tsemakh hadn't been afraid of admonishing his wealthy brothers-in-law and their customers; here he didn't even dare tell the poor Reb Menakhem-Mendl what he thought about arrogant scholars. And he would also have to watch his tongue when speaking to Reb Avraham-Shaye, that supposed lamed vovnik, one of the thirty-six hidden saints of the world.

As soon as someone in the beth medresh announced that Reb Avraham-Shaye was on Synagogue Street, Chaikl Vilner slipped out into the anteroom. Since he and his father had moved into the Vorobeys' apartment, he spent more time at home than in the yeshiva—all because of the landlady's daughter—and he had fallen behind in his studies of the Tractate *Kiddushin*, which everyone was studying this semester. Hence he didn't want to be present when the students pilpulized with the guest—they might notice how far behind he had fallen. From the anteroom he went into the side room and looked through the window at Reb Avraham-Shaye making his way along the deserted street.

The rabbi wore a light gray knee-length coat and held a cane in his hand. Head back, he proceeded slowly, as though counting the cobblestones with his stick. A village baker, wearing long ritual fringes but no jacket, sat on his porch with both feet propped up on a bench, resting after a hard night of kneading and baking. Seeing who was coming, the baker jumped to his feet. But Reb Avraham-Shaye didn't notice him and continued on his way, a serene glow on his face—as if he were delighted with the sunshine and the Talmud melody resounding from the beth medresh. But as Chaikl watched, instead of turning into the yeshiva Reb Avraham-Shaye headed down the hill to the rabbi's house. The new rabbi, Reb Mordekhai-Aaron Shapiro, came out on his porch to greet him.

He's not that old. Forty-five, maybe only forty. And I thought a gaon had to be an old man with a gray beard, Chaikl mused, doubly irritated: he was behind in his studies because of the landlady's daughter, and he was ashamed to show his face at Reb Avraham-Shaye's lesson because he couldn't display his learning prowess.

Synagogue Street was immersed in a noonday doze. Rays of sunlight fluttered on the whitewashed walls, on the shingled roofs, and on the porches. Chaikl looked at a dark blue window, one half shuttered, the other half covered with a colored curtain. He stared at a green fence around a little house and at two clay milk jugs drying upside down on the pickets. A man came out of his house and stopped in the middle of the street, as though the languor of the noonday sun had mesmerized him and he couldn't recall where he was off to. From a gate across the way, a cow poked out its white-flecked brown head and gazed dumbly at the man. At the other end of Synagogue Street, where the main road passed, a peasant cart drove by, leaving a dust cloud in its wake. Chaikl stared again at a square chimney capped by a round little roof. He surveyed a tall tree behind a house; its pale green leaves on thin branches winked at him. Seeing all these sights, he didn't notice Reb Avraham-Shaye leaving the rabbi's house. Chaikl saw him again only when his beard and hat flitted by the window of the side room.

Chaikl waited a few minutes, longer than necessary for the visitor to enter the beth medresh, and then left the side room, annoyed with himself at running away like a little cheder boy. But from the anteroom Chaikl saw that Reb Avraham-Shaye was still outside, standing on the lowest step and looking down at his cane. Local housewives stood at both sides of the entrance. Hearing from their husbands that the vacationing gaon was coming to the beth medresh, they had run out to look at him. The women seemed to be surprised and confused about why the rabbi wasn't going into the beth medresh. Realizing immediately that Reb Avraham-Shaye didn't want to pass between the women, Chaikl leaped outside and stood shoulder to shoulder with the visitor: then both passed the two rows of women and stopped in the anteroom.

The sun-tanned Reb Avraham-Shaye had a hawk nose like Reb Tsemakh Atlas, but it wasn't as large or sharply aquiline. His somewhat curly beard with its soft golden sheen grew at an angle—more under his chin than straight down, as though his beard too wanted to hide from people and not resemble a scholar's beard.

"Are you from the yeshiva?" he asked, smiling, his healthy white teeth gleaming from under his mustache.

"Yes, from the yeshiva," Chaikl answered, his gaze fixed on the rabbi. Reb Avraham-Shaye was on the short side, Chaikl noticed, but he had broad shoulders, strong hands, and thick fingers.

"The students are so immersed in their Talmud that it would be a sin to divert their attention. Which class are you in?"

"I'm Reb Menakhem-Mendl's pupil," Chaikl said, feeling a sudden need to confide in the rabbi. "I didn't come up with any new interpretations in my Talmud studies this summer," he stammered.

The visitor laughed gently. "One doesn't have to come up with new interpretations."

Strange, Chaikl thought; he was an author of books and yet belittled new interpretations. Chaikl became even more candid. "In fact, I've studied very little this summer. My friends know much more than I."

"If you didn't study, you can't be faulted for not knowing," the rabbi joked; then he became serious. "You probably know the Talmudic statement that when the Almighty created the world, he used the Torah as a guide for creation. The truth of the Torah is the only truth in all the world. And indeed why *haven't* you studied?"

"I brought my sick father here for a vacation and I have to help him," Chaikl croaked, but he knew he was lying; he was idling for another reason. Then, feeling it was beneath his dignity to defend himself, he shook his head impatiently and said, as befitted a true Navaredker, "Even though the truth of the Torah is the only truth, one can know this truth but not follow it. One can understand the truth in one hour, but to follow it—one must struggle a lifetime."

"Is that your own original thought?" the rabbi asked, astonished.

"I heard it from our rosh yeshiva, Reb Tsemakh Atlas."

" 'One can understand the truth in one hour, but to follow it one must struggle a lifetime.' That's a good saying," Reb Avraham-Shaye Kosover murmured. Suddenly a youthful ruddiness spread over his cheeks and his eyes twinkled cleverly as he looked at the youth. "It's a good saying, but it has nothing to do with sitting down and studying. If you're not in a hurry to get back to your father, come into the beth medresh." He slowly led the way to the door and Chaikl followed.

10

THE BRIEF VISIT at the new rabbi's house had caused Reb Avraham-Shaye great anguish, though he didn't show it when he arrived at the beth medresh. Reb Mordekhai-Aaron Shapiro had invited him into the living room, cited a few Midrashic epigrams, and served tea and cake. Reb Avraham-Shaye declined the food, stating that he was expected at the yeshiva and couldn't spend much time at the rabbi's house. And he immediately added, "The townspeople should be reminded to pay their weekly contributions. The wages aren't enough for the rosh yeshivas and they can't bring their families to Valkenik."

Reb Mordekhai-Aaron pulled his beard and replied, "I've heard quite a lot about one of the rosh yeshivas, Reb Tsemakh Atlas. He studied in Navaredok with my son and son-in-law. Had I been the rabbi here when he came to establish his little yeshiva, he wouldn't have done it in Valkenik. Tsemakh Lomzher, as he is called by the Navaredkers, is not fond of Torah, nor of Torah scholars."

The visitor spread his hands in amazement, as if to ask: How can a rosh yeshiva not be fond of Torah?

"Now you're in a rush to get to the yeshiva, so there's no time to talk. When I come up to your vacation house I'll tell you more," Reb Mordekhai-Aaron said as he escorted his guest out to the porch.

Reb Avraham-Shaye was vexed that the rabbi had begun by speaking ill of the principal. The rabbi's unexpected kiss when they bade farewell also irritated him. Reb Avraham-Shaye didn't like the rabbinic custom of kissing and embracing at every meeting and farewell. In fact, even when meeting a scholar after a long separation he only shook hands. He was ashamed to display his feelings and was flustered when others exhibited theirs toward him—especially in this case, since he had never met the Valkenik rabbi before, and the latter had already promised him a visit devoted to slander.

As he entered the beth medresh Reb Avraham-Shaye saw a delighted Reb Menakhem-Mendl Segal running toward him. A moment later the tall, reserved principal approached and stretched out his hand. Reb Avraham-Shaye cast an amiable, inquisitive glance up at him. He wanted the rosh yeshiva's appearance to demolish the Valkenik rabbi's slanderous comments about him. But Reb Tsemakh's fierce look immediately stabbed at his heart. Reb Avraham-Shaye also felt that Reb Tsemakh's palm clasping his hand was hard and domineering, strong, hot and dry. A shadow passed over Reb Avraham-Shaye's face, his nostrils dilated, and fear flickered in his eyes. He quickly removed his hand from Reb Tsemakh's as though he had touched a hot oven or pricked a finger.

Confident that the visitor would give a Talmud lesson, the students had set up a prayer stand for him between the pulpit and the Holy Ark. As soon as he entered, the students pushed forward from all sides to grab seats as close as possible to the prayer stand. The area between the Holy Ark and the pulpit was crowded with learners. Hats thrust on the backs of their heads, they were already pricking up their ears and wrinkling their brows, ready to hear new interpretations and ask questions. The two oldest students, Yoel Uzder and the prodigy Sheeya Lipnishker, elbowed their way up front, and between them slipped one of the youngest students, Melechke Vilner. Greedy and anxious as a young wolf, he wanted to sharpen his teeth by asking the first questions. But Reb Menakhem-Mendl came forward quickly and announced, "Our distinguished visitor has asked that you all return to your Talmuds and not take any time from your studies. He has no intention of giving a Talmud lesson."

The yeshiva lads sat by their prayer stands and looked on as Reb Avraham-Shaye began to edge his way out, accompanied by the two principals. Then he stopped at the bench where the beginners were studying and sat down next to a young pupil with a pale face and big black eyes. The surrounding boys fell silent and watched as the rabbi looked into the Talmud and asked the youngster to recite from the point he had left off. Seeing that the rabbi was short and had to bring his nearsighted eyes, his beard, and even his nose into the Talmud to see the large letters, the youngster lost his fear and began to recite:

"Our rabbis taught that if a man tells a woman, 'Be betrothed unto me with one hundred gulden,' and if she takes them and throws them into the sea or into the fire or anywhere else where they might get lost, she's not betrothed." The lad chanted quickly, as if he were running to win a bet.

"You're a scholar and you sing well, but you must learn to stop at each word and not be in a rush." Reb Avraham-Shaye laughed and stood up. It wasn't his way to pinch a pupil's cheek or pat his head, but his face beamed and a smile played in his mustache.

He passed a row of youthful little heads, all with earlocks, and stopped beside Melechke Vilner, who had moved his prayer stand forward.

"Oh, Melechke, how are you?" Reb Avraham-Shaye said delightedly, as though they were good friends.

"Thank God," Melechke answered, and looked around at the boys with flashing eyes so they would note that Reb Avraham-Shaye and he—praise be to God—were old pals.

Astonished, Reb Menakhem-Mendl blinked and asked the visitor, "How do you know Melechke?"

"What do you mean, how do I know Melechke? He came to visit me and threw questions at me. I barely managed to get him to stop." Reb Avraham-Shaye's blue eyes twinkled with laughter and everyone around smiled too. Only Reb Tsemakh Atlas stood behind the group and scowled even more anxiously.

As soon as the visitor and his escorts withdrew, the younger students surrounded Melechke. Although he had grown and matured somewhat and could already read a chapter of the Talmud, Melechke was still considered a spoiled only child and a show-off who thrust himself into the midst of older people so they would test him in Talmud and pet him. His friends couldn't understand why he hadn't told them that he had visited Reb Avraham-Shaye.

"I went to see Reb Avraham-Shaye Kosover to discuss Torah

with him," Melechke replied, "and I probably asked him about a dozen questions about the first page of the Tractate *Kiddushin*. So Reb Avraham-Shaye told me, 'Come into my house and we'll open my copy of the *Kiddushin* and look at that matter together. Then you can ask what you have to ask.' So we studied the page together, and all my questions were answered of their own accord. When we left his room, Reb Avraham-Shaye led me to the low window which faced the forest and told me, 'Climb out. Let's see if you can climb out of a window as nimbly and quickly as you can ask questions.'" Melechke spread his hands like an old Torah scholar and concluded, "Since I didn't hear any new interpretations from him, what was there to tell you? How I crawled out the window into the woods, and how he crawled out after me?"

The older students had expected that after Reb Avraham-Shaye finished with the youngsters he would come to them. The rabbi had indeed wanted to spend some time with the mature yeshiva students, but as time passed he sensed ever more sharply the principal's dissatisfaction with his visit. So he unexpectedly told the teachers, "I'll be leaving now. I just dropped in for a little while."

Tsemakh Atlas, who all along had followed the visitor in silence, suddenly began to speak. A cold luster was in his eyes and an unkind smile on his face. "The yeshiva students should have gone together to pilpulize with you, the young ones and the old ones separately, and then their trip would have been worthwhile."

"The time lost from Torah study in the long walk to and from my house would offset anything they might gain by listening to me," Reb Avraham-Shaye said, looking down at his cane.

"Could you perhaps come to the yeshiva once a week?" Reb Tsemakh asked. His face, lined by deep, vertical wrinkles, wore an odd smile. "A wagoner would pick you up and bring you back, and thus save you the walk back and forth from the forest to town."

"What are you talking about, Reb Tsemakh?" Reb Menakhem-Mendl cried, realizing that the principal wanted to show that the vacationing rabbi kept all his Torah to himself. "And won't a man perspire and get his fill of dust riding a wagon on a hot summer day? Don't you know that Reb Avraham-Shaye is not well?"

"Indeed, it would be difficult for me to come to town once a week," Reb Avraham-Shaye answered, his face flaming with embarrassment, as it usually did when someone mentioned his heart ailment.

Reb Tsemakh Atlas didn't say another word. But in his erect, reserved bearing—lips taut and hands behind his back—there was even more impudence than in his words. The corners of Reb Avraham-Shaye's mouth, his nose, his chin, even the lids of his eyes twitched and trembled nervously. For a minute he stood, head bowed, as though listening to the black, secretive depths of the principal's silence. But when he lifted his head, his face once again shone with the repose of the woods at dawn, when he strolled among the trees with his tallis on his shoulders.

"Good day," he said, bowing to the rosh yeshiva. His voice and gestures were gentle, conciliatory, and measured, as if he were retreating from the bed of a delirious man who must not be contradicted lest he become even more agitated.

Behind the pulpit Reb Avraham-Shaye stopped for a moment next to Chaikl and said, "I forgot to ask your name."

"Chaikl, Chaikl Vilner is my name," he stammered and looked sadly at the visitor leaving the beth medresh.

A few minutes later Reb Tsemakh was standing beside Chaikl, pleading with him as though the youngster must save him from a great calamity. "My goodness, Vilner, what's happened to you? During the winter you were a seeker and set an example for others. Now all of a sudden you've let yourself go. You either come late or don't come to the lessons at all. You're even late for prayers, and you don't study Musar with enthusiasm any more."

"I can't study Musar with enthusiasm because I no longer believe that Musar clearly outlines a man's path in life," Chaikl replied with anguish in his heart, and he turned back to the Talmud on his prayer stand. He saw that Reb Tsemakh, standing in the middle of the beth medresh, looked like a man who was lost in a wilderness and didn't know which way to turn. The student felt that his rosh yeshiva had himself not found the tranquility and understanding with which to guide others. Chaikl hid his face in his hands and thought of Reb Avraham-Shaye, who had enchanted him with his simple words and warm smile. But no matter how fervently he shut his eyes and clung ecstatically to pious thoughts, the hot eyes of the landlady's daughter blazed through him, and he knew that this had torn him away from Torah and Musar.

Reb Avraham-Shaye was at the other end of Synagogue Street and still asking his escort about Chaikl Vilner. Reb Menakhem-Mendl had much to report about his student.

"He's a hothead and as touchy of his honor as a red-combed rooster. That's why he's capable of a sharp, even rude reply. He still hasn't extirpated from himself the Vilna Butchers Street where he was raised. True, he's a talented youngster with a fundamental grasp of a problem, but occasionally he gets lost in thought and doesn't hear or understand a word of what's being said to him. Last winter he studied hard and delved into Musar. This summer he stopped studying Talmud, and his fire for Musar has gone."

"You're right, he's very touchy about his honor." Reb Avraham-Shaye laughed softly, following his cane with measured stride.

They left Synagogue Street and turned into the main road to the forest. Windows of houses on both sides of the road were half shuttered as a protection against the blinding sun. On the other side of the bridge that crossed the winding Meretshanke River, a blacksmith sat in front of his smithy, resting after work. Seeing the assistant rosh yeshiva in his long gray gaberdine and the vacationing rabbi in his frayed knee-length coat, the broadly built artisan with the smoky face rose to his feet, looking at the two short men. Reb Menakhem-Mendl nodded to the smith. Reb Avraham-Shaye realized that someone was greeting them.

"I'm very nearsighted, practically blind. Without glasses I can't see who's coming toward me and I don't know whom to nod good morning to," he said, annoyed at himself, and stopped in the middle of the road to say farewell. "Sheeya Lipnishker should be persuaded to go out and take a stroll every day. His diligence may have ill effects on his health. It would also be good for his studies if he took more time to reflect."

"I can't imagine his being persuaded to do that," Reb Menakhem-Mendl answered. He realized that Reb Avraham-Shaye didn't approve of Lipnishker's wild pilpuls. But Reb Menakhem-Mendl was disturbed by the very same question that troubled all the Valkenik yeshiva students. "Sheeya Lipnishker and Yoel Uzder said that you listened to their comments on your books and replied, 'You may be right.'"

"They came to refute and not to ask, so I told them they were right." Reb Avraham-Shaye smiled. "By the way, Yoel Uzder is indeed a scholar. But it's a sin that he's still unmarried. A proper match has to be found for him. Well, you've accompanied me far enough and done more than was called for."

"Please don't be angry at me, but you still haven't answered my question about whether I should stay in Valkenik to give Talmud lessons or go back to my family in Vilna and become a merchant again." Reb Menakhem-Mendl stopped, head down and feeling depressed.

Reb Avraham-Shaye gazed at length at the road, as though looking for an answer in the sand. He wasn't concerned about his honor, but he knew his place among the Torah scholars of Lithuania. Yet he had never met a Torah scholar who addressed him with as little reverence as Reb Tsemakh Atlas. Altogether the rosh yeshiva looked like a difficult man who was capable of quarreling and who loved to quarrel. If he was truly such a keen and perverse Musarnik, with little use for Talmud studies, then Reb Menakhem-Mendl must not leave. Without him the local yeshiva would fall apart or bring forth heretics. But on the other hand, his impression of the principal could have been a false one under the influence of the slander he had heard. In short, he would have to wait until the new Valkenik rabbi visited him and, as he had promised, offered more detailed information about Reb Tsemakh Atlas.

"It's not easy to advise a family man to leave wife and child; and it's not easy, either, to advise a Torah scholar to leave a place of Torah learning. Let me think about it," Reb Avraham-Shaye replied, after poking his cane into the sand in long deliberation. "Send your pupil Chaikl Vilner to me on Thursday. You don't have to take the trouble to come yourself. Don't say anything to your student. I'll answer in such a way that only you will be able to understand it."

Then the rabbi turned and took the narrow green footpath that led between the tall pines.

11

R E B   M O R D E K H A I - A A R O N   S H A P I R O   S P E N T a long time at
Reb Avraham-Shaye's vacation home. He drank tea, quoted
rabbinic sayings, talked about his young years in Volozhin, and
told his host why it had been advantageous to come to Valkenik
from Shishlevitz. It was only just before his departure, however,
that he began to speak at length about what his son and son-in-law
had told him concerning Reb Tsemakh Atlas.

"He broke his engagement to a girl from a religious household
and married one from a freethinking family. When his friends came
to persuade him to return to the correct path, he replied that his
only concern was the mitzvas between man and his fellow man.
And one doesn't even have to believe in the Torah precept, 'Love
thy neighbor as thyself,' he said. One can be a good man by
following the dictates of one's reason, and for that, one doesn't have
to be a believer. In brief, they say of him in Nareva, where he
studied, that he was never scrupulously observant of the mitzvas
and that he always talked to the students about doing good deeds
and not about being religious and praying and studying. In brief,
they say of him in Nareva that he simply lacks faith in the God of
Israel. They have no faith in his repentance there, either. If you
say: 'Didn't he leave a rich home after all and become a principal in
a small-town yeshiva?' they reply to this in Nareva: 'No wonder!
He studied Musar so long that he can't even have any more joy of
worldly pleasures!'"

Reb Mordekhai-Aaron Shapiro searched with all his fingers in
the hairs of his gray beard for an appropriate Talmudic comment so
as to end his visit on a good note. But as much as he tugged at his
beard, he couldn't pull out any Torah epigram; and as often as he
repeated, "In brief," he couldn't abbreviate his remarks about the
principal.

"My son and son-in-law have known him for many years. On the eve of my departure to Valkenik they told me to watch out. Be wary, they said. Keep away from him. On the one hand, he's capable of devoting his life to a cause; on the other hand, he's an embittered man who's capable of becoming an implacable foe. So I'm afraid he might persecute me, especially since he's a resident here and I'm just a newcomer. That's why I thought I should tell you this, so you'll understand why I don't want to become involved in local yeshiva politics and so you'll know how to handle him. I'm sure you'll keep this in strictest confidence, because otherwise it could be dangerous for me."

After this visit Reb Avraham-Shaye paced at length in the courtyard, talking to himself. "It's obvious that this Reb Tsemakh Atlas is a difficult man. It's also obvious that he's honest, which means he's a man who does only what he thinks he must do. His Navaredker friends, the rabbi's son and son-in-law, admitted that he can be utterly devoted to a cause. If he doesn't believe in God and in his Torah, why should a person like him disguise himself as a pious Jew with beard and earlocks and run a yeshiva? Nevertheless, it's possible for even an honest man to stick to something he no longer believes in because he has sacrificed so much for his belief and has nowhere else to go."

A downy-cheeked lad with long earlocks came running up to Reb Avraham-Shaye holding a Pentateuch. The child wanted to review a portion of the Torah with his uncle. The rabbi, who always spent his vacations with his sister and her children, stretched himself out, as was his wont, on the bench near the table in the courtyard, while his little nephew Berele sat on the other bench sweetly chanting the Hebrew text, "God said to Abraham, get thee out . . ." His chin resting on the table edge, Reb Avraham-Shaye heard the boy's silvery voice singing the biblical verses but saw Reb Tsemakh Atlas before his closed eyes—his burning glance, his gestures, his way of speaking. That he was a contentious man, one who didn't approve of toiling at Talmud and commentary study, was apparently true. But if in his talks to his students he had disparaged Torah learning, not to mention proclaiming his own doubts about the existence of the Creator, none of the pious students would have remained silent, especially not Reb Menakhem-Mendl.

The lad stopped in the midst of chanting the verses from

Genesis. Reb Avraham-Shaye opened his eyes and saw a visitor—Chaikl Vilner.

"Good morning! Reb Menakhem-Mendl told me that I'm supposed to get a message from you," Chaikl said, wondering why a gaon was, like a primer teacher, studying the Pentateuch with a little boy.

"Go, go, Berele. We'll finish the chapter later," the uncle told his nephew. Berele grabbed the Pentateuch and ran to the house.

To get Chaikl to undertake the mission, Reb Menakhem-Mendl had told him that Reb Avraham-Shaye had specifically chosen him. Reb Menakhem-Mendl had then asked Chaikl to leave as soon as he got Reb Avraham-Shaye's reply, so the rabbi would not lose precious study time.

Reb Avraham-Shaye asked Chaikl to be seated. "Rest awhile; you must be tired from the walk." Chaikl sat down on the other bench, and, as had happened at their first meeting in the beth medresh anteroom, now too he felt a need to talk to the rabbi candidly and confidingly.

"I'm not tired at all. I didn't even notice the distance I covered. I've never been in this forest before and didn't realize how beautiful it is. As I was walking I thought: Imagine, I might never have set foot in the Valkenik woods and never discovered how beautiful they are. Dense forests and inaccessible mountains covered with ice and snow exist in the world. People say there are stars that can't even be seen with a telescope. We don't know how many or what they look like. How can we say that everything was created expressly for man, for him to use and see the wonders of the Creator, if man knows nothing about the billions of stars, the ice-covered mountain peaks, and the dense forests? Then Maimonides was right when he said that the world wasn't created for man but was ordained by the Creator in His wisdom. The Ultimate Wisdom created everything for the sake of its own existence."

"Did you hear this from your rosh yeshiva or did you see this in Maimonides yourself?" Reb Avraham-Shaye asked.

The young philosopher was insulted: Did everything have to come from the rosh yeshiva? Sheeya Lipnishker and Yoel Uzder ran here to display their expertise in analytical Talmudic reasoning—so he would show his knowledge of philosophy.

Chaikl replied, "I myself read it in *The Guide to the Perplexed*, which my father has in his bookcase. I know that one isn't permitted to study philosophy until the age of forty because one might go astray. But I can—it won't hurt me. Our rosh yeshiva doesn't talk about philosophy at all, but he speaks constantly about man and his flaws. He feels that the world is composed of a minority of great people and a majority of little people. But I don't agree with this. Of course there are exalted human beings, but I don't at all agree with the notion that the world is composed of great and little people, like trees in the forest."

"Your rosh yeshiva is right, and not you." Reb Avraham-Shaye smiled from behind his mustache. "People are not only divided up like trees in the forest, they're also sorted out into large and small sizes like galoshes."

Chaikl didn't like the comparison between people and galoshes. But he did like the fact that Reb Avraham-Shaye listened to him, so he continued excitedly, "Everyone says that even a great man often has small flaws. Reb Tsemakh says that a great man can have only great flaws, not small ones, and that his greatness is apparent even in his flaws. Was there a greater sinner and corrupter than King Jeroboam? He persuaded the ten tribes to bow to the golden calves he had erected in Beth-El and Dan. Our sages say that God told him, 'Repent—and I, you and David will stroll together in the Garden of Eden.' And Jeroboam asked: 'Who'll be first?' And when the Divine Providence answered, 'David will be first,' Jeroboam refused to repent, because he didn't want to be second to King David. Reb Tsemakh points out a moral to this story. Any sensible person, any merchant, would have realized the advantage of being the second in the Garden of Eden, in the company of God and King David, over being the first in hell. And Jeroboam understood this no less than the smartest merchant. Nevertheless, he preferred damnation in hell to being second in the world to come, just as he didn't want to be second in this world. A great man, our rosh yeshiva says, is above all a man of great feelings: he is great and strong even in his flaws, and not small and weak."

"The Talmud too teaches us: The greater the man, the bigger his *yetzer ha-ra.* Your rosh yeshiva is right," Reb Avraham-Shaye said calmly from the other side of the table, then immediately fell silent. He saw that he didn't have to exert himself to get his visitor to talk.

"Still, I don't understand our rosh yeshiva. On the one hand, he considers Jeroboam a great man just because he was notorious for his pride and sensuality. But on the other hand, he has absolute contempt for all householders, all merchants, and just plain Jews who do good deeds, if their intent is to garner a bit of honor or if they have another ulterior motive. Reb Tsemakh never stops telling us that the greatest accomplishment of Navaredok is observing the principle that the impure worm of ulterior motive should not creep into our good deeds. The worst disease, says Reb Tsemakh, is the infection of egotistic self-interest."

"Noble people," Reb Avraham-Shaye interrupted, "are careful that their good deeds should be free of self-interest, but good deeds don't become invalid because of self-interest. On this point your rosh yeshiva and Navaredok are not right. Does it hurt anyone if a congregant donates firewood to the beth medresh and in return wants to be called up to the Torah?"

"Fundamentally I understand Reb Tsemakh," Chaikl said. "His view is that a man has to be great in good deeds just as King Jeroboam was great in bad deeds. Still, I can't persuade myself to have contempt for my parents just because they're shopkeepers." Chaikl bent over the table to the rabbi, who raised his head and listened. "My father used to be a Hebrew teacher. But after he got sick he stopped running a cheder, and my mother became a fruit peddler. If my mother has to go somewhere and my father takes her place, he sells more merchandise at higher prices. My mother says that the housewives have respect for my father's white beard, so they buy more and bargain less. My mother likes to have my father stop at the store for a while when he's on his way to the beth medresh so that passers-by can see that though she's a poor fruit peddler, her husband is a fine learned Jew. If a housewife asks her, 'Is he your father?' my mother says, 'He's my husband,' and then my father gets furious with her for telling the truth. He's ashamed that my mother is much younger than he." Chaikl's voice had dropped to a whisper from his previous shout and he fell silent, flustered and angry with himself. What was he babbling about? Reb Avraham-Shaye might even laugh at him and ask him what the point of all this was.

But instead of laughing or questioning him, Reb Avraham-Shaye removed from his jacket pocket a metal case containing a pair of eyeglasses. He slowly put on his glasses and looked at the youth with a gentle, barely visible smile. Chaikl didn't know why the rabbi had put on his glasses, but he sensed that he could continue saying what was on his mind, even if there were no brilliant ideas in his remarks.

"I was at the rabbi's house when the old Valkenik rabbi went to the Land of Israel, and then I joined the rest of the town in escorting him to the train station. The old gray-haired congregants never stopped crying. Recalling this, I still feel my limbs trembling. I thought then, and still think now, that there is a secret in the weeping of old people that a man discovers only when he's older. Even though I don't know the nature of the secret, I know there's a secret there. That's why I don't like our rosh yeshiva always talking about great men of spirit and scorning the everyday world."

"How old are you?" Reb Avraham-Shaye was still gazing at the round-faced, broad-shouldered youth with the dreamy blue eyes.

"I'm seventeen, but I know I look older. People don't believe I'm only seventeen."

"They're right. You are older. Maybe your mother registered you officially a couple of years after you were born," Reb Avraham-Shaye joked. He removed his glasses and replaced them in the metal case. "Chaikl, come into the house with me and have some tea and cookies."

Chaikl Vilner was pleased that the author of *The Vision of Avraham* joked with him, spoke intimately to him, and called him by his first name. They went through the dining room into a separate room in the middle of which was a long table laden with books. Two iron beds stood alongside the walls. The window faced a foothill covered with pine trees and vegetation, which made the room rather dark. Chaikl was awed by the rustling of the pines and the narrow patch of sky between the branches. He imagined he was in the secret cave of a hidden saint. A pious silence hovered in all the corners. But Reb Avraham-Shaye Kosover didn't look at all like an ecstatic Kabbalist in a cave.

"Sit down, Chaikl. Do you like tea with granulated or lump sugar?"

Chaikl leaped up. "No, no, I'm not thirsty. I don't want tea. I don't want to take any more of your time from Torah learning. I'm going to leave right now."

"Stay where you are," Reb Avraham-Shaye commanded, and left the room.

Chaikl looked around and saw a net of sunbeams. Interwoven with the shadows of the green pine branches, the sun's rays fluttered and quivered on the wall with an ethereal secretiveness, and in mute vibration rebuked him: The saintly gaon who is spending time with you couldn't possibly imagine that you spend every evening sitting in the little garden with the landlady's daughter and kissing. . . . Chaikl turned away from the wall and quickly began browsing through the books on the table. At that moment he was prepared to sneak out of the cottage and flee. But the rabbi soon stood at his side, holding a glass of tea in one hand and a plate of sugar cookies in the other.

"The tea is from a vacuum bottle and not very hot." He placed the refreshments on the table and lay down on the low bed by the window.

12

REB AVRAHAM-SHAYE was lying on his side, his hand beneath his chin. His cheeks were drawn and two deep wrinkles cut across the length of his forehead and the bridge of his nose. His brows tightened sternly, and Chaikl found no pleasure in the sugar cooky and the sweet tea. Then the rabbi's face suddenly changed again. He spoke slowly, clearly, and his sharp, penetrating eyes looked off into the distance.

"You told me before that your rosh yeshiva is always talking about people's flaws. But constant looking for faults in oneself and in others can occasionally bring the faults to the surface. The bad traits lie within us, at times knotted up and dormant. If you touch them, you provoke them, and they stick their heads out and begin biting like angry little beasts. Sometimes you can influence a man to improve by considering him a better man. Then he strives to show that he is indeed a better man. But if a sensual or irascible man notices that you see through him, and especially if you provoke him, he no longer strives to overcome his flaws and makes no effort to appear to be a better person. And frequently a person can persuade himself to improve by seeking virtues, not faults, in himself. Every man is a village of good and bad Jews, and of many bad and good inclinations. So we first have to weigh when it is proper to start a quarrel with oneself and when not. Sometimes the greatest fault is—looking for faults in yourself."

Suddenly downy-cheeked Berele appeared in front of the low window that faced the hill. At the side of the window stood another lad with a broad double chin. A moment later a third little rascal appeared; he was the tiniest of the lot, with soft red lips and a dimple under his nose. All three, with skullcaps on their shaven heads and big, thick earlocks, gazed with curiosity at the stranger. From his bed along the wall Reb Avraham-Shaye couldn't see his three nephews, but he noticed that the half-dark room had become even darker and he heard their secretive whispering. He burst out laughing, and all three pranksters fled from the window, twittering like the swallows that flew about under the high dome of the old Valkenik synagogue.

Reb Avraham-Shaye pressed his back to the wall, breathing heavily, softly at first and then with a groan. "Occasionally I feel a pressure in my heart and I have to groan," he explained and continued weakly: "As man is infected with pride by contemplating his real or imagined virtues, in like fashion he falls into despair and feelings of inferiority by constantly thinking about his real or imagined faults. The strength that can lift man up is inherent in the acquisition of wisdom. The world is a festively decked table and the intelligent man yearns to enjoy it. But unclean desires drive off the desire for wisdom. Hence studying Torah is the only sure and proven way to prevail over our bodily wants. Self-infatuation and pursuit of various pleasures, especially forbidden pleasures, are deeply rooted in man's nature. They cannot be totally uprooted without man himself being destroyed in the process.

"The proper path for perfecting one's character isn't to tear the innate desires out of oneself, but to make them better and more beautiful. A rational man doesn't have to undergo torments to uproot his passion for honor; he just doesn't seek honor from the masses. Instead of the noisy seekers of honor and dispensers of honor, he wants to be recognized by men of culture, even by those who are no longer alive. He wants them—from the other world—to approve of his thoughts and decisions here in this world. A man shouldn't shout into himself day and night that one must not love oneself. Let him love himself, yes, but in an intelligent way— through love of wisdom and Torah. Next to the ocean man feels insignificant. But next to the Torah, which is greater than the ocean, man does not feel insignificant, because he is as great as his grasp of the Torah. The Torah cleanses the sensitive man, the intellectual man, of pride and anger: it makes him modest and patient; it inspires him to seek spiritual uplift and not vulgar physical pleasures. Attempting to uproot from oneself the baser desires solely by the strength of one's own will and by studying Musar books in the dark can only bring one to an opposite result—the baser desires become even stronger, just as the shadows increase in the beth medresh, the fewer lights there are. Screaming and studying Musar out loud to drive away the *yetzer ha-ra* is as effective as sweeping shadows away with a broom. But when the lamps of Torah and wisdom are lit in one's mind, the shadows disappear of their own accord.

"The Creator and his Torah trust man much more than the Navaredker Musarniks trust man." Reb Avraham-Shaye chuckled while intently inspecting his fingernails.

"That's exactly the opposite of what our rosh yeshiva says," Chaikl exclaimed with boyish glee. "Reb Tsemakh says that bad traits aren't supposed to be beautified or adorned, but rather totally uprooted. And if one doesn't study Musar one can't be absolutely sure that the *yetzer ha-ra* won't crawl even into our toiling at Torah, like a worm crawls into the heart of a beautiful apple. In fact it was on this topic that our rosh yeshiva gave a very profound talk the day before yesterday. He spoke about the superb man of virtue who studies Torah for its sake and flees from honor. But though he flees honor and doesn't care at all what people say about him, he sees that the world recognizes him, nevertheless, and has great respect for him. Accordingly, that saint will continue to flee from honor; he'll live in poverty and will do everything for the sake of heaven. But quietly, perhaps in secret even from himself, he will remember that he must not spoil his own great reputation as a saint. He began solely for the sake of Torah; in loneliness he began; quietly, hidden from the entire world, did he begin as a servant of God. But since the world beat a path to his door against his will and he became famous, he remembers that he has to be careful of this fame and not step out of the bounds of his self-imposed sacred wall, lest his reputation as a man of great modesty and as a holy and pure man suffer."

The young Musarnik was unaware that his finger was pointing at Reb Avraham-Shaye as he seethed and fumed with Reb Tsemakh's fire, spoke his words, and used his gestures. He didn't begin to understand what and whom his principal had been talking about. He just liked Reb Tsemakh's zeal and fervor and his ability to draw out and elevate a man's spiritual strength.

"When did your rosh yeshiva deliver this talk?" Reb Avraham-Shaye asked. Red blotches had appeared on his face.

"The day before yesterday, the day after you visited the yeshiva," Chaikl replied heatedly and grew even more impassioned, gesticulating with both hands. "Reb Tsemakh also recently delivered a very profound talk about faith. As bad an opinion as we have about the skeptic, he said, the skeptic is not as good-for-nothing and not as inconsequential and as small as the sensualist who needs a God so as to have pleasure from his sinning. This sensualist wouldn't have his worldly pleasure if he didn't believe that there was also another world. While sinning, his very skin trembles out of fear that he may lose the other world; but he consoles himself by saying that there will be time to make up for it. Never mind, he'll repent later. And when he does repent, he greatly enjoys beating his breast and saying, 'I have sinned,' and takes pleasure in the dirty tears he sheds while confessing. The sensualist also enjoys fasting. In fact, he's delighted that he'll be flogged in the world to come—as long as he's not deprived of the hope that after the prescribed number of lashes and other punishments he'll tear off a hunk of meat from the Wild Ox of Paradise and drink a jugful of the messianic wine. . . ."

"Enough! I have no more strength!" Reb Avraham-Shaye gave a sudden bitter, anguished cry and immediately burst into soft, sad laughter.

He closed his eyes and thought: That Reb Tsemakh Atlas, with his erect bearing and acerbic thoughts, is no doubt a broken man. He tortures himself and is bitter toward others because he lacks faith. But he suffers in the dark so that no one knows; in his talks to his students he doesn't reveal his doubts. In any case, attempting to remove him from the yeshiva he founded might destroy him, God forbid. Still, one shouldn't trust him to lead a place of Torah learning. Menakhem-Mendl must remain with him. The latter is so naïve that he apparently doesn't understand his friend at all.

"You told me, Chaikl, that all the old congregants wept bitterly when the Valkenik rabbi left for the Land of Israel, and you understood that there is a secret a man discovers only in his old age. Since I'm much older than you, I'll reveal that secret." Reb Avraham-Shaye spoke with strangely luminescent and radiant eyes. "The congregants cried out of great love for the Torah and out of sadness that the rabbi who had studied Torah with them was leaving. Surely you've seen Jews bathed in tears at a funeral, or at a eulogy for a Torah scholar, even though they never knew him and even though he died at a venerable old age, eighty or more, sometimes even ninety or more. The Jews cry out of love for Torah. Jews love a Torah scholar, a man of pure heart who always sits and studies; they don't like a faultfinder. Not everything we know about a man should be said to his face."

Reb Avraham-Shaye adjusted the pillow under his head and stretched out on his back, exhausted by the long conversation. "Your teacher, Reb Menakhem-Mendl, sent you here on a mission. Tell him, then, in my name, that as he himself wishes it, let things be as they have been up to now. That's what you're to tell him. Will you remember?"

"I'll remember," Chaikl said. If he remembered sections of philosophical treatises from the third part of *The Guide to the Perplexed* and many pages of the Talmud, why couldn't he remember a few words? The subject of Reb Menakhem-Mendl's inquiry and what the answer meant didn't interest him at all.

"Do you like to swim?" Reb Avraham-Shaye asked.

"Yes, but the water is still too cold now."

"When the water turns warmer, come to see me about one o'clock some afternoon and we'll go swimming together. Now go. I'm exhausted."

On his way back through the forest, Chaikl no longer stared at the trees; he didn't look for wild strawberries among the low-lying foliage, and he paid no attention to the birds' chirping. He thought of the rabbi and how right he was that Jews love Torah. Chaikl had often seen the simple folk and even the fresh punks from Butchers Street respectfully making way for a Torah scholar; loudmouthed market women assumed a pious demeanor when they saw a Jew in a rabbinic gaberdine passing by. During winter nights old men sat in the beth medresh over their books and talked about scholars while studying. Although Chaikl wasn't overfond of the congregants of Reb Shaulke's beth medresh because of their contempt for him and their grudge against his father, the maskil, he listened to their talk about gaons and their miracle stories about hidden saints. The reverential awe for Torah shown by Jews with white beards, brass-rimmed spectacles, and bristly root hairs on their noses— their whispering and pious gestures—blended in Chaikl's thoughts with the shadows of the hanging lamps and with the dark gold flame of the Eternal Light illuminating the pulpit at the dark eastern wall like a sun risen in the middle of the night . . . In his meeting with Reb Avraham-Shaye, Chaikl felt the greatness and simplicity that were consistent with what the old congregants had whispered about the great scholar.

Overjoyed at the answer he received, Reb Menakhem-Mendl couldn't stop wondering how Reb Avraham-Shaye had known that he wanted to remain in Valkenik and not return to Vilna to become a merchant again.

"Is that what he really said? Using these words—'That as he himself wishes it, let things be as they have been up to now'?"

"He told me those very words two or three minutes before I left. But before that he spent two whole hours talking with me. He also invited me to his room and served me tea and sugar cookies. You see!" Chaikl crowed his triumph over the entire yeshiva.

"And of the two of you, who talked more, you or he?" Reb Menakhem-Mendl asked, feigning innocence.

"First I spoke awhile and he listened, and then he spoke awhile and I listened to him," Chaikl replied, looking as elated as Reb Menakhem-Mendl was dumbstruck—astounded that it was with Chaikl that the solitary and reticent rabbi had conversed for two hours.

13

KREYNDL, FREYDA VOROBEY'S DAUGHTER, spent most of
her time sitting by the window looking out at Valkenik with anger
and derision. She couldn't operate a sewing machine, and serving
as a maid was beneath her dignity. So she dreamed and waited for
her cousin from America to come and take her across the sea, and
quarreled with her mother for having a sweet tooth.

"You take the ten or fifteen dollars we get each month and spend
a good part of it on sugar cookies and chocolate. Me, I can't
stomach sweets," Kreyndl would shout.

"Because you're a witch," Freyda would shriek back.

These shouts were heard from the synagogue courtyard to the
river's edge.

But since the Hebrew teacher from Vilna and his son had moved
into their house, the loud screaming at the Vorobeys' had stopped,
and Kreyndl no longer sat by the window in the large room looking
bitterly out at Valkenik. She closed herself into her little alcove and
from behind its red curtains peeked in on Chaikl's father as he
immersed himself in a book. On the basis of his appearance, she
was trying to guess whether he would be opposed to his son's
marrying her.

Reb Shlomo-Motte liked to walk in the outskirts of town at
dawn. He went to sleep at ten, when everyone else was still awake,
but from then on absolute silence reigned in the apartment. Freyda
didn't let her son Nokhemke say a loud word. She fed him in the
kitchen and bedded him down there. He too got up early, for he
worked at the cardboard factory beyond the woods. Freyda would
stay in the kitchen, sitting on the bench next to the oven. She dozed
off with one eye and one ear; the other eye and ear stayed awake.
The mother was on guard lest a neighbor come in and find the
young scholar in Kreyndl's room.

As soon as Reb Shlomo-Motte fell asleep, Kreyndl would poke her head out between the curtains and sear Chaikl with her eyes. Every evening Chaikl would first turn away and gaze at the weakly burning kerosene lamp. The shadows on the wall reminded him of dark accusers, born of his sinful thoughts and deeds, who would later bear witness against him. He reviled himself for sitting at home and not going to the beth medresh to study. But his glance again met the eerie, feverish glint of Kreyndl's eyes, which at once insisted and raged. He looked at his sleeping father's snow-white beard and slipped into Kreyndl's room.

Chaikl grumbled, "Leave me alone," but he was already panting, for a pair of long bare arms were wrapped around his neck, and powerful, crooked teeth bit into his lips. The girl, a head taller than he and two years older, hurled herself at him, her body as hot and dry as a sun- and sand-scorched cactus.

Aroused by her kisses and the press of her body, he dragged her to the wide wooden bed that took up half the room. Kreyndl didn't resist but said through clenched teeth, "Remember, it'll be your headache!" and Chaikl let her go at once. Inflamed with desire, his veins popping in his head, he was ready at that moment to marry "the princess of the imperial family," as she was known in town. He didn't care what family she came from. But he was sobered by her boorish, fish-market remark that if something happened to her it would be his headache. He grimaced in disgust. A great black alley cat seemed to be sitting on her wooden bed in the dark corner, looking at him with its wild eyes and yawning with its red tongue out. Chaikl felt like returning to his room and going to sleep, but Kreyndl wanted him to crawl out with her into her garden.

The little window in her alcove faced a small enclosure formed by the walls of stables, granaries, and storehouses, the rear wall of the bathhouse, and a part of the guest house. The community-owned lot was strewn with rotting wood and old scrap metal and was overgrown with weeds. Only one tree grew there, a lonely willow with a crooked trunk and low-hanging branches that had seemingly strayed from the nearby river bank. Kreyndl had put a bench under the tree and spent half her nights there. She also had access to the little yard via the narrow passageways between the houses, but she preferred climbing out the window to make it seem more clandestine. From the time she began her love affair with the student, she had demanded that he sit on the bench with her.

Chaikl was afraid they might be seen there, but Kreyndl laughed at him. "The townspeople don't even know there's a willow tree in the yard, and they know nothing about the bench there." Then, as quick and supple as a snake, she slipped her long, thin body through the window. The pudgy, broad-shouldered yeshiva student, however, followed with difficulty and just barely managed to squeeze through. Gradually his fear that they might be discovered there subsided. Once outside, Chaikl felt more secure than in the house, where his father was sleeping and might wake up any minute.

Somewhere along the river bank young people were walking, laughing loudly, and singing in the efflorescent night. The Cold Shul towered over all the walls and fences and gazed down into the enclosed yard where the couple sat. The arched windows and the square ones glowed with a mysterious blue light. The lacquered shingles of the turreted roofs glittered greenly in the night, like the reflection of water filled with vegetation. The longer Chaikl looked at the shul, the farther away he felt from the girl at his side. When he wasn't kissing her hotly and feverishly, she disgusted him. What did she want of him? Her straight-combed hair was greasy and smelled of kerosene. He couldn't believe that in this day and age a girl would still wash her hair with kerosene. Her upper lip felt like a prickly hairbrush. Her skin was rough; she was as hard and lean as a board.

"Why are you moving away from me?" she whispered, and, frightened, he inched closer to her, as if he were already her captive. "My mother's sister in America fooled me," she grunted angrily. "Instead of sending her son to take me to America, my aunt sends silly letters and ten or fifteen dollars a month."

"How did this aunt of yours fool you? She never promised to take you to America."

"She fooled me, fooled me." Kreyndl stamped her feet on the soft, refuse-laden ground of her garden. "If I hadn't depended on that fool aunt of mine and my cousin, I could have gone to Vilna or Warsaw. I would have been a saleslady in a big women's shop, worn high heels and a hat with a feather, and paraded around with big-city cavaliers. I don't even want to speak to the fellows in this smelly town. But in America I'd be even better off than in Vilna or Warsaw. I hear people say there aren't enough women in America. They're looking for nineteen-year-old girls there. But my aunt fooled me, she fooled me."

The couple then crawled back through the window into the cottage. Chaikl regarded her bed with horror, as if it were made of the boards of a gallows. He tiptoed out of her room, looking around and listening. His father was asleep, and in the kitchen the landlady was still awake on the oven's earthenware bench. Freyda twisted and groaned as though she'd given up ever having joy in her daughter. Her sitting on guard by the door made Chaikl realize that Freyda too expected him to marry Kreyndl. Now he was really terrified. Kreyndl might even claim that he too had fooled her, as her aunt had done. And what would his father say? Chaikl couldn't tell whether his father knew what was happening at night and didn't want to interfere, or whether he knew nothing because he slept so soundly.

Chaikl's hatred of Kreyndl grew daily: Has she gone mad? Me become engaged at seventeen? Finding another room was the only way out. But if he moved, the girl would evict his father too. His father paid only for food here, and renting a room elsewhere would be difficult. First, all the houses were full, for every landlord had his steady summer guest. Second, his father didn't have that much money. What should he do? Chaikl racked his brain and couldn't find a way out. After his long conversation with Reb Avraham-Shaye he became very embarrassed: How could he look Reb Avraham-Shaye straight in the eye and debate lofty matters with him when he did such improper things at night? His shame at deceiving a saintly gaon changed to fear: Perhaps Reb Avraham-Shaye knew? A man like that had divine intuition. . . . Terror-stricken at the disgrace if Reb Avraham-Shaye Kosover knew his disgusting, sinful secret, Chaikl was prepared to leave his ailing father and flee to the farthest corner of the world.

14

THE WOMEN IN TOWN were the first to sense that Kreyndl was having a love affair with the yeshiva student who lived in her house. Otherwise, why would Bentzye the Apostate's daughter be keeping a student and his sick father? Freyda Vorobey busily ran from store to store shopping for her tenant with cash. Her face shone with joy at being able to cook and manage a household. She continuously warned the saleswomen, "The granulated sugar has to be soft and thin—it's for my tenant. I want the best shmaltz herring—it's for my tenant. I want the cheese to be absolutely dry, hard and salty, just the way my summer tenant likes it."

"Why are you making such a fuss over your summer tenant? Do you get any benefit from him?" the women shopkeepers asked.

"What sort of benefit should I get? I'm just doing it for the sake of a mitzva." Freyda blinked idiotically, in fear of her daughter, who had called her a blabbermouth.

Saleswomen later whispered among themselves, "Did you see how scared Freyda the American became? It's as sure as gold that she has her eye on the student. Just like she can't understand her bills when the storekeeper points to things she's bought on credit and then she says it's a phony set of figures; and just like she can't make out how many zlotys there are in ten dollars—so the American can't understand that a tenant isn't necessarily a son-in-law."

Housewives laughed good-naturedly and seamstresses and maids bristled with rage: "Wagoners aren't good enough for Kreyndl. She's waiting for her cousin from America. But since her cousin isn't coming, a yeshiva boy is all right for her—anything, so long as it isn't a wagon driver."

In the evenings the girls began strolling more frequently around

Freyda Vorobey's house. At ten at night, they noticed, it became
dark there. One long-legged wag of a girl in a rustling skirt dashed
into the house. "Excuse me, Freyda, isn't my mother here? And I
thought my mother was sitting here chatting!"

The usually genial Freyda leaped up in a rage and began waving
her hands as though putting out a fire in a pot of fat. "Shh! Be still!
I don't want you to wake up my tenant!" The wag dashed back
outside and told her friends, "The lamp's been turned down and
the white-bearded tenant is asleep. But the yeshiva boy is nowhere
to be seen—he's probably in Kreyndl's room. And Freyda Vorobey
is sitting in the kitchen on the lookout, it seems, against the evil
eye."

On a dark blue night saturated with drunken voices from the
nearby village and far-off surreptitious sounds—a night full of
white-blossomed trees and pungent aromas from the surrounding
fields—several youths, boys and girls, sneaked into the enclosed
yard and sent a spy up to Kreyndl's window. The latter returned
gleefully: "The couple is sitting in the little room all lovey-dovey!"

The young people began approaching the house from all sides.
Everyone wanted to have a look. The Cold Shul up on the hill
gazed over all the walls into the courtyard. Chaikl sniffed its musty
wooden odor and heard within him the old shul groaning and
warning him: "Watch out, lad!" But the young witch had already
drawn him into her room, choking him with her kisses. Suddenly
he heard soft, furtive steps and low voices.

"There's someone out there! They're watching us!" he whispered, shuddering.

"You're imagining it. You're afraid. A man, and you're such a
coward!" Kreyndl stopped kissing for a moment and spoke loudly
to show him that his fear was completely unfounded.

The next day congregants in the beth medresh were already
shaking their heads: "If the yeshiva student is ready to marry
Bentzye the Apostate's daughter, let his father worry about that.
But spending entire nights with her in a dark room? Ugh!
That's disgusting!"

Leitshe the cook was especially resentful. Since Gedalya Zondak
had begun screaming all over Valkenik that his son-in-law was a
lazy good-for-nothing bum because he didn't want to study or go

into business, Leitshe had asserted that she thanked God that Zondak's daughter had snatched that bargain Yosef Varshever out of her hands. But now the young cook was carrying on in an inexplicable fury. "Chaikl Vilner is as much of a scoundrel as my ex-fiancé, Yosef Varshever. As soon as he came here at the beginning of winter I noticed that he didn't hate girls. But what does he see in her? That Kreyndl is just a skinny, dried-up tapeworm."

Her older sister, Rokhtshe, shrugged and said nothing. Did Leitshe think she had a monopoly on all the yeshiva students who ate in the kitchen? And why was Chaikl Vilner a concern of hers? He was still only a boy.

Leitshe, however, didn't say a word to Chaikl himself. The cooks had learned from the students something about proper behavior and keeping silent. Chaikl's friends offered no hint either. They just spoke to him less frequently and avoided his eyes. But he sensed this change toward him, and his throat constricted; he felt that he was choking, as if his windpipe had been filled with sand. To pretend he knew nothing was against his nature. And precisely because he felt guilty and ashamed, he had no intention of going around with lowered head. While eating in the kitchen and studying Talmud in the beth medresh he looked angry and ashamed, as though informing everyone: I know I'm a sinner, but I don't want to repent.

Eating supper Friday night at Reb Hirshe Gordon's house, Chaikl first felt the full impact and realized the extent of the disgrace he had brought upon himself. The lady of the house welcomed him with her usual warmth, but her eyes flickered with the false show of a woman who sees a young lad naked and, to avoid feeling embarrassed, pretends indifference, as if he were still a child. Reb Hirshe's wife considered it an affront to her dignity that the student who ate Sabbath meals at her home was dallying with a girl from a lower-class family. Reb Hirshe himself, as was his wont while eating, looked into his book and occasionally said a few words to Chaikl, as calmly and distantly as usual, as if aware of nothing. But Tsharne giggled throughout the evening.

Tsharne had long since ceased being a temptation for Chaikl. It made him wonder: Here he was looking at her high white forehead, her brown hair with its reddish sheen, her big, light green eyes—and felt nothing! She interested him no more than a rosy-cheeked girl pictured on candy wrappers. He was happy that she didn't know he had once imagined her as the *yetzer ha-ra* disguised as a Holy Ark. In his heart he had laughed at her short chubby figure and called her a calf. But now the calf was laughing at him with demonic glee. Finally her mother, eyes lowered, began to smile. Reb Hirshe Gordon's wrathful look at his daughter ordered her to be still—at which her gales of laughter increased. Since her father hadn't asked her why she was laughing so hard, Chaikl realized that Reb Hirshe knew the reason. Tsharne was convulsed with laughter because he was involved with a skinny, wizened girl, a sourpuss with foxy eyes. How he loathed both Tsharne and Kreyndl at that moment! He left the house weak in the knees and just barely made it home.

This time he didn't wait for the witch to lure him into her little room; he burst in, out of breath. "You see, the whole town knows already," he panted.

"So what? Are you ashamed of me?" she muttered. Her glossy, greasy hair, washed in honor of the Sabbath, exuded its kerosene smell. "Sarah the Blind Eye wished me *mazel tov* today. I told her not to get any headaches over me. In fact I'm glad everyone knows. Let my enemies know and burst."

Chaikl's hatred of her so engulfed him that he couldn't find words to reply. Previously she had always told him not to be afraid, she wouldn't gobble him up or force him to marry her. Now she spoke as though they were already engaged. He promised himself not to look at her again and strode out of the room. Freyda rose from the kitchen bench and craned her neck forward in fright. She realized that the couple had quarreled. Chaikl now looked with hatred at the good-hearted landlady too. What a clod! The mother is a clod and the daughter is a long, thin beanpole, a scarecrow. He sat down on his bed, opposite his father's, and removed one shoe. As he pulled the other off, the lace became entangled and the bow knotted. In a temper, he broke the shoelace and flung the shoe to the floor, the way he wanted to break up with Kreyndl and fling her away from him.

The next morning he didn't know what to do with himself. If he sat at home with his father, Kreyndl would be there, and he couldn't bear looking at her. If he sat in the beth medresh and studied, he'd be ashamed before his friends. So he went to the Cold Shul, which had recently been reopened for summer worship but was deserted between Morning and Evening Services.

Chaikl stood in the front of the shul looking up at the narrow windows and the high ceiling. At the top of the Holy Ark little carved lions held the Ten Commandments with their front paws. Seeing the tiny flaming tongues in the lions' open mouths and the childlike curiosity in their eyes, Chaikl imagined he'd studied in cheder with them as a child. From the high windows, strands of light illuminated the eagles painted on the ceiling and seemed to bring them to life. The winged creatures, with crowns on their heads, held lulavs and esrogs in their claws. A sunbeam landed on a hammered copper tray, and in the depths of the metal a memorial candle was set ablaze. The pillars around the pulpit rose up to the sky. The steps descending from the anteroom into the synagogue led his imagination deeper into covert subterranean caves. The open staircase in the shul, which spiraled like a screw up to the innermost balcony, transported him to a blue infinity, where bronze hanging lamps and silver candelabra sparkled like stars. What a palace! What a secret, otherworldly palace amid a dense wood that had existed since Creation!

Chaikl's glance fell on a meshed window in the women's gallery and he froze in fear. A pair of coal-black eyes were watching him through the screen; a pale man with a black beard—the rosh yeshiva! With a finger Reb Tsemakh Atlas beckoned him to come upstairs. Chaikl dashed to the exit, ready to flee as if from a corpse in the cemetery. But the big broad iron door of the anteroom seemed far away, at the end of the world. He wouldn't reach it in time. . . .

He heard the principal's voice. "Come up, I must tell you something." Chaikl, frightened, wanted to run—he knew quite well what Reb Tsemakh was going to say.

15

THE SECLUSION in the Musar room had been a torment for Tsemakh Atlas; he felt hemmed in as if in a four-by-four cell. Moreover, from the window he could see half the town and hear the tumult of the nearby market place. When summer came and the Cold Shul was reopened, Reb Tsemakh had settled down in its women's section, a long, narrow corridor that spanned the length of the shul's northern wall, where he could pace back and forth for hours on end. Sometimes he would sit benumbed over a Musar book with his head leaning against a prayer stand. At sunset the little meshed windows of the women's gallery became braided golden bars; then slowly darkness fell. The eerie rustling of the descending twilight awakened him. He rubbed his eyes and always came to the same conclusion: he had not found his path in life.

Though he had found no answer during his solitude, he spent every free hour there and took pleasure in tormenting himself. That morning he had arrived early, almost running from the beth medresh to avoid meeting and speaking to Chaikl Vilner. Reb Menakhem-Mendl had often urged him to talk sternly with Chaikl. But since the scandal—as Reb Menakehm-Mendl called the Chaikl-Kreyndl affair—had become public knowledge, Reb Tsemakh had again begun to ponder his meetings with Ronya in the dark dining room. He always thought about them with longing, anxiety, and chagrin, as if he regretted withstanding temptation during those nights. Hence he didn't want to moralize to his pupil about a sin of which he was not innocent himself. But the Vilner had seemingly pursued him into his hiding place—and Tsemakh felt in his heart a flame of yearning to wage war against his pupil and himself.

"Are you studying Musar by yourself?" The principal sat down on a bench, spreading the skirts of his long gaberdine, as though preparing himself for a lengthy talk.

"I came into the shul to look at the carvings. The man who carved the lions, eagles, deer, and leopards is a great artist."

Reb Tsemakh Atlas scratched desultorily under his chin and replied, "A Talmudic sage said: 'Be as strong as a leopard, as light as an eagle, as fleet as a deer, and as brave as a lion to do the will of your Father in heaven.' Indeed, because of this remark these beasts are drawn on shul walls. But I'm surprised at your going into such ecstasy over a carver just because he whittled a lion and a deer! Was he a man of good character? If not, then none of the artist's wizardry is of any value."

To the principal's scornful remarks Chaikl responded with even greater scorn. "First of all, an artist is not a wizard. Second, it makes no difference whether he has a good character or not as long as he's a master of his craft. Reb Avraham-Shaye is altogether opposed to the practice of breaking one's bad character traits. He holds that these traits shouldn't be uprooted but made better or more beautiful. He also opposes too much delving into one's soul, and especially burrowing into another person's. In general, he says, we shouldn't tell a person everything we know about him."

"Oh? Is that so? So you too are running to the vacationing rabbi?" Tsemakh Atlas scratched more vigorously under his chin and his armpits like a bedraggled pauper who has slept in his clothes on a hard beth medresh bench. "You say Reb Avraham-Shaye disapproves of uprooting bad traits—he'd rather make them more beautiful. He also opposes too much delving into one's soul and disapproves of telling the whole truth. What else does Reb Avraham-Shaye disapprove of? Sit down, Vilner. Here on the bench. Sit down and tell me what else he disapproves of."

Chaikl's yeshiva friends occasionally ridiculed him for his naïveté and gullibility. But if he lost his confidence in and respect for someone, spite and malevolence replaced naïveté. Now Chaikl replied with malice aforethought: "Reb Avraham-Shaye doesn't believe that good deeds become invalid because the doer has motives of self-interest. He doesn't think that self-interest, as it's known in Navaredok, is a vicious itch at all, and that one must constantly scratch it. Whoever does that, he says, is really scratching a pestilence into himself."

"It sounds like you had a very high-flown discussion." Reb Tsemakh swayed back and forth, then suddenly his fiery eyes blazed at his pupil. "During your talk on these grandiloquent matters did you by any chance inform him that you spend night after night in a dark room with your landlady's daughter and that all of Valkenik is already talking about the desecration of God's name? Does Reb Avraham-Shaye know about this?"

Chaikl was so shocked, so dumfounded by the unexpected question and its rancor that his lips went dry and a mist fogged his eyes.

"You're crying!" Reb Tsemakh said triumphantly.

"Who's crying? Me?" Chaikl shrieked, in a rage at not being able to contain his tears, and he bit his lips to keep from bursting out in sobs like a little boy. But instead of becoming more tender, the rosh yeshiva stoked up his wrath and spoke with bitter disdain, as though delighted that he could still cause a youngster to break down, could still bring an insolent student to tears.

"A sensualist cries out of self-pity. A sensualist is a good sort by nature; and if he gets what his heart longs for, he begrudges no one else any pleasures. But if he doesn't get what he wants, the good-natured sensualist turns ruthless. He becomes blind—deaf and blind to the entire world. Yet for his own desire he has a thousand ears to hear and a thousand eyes to see, and he weeps only for his own failure. A stranger who doesn't know why the sensualist is crying might even think that the man is shedding bitter tears over the Jews and the Divine Presence being in exile, or that his eyes are brimming with hot tears over the destruction of the Holy Temple or the suffering in this world. Who would imagine that this weeper was a glutton and a drunkard? And because the Divine Providence doesn't submit to him, he submits to himself and wails. He eulogizes his own unfulfilled desires as if they were a baby that died in the cradle, God forbid. In a fury he weeps, he grates his teeth, he stamps his feet, he actually melts with tears and wailing over his failure. Basically, this sensualist's feelings stopped at the child's stage, so he remains at once a child and a wild beast. Even if the Creator himself were to come to him and say, 'My son, my child, don't cry. The earth has more skulls and bones in it than people walking on it. And all these dead men once burned with lusts. But life taught them forbearance, and death spread earth on all their plans. Believe me, my child,' God would say to him, 'believe me, the one who knows the impulses of all creatures, that one can stay alive without the pleasure you lust for. Wipe your tears. Within a day, you yourself will see that there are many other pleasures on this earth, and I shall give them all to you. All of them except that pleasure which you now want. That pleasure I cannot grant you.' If Divine Providence were to speak thus to the promiscuous pleasure seeker and pathetic sensualist, the latter would whine and wail and rant: 'Grant me *now* the pleasure that I want. I don't want any other pleasure. Only *this* one. Just *this* one!' Since he didn't learn Musar and made no attempt to break his own will, he doesn't know that one can deny oneself; he hasn't got the slightest conception that it can be done." Tsemakh was shouting now. "But he who has studied Musar knows that one can deny oneself desires real and imagined!" Tsemakh heard the echo of his shouts reverberating in the empty shul as if it had come from his own inner depths.

"Well, Vilner, are you going to move out of that room?" The principal smiled, somewhat ashamed of having directed at his pupil the words of admonishment meant for himself. "Your father can stay on there, but we'll find another place for you."

Chaikl knew that he could stem Reb Tsemakh's wrath by telling the truth: he was afraid of moving out of his room for fear of having to look for another apartment for his father; and, moreover, lately he wasn't even looking at Kreyndl any more. But he wanted to take vengeance on Reb Tsemakh, who had brought him to tears and had even compared him to a pathetic sensualist.

"I don't have the slightest intention of moving out," Chaikl said, seething with cold fury, as one's face burns in a frost. "And why should I resist temptation, if you didn't?"

"What didn't I resist? What do you mean?"

"I mean what I mean." Chaikl hesitated for a moment over whether to say it or not. "I mean your wife." ·

Tsemakh stared at him in mute amazement. He couldn't believe that Chaikl Vilner would display so much impudence. His now ashen face perspired. "I know it from experience," he murmured and sadly shook his head. "That's why I know one must resist temptation, because I couldn't. You see, Vilner, you quoted Reb Avraham-Shaye's remark that we shouldn't tell a man everything we know about him. But still you couldn't restrain yourself and told me something that you know very well you shouldn't have said." Reb Tsemakh fell silent and with glazed eyes looked toward the door of the women's gallery as though he couldn't stand his way of life any longer and were waiting for someone unseen to come and redeem him.

"Forgive me," Chaikl stammered.

"I forgive you. A moment ago you didn't have the strength to keep still, and now you don't have the strength to bear the responsibility for your inability to keep still. In Vilna I saved you from the drunken tobacco merchant who wanted to beat you. Now I wanted to save you from your own drunkenness. But if you can't bear to hear the truth, then go and do what you want."

Chaikl made his way to the door haltingly, listening to the floor boards creaking beneath him. The wooden groaning pierced his ears and plucked at his heart. The farther he went, the longer the women's gallery seemed to become. Dazed and drained, he barely managed to make his way outside.

Tsemakh sat with his eyes closed, thinking that the mistakes he had made were taking their revenge on him by way of his students' remarks. During the winter Yosef Varshever had accused him of breaking off the match with his first fiancée in Amdur. And now Chaikl Vilner had called him to account for giving in to his desire and marrying the other woman in Lomzhe. What was Slava doing? He didn't hear from her and she didn't hear from him, just as if they had long been divorced.

He opened his eyes, and his glance fell on one of the little windows of the Cold Shul, where the impressionable Vilner had stood earlier, greatly moved by the wood carvings. Tsemakh recalled that even during the first months of their marriage, Slava would tell him that he lacked a feeling for beauty; for him everything under the sun was either good or bad and permitted or forbidden. "I just never thought of it," Tsemakh would reply. He considered the feeling for beauty an addiction, a fantasy, an amusement for oversatiated idlers. He rose slowly and approached the window to see the carvings in the men's section below. Perhaps he did lack an important sense that prevented him from understanding the world, people, and his own students.

Opposite him, on one of the shul's pillars, hung a large cardboard poster with the Thirteen Articles of Faith. From up in the distance a sheaf of sunbeams fell like lances and illuminated the Torah-script letters. In the surrounding silence the sunlit placard seemed to Tsemakh like an unfurled scroll being given to him from heaven. His eyes wide open, he stared through the grated window at the black script and read the first of the Thirteen Articles: "I have perfect faith that the Creator, blessed be His name, is the Author and Guide of everything that has been created; and that He alone has made, does make, and will make all things."

He stumbled back to his prayer stand and sat on the bench with lowered head: Slava had told him that he lacked a feeling for beauty; later she had accused him of being unable to love a woman. Students complained that he demanded of others greater honesty and piety than he himself possessed. Even Reb Menakhem-Mendl was rather hostile to him and charged that he lacked respect for gaonim and lacked love for diligent students and Torah. The truth was that he lacked something greater—simple belief in the first Article of Faith.

16

"I COULDN'T CONVINCE the Vilner," Tsemakh told Reb Menakhem-Mendl. "But I don't think we should say another word to him—otherwise he might get angry and leave the yeshiva altogether."

"Let him go. The sooner the better. That way he won't corrupt the other boys," Reb Menakhem-Mendl replied.

"I'd rather see you go than have Chaikl Vilner leave the yeshiva and be pulverized out in the world," Tsemakh shrieked and hastily left the beth medresh, fleeing from his own rage before it could explode into an even nastier remark to his friend.

Although shaken by the assault on him, Reb Menakhem-Mendl

wasn't intimidated. His role in the yeshiva was no smaller than Tsemakh Atlas', he told himself, and he left for the old pitch factory to call on Reb Avraham-Shaye Kosover.

Reb Menakhem-Mendl found him in his room in a strange position. The iron bed was so laden with books that it sagged to the floor in the middle. The rabbi sat cross-legged on the floor, writing his commentaries in a thick notebook placed on the edge of the bed. Seeing his visitor, Reb Avraham-Shaye rose and his face lighted up. But Reb Menakhem-Mendl, vexed that he was once again depriving the rabbi of precious study time, reported with heavy heart the scandalous news concerning Chaikl Vilner.

"All of Valkenik is talking about how he spends nights sitting in a dark room with his landlady's daughter."

Red blotches appeared on Reb Avraham-Shaye's cheeks; he looked amazed, as though he couldn't imagine that Chaikl was capable of such stupidity.

"Reb Tsemakh talked to him but couldn't influence him. Still, he doesn't permit that bad student to be sent away from the yeshiva," Reb Menakhem-Mendl groaned.

"Then your principal is a great man indeed," Reb Avraham-Shaye said loudly, as if the words had been torn out of his throat against his will.

"I don't see any greatness in this," Reb Menakhem-Mendl snapped indignantly. "I stayed in Valkenik to teach Talmud and didn't return to my family in Vilna because of your advice. So I came here to tell you how my staying on in the yeshiva is being appreciated. The principal, my former friend, shouted at me: 'I'd rather see you go than have Chaikl Vilner leave the yeshiva.'"

"Is that what he said?" Reb Avraham-Shaye shook his head as though seeing even more greatness in this remark.

Upset that Reb Avraham-Shaye praised the principal's behavior, Reb Menakhem-Mendl said bitterly, "Back in Vilna I was the first to interest Chaikl in Torah learning. I left my little shop every day and ran to Reb Shaulke's beth medresh to study a page of Talmud with him, even though I saw that he didn't have the modest demeanor of a ben Torah. But now we're not merely talking about him. If we let him do what he wants, other students might do likewise, claiming that there's no discipline and everyone can do what he pleases. The result will be that the congregants will stop supporting the yeshiva."

"Of course he shouldn't stay at the local yeshiva any longer, but he shouldn't be driven away from Torah study." Reb Avraham-Shaye paced the room several times and then stopped in front of Reb Menakhem-Mendl, his hands folded on his chest. "Tell the boy I've asked that he come to see me. I don't want him to suspect that I know anything about his behavior or that I plan to chastise him for it. So tell him the truth—I've invited him because I like him very much."

Returning to town, Reb Menakhem-Mendl mused: I should have remained a merchant of shoemakers' supplies. He couldn't understand how Chaikl Vilner could be liked after behaving the way he had, and he couldn't understand Reb Avraham-Shaye either. On the one hand, the scholar had agreed that Chaikl should no longer remain in the Valkenik yeshiva. On the other hand, he had said that the boy shouldn't be driven away from Torah learning. Then who would accept him, the yeshiva in Radun or in Kletzk? Or perhaps Damir would want to snatch him! Nevertheless, Reb Menakhem-Mendl brought Chaikl Reb Avraham-Shaye's invitation.

Chaikl winced. "Why all of a sudden? What does he need me for?"

"I don't know. He just told me he liked you very much." Seeing that the student still looked at him suspiciously, Reb Menakhem-Mendl tugged at his little beard. "I'm ready to swear that he said he liked you very much and wants you to visit him. You still don't believe me?"

Chaikl knew that Reb Menakhem-Mendl wouldn't swear falsely. This meant that the vacationing rabbi hadn't yet learned of the incident with the witch Kreyndl. Bursting with impatience, Chaikl didn't wait for the next day but ran immediately to see Reb Avraham-Shaye.

In the courtyard the rabbi's little nephew Berele said that his uncle was in the woods and pointed the way. Chaikl crossed the road and climbed the hill through the tall ferns. He stopped at a place full of sawed-off tree stumps. White wood chips glinted in the sun like glass splinters. There was a scent of resin and dry sawdust.

Chaikl went deeper into the dense forest and saw little red dots slyly winking at him from among the green leaves. "Wild strawberries!" he cried out, and he sat down on the ground to pick and eat the red berries that reminded him of green-bearded midgets with Turkish fezzes. Then, among the slender trunks of a sparse young grove, he suddenly spotted a man in a skullcap lying on the ground.

Reb Avraham-Shaye was resting on a blanket, head propped with his left hand, while in his right he held a small Talmud close to his myopic eyes. From the hill the red-brick cardboard factory was visible; and one could hear the din of the saws and wheels and the roar of the river flowing under the wooden bridge. Behind a green meadow on the other side of the forest stood a high, even wall of tree trunks. The sun was slowly setting and the trunks glowed like copper pillars in a blaze of fiery red.

"Reb Menakhem-Mendl said you wanted to see me," Chaikl declared; then a boyish thought suddenly flashed; was this why the vacationing rabbi had sent for him? "When I was here last time, you said we'd go swimming the next time I came. But the water is still too cold."

"Yes, the water is still too cold. Besides, we won't go bathing during the Omer days before Shevuos." Reb Avraham-Shaye raised his nearsighted eyes from the Talmud. "Why are you standing? Sit down."

Chaikl sat down on the blanket, gaping open-mouthed like a golem. Reb Avraham-Shaye looked at him with a half-mischievous smile, as though contemplating tickling him or tweaking his ear. When his smile had disappeared into his gray-streaked golden mustache, he spoke very softly, almost inaudibly:

"It is my wish that we study together."

Chaikl always remembered imagining that the entire world had stood still at that moment, completely transfixed. Reb Avraham-Shaye Kosover's words entered his heart and remained there always, like a lake that forever mirrors the surrounding shores.

A deep blue sky, astonished at its own primordial blueness, stretched over Chaikl's head. The green meadow, surrounded by tall pines aglow with the dark red fire of sunset, reminded him of Friday night in the Cold Shul, when all the hanging lamps were lit. But a moment later Chaikl looked apprehensively at the clear sky, wondering if a peal of thunder would proclaim him a sinner and a corrupter. There was no need for thunder; of his own accord he would soon begin to tell the whole truth about his transgression. Shaken and ashamed that he still lacked the courage to report his misdeeds, Chaikl rudely grabbed the rabbi's hand, like a merchant in the market slapping another's palm to conclude a deal.

Reb Avraham-Shaye pushed Chaikl's hand away and laughed. "My, are you wild!" For a moment he strained his eyes toward the trees, as though looking for a shortcut through the dense wood. "If you came here every day and then returned to town you'd be wasting precious study time. However, you could stay here with me and sleep in the other bed in my room. Let me think about it. But this coming winter, with God's help, we'll study together in Vilna." He turned the pages of his Talmud and handed it to Chaikl. "It's still light enough. Let's go over a passage of the Mishna so that your trip will not have been in vain."

As a youngster Chaikl had studied the first chapter of the Tractate *Baba Metzia,* which begins, "Two men are holding one tallis." Therefore he read the paragraph slowly and carefully, expecting the rabbi to pose a difficult question at any moment. Reb Avraham-Shaye, however, listened silently. He didn't even look into his little Berlin edition of the Talmud, as if his intent were solely to hear Chaikl's voice.

"Good, now go back home. It will be dark by the time you get to town."

Chaikl did not emerge from his trance until he was out of the forest and among the houses in town. "Instead of saying he would teach me," Chaikl mumbled to himself, "the rabbi said, 'It is my wish that we study together.' He and I together?"

17

THE LANDLADY'S DAUGHTER was waiting for Chaikl to come and make up—he would talk to her, Kreyndl planned, and she wouldn't respond. But she saw that he didn't even look at her. Kreyndl began bustling about him, throwing piercing, angry glances at him like a deaf-mute. But Chaikl turned his back on her and thought of her as a gaunt stork with a broken beak. He felt somewhat guilty toward her because he had kissed her and now he was humiliating her, but he didn't want to kiss her out of duty, and he had never felt any commitment to the girl. The gossip in town had totally destroyed any desire in him.

After his conversation with Reb Avraham-Shaye in the forest, Chaikl took steps to conduct himself as befitted a pupil of a saintly gaon. He had to be serious and respond sedately, with measured words, only when he was spoken to. He even overcame the *yetzer ha-ra* and did not brag to anyone that he would be studying with Reb Avraham-Shaye Kosover.

He recited the Evening Service by himself in a corner of the beth medresh, swaying piously. Then he went home, looking like an emissary from the Land of Israel who doesn't let weekday matters cross his lips on the Sabbath. His father was already asleep, and the landlady as usual was sitting in the kitchen on the earthenware bench by the oven. Lately her son had stopped coming home to sleep. To avoid being late for work in the morning, Nokhemke slept in a house near the cardboard factory. Nevertheless, Freyda didn't lie down to rest. She waited for her lodger and looked at him pleadingly, silently begging him to make up with her daughter. Kreyndl opened wide both halves of her curtain and poked her head and shoulders out. Her tempestuous eyes now smiled at

Chaikl. She cast coquettish glances at him, hinting that he should come into her room. Seeing him turning away, she cupped her mouth with both hands, like someone shouting across a river, and whispered something that he neither heard nor wanted to hear. Finally she grew sick of pleading and abruptly drew the curtain. Chaikl heard her climbing out of the window into the yard, as if to show him that she could have a good time by herself on the bench beneath the willow tree. He undressed under his blanket so that the landlady wouldn't see him in his underwear; and like an old recluse he pressed his eyes shut while reciting his bedtime *Shema Yisroel.*

He woke up terror-stricken and began to twist about like a beast in a net. Long naked arms were enveloping him; hot dry lips were pressed to his mouth, gagging him. Kreyndl had lain down to sleep, but, intoxicated by the spring night and driven wild by humiliation because Chaikl no longer looked at her, she had left her room barefoot and, wearing only a shift, hurled herself at him, kissing, embracing, and biting. Her teeth chattered with fear, rage, and anguished longing. Still, she didn't forget that the old Hebrew teacher was sleeping in the room, and before flinging herself at Chaikl's bed she put out the light.

A bluish light striped in through the shutter crevices. Chaikl saw Kreyndl's smoldering face and the black hair scattered over her thin shoulders. He tried to push her away, but she burrowed into him with her bony elbows and panted through clenched teeth, "Shut up! Shut up!"

She stretched out next to Chaikl and pressed against him. He heard his heart beating against her chest and felt her lean, hot body. Afraid that his father might awaken, he didn't dare struggle, and his resistance gradually weakened. Now his body seethed along with the girl's. A drunkenness inundated his mind; her outspread hair entangled him like seaweed.

Suddenly Chaikl heard a stifled voice. Freyda stood over her daughter, wringing her hands and whispering, "You crazy loon! What are you doing? His father'll wake up!"

As a thunderbolt swiftly brightens a patch of cloudy sky, so the sunset in the forest where Chaikl had talked and studied Mishna with Reb Avraham-Shaye flashed in his mind. Mustering all his strength, he pushed Kreyndl off his bed, but she landed on both feet and stretched her bent fingers at him, nails bared like claws, as though ready to scratch his eyes out.

"You snake in the grass! You bench warmer!" she rasped and fled into her room.

"I wish I were six feet under and done with these troubles," Freyda groaned and ran out.

The yeshiva student sat on his bed and listened to Kreyndl's sobs, which grew louder and louder until she broke into shrill, raucous weeping. Reb Shlomo-Motte sat up in bed and shook his head. The louder Kreyndl cried, the more the old man shook his head and sighed, out of sympathy with the girl and anguish at the disgrace his son was bringing upon him. Chaikl could stand it no longer. He threw on his clothes and put on his shoes and hat, ready to flee.

But his father muttered in a rage, "Stubborn and rebellious son! It's too bad your mother's not here. She'd see how worthwhile it is to sell fruit all day until her feet collapse just so she can support her yeshiva boy. Go quiet the girl."

But Chaikl ran out of the house—and bumped into the landlady, who stood shivering in her flimsy dress. He thought that Freyda too would scold him and demand justice for her daughter. But she stretched her hands out to him and pleaded, "Don't move out! As long as you and your father live here with us, everyone has respect for me."

Chaikl didn't answer; he strode up the hill to the synagogue courtyard. Kreyndl's loneliness and her tears of humiliation pursued him and gnawed at his heart. He'd never before heard the irascible girl crying.

Chaikl stopped and looked around. Where should he go? The beth medresh and the Cold Shul were dark. If he went to the guest house, where he had slept during the winter months, his friends would ask him why he had left his room. Chaikl sat down on the steps of the beth medresh. He pulled up the collar of his jacket, sleepy and feeling a cramp in his knees from the cold. Synagogue Street and its two rows of houses seesawed in a white mist before his eyes.

Tsemakh Atlas was walking around outside the shul; he couldn't sleep: Chaikl Vilner had told him that he, the rosh yeshiva and student of Musar, couldn't resist marrying a woman who didn't suit him—but could he resist now? He couldn't drive away the thought that the fund raiser Azriel Weinstock had departed for distant lands and Ronya was alone again. . . . Tsemakh rubbed his eyes. Was he imagining it, or was it a ghost or a demon? On the beth medresh steps sat Chaikl Vilner, huddled into himself with cold. Seeing his rosh yeshiva, he jumped up; the two stared at each other. Tsemakh realized at once that to avoid temptation Chaikl had either run away from his room or hadn't gone there at all. He put his arm around the youth's shoulder and spoke to him tenderly, as if he were a long-lost younger brother.

"Tonight you'll sleep at my place and tomorrow we'll find you another room. If you like, you can share mine. My room at Reb Yisroel the tailor's has two large beds."

"No, no, I don't want to." Chaikl shivered with cold and, since he was drowsy, told Reb Tsemakh what he hadn't told even his father. "I'm going to move out anyway and move into Reb Avraham-Shaye's house. He told me, 'It is my wish that we study together.' And I'm going to study with him next winter, too."

The principal remained silent for a long while. Then he put his arm around Chaikl's shoulder again and spoke confidingly to him. "For now you don't need a gaon as a teacher. You need an environment of good and pious friends in a yeshiva. If you live in a big town and not among Torah scholars, you'll be pulverized."

Chaikl felt Reb Tsemakh's beard over him like a piece of warm wool. "I won't be pulverized in Vilna," he replied with youthful impatience. "I'll eat at home, not at strangers' tables, and I'll study with Reb Avraham-Shaye."

"All right. We'll see. In any case, you can sleep in my room tonight," Reb Tsemakh urged.

"No, no, I don't want to," Chaikl cried out, and he headed for the river bank, as though afraid to become indebted to his rosh yeshiva for the invitation, as he had become indebted to his landlady and her daughter.

18

CHAIKL LAY ILL with a cold and an earache from having wandered around outside during the night. Freyda Vorobey served him hot tea and raspberry jam to reduce the fever. She gave him strained camomile tea to rinse his swollen throat, and stuffed his ears with cotton dipped in oil. On the third day the sick youth woke up in a sweat but no longer felt any pain in his ears. The swelling in his throat had subsided too. Reb Shlomo-Motte sat at the table gazing into a holy book. He was still angry with his son for wandering about all night long and catching cold. First he had played around with the girl and now he had suddenly become a little saint.

Chaikl left his bed to wash up and then returned to say his prayers. He had just begun to put on his tefillin when Kreyndl's voice came from the curtained alcove. "He got sick just to get even with me."

Her mother, in the little room with her, asked Kreyndl to speak more softly. At which Kreyndl purposely raised her voice so as to be heard in the next room. "The old man can stay, but his brat's got to move out right away. If the old man can't live without his darling boy, then they can both pack up and go."

"You won't live to see the day. Meanwhile, I'm still boss here!" Freyda pounced on her daughter.

Kreyndl ran out of the alcove to embarrass her mother before her tenants. "Candy nibbler! You squander all the dollars we get on sweets and you write your sister that we don't have enough money for bread. I don't want to see a trace of him here any longer!" She pointed at Chaikl and ran outside.

"Let your daddy who's living with a peasant woman support

you. Go be a maid. Meanwhile, I'm still boss here!" Freyda banged her fist against her thin chest and followed Kreyndl.

Chaikl sat in his tefillin, depressed at having to hear all this, especially while he was praying. From behind him his father's voice pierced him like a spear. "You should have weighed your actions beforehand. Now you see what you've done?"

Chaikl quickly turned to his father, holding his head tefillin to keep it from falling off. "It's your fault! I moved in here so you'd have a free room. Now everyone in town is laughing at me, and none of the students even look at me. I'm not going to eat at Reb Hirshe's house any more, and I won't set foot in the yeshiva kitchen during the week."

Reb Shlomo-Motte leaned both elbows on his open book and smacked his lips sarcastically. "Excellent! I said all along that your going to the yeshiva was a blunder, like a three-legged chicken. If you return home and learn a trade, you'll give your mother more joy than she has from you now."

"I *am* going to remain a ben Torah, and I'll even be a student of a great gaon, the author of *The Vision of Avraham*. This summer Reb Avraham-Shaye is going to teach me at his vacation house, and during the winter I'll study with him in Vilna," Chaikl said, revealing the secret he had kept from his father.

The old teacher remained hunched over, his hands tucked into his sleeves, as if it were still winter for him. By the light of day his white head and beard looked like frozen snow piled in a shady corner while spring torrents were already flowing all around. Reb Shlomo-Motte had heard much about Reb Avraham-Shaye from the various congregants in the beth medresh. Deep down, he wasn't impressed by a rabbi who wrote new interpretations as though the interpretations in the old commentaries didn't suffice. Now he'd just heard that this man who lived apart from the whole world had become Chaikl's new guide in life. Everyone had influence and mastery over his son except him, his father.

Chaikl too was sadly silent. Reb Avraham-Shaye had said he would have to think over the matter of Chaikl's moving into the cottage. Kreyndl was evicting him from his room. He was ashamed to go to Reb Hirshe Gordon or the yeshiva kitchen. Where would he eat on Sabbath and during the week? His only recourse was to go back to Vilna and put off studying with the rabbi until he returned from Valkenik. But what would his mother say if he came home in the middle of the summer? And how could he leave his sick father alone? Chaikl wrapped up his tefillin and looked out the window over his bed.

In the sun-sparkling gold and green distance flowed the Meret-shanke River, full and rising over its banks. In mid-river the current gleamed and trembled like silver strings; at the opposite bank the water scintillated between gray and indigo, reflecting the town cemetery, which was overgrown with weeds, shrubs, and little trees. Chaikl turned his head back to the synagogue court-yard. On the turreted roofs of the shul birds were twittering. They flew down to the ground looking for seeds, then flew back up to the roofs. Through the open windows of the beth medresh the Talmud chants floated out and fused with the warbling winged choir, the trembling sunbeams, and the rustling trees near the river.

The Talmud melody tugged at Chaikl's heart. He had been rejected by his friends; none of them had come to visit him while he was sick. He had no choice now but to leave town. Instead of sitting in a yeshiva with boys his own age, he would have to study among irritable, grumbling old men in Reb Shaulke's beth medresh in Vilna. He thought of the constant uproar on Butchers Street— the crowded courtyards, the shouts and vituperations of the women shopkeepers, the sweaty, stifling heat of the hot, humid summer days, and the smell of raw meat and the raw, vulgar words of the butcher boys. With yearning eyes, as though he had already bidden farewell to Valkenik, he gazed at the green pastures, at the river, and once more at the old wooden shul.

Reb Menakhem-Mendl Segal ran past the window. A moment later he opened the door to the house and cried out in amazement, as though incredulous at his own announcement, "Reb Avraham-Shaye has come to pay you a sick call."

Chaikl jumped up but, realizing at once that he wouldn't have time to dress, remained in bed, eyes fixed on the door as during childhood Seders when the door was opened for Elijah the Prophet. Reb Shlomo-Motte rose quickly too, and out of respect for the rabbi removed his workaday stiff-visored cap and donned a high skullcap. Despite being an obdurate maskil, he was surprised and pleased that a famous gaon was interested in his son.

Following Reb Menakhem-Mendl, Berele with his big, billowing earlocks came into the house, and behind him was Reb Avraham-Shaye, cane in hand, wearing his threadbare gray gaberdine.

"I heard from Reb Menakhem-Mendl that you caught a bad cold. That doesn't become you, Chaikl! I thought you were a veritable Samson!" He stretched his hand out to the white-bearded man. "You're probably Chaikl's father. No doubt he has told you that I want to study with him."

Reb Shlomo-Motte answered sedately, with dignity and with courtesy toward the visitor: "Chaikl's mother will be very happy that her son will be studying with a great rabbi. But since I'm an old Hebrew teacher, I know that no matter how great the teacher, success also depends on the pupil."

Reb Avraham-Shaye laughed and at once sat down in a chair by the table so that the old man would sit too.

"It depends even more on the pupil than on the teacher, and that's why I'm only taking your son for a trial period. He will live at our cottage and sleep in my room."

The walls and ceiling swayed before Chaikl's eyes. He soared up to the sky and just managed to keep from shouting with joy. Now he wouldn't have to return to Vilna or wander about in Valkenik, rejected and humiliated. But Reb Shlomo-Motte sat mutely at the edge of his bed, looking like a man weighing a difficult decision. Outside, meanwhile, a group of younger yeshiva boys had gathered. They had run down from the beth medresh to see if Reb Avraham-Shaye had indeed come to pay a sick call on Chaikl Vilner. The landlady and her daughter, who had been quarreling softly outside, returned to the house and stared open-mouthed at the visitor. Noting the crowd of young scholars outside and the reverential silence within, the women had realized that the guest must be an exalted person. Chaikl sat holding his breath, fearing that Kreyndl might say something.

"If you agree, your son can come to us for Shevuos," Reb Avraham-Shaye began again. His cheeks were red; he didn't like to coax and persuade anyone. "Shevuos, when our Torah was given to us, is an auspicious time to begin Torah study."

"I agree," Reb Shlomo-Motte replied, "but I don't understand how it will work out. All week long Chaikl eats in the yeshiva kitchen and on the Sabbath he eats at the house of a local congregant. Will he have to go back and forth from the forest every day?"

"I won't give him an excuse like that for wasting time," Reb Avraham-Shaye joked. "Since he's going to stay at our house, he'll eat with us on Sabbath and during the week too. But I won't snatch him away completely. I'll let him come to see you."

Reb Shlomo-Motte said no more and the visitor bade him good-bye. Reb Avraham-Shaye went to the door, escorted by his nephew Berele and by Reb Menakhem-Mendl, who had remained silent throughout the visit. Although Reb Menakhem-Mendl had a scholar's faith that the gaon knew what he was doing, he nevertheless felt that Chaikl wasn't worthy as yet of becoming Reb Avraham-Shaye's pupil. He also felt that a gaon shouldn't come to visit a mere boy. It was beneath his dignity as a Torah scholar. But Freyda beamed with joy that such a distinguished man had come to see her tenants.

"Thank you, rabbi, for coming to my house," she said, letting the visitor know she was the landlady. Her daughter gaped at Chaikl as though she hadn't imagined that he knew such great men. Freyda and Kreyndl followed the visitor outside.

Chaikl took advantage of the minute alone with his father to ask him in a trembling voice, "What will happen if he discovers what they're saying about me in town?"

"You're a fool! He knows already. That's why he came to take you to his house, so you won't have anything more to do with the girl or run around outside at night and get sick." Reb Shlomo-Motte sat with both hands pressing the edge of his bed, sighing with relief. He felt as if a burden had been removed from his back. He would be able to remain here and Chaikl would live in the forest. His teacher would probably look after him during the winter too, and then his mother wouldn't have to support him from her fruit baskets. Reb Avraham-Shaye is no doubt an even greater opponent of the Haskalah than other religious Jews, thought Reb Shlomo-Motte. But he is a very clever and noble-hearted man—an altogether different sort from that Tsemakh Atlas.

19

TSEMAKH ATLAS SAT ACROSS the table from Reb Avraham-Shaye in his courtyard and said, "Nowadays even rabbis aren't depending on ancestral merit; they're not keeping their children at home but are sending them to yeshivas, especially those that are far from a railroad, away from the world. For Chaikl Vilner, then, a large town would surely be an open door into the wide, secular world. His father belongs to that generation of maskils who to this day haven't regretted their former ways. Even his honest and pious mother might be envious of other poor women whose children help to support them. Wild energies rage in Chaikl Vilner that have to be uprooted like weeds—and it wouldn't be a bad idea if he were fenced in. He should be constantly in the environment of friends whom he would want to emulate in Torah studies, in good behavior, and in fine character traits."

"In your yeshiva he was surrounded with Torah scholars and students of Musar, so why didn't he conduct himself in the proper manner?" Reb Avraham-Shaye asked.

"Nevertheless, he did flee from his room one night so as not to remain alone with the girl. But if he's not in the company of yeshiva students and has no need to feel ashamed, he won't flee from a temptation. Reb Menakhem-Mendl probably told you that I found Chaikl Vilner sitting on the steps of the beth medresh."

Reb Avraham-Shaye nodded and Tsemakh angrily spat out his words one by one. "I know that Reb Menakhem-Mendl comes and tells you everything that's happening in the yeshiva. I told him to his face that since he didn't want the Vilner to stay in the yeshiva, he persuaded you to take him as a student."

"You're suspecting an innocent man. Reb Menakhem-Mendl did indeed tell me about his student's behavior and that he had fallen ill from wandering around outside all night. But he did not urge me to take Chaikl as a student; the idea never crossed his mind. On the contrary, I noticed that my going to town to visit the sick boy didn't please Reb Menakhem-Mendl at all. He thought even that was too much." Reb Avraham-Shaye rested his chin with its soft beard on the edge of the table and frowned slightly, as he did upon discovering a text-mangling printer's error in Rashi's commentary. "I don't understand. Since you found your student wandering around at night by the beth medresh and realized he didn't want to spend the night in his room, why did you leave him outside?"

"I pleaded with him to sleep in my room, but he absolutely refused. He's still a child! Even if he is going to be your pupil, isn't he still allowed to spend the night in my room?"

"Maybe he was afraid you'd admonish him." Reb Avraham-Shaye smiled.

"And you told him nothing? You didn't reprimand him at all?"

"I? Never!" Reb Avraham-Shaye laughed. "If I had given him the impression that I knew anything, he would have run away from me too. Well, how did he react to your reprimand?"

"He answered impudently that he wouldn't move out of his room. . . . Now I understand! He ran away from the house and from the girl for your sake. But I can promise you that this is temporary; it will last only as long as he considers it a great honor to be your pupil. Once he gets used to you, he'll no longer have your image before his eyes during a moment of temptation. His hot blood won't calm down just because his teacher is Reb Avraham-Shaye Kosover. Even if he does become a diligent ben Torah, I can't imagine how the Talmud and its commentaries will be able to protect him from the yetzer ha-ra in all its shapes and forms."

Reb Avraham-Shaye, sitting opposite Tsemakh, listened, his face flaming. His skullcap had inched to the back of his head. He began in a shrill voice, pointing his finger at Tsemakh: "What? A rosh yeshiva can't imagine how Torah study can save someone from the yetzer ha-ra? The Talmud says: If you encounter that blackguard, drag him to the beth medresh! When one studies the Torah, one's mind fuses with that of Moses on Mount Sinai. Studying the Mishna, one unites with the sages of Yavneh and converses with them as if they were alive. A youngster pores over his Talmud in Vilna and muses that he's in Babylonia, sitting in the great Talmudic academy of Nahardea, in the beth medresh of Rashi and his scholarly descendants. Whoever carries so many eras of Torah and wisdom in his heart and mind considers the world and all its pleasures only a pauper's hospice."

Tsemakh could no longer sit still. He walked around the table as if he wanted Reb Avraham-Shaye to hear him from all sides. "If man were naturally drawn to a higher life of spirituality, the Talmud and its commentaries would suffice. But matter, man's body, drags everyone down, even the noblest ben Torah. A Torah scholar can be an evil genius and pilpulize a dispensation for his every desire. But when these wormish lusts assail man, only one solution remains: cast off all clothes, stand naked—study Musar. Only by looking deeply into oneself can one know if the intent is pure, or if it's self-interest hurling quotations from the Talmud and its commentaries and shrieking: 'Yes, it's permitted! Yes, you can do it!' The *yetzer ha-ra* can put on a pure blue tallis whose fringes and fine gold collar are woven through with the holy words of the Talmudic sages. But in those piety-glazed eyes the swinish calculation of self-interest still burns. And the more ecstatically he prays, the more hypocritical he is—that pious demon garbed in the defective tallis of self-interest."

Reb Avraham-Shaye laughed delightedly. "The *yetzer ha-ra* can also put on a tallis woven from a Navaredker sermon and moralistic talk." He recalled that Chaikl had recently repeated his teacher's talk with similar passion and in the same style. But these harsh and fervid Musar sermons hadn't protected the student—and who could know whether they were protecting his teacher?

Reb Avraham-Shaye stopped laughing and continued in a low, pained voice, "Consider a married ben Torah who is burdened with the problems of livelihood and raising children, not to mention that he may think he has made a poor match with his wife, his business, and the small town he lives in. Who can console him? What can encourage him? During his youth he studied Musar fervently and drove off the *yetzer ha-ra* from himself with staves. Now he is no longer young, he's saddled with a family, and he's stuck in some provincial town without friends of quality near him—can he now study Musar with fiery enthusiasm? He will shriek into himself as if into a cellar and cry out as though in a wasteland. He will have to warm himself with memories of his youth. And when he recalls his old triumphs over the *yetzer ha-ra* his heart will grow even heavier. Wrangling with great desires gives a man a feeling of greatness and festive joy, even when he stumbles and falls. But when a ben Torah who has married becomes a shopkeeper or a merchant in the market place, his temptations become petty. Day in and day out he has to give honest weight for a pound of grits; he must not stretch the cloth on the yardstick; and he has to know how to get along with his family, his townsmen, and the village peasants. So when temptation confronts him in his house or store or in the market, he won't run to the beth medresh to consult the *Code of Law* and the *Path of the Upright*. These texts have to be open books in his heart from the time he sat studying in a corner of the beth medresh. The light of the Torah of his young yeshiva years has to illumine his path later, when he's in his store amid village peasants and barrels of herring. Perhaps in his youth this diligent scholar hadn't been one of the noted Musar students; he gained no reputation for his accomplishments or penetrating ideas. But the little candle before his nighttime Talmud lights his way for a long time thereafter, while his fiery Musarnik friends who took the world by storm have long since been extinguished."

Tsemakh Atlas did not believe that Reb Avraham-Shaye had divine insight, yet he spoke as though he knew everything he himself had experienced and was still experiencing. Tsemakh stood straight, his hands behind his back. Despite his pallor and his trembling lips, he replied with a firm voice. "Reb Menakhem-Mendl Segal was that sort of ben Torah when we both studied with our teacher, Reb Yosef-Yoizl Hurwitz, the Old Man of Navaredok. Nevertheless, Reb Menakhem-Mendl would rather live an anguished life in the Valkenik yeshiva than be a merchant in Vilna. He had sold shoemakers' supplies for so long he felt that the light in him was beginning to dim. Now as to Chaikl Vilner—and it's about him that I've come here—he is not at all the sort of scholar you depicted. A singular danger lies in wait for him—the feeling for beauty. With his poetic fantasy he beautifully embellishes what he likes, or persuades himself that he likes, until he becomes intoxicated and seduced by it. That's why he, more than any other youth, must constantly be in the midst of the seething of the Musarniks. And you, Reb Avraham-Shaye, please forgive me, but you have too much faith in people."

"Because I have faith in the Creator and his Torah, I also have faith in people—though not in every one of them."

"Do you mean *me?*" Tsemakh felt huge drops of perspiration on his forehead.

"You give your students lectures that they ought not to hear. Even if they don't understand the intent of your words now, they'll remember what you said, and in time they'll discover what you wanted to hide from them."

"What do I want to hide from them?"

"Your own doubts. You're too strict. You're an extremist because you yourself are drawn to a strange shore. . . . I understand. You're suffering too, and you're suffering immensely. But you must be careful in your talks to the students. Please don't be angry, but I have no more strength to talk or listen."

Reb Avraham-Shaye lay down on the hard bench, breathing deeply with an occasional groan. Tsemakh Atlas looked at the author of *The Vision of Avraham* but couldn't open his mouth to reply. He nodded mutely and left the courtyard.

On his way back to town he walked slowly, looking down at the road, as though he had lost a precious object along the way and were certain it was somewhere nearby. But he could not sift through so much sand and dust to recover what he had lost.

GLOSSARY

AGUDAH	The ultraorthodox religious party, opposed (in the time of the novel, but not nowadays) to Zionism.
ALEPH BEYS	The Hebrew alphabet.
BAAL TEFILLA	A congregant who leads a prayer service; not a trained cantor.
BAR MITZVA	The age of thirteen, when a Jewish boy is called to the Torah for the first time and assumes adult responsibility for his conduct.
BEN TORAH	A yeshiva student; a Torah scholar. Literally, son of Torah.
BETH MEDRESH	A house of study; also used as a place for prayer.
CHALLA	The braided bread made of white flour, used for Sabbath and holidays.
CHEDER	Hebrew school—in European villages, usually a room in a teacher's house—where children are taught Hebrew, prayers, and the Pentateuch.
CHESHVAN	The second month of the Jewish calendar, following Tishrei with its cycle of holidays. There are no holidays during this late fall (October–November) month.
CHOLENT	A hot meal, usually consisting of beans and meat, cooked on Friday and kept warm to serve on the Sabbath.
CHUMESH	The Five Books of Moses.
CODE OF LAW	See *Shulchan Aruch.*
DAYS OF AWE	The ten-day period of High Holy Days between Rosh Hashana and Yom Kippur.
DYBBUK	The soul of one person which has entered another.

EATING DAYS   The system in Eastern Europe of assigning yeshiva boys
                       a family with whom they could eat one day each week.
                       A yeshiva lad was fortunate to have seven eating days.

ELUL   The month (August and part of September) preceding
                       Rosh Hashana.

EREV YOM KIPPUR   The Eve of Yom Kippur, the Day of Atonement.

ESROG   The citron used in services on Sukkos, in conjunction
                       with the lulav.

GAON (PL. GAONIM)   Great scholar.

GEMARA   Part of the Talmud, the commentary on the Mishna
                       (Oral Law).

GOLEM   Clod. Literally, a creature of clay.

GUT SHABBES   A greeting: A good Sabbath!

GYMNASIUM   The European high school.

HAGADA   The book used for the Passover Seder, recounting the
                       Exodus from Egypt.

HALAKHA (HALAKHIC)   The Jewish law.

HANUKA   Holiday of Lights, celebrating the rededication of the
                       Temple by the Maccabees.

HASID   A follower of a certain Hasidic rebbe. The Hasidim were
                       known for their accent on joy, dancing, and singing in
                       their worship of God, rather than on religious study.

HASKALAH   The Enlightenment, which sought to bring to the Jews
                       secular learning and knowledge of languages.

HAVDOLA   Prayer said at the end of the Sabbath.

HIGH HOLY DAYS   Rosh Hashana and Yom Kippur.

HOLY ARK   The ark at the eastern side of the synagogue where the
                       Torahs are kept.

IYAR   The month after Passover. Late spring (May–June).

JUDAH MACCABEE   The leader of the Hanuka rebellion in Palestine during
                       the second century B.C.E.

KABBALA   The medieval mystical texts interpreting the Torah. One
                       who studies the Kabbala is known as a Kabbalist.

KABOLAS SHABBES
  PRAYERS   Friday night service of Psalms and songs preceding the
                       Evening Service.

KADDISH   A prayer that marks the conclusion of a unit in the
                       service; it is also recited as a prayer for the dead.

KASHRUT   One who eats kosher foods and observes the Jewish
                       dietary laws keeps kashrut.

KIDDUSH   Blessing recited over wine at the beginning of the
                       Sabbath or holiday evening meal.

KITTEL   The white gown worn by the cantor and members of the
                       congregation during the High Holy Days and during
                       the Passover Seder.

KOHEN — A descendant of the Levites; a member of the priestly class.

KOL NIDREI — The opening prayer, with its world-famous melody, of the night of Yom Kippur.

KOSHER — See *Kashrut.*

LAG B'OMER — A day of festivity, especially for children; they are released from their studies and taken into the fields and woods.

LAMED VOVNIK — One of the thirty-six hidden saints upon whose righteousness the world continues to exist.

LATKES — Pancakes.

L'CHAYIM — To life! The traditional Jewish toast.

LITVAKS — Jews who come from Lithuania and who are traditionally thought of as being more reserved and scholarly than Jews from other regions.

LULAV — The palm branch adorned with myrtle and willow branches that is used in conjunction with the esrog during Sukkos.

MAIMONIDES — The great philosopher, physician, and sage (1135–1204), author of *The Guide to the Perplexed* and the *Mishneh Torah*, a codification of Jewish laws.

MASKIL — A follower of the Haskalah, the Jewish Enlightenment movement.

MAZEL TOV — Congratulations! Literally, "good luck."

MENORAH — A synagogue candelabrum holding seven candles. A Hanuka menorah holds eight candles.

MEZUZA — A rolled piece of parchment containing Torah verses and inserted in a wooden or metal case; affixed on the doorpost of Jewish homes and synagogues.

MIDRASH — Rabbinic commentary and explanatory notes, homilies, and stories on Scriptural passages.

MIKVA — The ritual bath, used separately by both men and women.

MINYAN — The quorum of ten adult males needed for synagogue services.

MISHNA — The body of oral law redacted *c.* 200 C.E. by Rabbi Judah.

MITZVA — A Torah precept or commandment; a good deed.

MIZRACHI — The religious party that supported Zionism.

MOHEL — The man who performs circumcisions.

MUSAF — The additional service (after the Morning Service) recited on Sabbaths and holidays.

MUSAR — A nineteenth-century movement in Judaism to educate the individual to strict ethical conduct; it also became a trend in certain yeshivas.

MUSARNIK	A follower of Musar. (See above and Introduction.)
NAHARDEA	A city in Babylonia famous for its Talmudical academy.
NEILAH	The concluding service of Yom Kippur.
OMER DAYS	The seven weeks between Passover and Shevuos. During this period no music is played, nor are weddings performed, except on Lag B'Omer.
PASSOVER	The eight-day festival during Nissan (March–April) that commemorates the Jews' freedom from Egyptian bondage.
PENITENTIAL PRAYERS	Prayers recited prior to Rosh Hashana.
PENTATEUCH	The Torah; the Five Books of Moses.
PILPULIZE	To split hairs, especially in a discussion of a Talmudic text.
RAM'S HORN (HEBREW: SHOFAR)	Blown several times during Rosh Hashana and once after the Neilah service at the end of Yom Kippur.
RASHI	The great commentator of the Bible and the Talmud (1040–1105).
REB	Mister. Used in conjunction with a first name, it is used when speaking to adults.
REBBE	Spiritual leader of a group of Hasidim.
REBBETSIN	The wife of a rabbi.
RITUAL FRINGES	A four-cornered, poncholike garment put on over the head and worn underneath the shirt by male Jews who observe the biblical commandment to wear a garment with fringes (Numbers 15:37–41).
ROSH HASHANA	The Jewish New Year, celebrated the first and second days of Tishrei. Rosh Hashana and Yom Kippur are the most solemn days of the year.
ROSH YESHIVA	The academic head of a yeshiva.
SHEVUOS	The Feast of Weeks, celebrated on the sixth and seventh of Sivan (May–June), seven weeks after Passover. It marks the day on which the Torah was given.
SHOFAR	See *Ram's horn*.
SHOLOM ALEICHEM	Peace to you. Used as a greeting in Yiddish.
SHUL	Synagogue.
SHULCHAN ARUCH	The collection of laws by Joseph Caro, *The Code of Law*.
SHVAT	The winter month (February–March) which contains the festival Tu Bishvat.
SIDDUR	The prayer book.
SILENT DEVOTION	One of the central prayers in the Jewish service, recited while standing.
SUKKOS	The Feast of Tabernacles, celebrated for seven days (nine, including Shemini Atzeres and Simkhas Torah) starting the fifteenth of Tishrei. It commemorates the

Jews' living in *sukkos* during their wandering in the desert.

TALLIS — The prayer shawl worn by adult males during the Morning Service. Most men wear the prayer shawl only after their wedding, hence one can easily spot a bachelor.

TALMUD — The body of written Jewish law, comprising the Mishna (in Hebrew) and the Gemara (mostly in Aramaic).

TALMUD TORAH — The school in which children are taught Hebrew, the prayers, and the Pentateuch.

TEIGLAKH — A sweet baked confection made of honey and dough.

TEFILLIN — Phylacteries used in morning prayers. These are square boxes with leather thongs, containing Scriptural passages worn on the arm and head during morning prayer daily, except Sabbath and holidays, by male Jews over thirteen.

TEN DAYS OF REPEN- TANCE — The ten-day period beginning with Rosh Hashana and ending with Yom Kippur; a time when the Jew is supposed to examine his moral and religious state of being and change his ways.

THIRTEEN ARTICLES OF FAITH — A series of thirteen statements, each beginning with "I believe," originally formulated by Maimonides, and recited now by all Jews.

TISHA B'AV — The ninth day of the month of Av (July–August), marking the destruction in 586 B.C.E. and 70 C.E. of both Temples in Jerusalem.

TISHREI — The first month of the Jewish year.

TORAH — Not only the Five Books of Moses, and by extension the entire Bible, but the entire complex of Jewish learning comprising the Talmud, the Commentaries, rabbinic writings, etc.

TRACTATE ERUVIN — One of the tractates of the Talmud.

TRACTATE NEDARIM — One of the tractates of the Talmud.

TRACTATE SABBATH — One of the tractates of the Talmud.

TSITSIS — See *Ritual fringes.*

TU BISHVAT — Jewish Arbor Day, which falls on the fifteenth of Shvat; a day when Hebrew school children were treated to nuts, dates, carob, and other fruits of Palestine.

VILNA GAON — The great sage of Vilna, Elijah ben Solomon Zalman (1720–1797).

VILNA TALMUD — A famous edition of the Talmud printed in Vilna.

YARMULKE — A skullcap worn by Jewish boys and men.

YAVNEH — A town in ancient Palestine that became the center for

Torah study after the destruction of the Temple in the year 70.

YESHIVA   A Talmudic academy.

YESHIVA BOKHER   A student at a yeshiva.

YETZER HA-RA   The evil inclination in man; his bad impulses. At the beginning of the novel the interpretation given to *yetzer ha-ra* is "the evil tempter"; but *yetzer ha-ra* can also be seen merely as the tendency in man to do forbidden acts.

YOM KIPPUR   The Day of Atonement, the holiest day in the Jewish year.

ZOHAR   One of the most important texts of the Kabbala.

Temple Israel

Minneapolis, Minnesota

In honor of the Bat Mitzvah of
LORI BETH KING

January 15, 1977